The sate[...]
under the steady
barrage of rounds

Staying low, Ryan knew that attacking meant certain death. Pawing through the bloody clothes of the corpses piled under the dish, the one-eyed man found the wrong end of an AK-47, a bent knife and a single gren.

Bullets zipped through the trees on either side, the cross fire closing in like the mandibles of an army of killer ants. Ryan tried to gauge the distance to the fuel dump. The resulting blast would obliterate the whole outpost, chilling him as well as the blue shirts. But if Ryan Cawdor was going to die, then he would take Overton and his troops along for the ride.

Ryan pulled the pin and prepared to charge.

"We go in pairs," Ryan directed, surreptitiously cau-

**Other titles in the
Deathlands saga:**

JAMES AXLER

DEATH LANDS®

Gemini Rising

THE BARONIES TRILOGY BOOK 1

A GOLD EAGLE BOOK FROM
WORLDWIDE®

TORONTO • NEW YORK • LONDON
AMSTERDAM • PARIS • SYDNEY • HAMBURG
STOCKHOLM • ATHENS • TOKYO • MILAN
MADRID • WARSAW • BUDAPEST • AUCKLAND

With great respect and admiration to Don Pendleton, the granddaddy of us all.

First edition July 1999

ISBN 0-373-62546-4

GEMINI RISING

There is not one people in the history of the world to whom gaining their independence had not brought forth the tortures which ancient poets and theologians reserved for the damned.

—Sir Winston Churchill
The Gathering Storm, 1936

THE DEATHLANDS SAGA

This world is their legacy, a world born in the violent nuclear spasm of 2001 that was the bitter outcome of a struggle for global dominance.

There is no real escape from this shockscape where life always hangs in the balance, vulnerable to newly demonic nature, barbarism, lawlessness.

But they are the warrior survivalists, and they endure—in the way of the lion, the hawk and the tiger, true to nature's heart despite its ruination.

Ryan Cawdor: The privileged son of an East Coast baron. Acquainted with betrayal from a tender age, he is a master of the hard realities.

Krysty Wroth: Harmony ville's own Titian-haired beauty, a woman with the strength of tempered steel. Her premonitions and Gaia powers have been fostered by her Mother Sonja.

J. B. Dix, the Armorer: Weapons master and Ryan's close ally, he, too, honed his skills traversing the Deathlands with the legendary Trader.

Doctor Theophilus Tanner: Torn from his family and a gentler life in 1896, Doc has been thrown into a future he couldn't have imagined.

Dr. Mildred Wyeth: Her father was killed by the Ku Klux Klan, but her fate is not much lighter. Restored from predark cryogenic suspension, she brings twentieth-century healing skills to a nightmare.

Jak Lauren: A true child of the wastelands, reared on adversity, loss and danger, the albino teenager is a fierce fighter and loyal friend.

Dean Cawdor: Ryan's young son by Sharona accepts the only world he knows, and yet he is the seedling bearing the promise of tomorrow.

In a world where all was lost, they are humanity's last hope....

Chapter One

"Git!" the first sec man snarled, leveling his blaster.

Dressed in tattered rags, with strips of cloth wound around their feet as crude shoes, the couple before him whimpered in fear but didn't move an inch, so the sec man worked the bolt of his weapon, chambering a round.

"We just want to get out of the cold, sir...." the man began, raising his empty hands.

Without a word, the other sec man worked the bolt of his old BAR rifle. The wooden stock was bound with gray tape, the lens in the scope badly cracked, but the barrel was twice as wide as that of the hunting rifle and shone with fresh oil.

"Move away slow, liar," the first guard ordered, edging closer to the gate of the ville.

The wall surrounding the town was built of everything, bricks at one point, cinderblocks at another, field stones and notched logs here and there. But the patchwork barrier stood ten feet tall, and the top glistened with jagged broken glass. The only visible entrance was a wide gateway, the arch lined with bricks supporting two thick wooden doors hung on six mismatched hinges. The left door was bolted into place, closing off half the entrance. The second was open, allowing a glimpse at the houses and structures within. To the left rose a high mound of busted shale, and to the right was a huge excavation, a stone quarry whose stepped slopes extended hundreds of feet deep to a calm pool of muddy water. In the distance, dark mountains stretched above the thick growth of green forest and disappeared into the gray autumn clouds.

"Liar?" the pregnant woman gasped. "Oh, but sir, I can promise you that—"

"You said you two walked here from Culbert ville," he interrupted. "That was stupid. First off, I never heard of the place, and secondly your shoes and pants ain't dirty enough."

The second guard took over. "Plus you claimed not to have eaten in a week. Ain't no traces of hunger on your faces."

"Liars and cheats don't get into our ville."

The man wet his lips, turning to look at each of the armed sec men in turn, while the pregnant woman shivered and hugged her thin coat closer to her body.

"But, sir," she whimpered, "I'm close to birthing and the babe will die in this cold."

"Don't care. I said git!" the sec man shouted, his breath foggy in the early-morning chill. "Unless you wanna take an air dance like those horse thieves!"

The couple darted a glance to the gallows, which extended over the stout wall surrounding the ville. A pair of human figures dangled at the end of thick knotted ropes, while a crow sat on one man's shoulder pecking at his face. Hands bound behind his back, the other weakly struggled to scare away the rest of the black birds circling closer and closer. A strip of bark hung about his neck with his crime scrawled there for all to read.

"Mebbe we can make a deal," the man said softly, his tone and demeanor changing subtly.

"Last chance," the first sec man stated without emotion, his callused hands tight around the stock of his rebuilt weapon.

"How would you like some of this?" the woman asked, lifting her skirts.

The guards started to back away, but forced themselves to look just in case it was a diversion so she could draw a weapon. But the woman was naked underneath the many layers of shirts and dresses except for tall boots and a padded belt around her flat stomach to simulate pregnancy.

"What's the bitch…?" The sec man seemed confused.

"Few outlanders want to rape a pregger." She smirked, easing open a tiny pocket on the pack and withdrawing a little bottle filled with white powder. "Now, just a pinch of this will make ya more happy than ten women, and you can sell the rest."

"That's paradise for free!" the man added, grinning eagerly as if he had a done deal. "Just let us inside to spread around some of the joy. Okay?"

"Jolt," the guard said in horror, and then he spit as if the word itself were unclean. "Stinking drug dealers."

"Light 'em up!" shouted his partner, and both men fired.

The smugglers were so close the flame from the muzzles actually reached their faces. The .22 long round from the hunting rifle blew away a piece of the woman's forehead, and the gushing corpse staggered backward from the gate, her hands clawing the air. Bleeding from a terrible wound where his ear used to be, her companion snarled in bestial rage and drew a massive black automatic pistol just before the second sec man cut loose.

The big-bore rifle stuttered three times so fast it almost sounded like one shot. The trip-hammer blows of the military cartridges opened his chest wide, and he joined his wife on the frosty ground, steam rising from the red blood pumping out of the gaping holes in their flesh.

The first sec man stood alert and watched for signs of treachery from friends hidden in the bushes, while the second guard ransacked their pockets, taking only a small derringer from the woman and the big handcannon from the man.

"Never seen its like," the first guard said. "What is it?"

"A .44 Automag," his comrade replied, dropping the clip and looking inside. "Big motherfucker. Damn, only three rounds."

Impressed, the first man whistled, his breath visible in the cold. "You could trade for a good horse with that monster."

The man grinned as he tucked the gun into his belt. "My idea exactly."

"Now, my daughter would like that palm blaster."

"Well, it's my turn to get paid, but I missed with the first shot." He tossed over the derringer. "So it's yours. Fair deal?"

"Fair deal," the sec man responded, tucking the tiny blaster into a pocket. "Thanks. Okay, let's drag this scum to the quarry and feed the rock rats."

"Don't know if they'll eat this kind of garbage, but at least it will get them off the road."

Just then, the woman trembled and moaned.

"Well, shit," the second guard complained, sounding annoyed. "The bitch is still alive."

Angrily working the bolt on his rifle, the other guard pressed the hot muzzle to her face and fired again with explosive results.

"Not anymore," he stated, wiping some gore off his face with a sleeve.

WATCHING THE GUARDS tumble the bodies into the pit, Ryan Cawdor adjusted the focus on the antique brass telescope, careful not to disturb the bushes he was hiding within and give away his position.

The telescope was an amazing little thing they had found in the ruins of the Virginia Beach Naval Station. Apparently, the base had been in the process of building a gateway when skydark hit, and thus the job was never finished. When the companions had jumped into the partially constructed mat-trans chamber, every working circuit in the complex blew and they barely managed to escape before the building burned to the ground. Afterward they dutifully searched the ruins of the base, which included several smashed warships lying scattered about hundreds of feet from the beach. A nuke had to have hit offshore and blown the crafts inland. All of the weapons and food were long gone from the base and the vessels, naturally, but Ryan had found this telescope. The unbreakable plastic lens was heavy, but the scope compacted smaller than binocs and was perfect for a one-eyed man.

Fighting back a shiver, Ryan tried to ignore the cold that seemed to be seeping into his very bones. He was dressed in a fur-lined coat, but with only a thin flannel shirt, denim pants and worn Army boots. The comfortable clothing was perfect for the dry desert of southern

California, but useless against the damp chill of a Virginia autumn. The heavy metal of the Steyr SSG-70 rifle across his back and the blaster at his hip seemed to be leeching away what little heat his body generated. The weapons felt like lumps of ice pressed against his skin.

Worse, the damp cold was making an old wound ache. Ryan gently rubbed the back of his hand against the leather patch where his left eye used to be. Sometimes in nightmares he could still see his brother's knife descending and feel the terrible starlight of pain that haunted him for so many years afterward.

"What happened?" asked J. B. Dix, squinting between the leaves of the bush at the ville below. "I heard shots."

Dressed in loose neutral-colored clothing, Army boots and a brown leather motorcycle jacket, the wiry man blended in perfectly with the mottled browns and greens of the forest. An Uzi submachine gun hung off his left shoulder, a Smith & Wesson M-4000 shotgun was slung across his back and his backpack bulged with explosives. Their old boss, the Trader, had nicknamed him "the Armorer" long ago, and the title fit John Barrymore Dix perfectly. There wasn't a weapon in existence the deadly man couldn't fire or repair with his eyes closed.

"Guards chilled them both," Ryan said aloud.

"Dark night! The pregnant woman, too?" J.B. asked in shock.

Nodding, Ryan passed over the telescope. "She was a fake, smuggling something in a belly pouch. Looked like jolt."

"Druggies, eh?" Taking the brass instrument, J.B. pushed his battered fedora to the back of his head so that he could slide his wire-rimmed glasses up on his forehead to use the long-eye. "Hope the guards did them slow and painful. Jolt dealers trade on the misery of others and deserve whatever they get."

Shrugging his shoulders to adjust the rifle hanging across his back, Ryan agreed. Jolt was the curse of the new world. The drug was horribly addictive and promised a death slower than rad poisoning.

The very thought reminded Ryan to check the miniature rad counter pinned to his collar, but the meter read clean, showing only a normal background count from the polluted orange sky. Any nukes used in this area had to have been "clean" bombs, the deadly radiation long dissipated.

"So what do you think?" Ryan asked, tugging on the fur collar of his coat. The wind was soft, but every gust cut through his clothing as if it were paper. They needed to get out of the cold mighty soon, before hypothermia cut them down.

"Looks good," J.B. stated at last, lowering the yard-long telescope and compacting it to the size of a soup can. "Lots of families, no slave pens or cannibal roasting pits. I think we should do it."

Brushing the black curls off his scarred face, Ryan grunted his agreement. "This ville is our best chance. Let's go."

Rising, the two men moved stealthily into the woods. The ground was lightly frosted with twinkling ice, and every step they took crunched softly, betraying their movements. Following an old game trail, they soon came upon a small clearing hidden behind a thick copse of oak trees.

A wide hole had been dug into the stony ground, with a small fire crackling in the middle of the shallow pit. Four people huddled close to the flames, the earthen walls containing and reflecting the meager heat so that even a small campfire would keep them warm through the bitter night. Ryan knew that the depression also helped to hide the light of the blaze from the armed sec men of the ville below.

An owl called softly, announcing their presence just before J.B. shook the branches on a thorny bush and Ryan whistled sharply twice. The people in the hole looked over the rim of the pit with their blasters drawn.

"Hey, Charlie," said a redheaded woman, dressed in a shaggy black fur coat. The S&W .38 revolver in her hand wasn't pointed directly at them, but her slim finger rested on the trigger nonetheless.

"The name is Adam," Ryan answered, giving the code name for all-clear, and the others visibly relaxed.

Entering the clearing, Ryan and J.B. noticed a small movement in the bushes nearby. It was the source of the owl call.

"Dean is getting better all the time," J.B. said. "I can barely spot him anymore."

"The kid is good," Ryan agreed. Cupping stiff hands around his mouth, he gave the call of a lake bird and within a few ticks his son appeared from the trees. There were leafy vines wrapped about his dark cloth and a slim black pistol in his hand.

"Nobody followed you, Dad," Dean reported, holstering the Browning Hi-Power.

Ryan allowed himself a small smile. "Good work. Take a break and get warm. We're going for the ville."

"Hot pipe!" the boy cried, and hopped into the fire pit, landing dangerously close to the flames. He flopped down on a rock and shoved his face toward the warmth, breathing in the waves of heat like a fish gasping for air.

Stepping into the pit a bit more carefully, J.B. went straight to the stocky black woman and gave her a kiss on the cheek. "Hey, Millie. This ville looks okay. No sign of slave pens like the last two."

"Thank goodness," Dr. Mildred Wyeth sighed wearily as she whittled on a tree branch with a wicked-looking knife. "Any chance we can trade for horses or a wag?" she asked hopefully.

"That depends upon how willing they are to be reasonable," J.B. said gruffly. He removed his fedora and smoothed his sandy hair. "But we'll get you some transport."

"The ville seems to be a trading post," Ryan stated, squatting on his heels. "We saw a caravan of wags and horses being prepared. Long as we can pay, there will be no trouble."

"War wags?" Krysty Wroth asked, concern in her voice. Her sentient hair was coiled tightly about her head in response to her tense mood.

"No, just trucks and some vans. Nothing special."

"Good."

"How's the foot?" Ryan asked, basking in the heat of the fire.

Sheathing the blade, Mildred used the branch as a crutch to lever herself erect. Experimentally, she put some weight on her bandaged foot and hobbled a few steps, then sat on another flat rock with obvious relief.

"Better," the physician replied. "Swelling is going down. Feel like an idiot spraining my ankle jumping from that ship we were searching."

"Thank Gaia it wasn't broken," Krysty said.

"Well, landing on top of John helped a lot." Mildred smiled, straightening her leg carefully.

Adjusting his glasses, J.B. grinned. "Glad to be of assistance."

Ignoring the banter, Ryan watched her face, noting the pain she was trying to hide. "Think you can make it to the ville?"

"To get out of this cold, I'd walk barefoot over live sting-wings," she growled. "Hell yes, I can make it. I'm ready to go right now."

"Sit down—we're going to wait for a bit before going," Ryan said, rubbing his unshaven jaw. "J.B. and I need to warm up some in case there's trouble, and we want to give the guards enough time to finish burying the dead."

"And divide the loot," J.B. added, resting his Uzi on his lap. He paused for a moment, listening to the sounds of the forest, then slowly relaxed.

"We heard the shots. Who got chilled?" Krysty asked, her long fiery hair waving softly around her shoulders as if stirred by secret winds only she could feel.

"A couple of outlanders trying to get inside the ville," Ryan replied, feeling his muscles loosen under the waves of heat from the tiny fire. He rested a hand on the ground and discovered the surface was warm to the touch. This pit idea of Doc's worked great. Doc Tanner was a gold mine of clever ideas. "Smugglers, we think. Man and a woman. She was dressed like she was pregnant, but it was only a bundle of white powder strapped to her belly."

"Shot her on the spot," J.B. added, using a hand-kerchief to polish his glasses. "Very fast on the draw, these guys. Not good marksmen, but bastard fast."

Pausing in his work of sharpening a leaf-shaped knife

on a whetstone, Jak Lauren looked up and said, "Close enough, speed all need."

Born and bred down in the nuke-blasted ruins of Norleans, the teenager was the color of snow, hair and skin alike. He wore military fatigues with bits of metal and glass sewn into his camou-colored vest. A blue-steel handcannon rested on his right hip, and more than a dozen knives were hidden on his person. Another was sheathed on his belt, and a small knife peeked out from the top of his left boot.

"What was it, jolt?" Krysty asked.

Ryan shrugged. "I have no idea, but that sounds right. What else could stir such hatred with a glance?"

"Did they have horses?" Mildred queried. "If the ville now has a spare pair, we might get them at a price."

"The druggies were on foot."

"Damn."

Stirring the small fire with a green stick, Dean glanced at his father, then tossed some more seasoned branches onto the flames. As a small child, he had been taught that only dry wood went into a campfire. Green wood was still alive and full of sap, which made it smoke and give away your position. That could get you chilled, or worse. Out in the Deathlands, there were a lot of things more horrible than merely dying.

"Too bad the destroyer we found didn't have any working Hummers," Dean commented, poking the hot embers. "Or even a motorcycle. Just planes."

"If found working Hummer," Jak said, "how get out sideways boat?"

Wiping his face with the cloth, J.B. barked a laugh. "I'm not going to catch a bastard jeep like I did Millie."

Jak almost smiled at the Armorer's rare wit.

"Odd, though, the way the base and each of the ships had been stripped so thoroughly," Ryan muttered, flexing his fingers with greater ease. The chill was slowly leaving his bones, and circulation was getting back to normal. "You would think if the vessel was caught in a nuke tidal wave, the whole crew should have died when it hit the beach," he finished aloud.

"Scavs," Jak said, as if that ended the matter.

"I agree," Krysty added. "A prize like those ships wasn't going to be left alone for very long. Even if there were no blasters, the tools and such were worth a baron's ransom."

"Too bad that comp disk we found last month was encoded." J.B. wrapped his handkerchief around the bare metal grip of a coffeepot and poured the contents into a battered tin cup. He took a sip and tried not to grimace. Springwater, tree bark and some river moss. Mildred said it was nourishing, chock-full of vitamins, but it definitely failed in the taste department. He supposed this was a case of whatever didn't kill you made you stronger. "Sure would have been nice to jump to any redoubt we wanted."

"The redoubt at Wizard Island at Washington Hole?" Dean asked, scratching his neck.

Tugging his fingerless gloves on tighter, Ryan accepted a cup of the steaming brew and drank it without expression. Food was fuel, and he would eat anything that didn't kill him first. Even this medicinal dreck. "If we could have jumped there, it would have shaved weeks off our journey to Front Royal."

"But first mayhap we would have visited the old Alaska redoubt first," Doc Tanner rumbled in a deep bass. Tall and slim, the white-haired man wore a long frock coat and a frilly white shirt from another era when the style of a man's clothing was a vitally important issue. An ebony walking stick lay across his lap, the silver lion's head shining like a mirror in the reflected light of the campfire.

"Huge place, biggest redoubt we've ever found," Ryan said, frowning. "Over a mile wide. Big as an underground shopping mall."

"Like the Freedom Mall?" Dean asked. His face was red from the firelight, making the boy seem years older, almost an adult.

His father nodded. "Yeah, and just as bad."

"Worse," Krysty countered, her hair flexing and moving in dark remembrance. "Much worse. Thank goodness that hellhole got what it deserved."

"Indeed, the Keeper of the Alaskan redoubt couldn't have been more insane if he had been his own father," Doc said grimly, his hands tightening their grip on his walking stick. There was a click and the handle came free, exposing over a foot of shining steel blade. "However, I fondly recall that is where we got most of our blasters from originally, and there was a lot more there to be taken. And of course there was dear, dear Lori."

Closing the swordstick and twisting the handle to lock it tight, his face softened. "Ah, poor Lori Quint, I do sorely miss her company sometimes."

Nobody spoke for a few moments out of respect for a friend no longer among the living. It had been a terrible way for anybody to die.

"Travel right direction?" Jak asked, changing the subject. The teenager didn't care if there were a million blasters elsewhere. They were here, and what ammo they carried in their pockets was the reality of the day. Dreams were for the dying.

Loosening his collar, J.B. squatted by the fire, savoring the warmth. "I double-checked our location on my minisextant. It's slightly more than a hundred miles to Front Royal, north by northwest."

"Right through the heart of some bad mutie territory," Ryan noted, holding the cup in both hands to absorb its heat better. He took another sip. "We'll never make it on foot."

"So this little ville is our best bet," Mildred said, grimacing as her foot painfully throbbed. She had slammed her ankle in the fall and received a bone bruise along with the sprain. Neither was life threatening, just painful.

"Our only bet," Ryan corrected, looking over the others. They weren't sick yet with the wet coughs, or starving, either. But their food was low, and hunting had been very poor in this area. The backpacks held some self-heats and jerked meat that hadn't gone bad yet, maybe enough chow for a week. Shelter and food were top priorities. Both could be gotten at Front Royal, if his home ville was still standing.

Strange rumors had been plaguing them for months about trouble at the Virginia ville, but Ryan had discounted the news. His nephew, Nathan Freeman Cawdor, was a more than competent baron and could handle any problems that came his way. But in Utah, then California, clear across the continent, they had again heard tales of people fleeing the ville from the tyranny of a savage baron. Even simple stories got garbled over the long distance, but the third time Ryan heard the same tale, it was clear that something was horribly wrong in Virginia.

Mildred and Dean hadn't been with them the last time they had gone this way. Just as well. He had faced many coldhearts and mad killers before, but his own brother Harvey was near the top of that shit list.

"If we can't trade for a wag, why can't we just walk? We could make a litter and drag Mildred along behind us," Dean suggested, drawing in the dirt with a stick. "She wouldn't slow us much."

"We would never make it to Front Royal," his father stated. "Autumn is here and in the hills the temperature drops to killing levels at night. Plus there are snow leopards and ratters, muties who live under icy ground. Bastard things attack only when you are standing right smack on top of them."

"Frag them," Jak snarled, a knife dropping from his sleeve and into his hand in a reflex action. He flipped the blade once, catching it by the handle and sliding it away again.

"Leopards, in this part of the world?" Mildred asked, arching an eyebrow. "You sure about that?"

"Don't know if they are, but that's what they're called." Ryan threw the dregs of his drink onto the fire, dampening the dying flames. "Come on, let's get going before night falls and they close the gates until dawn. Another night out here and we won't have to worry about muties."

Throwing dirt on the campfire, the companions gathered their belongings and savored the tapped heat of the fire pit until the evening wind started to leech it away again. Climbing free, Ryan and the others checked their weapons and started deeper into the woods until they were a good quarter mile from their camp before angling down the hillside toward the road.

Behind them, something only vaguely shaped like a human stirred in the trees, then was gone.

Chapter Two

Zigzagging down the snowy side of the hill, the companions reached the road and spread out in a standard two-on-two defense pattern. The paved surface was badly cracked and full of holes, but still a lot easier to traverse than the rough ground. A rusty sign on a badly dented metal pole warned that no CB or cellular phones should be used for the next ten miles.

Taking a curve in the cracked road, Dean eagerly pointed as the irregular top of the shale hill became visible above the trees.

"We're close, so be ready for trouble," J.B. warned, unwrapping the tape from the handle of a grenade. "Just 'cause the sec men may greet us with a grin doesn't mean they won't kill us anyway."

"'Aye, that one may smile, and smile, and be a villain,'" Doc rumbled, pretending to lean heavily on his swordstick as if he were old and weak.

"*Hamlet,* act 1, scene 5," said Mildred, stepping around a deep pothole in the rough surface. The summer rains must be very fierce in this area. "You ever saw the Mel Gibson version?"

Doc shook his head. "Indeed, no, madam, the name is unfamiliar to me. But then, the few motion pictures that I have seen were on laser discs and videos in the archives of the redoubts. Movies were a bit after my time."

"Yeah, well, he blew the Kenneth Branagh version to hell and back."

"These people, they fought over a movie?" Dean asked, trying to follow the adult conversion. He knew that both Mildred and Doc were born before skydark, and he often had a trip-hard time following their conversations.

"Fight? In a way," the physician mused.

"And Gibson won?"

She smiled. "Kicked the living shit out of Branagh."

Shifting the position of the Browning in his belt, the boy made no comment. Old fights by dead sec men held no interest for him.

Accepting the rebuff, Mildred shrugged to adjust her heavy medical bag. Or rather, what she called her medical bag since it held no proper surgical tools—just boiled cloth and strong string, leather strips to use as a tourniquet, a small sharp knife, a few herbs and moss she knew helped ease itching and minor infections, some plastic-wrapped tampons reserved strictly for deep bullet wounds, a plastic bottle of alcohol, a bag of sulfur and one small tin of aspirins. Not much, hardly anything, but it was a start. Before she went into cryo-sleep and awoke in the next century, Mildred had been a highly trained physician. But without tools and chems, there was little the doctor could do but offer a smile to the dying.

The road rose in a gentle swell, bringing the wall and gate of the nameless ville into view. A gurgling creek flowed alongside the road, leading toward the huge, gaping crater of the stone quarry. To their left was a ragged pile of busted shale rising a hundred feet tall. It was no more than a molehill, really, compared to the Shen Mountains cresting over the western horizon.

The gentle wind was pushing the corpses hanging from the gallows to and fro like a clock pendulum, the flock of crows taking flight and landing again as they tried to feed on the dead humans without interruption. A sudden flurry of movement at the gate caught Ryan's eye, and he noted the guards stuff loaves of steaming black bread into the pockets of their coats and frantically ready their blasters.

The companions paused for a while until the guards at the gate were prepared for visitors, then proceeded at a slow pace, watching the bushes for snipers or traps.

"Remington .22 hunting rifle on the left," J.B. said softly, fingering the HE grenade in the pocket of his leather jacket. "Slow, jams a lot and not very accurate."

"The other looks military," Dean commented, hands in his pockets, his fingers tight on the grip of his blaster.

"It is," replied his father, easing the safety off his longblaster. "That's a BAR, Browning Auto Rifle, .30 long and one of the best blasters around. We're already in range, so stay sharp."

"Wonder if they are thinking the same as us," Krysty muttered as they started forward again.

"Smiling villains?" Jak asked with a scowl.

"Yeah."

"Damn well should be," Doc stated, clicking back the hammer of his monstrous LeMat pistol. "Unless they are total fools."

As the companions came abreast of a busted stone lintel lying on the berm, the big guard with a beard called out to them.

"That's close enough, outlanders." Oddly, the man's eyebrows and the hair under his hat were burnished crimson, like polished copper, but his beard was jet-black. "What do you want?"

Ryan noticed that the second guard was a good distance away from the first, and stationed behind a water barrel for additional protection. Smart. These men knew their jobs, even if they were poor shots. There were only faint traces of blood on the ground, a few insects scurrying to quickly harvest the nutrient-rich soil before it dried.

"We're just travelers who want to get out of the bastard cold," he said, blunt but friendly.

"Well, outlanders be welcome," the sec man said carefully. A wisp of steam rose from the hot bread in his pocket, the tantalizing smell a knife in Ryan's rumbling stomach. "Always ready for a bit more trading is the baron."

"Fair enough. This place got a name?"

"Rock ville."

Not a particularly original name for a ville built in a stone quarry, but Ryan made no comment. He had heard worse.

"We got goods to trade," J.B. announced, his empty hands hanging open at his sides. But the Uzi was there on his shoulder for the world to see, along with the scattergun.

"I suppose so. Got enough blasters showing, it's the truth. Mercies, I suppose?"

"Mercies?" Krysty spit in disgust.

"Hardly," Mildred snapped.

"We fight only to defend ourselves," Ryan said, feeling his temper rise to the insult. "Not for jack or a cut of the booty."

"A man who sells his honor, sells nothing," Doc stated forcefully.

"Sounds good, because we don't take big-ville jack here," the bearded guard said gruffly. "The barons might trade with it, but out here we only take what can be used. What you have, furs or fuel?"

"I can hear from your bellies it ain't food," the second guard added, his blaster still held level and ready as if expecting treachery.

Slowly reaching into a pocket, Ryan pulled out a cardboard box marked Remington. "Got full box of .38 longs here. Fifty live rounds with no corrosion. That buy us food and beds for a night?"

Both of the sec men burst into laughter and visibly relaxed.

"Shit and bedamned, One-eye," the bearded man said, "that'll buy the lot of you the best rooms and food we got for a week, plus a night with Mad Jennifer, the tightest piece of ass this side of the Shens."

"No, thanks," Krysty stated coldly. "We brought our own."

"And the name is Ryan."

"Russell," said the man with a beard, then he jerked a dirty thumb at the other sec man. "And he's Einstein."

The skinny guard grunted in acknowledgment and stepped away from the gate, clearing the entrance. "Well, it's almost dusk and time for our supper, so come on in if you're going to stay for the night. There ain't no toll coming or going. This ain't Front Royal, you know."

As he walked past the man, the unexpected words hit Ryan hard, but he forced his face to stay neutral and kept moving along with the rest of the companions. The thick wooden gate closed behind them with a boom, and the sec men locked it with a rusty steel chain. The wind cutting through their clothes noticeably lessened, and everybody stood a bit taller.

"Did you hear that about Royal?" Krysty asked, easing down the hammer of her wheelgun. "Wonder what that was about?"

"Tolls on travelers—that doesn't sound like Nathan," Ryan said thoughtfully.

"Mebbe he's not in charge anymore," Dean said. "Or there was a famine or something."

Brushing back his long black hair, Ryan chewed that over. "A famine," he finally stated. "Possible."

"You called him nephew," Mildred said, turning up her collar. "Is he blood kin?"

"Son of my dead brother."

"Kin helps kin," the woman said as if that were an immutable law of the universe.

Ryan didn't reply, his scarred face somber in dark thoughts.

Pausing at an intersection of two streets, the companions studied the layout of the ville. The town was laid out in neat rows of log cabins, stores and homes, dark smoke curling from a dozen crude stone chimneys. A flagpole stood in the middle of the ville common, but no flag fluttered from the top. A Revolutionary cannon sat at its base, the antique surrounded by a circle of sandbag walls, a stack of iron balls conveniently nearby. It was clearly a functioning piece of city armament.

A big horse corral was off to the side, and a small paddock for cattle stood empty next to a butcher's slaughterhouse. Blocks away, the water wheel turned steadily, creaking loudly in protest as it endlessly worked at whatever was going on inside the building alongside. The windows were covered with shutters and the one door closed. No smoke rose from that chimney.

Numerous folks bundled against the night were scurrying from house to house, carrying wood for fireplaces or toting wicker baskets that steamed in the dwindling light.

High on the side of the slag pile was a wooden cabin, with a zigzagging staircase scaling the jagged slope to reach the small building. As Ryan stared, there came a brief wink of reflected light.

"Somebody with binocs watching us," J.B. cautioned, glancing sideways.

"I saw," Ryan replied, maintaining his stride. "Stay loose."

"Indeed, sir," Doc intoned in his deep stentorian voice. "We are coolness personified."

Jak gave a noncommittal grunt.

"Hey! There's the inn," Mildred announced, hobbling along on her crude crutch. "About freaking time."

Situated on a corner across the compound was a brightly lit building, with horses and bikes parked in front. A sign was suspended from the overhanging roof with an actual knife and fork nailed to the board.

"You tired?" Krysty asked, sounding concerned. It was obvious that the bad ankle hurt a lot more than Mildred was letting on.

Holding back a wince as her tender foot accidentally touched the uneven ground, Mildred forced a smile. "No, just starving."

"Smells good," Dean said, eagerly sniffing the cold air.

Walking slowly across the compound, the companions went around the sandbag nest, coming close to the gallows and the hanging men. Only heads were visible over the top of the ville wall. They could hear the anguished sobs of the live prisoner as the black crows pecked at the bleeding scabs on his cheek and neck. His left ear was completely gone, as were both eyes, the empty sockets oozing blood and a clear viscous fluid. The facial bones of his dead partner showed white through the gaping rifts in his tattered flesh.

Pausing in midstep, Ryan turned on a heel with his 9 mm Sig-Sauer in hand. The silenced weapon coughed once, and a hundred paces away the head of the prisoner exploded in a grisly spray of bone and blood. Gingerly picking the hot brass off the ground, Ryan pocketed the spent cartridge.

"Dad," Dean began, sounding puzzled.

"That's no way for anybody to die," the elder Cawdor said in a voice of broken granite. "You got an enemy, you kill him. Torture only makes you worse than them."

He looked hard at the boy. "The Trader taught me that. Now you know it, too."

Not quite sure he fully understood, Dean nodded and decided to think long on this event since it was important enough for his father to waste a live round on a total stranger.

"Good shot," J.B. commented dryly, walking abreast of his friend.

Holstering his blaster, Ryan merely replied, "The wind was with me."

Past the compound, the muddy road displayed random patches of gravel and macadam under the thick covering of red dirt, showing that this had once been a paved street. A big man in a heavy bearskin coat watched them cross the avenue, with an expression of extreme dislike. Krysty paused to stare at the man, he turned to walk away quickly, his massive shoulders hunched against the mounting winds.

"Real friendly folks," she muttered, checking the draw of her blaster as a precaution.

A couple of rusty bicycles leaned against the front of the inn, a lump of canvas in the street covering a mountain bike with studded tires. An old gray swayback horse was tied at a concrete post, the reins stretched to the limit so that the animal could slurp noisily from a mossy water trough. Its saddle was merely ropes and blankets, the reins spliced leather belts. A mangy German shepherd was asleep under the horse, and as the companions approached, the dog awoke with a start and growled softly, baring dingy yellow teeth until they went past and stepped onto the wooden porch.

A handmade sign bid guests Welkom Too Cords Tavern, but the companions were impressed that somebody in the ville could write at all. It was rather a lost art these days. Throwing open the door, Ryan found himself facing a rain-stained sheet of plywood and realized it was a buffer to cut the wind from getting inside.

"Pretty smart," he said in admiration. "Got to use that trick myself."

Entering the inn, the companions separated, automatically going around opposite sides of the buffer so as not to offer a group target. Inside, the inn was a lot larger than it seemed from the street, the single huge room filled with redwood picnic tables salvaged from predark days. A few had been expertly repaired with a lighter-colored wood, but every one was in good condition, offering seats for six at each. Old faded advertisements for beer companies adorned the walls. Most featured amazingly busty blondes in string-bikini swimsuits skiing down snowy mountains. Two fieldstone fireplaces stood at opposite ends of the room throwing out waves of heat, and a bar spanned the back of the building, rows of different shaped bottles filling the shelves, the mirror behind long gone.

The ceiling was festooned with fluorescent light fixtures reminiscent of bygone days. Now oil lanterns stood on every table with a customer. The rest dark and deserted.

More than a dozen men sat at the communal tables, slurping soup from wooden bowls or drinking from battered tin cups. A tall spindly man with a red beard was working as the barkeep, filling mugs with frothy beer. Cleaning off a dirty table was a young girl with midnight-black hair and figure she barely could keep within the tight clothing. Jak almost stumbled when he saw the pretty waitress, and bumped into an occupied table hard enough to rattle the plates.

"Sorry," he apologized, backing away, not taking his sight off the waitress.

Crossing the room, Ryan chose a table slightly away from the locals, but with a good view of the front door. As the companions took their places on the attached bench, the raven-haired waitress hurried over from behind the bar and lit the table lantern with a smoldering piece of oakum. The light had a faint yellow tint, both from grease on the flume and the dirty oil in the basin.

"Well, well, been a while since we last had outlanders in town. Welcome to the Hilton," she said, placing both hands on her hips. "I'm Lil. That's Cord, my pa, behind the bar with the shotgun. What'll you have?"

"You got rooms, as well as food here?" Krysty asked, sliding off her heavy coat.

"Sure." Lil frowned. "Upstairs on the second floor. They're clean and not too many bugs. But this ain't no gaudy house. We serve food and booze. Nothing more.''

"Good," Ryan said, placing the box of ammo on the table, removing half the rounds, then sliding it over. "Food and three rooms for two nights."

Expertly, the waitress caught the box as it went off the end and suspiciously examined the ammo before tucking it away into her apron. "Cord will test them tomorrow," she said. "If these are loaded with dirt instead of powder, the sec men will toss you into the pit."

"They're good," J.B. stated, tilting back his hat to a more comfortable position.

Lil looked over the group, then smiled. "Yeah, they are. One thing I can spot is shams."

"Thank you for the compliment, dear lady. And pray tell, what is the bill of fare?" Doc asked, beaming a smile with his strangely perfect teeth.

She stared blankly at the man.

"What's for food," Mildred translated, kicking the time traveler under the table.

"Oh, gotcha." Her face brightened. "Well, we got rabbit stew. It's fresh today and pretty damn good. There's cold mutton, and we can toss a few taters into the fire for ya. Bread and onions, of course, but we're out of venison jerky. There is plenty of drippings and stale bread, but you paid for better than that slop. No pies till spring, but we got some apple butter left. Some smoked bacon, plenty of salted fish."

"What kind of fish?" Krysty asked, fanning out her hair with both hands to hide the fact it was spreading all by itself.

Lil shrugged. "River fish."

"Not from the quarry, is it?" Mildred asked pointedly. "Where you toss cheats and maybe your night soil?"

The woman pursed her lips tight. "That could be," she finally admitted sheepishly, clearly embarrassed at getting caught.

"I'll go with the rabbit stew," Ryan decided, laying the Steyr on the table. "Big bowls and plenty of bread."

The rest followed the choice, with Dean adding apple butter to the order.

"For dessert," he explained.

"What there to drink?" Jak asked, feeling his muscles loosen from the waves of heat coming from the fireplace.

"Water, sassafras tea, hot or cold—your choice. Cook has something he calls coffee, but nobody else agrees."

"I said to drink," the teenager repeated.

She laughed. "Beer and 'shine at the bar, if you got more ammo or something else to trade. We don't take big-ville jack here."

"Why not?"

Lil shrugged as if the question were unanswerable.

"Any place we can wash before our repast, dear lady?" Doc asked politely.

The waitress looked at the oldster with newfound respect. "To the right of the bar, there's a tub and some towels. Lav is out back behind the woodpile. I'll get the food." Lil walked away, her shapely hips moving in the age-old rhythm of dodging tables and the fumbling hands of drunks. She disappeared into the rear of the building and returned a few ticks later to start wiping down the bar counter.

"We go in pairs," Ryan directed, surreptitiously easing off the safety on his rifle. "One person stands guard while the other washes. Nobody goes anywhere alone."

"You feel it, too," Krysty said, glancing around. "They seem kind of tense here about strangers."

"Maybe lots of coldhearts in the area," Mildred speculated, placing both hands on the tabletop. "After the Freedom Mall fell, there must have been sec men who survived and went looking for work."

"Mebbe that's the problem with Front Royal," J.B. suggested, passing the physician a grenade under the table. She took the ferruled sphere and tucked it into her medical bag, still draped across her shoulders.

"No sense guessing," Ryan said, rising from the table with blaster in hand. "We'll find out soon enough. I'll hit the wash first. Krysty?"

"Right with you, lover," the woman replied, and they headed into the back room. A score of eyes watched them leave.

"Going for drink. Right back." Jak stood and brushed the wild tangle of snowy hair off his face.

As he walked to the bar, a few of the patrons chuckled as the albino passed, so Jak brushed back his jacket to expose the .357 Colt Python riding in his belt. The laughter died, and the men turned their attention to the food and drink on their tables. A group started dealing cards, while another took out a harmonica.

There were no stools at the bar, so Jak rested an arm on the counter and laid down a handful of spare cartridges. The oddball-sized rounds fit none of the weapons of the companions and so were good only for trading.

"Whew, quite a pile there, Whitey. What'll it be?"

"Two fingers 'shine," the teenager replied. "Nothing ground level, either. Old and copper or forget."

"Wouldn't sell dirt 'shine to a mutie," the barmaid scoffed, her hands busy below the counter. "It's all clean brew."

He winked. "Taste will tell."

Murmurs sounded from the dining tables, and Jak assumed it was just the card players arguing over a deal.

Placing a ceramic mug on the bar, the raven-haired beauty retrieved a clay jug from one of the shelves on the wall. Working the wooden stopper loose, she hoisted the big container on a shoulder and poured two jiggers into the cracked IBM logo mug.

Visually inspecting the brew, Jak took a sniff, then sipped and nodded in satisfaction. "Good stuff, no priming."

She was impressed. The outlander didn't have the look of a boozehound, but he sure knew his 'shine. The woman leaned an elbow on the counter, their arms almost touching. "What's the handle?"

"Jak Lauren."

"Lily DuQuesne. 'Tiger' to my friends."

Strange, he could have sworn she said Lil out on the floor.

"We friends," he said, nudging her arm.

"I'll bet we could be, at that. You work 'shine?"

"Yeah," he said, taking another sip. "Down bayou ran own."

"A man of few words, I see."

He nodded.

"I like that." Lily smiled, looking him deep in the eyes. Damnedest thing, they were as red as the dawn. She felt the urge to caress his cheek and stayed her hand by force of will.

Jak saw that her eyes were a deep emerald green, just like that old jade he found once in a predark museum.

She was almost as lovely as his Christina.… The memory of his murdered wife cooled his passion completely, and the teenager stood back a bit from the ravishing woman.

Instantly, Lily felt the mood change, and she could see some dark memory cloud his face. Instinctively, she understood it was for a deceased love or family member. Hell's bells, everybody lost kin these days, especially with all the trouble at Front Royal. Taking his mug, she poured another two jiggers without being asked.

"So what did you use for sweet?" she asked, pushing the mug closer.

He drained it in a gulp, then slowly faced her again. "Beets," Jak replied without a trace of warmth. He was just answering a question, nothing more. "Honey when could."

"How did you make it taste old?"

Without meaning to, the teenager grinned. "Touch of iodine," Jak admitted.

"Yeah, you've done 'shine. Here, next round is on me." Lily started to pour a third drink.

"Two is limit," Jak said, snaking his hand across the counter to touch her arm. The woman's skin was a light, creamy pale—a peaches-and-cream complexion, he had heard Mildred call it, but she looked tan when compared to his white skin.

She patted his powerful hand. "I'm no gaudy slut."

The albino smiled. "Then free?" he teased.

Lily frowned in mock anger, then laughed out loud and this time playfully squeezed his forearm to feel the hard muscles beneath the camouflaged military jacket. "Strong," she purred. "I do like them strong."

Relaxing under the powerful 'shine, Jak stroked her

cheek. "Soft," he whispered deep in his throat. "Like a flower petal."

Lily smiled and removed the sweaty cloth around her neck, exposing a wealth of cleavage. "You have no idea," she whispered.

"Hey, Lily!" called out a big bald man, stumbling from the dining tables. He banged his mug on the counter, cracking the plastic. "Stop fondling that stinking mutie and come serve a real man!"

A knife slid from his sleeve into his palm as Jak turned with an expression of white-hot anger. Dropping a tray, Cord grabbed his shotgun just in time to cover the dozen men as they rose from their tables, fisting a wide assortment of blasters.

"Everybody freeze!" Ryan thundered from the corner of the room as he loudly worked the bolt on his longblaster.

Chapter Three

"Nobody move!" J.B. added, working the bolt on his Uzi, the noise supernaturally loud in the room.

Silence reigned for several moments, the only sounds the gentle crackle of the fireplace and the thudding of human hearts.

The hill men waited, gauging their chances. Ryan and Krysty stayed motionless at the washroom door ready for the first killing move. Cord kept his blaster pointed at nobody in particular, prepared to chill whoever started the fight that would surely wreck his bar.

Inch by inch, Jak eased his knife forward until it was pressing against the neck of the bald man.

"What the—?" he gasped, and darted a hand for his blaster. But there was only empty leather on his belt.

As slow as molasses, Lily pressed the barrel of the snub-nosed Police Special .38 wheelgun against his head. "Looking for this, Phillipe?" she said without apparent emotion.

His hand still reaching at his belt, the mercie curled a lip at the barmaid. "Fucking bitch," he whispered.

Ruthlessly, Jak nudged his hand forward a hair, and blood began to well around the knife point buried in the man's throat.

"Hey, you got me, I give. It was only a joke," Phillipe said, forcing a smile as he raised his hands in surrender. "Just a joke."

"You sure now?" Lily asked, clicking the hammer backward.

The table of mercies watched the scene closely. Ryan and the companions watched the mercies. Cord kept his eyes on his daughter.

Sweat beaded on Phillipe's forehead, a rivulet of blood trickling into his dirty shirt. "A joke," he repeated.

"Wouldn't start a fight here. We're drinking, for God's sake! I was jazzing the kid. No harm done, right?"

Keeping her thumb tight on the spur, Lily eased down the hammer until the double-action was at rest. "Okay, then, Phillipe. Nobody could get insulted from just a joke. Right?"

"Yeah, sure. Absolutely."

Everybody in the room relaxed a notch. Fingers were removed from triggers, and barrels shifted aim. Jak removed the blade from Phillipe's throat, and the man eased his stiff position.

"All right, show's over," Cord stated, resting the shotgun on his shoulder. "You new folks already paid, so back to your table, the food will be out soon.

"On the other hand," he said roughly, "you mercies had better get back to the stables. Ya want to be fresh when the caravan leaves in the morning."

"You chasing us out?" demanded a burly man, his long greasy hair tied back in a ponytail.

"Not me. This is." Cord patted the scattergun.

Krysty grunted slightly, but Ryan said nothing, letting the big barkeep handle the problem. His targets were already chosen, and the Deathlands warrior already had four pounds of pressure on the six-pound trigger.

Phillipe touched his throat, the fingertips coming away stained red. "We paid for our drinks, too, Cord!"

Chewing that over, Cord relented. "Fair enough. But that is your last round. Lily!"

"Bar's closed," she announced, tugging on a cord and ringing a small brass bell hidden up in the rafters. "Bar is closed!"

"When you men have finished what's on the table, leave," Cord said, pulling a chair closer and taking a seat. "I'll just sit here till you're done."

Holstering the blasters, the mercenaries sat back down at the table and started grumbling among themselves.

Their weapons still at the ready, Ryan and Krysty walked slowly along the counter, keeping their faces toward the drunk mercies until reaching their own table.

"My blaster," Phillipe said, holding out his hand.

Lily clicked down the safety and tossed it to him.

Catching the weapon, he turned toward Jak only to see the teenager's Colt Python out and pointed at his groin.

"Go for it," Jak said. His head was tilted forward, the snowy hair masking his face. It was an unnerving sight.

Phillipe felt the blood pound in his temples, then by sheer force of will, returned the blaster to its holster. Turning, he walked to the picnic table as if he didn't have a care in the world.

"Close," Jak said, putting away his blaster and shoving the knife up his sleeve again. "Cold man. Solid ice."

"Too damn close," Lily stated, resting an elbow on the counter and revealing a tiny .22 derringer in her other hand. "But those damn mercies have been causing trouble since they arrived last week. Stephen is a cheap bastard and hires anybody with muscles to ride blaster duty with his convoy. Damn fool.''

''Thanks,'' the teenager said, then pulled the woman close and kissed her hard and long. When they broke, her face was flushed, and she kept starting to smile and fighting it down.

''We'll do more of that later. In my room.'' She placed an iron key in his palm, her fingers warm on his skin. ''Top of the stairs, last door on the left.''

Jak tucked the key away. Brushing away his long hair, he picked up the mug and drained the last few drops of 'shine.

''Now go eat,'' she said, openly smiling at last. ''Man needs to keep his strength up.'' For some reason, she seemed to stress the last word.

Since it finally seemed safe to move, several of the other patrons rose from their tables and headed for the plywood blocking the door, a short cold breeze announcing when each hurriedly departed.

Hiding the derringer in her clothes, Lily went into the aft room and returned almost immediately carrying a heavy tray laden with food. Jak followed her to the table and took a seat between Mildred and Doc. Blasters were lying on the wood slats to forestall any further interruptions.

The mercenaries across the room noticed the arsenal of blasters, and spoke softly among themselves. Phillipe seemed to be holding court, with the others listening closely.

With the tray braced on a hip, Lily dished out the food efficiently, as if this were a chore done a thousand times before, then returned to the steamy kitchen. One tick later, the raven-haired beauty came out again and went behind the bar to start wiping down the counter with a damp rag.

"That barmaid saved a lot of lives," Ryan said, using his own spoon to sample the stew. The food was hot, thankfully, and even had a few herbs floating about, but there was a lot more vegetables than meat, and grease seemed to be the primary ingredient, even above water.

"Yeah, theirs," Jak growled, dipping the black bread into the brimming bowl and biting off a mouthful. "Bad!"

"We've eaten worse," Mildred reminded him, forcing down another swallow. Her foot was throbbing painfully, and she did her best to ignore that and concentrate on eating. The physician debated taking an aspirin, but held off taking one until later so she could sleep.

"Not by much," Krysty said, chewing on a piece of gristle.

"Bacca would not have been pleased," Doc noted sourly.

He scanned the tabletop. "Any chance of some salt, my good doctor?"

Mildred reached into a pocket, extracted a small container and slid it across the rough wood. "Our last," she warned.

"Thank you." He applied a sprinkling. "Pepper?"

She barked a laugh.

"I'll take that as a negative," Doc said sadly. Such was understandable. Salt could be garnished from the ocean, while pepper had to be specially grown, dried properly and then finely ground. He recalled that in ancient Rome during the reign of Augustus Caesar, soldiers were often given the choice of a pound of black pepper for their monthly wages, or a pound of gold, the price of the two being equal. Most took the pepper.

"Over here," Dean said, and the salt began to make the rounds.

In spite of the lack of additional condiments, the companions dug into their meal with gusto. Hunger was always the best sauce.

"Damn mutie," Krysty whispered, using her tarnished spoon to push away a glob of grease to reach the thin stew underneath.

"Huh?" Dean said, arching an eyebrow.

"The mercies are discussing us," she replied, not lifting her head or motioning in that direction. Her hearing was much better than a norm's, and while she was missing the occasional word, most of what the mercies said was perfectly audible.

"Not favorably, I would guess," J.B. said, ripping apart some bread. Taking a bite, he frowned but chewed and swallowed anyway. Acorn bread. Dark night, he hated the stuff. The Trader used to love it and often went out of his way to get more of the delicacy. J.B. would trade his away for cigars, or spare brass, or anything else available.

"They're talking about chilling us to get our blasters," Krysty answered, dicing a potato. The tubers were brown on the inside, but not black with rot, so she ate them anyway.

"When?" Jak asked, chewing on a bit of overcooked rabbit. He started to spit it on the floor when he saw Lily glancing his way while she was storing the bottles from the wall shelf. She winked, and the teenager swallowed the inedible bit of fat and smiled as if the meal were fit for a baron.

"Soon," she replied. "They've also been watching how much we've been drinking."

Ryan swallowed to clear his throat. "Ambush?"

"When we go to the lav," Krysty said, wiping her mouth clean on a pocket rag.

"Thought as much," Ryan said sourly, pushing away his bowl. "We hurt their pride, and now it's a matter of honor to get us. Triple-stupe fools. Okay, if they're going to do a night-creep, then we choose the time and the place."

"Well, this table is no good," J.B. said, running his hand over the surface. "But the one behind us should do."

"Agreed. Jak?"

"Yeah?" the teenager replied, pausing in the act of picking his teeth with a sliver of wood. Lily was beautiful, but apparently couldn't cook to save her life. He damn near broke a tooth when he found buckshot in the meat.

"Go flirt with the barmaid and warn her there's going to be a fight. Nothing we can do."

"And dally a bit," J.B. added. "Don't make it seem you're just there to deliver a message."

"Gotcha." The teen rose and walked casually to the bar, smiling and radiating charm.

"Tight quarters," Mildred noted, measuring distances with her eyes. "Not much room for maneuvering." Out of sight below the table, she took J.B.'s hand and gave it a squeeze. He replied in kind, maintaining the contact for much longer than necessary.

"Better here," Ryan stated, ladling more stew into his bowl to make it appear they weren't going anytime soon. "Outside, their numbers would work against us.

Twelve to seven aren't the best odds. But we'll be ready long before they start to leave and then—''

''There they go.'' Dean pointed with his wet spoon.

The mercies across the room were rising from their two tables, pulling on heavy coats and murmuring among themselves in guttural voices.

''Move fast, people,'' Ryan directed, taking the lantern from their table and placing it on the fireplace mantel.

Quickly, the companions stepped free from the confining bench-and-table combo, moving to other tables for protection. Turning away from the cheery fire, Ryan watched the departing men head for the front door and loudly said, ''So you're going to ambush us in the alleyway, are you?''

Already past at the plywood, Phillipe jerked his head back into view with a shocked expression.

''Shit-fire, boss, they know!'' said one of his crew, dropping his bedroll.

''Ace them!'' cried another, drawing a brace of wheelguns from underneath his long coat. One blaster misfired, only spraying burning sparks, but the other boomed, and something slammed into the poster on the wall behind them.

Mildred flipped over the new table, and the companions ducked for cover as the first fusillade of rounds hit everything near them. The solid redwood table bucked and jumped from the impacts, but no holes appeared in the thick planks.

The barrage stopped for a tick, and J.B. fired the Uzi in a long burst. A line of holes crawled across the plywood barrier, splinters exploding from the furious assault of the 9 mm rounds. One man grabbed his face and spun away, spraying blood. Another dropped to his knee and clutched a wounded leg, but still fired his weapon.

"Corner!" Phillipe shouted, and the mercies retreated quickly.

Their leader grabbed the lantern and the others flipped over the old table and used it as a shield as the mercies backed into the corner where nobody could get behind them.

"Mine!" Jak shouted from the bar. The teenager leaned over the counter, holding his huge Colt Python in both hands. The powerful .357 pistol spoke three times, the big-bore wheelgun punching holes straight through the replacement pine boards in the repaired table.

A screaming man stumbled into view clutching the ruin of his belly, his hands full of writhing intestines. Krysty took careful aim and shot him in the heart. The noise stopped instantly, and the corpse slumped to the floor in a spreading pool of red fluid.

Sitting on her medical bag to keep pressure off her foot, Mildred sniped at the others with her ZKR target pistol. Dean aimed for the floor, trying to hamstring the mercies, while J.B. and Ryan maintained a steady holding fire. Trapped, Phillipe and his crew could do nothing until the barrage of lead eased enough for them to chance fighting back.

Switching the selector pin on his two-barrel LeMat, Doc triggered the monstrous handcannon, its blackpowder roar deafening in the confines of the spacious room. A foot-long tongue of flame reached out from the pitted muzzle, and a fist-sized hole appeared in another pine board. A gasping mercie stumbled into view, moving backward, and went out the window in a crash of glass. Instantly, a bitterly cold wind blew into the bar as a woman began to scream outside.

With one of his dead crew propped in front as cover, Phillipe was firing a MAC-10 machine pistol through the narrow slot between the table and the attached bench. But the blaster constantly stopped, and he kept working the bolt to clear a jammed round from the ejector port. Oddly, he seemed to be aiming for the fireplace mantel.

Slamming a fresh rotary clip into the Steyr, Ryan realized the man was going for the lantern, trying to start a fire and force them into view.

"Cover me," he shouted, and the companions began wildly shooting as fast as possible, forcing the others into hiding for a moment. Moving fast, Ryan stood and swept the lantern into the fireplace in a single movement. The glass basin shattered as it hit the burning logs, and the oil ignited into a raging fireball that swelled out into the room for a single heartbeat, then the flames died down to normal.

"Fuck this," somebody growled, and a wiry man darted from the corner, heading for the riddled sheet of plywood trying to escape.

Slamming in a fresh clip, Dean snapped off two shots, catching the mercie in the boot. Yowling with pain, the man went down and started crawling for the door until Krysty finished him off with a round to the head.

Bottles burst on the wall behind him as Jak emptied his Colt into the table, making lots of holes in the soft pine, but no screams sounded. The mercies had gotten wise and were avoiding the weak spot in their defense. Then a man dived under a nearby picnic table and kicked it over. Safe behind the solid redwood planks, he dragged the heavy furniture toward the damaged table.

"They're fortifying their position," J.B. snapped, reloading the Uzi with a spare clip from the ammo pouch on his belt.

"We have grens," Krysty suggested, thumbing fresh rounds into the cylinder of her open wheelgun. She eased the loaded cylinder shut and clicked back the hammer looking for new targets.

Longblaster to his cheek, Ryan fired a fast five times at the moving table and didn't get penetration. That was the very reason he choose to fight inside—the hundred-year-old redwood was a hell of a shield. "Can't use explosives," he said, working the bolt and inserting another clip. "The concussion would kill us, too."

"Not necessarily," Mildred stated, lowering her piece.

Peeking out from around the side of the battered table, Doc fired once more with extreme care. His titanic LeMat held nine shots, but then took minutes to recharge, and he was down to three remaining loads.

"A bait-and-switch?" Doc asked, waving the barrel to disperse the volumes of acrid smoke pouring from the hot maw of the blaster.

"Sure."

"Do it," Ryan ordered, passing Doc the loaded rifle and drawing the SIG-Sauer P-226 from his belt.

Holstering her weapon, Mildred took the grenade from her pocket, unwrapped the tape holding the arming lever in place, then stood and threw the unprimed military charge. The sphere bounced off the side of the fireplace across the room and neatly rolled behind the enemy table.

"Gren!" a man screamed, backing away from the explosive.

The silenced 9 mm pistol coughing softly, Ryan shot him in the chest as the rest of the mercies raced away from what they thought was certain death. J.B. got two more with the chattering Uzi, Dean wounded another in the shoulder, and Doc blew away the gun-filled hand of the fourth.

Suddenly, a limp man dived clumsily for the window, and everybody concentrated on stopping him. At the same moment, Phillipe made a dash for the exit from the other end of the long table, hosing lead from the MAC-10 and wildly firing somebody else's revolver.

The bastard had thrown a corpse as a diversion! Ryan trained his blaster on the fleeing man, when a blur moved across the room and the handle of a knife sprouted from the throat of the mercie chief. Clawing at the hideous wound, crimson pouring down his shirt, Phillipe stumbled against the wall and the companions shot him enough times to make sure he stayed down. The body jerking like a mad puppet under the concentrated barrage of flying lead.

As the assault slowed, Phillipe fell face forward onto the dirty floor, driving the blade out the back of his neck. Blasters clenched in a death grasp, the dying leader of the mercies twitched once and went still.

Walking out from behind the bar, Jak crossed the room, kicking spent shells musically out of his way. Flipping the dead man over, Jak retrieved his knife.

"Any more?" Ryan asked, slamming a fresh clip into his blaster.

"One hiding in the corner," J.B. said, straightening his glasses. "See the blood trail?"

Sitting at a table, Doc took this opportunity to start

cleaning the chambers of his weapon prior to recharging. Burned gunpowder rained to the floor like black snow as he purged the holes with a brass brush.

"Come out, you," Ryan called, walking closer. "We want to talk."

"F-fuck y-you," a frightened voice stammered, and some bullets spilled into view from behind the bullet-ridden table as the trapped man fumbled trying to reload his weapon.

"Shit, shit, shit," he softly cursed. "Shit!"

Suddenly a thunderous discharge shook the room, rattling the windows and ringing the brass bell suspended above the bar.

Spinning toward the newcomer, the companions saw a group of heavily armed men walking around the smashed plywood barrier and bleeding corpses. Striding at the front was a short, crew-cut man with a dour expression, brandishing a smoking double-barrel shotgun.

"What the bloody hell is going on here?" the small man demanded, cracking the breech of his blaster to dump the spent shells onto the littered floor. They hit with a soft clatter and rolled away still smoking slightly.

Easing the safety off the Uzi just in case, J.B. noted the empty rounds as homemade reloads, and expertly done. Somebody in the ville really knew blasters.

The other men spread out across the room, taking strategic positions, their bolt-action rifles tight in their grips. Ryan listed them immediately as seasoned sec men.

"Them! They chilled my crew," the wounded mercie said, rising weakly to his feet, a hand clutching a bleeding shoulder. "We were just eating our dinner, and those mutie-loving freaks opened fire on us!"

His pale face a mask of rage, Jak started grimly forward. Lily stayed him.

"That's a lie," Ryan said calmly, holstering his blaster.

"That's what you say." The mercie glanced around. "How about it, Lily?" he asked bluntly.

"He's telling the truth, Monty," the barmaid stated. "Those damn mercies started the fight. I heard them talking about chilling the strangers to steal their blasters."

"Yeah?" Monty asked, sliding fresh shells into his sawed-off and snapping the breech closed with a jerk of his hand.

"Yeah," she repeated. The woman radiated a fury that was almost detectable over the heat from the fireplaces. "The outlander with the patch called them on it, and they started shooting."

Monty looked at Ryan, "A fair fight, then," he said slowly.

Lily snorted. "No, it wasn't. He didn't have a blaster in his hand till they started shooting."

Sliding the sawed-off shotgun into a wide holster hung over his shoulder, Monty hooked his thumbs into his wide leather belt and studied the one-eyed man for a minute before speaking.

"You don't look insane," he ventured thoughtfully. "But I have been fooled before. What's your version of this, Cord?"

The barkeep placed his shotgun on the shelf behind the bar. "It's as she said, Chief."

"Two for, one against," the sec chief said, and he gestured at the companions. "Looks like you folks can go about your biz."

"Planned to," Ryan stated, crossing his arms. "And I want to talk with the survivor."

"After I'm done with him." Monty advanced upon the skinny man bleeding by the fireplace. The mercie was almost twice the height of the tiny sec man, but there was no question who was in charge.

"However, you are going in the hole," Monty announced, looking up at his prisoner. "Lying to a sec man in this ville is a crime. Ten lashes."

"Y-you can't p-put me in chains," the frightened man stammered. "I'm bleeding! Shot!"

"And another ten for challenging my orders," Monty said, jerking the big man toward the door. "Harold, get this triple-stupe slackbrain out of here before I waste a round and chill him myself!"

A redhaired sec man took the prisoner by the collar and marched the trembling man outside into the cold dark night.

"Mercies," Monty growled, running a callused hand over his flat-top hair. "Bloody pains in the arse."

"Excuse me, sir, are you of British descent?" Doc asked curiously, sliding the LeMat back into its greased holster.

Lowering his head in the manner of a bull about to charge, Monty glowered at the oldster. "What about it, Yank?"

"Why, nothing, sir," Doc replied, smiling politely. "I was merely curious."

"Remember what it did to the cat," the sec chief said brusquely.

"Zed, block the busted window with a table. Thomas, give me a report."

The wind blowing steadily around him, a bald sec

man shoved an upright table in front of the hole, and the breeze dropped to fitful gusts around the edges.

Kneeling on the bloody floorboards, a black sec man rose from examining a pile of corpses. "They're all dead, that's for damn sure."

"I got eyes, man. How about the blasters?"

"Quite a selection here." Thomas lifted a handful of sticky weapons. "Autos, wheelguns and a grenade."

"A what?" Monty strode toward the man in his curious gait, reminding Ryan of a sailor on a ship at sea. "A gren. Well, I'll be damned. And the pin hasn't been pulled. Wonder why."

The small chief stared directly at Ryan. "They hid behind a table, and you flushed them out with a dud," he announced. "Pretty clever. Any chance you folks planning on staying in town for a while? I could use some more sec men. Winter is coming, and that means coldhearts will be hitting us for supplies soon."

"Just passing through," Krysty replied, her hair flowing as though still being stirred by mountain winds.

If Monty noticed anything, he made no comment. "Yeah, expected as much. North or south?"

"We haven't decided yet," Ryan answered quickly.

Monty scowled. "Right."

"Chief, about my place…" Cord started.

The leader of the sec man raised a hand. "Way ahead of you. The ville gets the usual half, and I'm sure these fine folks who don't shoot first in a fight will be happy to give you the rest to pay for the damage to your home. Fair enough?"

"Fair enough," Ryan agreed.

Wearily rubbing the back of his neck, Cord beamed a smile. "Thanks. That will help."

"And don't wait so long calling for help. That's why I'm here."

"Understood, sir."

"Ah, any chance you might consider using one of the blasters on that so-called cook of yours?" Monty asked.

"Tried it," Cord said deadpan. "Shooting only makes her mad and cook worse."

Monty cracked a smile. "Well, it was worth asking."

Slinging the Uzi, J.B. said, "The bar gets half of their property? Odd policy."

"That it is," the sec man agreed, loudly cracking his knuckles. "But I find it holds down trouble when folks know their blasters and clothes get divided afterward."

Just then a fat man pushed his way into the bar through the crowd of sec men. The newcomer was wearing an Aussie digger hat with a feathered plume, creased gray pants tucked loosely into polished boots and a heavy trench coat with natty embroidery on the sleeves and collar. There was no sign of a blaster or any other weapon.

After staring in horror at the bodies, the fancy-dressed man headed straight toward Monty and nearly fell as his shiny boots slipped in a slick puddle of congealing blood.

"Hello, Stephen," Cord said as if a vomiting dog had walked into his establishment.

"How many dead?" Stephen demanded, yanking off his hat and clutching it in his smooth hands. "Six? Eight?"

"Eleven," Monty answered without interest. "And one in the hole."

Stephen went pale. "Black dust, that's the lot of them. What am I going to do now?"

"Not my problem," Monty said, pouring himself a shot of 'shine from a jug on a table. He took a sip and sighed all the way down to his boots. "God, it's a cold night."

"Monty, you have to help me," Stephen pleaded, wringing the hat as if it were wet laundry. "Phillipe and his crew were my blasters for the journey north. Without them, I can't go."

"So?"

"So I should get all of their blasters as partial payment."

The sec chief of the ville rubbed his chin, the only visibly large thing about the tiny man. "Stephen, you're always bitching and whining, constantly trying to get more than your fair share of everything, and I'm more than sick of your endless crap. If it wasn't for the local folks traveling north with you tomorrow, I'd toss you and the whole damn caravan into the quarry with the rest of the night soil. I'm not short-changing Cord because you chose coldhearts for protection."

"But without them, I'm out of biz!"

"Tough."

"Damnation, where am I going to get more troops now?" Stephen raged, shaking a fist. "We have to leave at dawn if we're going to make Front Royal by end week."

The companions paused in their reloading.

"Where was that?" J.B. asked in surprise. "Where you going tomorrow?"

Monty pricked his ears at the reaction, but said nothing.

"Front Royal, big ville a hundred-plus miles north of here." Stephen suddenly seemed to register the presence of the companions. "Who are you folks? Friends of the deceased?"

"Hardly. These are the ones who chilled your top-notch crew," Monty snorted, taking another sip.

The ville sec men were already stripping the bodies of usable clothing and boots before rigor made the limbs too stiff to bend.

"And you're leaving tomorrow?" Mildred asked, sitting on a bench massaging her bandaged foot.

"At dawn," the sec chief replied. "Not a tick later."

Stephen glowered but said nothing.

"We were planning on traveling north," Ryan said, approaching the caravan owner. "Mebbe we can cut a deal."

"Just the seven of you?" Stephen sneered in contempt. "And three of those a whitehair, a kid and a crip? Bah, I can't carry any more passengers. Besides, I need at least a dozen blasters to make it through the badlands."

Slamming down his mug, Monty laughed. "Stephen, you are a total ass. These seven chilled your twelve and gave them the first shot."

"Really? Well, then, mebbe..." the fat man said thoughtfully, a crafty expression forming on his plump face. "So what would you charge for the trip? And remember, I already paid for mercies once already!"

"Cheap bastard," Cord muttered at the bar, pouring the contents of a broken bottle into an undamaged empty.

"No charge. Not even a slice of any goods found. We're not mercies," Ryan said, as if the word were unclean. "We go as passengers. Passengers, mind you. But if there's any trouble, we'll be more than willing to help defend the caravan."

"You turning down jack?" The fat man seemed scandalized at the very idea.

"The man who sells his honor," Doc intoned, as if delivering a lecture, "sells nothing he ever truly owned."

Stephen chewed that over for a minute, then extended an open hand. "Done, sir! Glad to have you on board."

Hesitantly, Ryan shook on the deal, not sure if he had solved a lot of their problems or just invited a whole new set.

Chapter Four

As Ryan and Stephen talked over coffee in the dining room about the details of the journey north, Jak took the opportunity to go into the kitchen. The huge iron stove was blazing with heat, with a full cord of split wood nearby for easy access. Pots and pans festooned the ceiling, and plates and mugs were stacked in a plastic rack above a chipped enamel sink. There was no sign of the cook.

Moving down the aft corridor, he went straight to the last door on the left and knocked softly. A female voice bid him enter, and Jak used the iron key to let himself inside.

The room was dimly lit with candles, and Lily was standing near a canopy bed, the heavy blankets pulled back. Her work blouse was undone, showing that she was wearing nothing underneath. As he closed and locked the door, she slid her arms around the pale youth, and they deeply kissed. His hands glided down her muscular back to cup her buttocks, and Jak brought her closer, tight against his body.

A figure moved in the darkness.

With a curse, Jak pushed the woman aside and drew his Colt Python and moved to the corner to protect his back. Lily gave a low laugh as the figure stepped into the flickering light, and the teenager gasped.

"Twins?" he said, lowering his blaster. Suddenly

feeling like a fool for not figuring it out, he holstered the piece quickly.

"Sorry."

"You didn't think one woman could handle all the work in that tavern, did you?" Lil laughed, undoing the red ribbon in her black tresses. The ebony cascade tumbled past her shoulders, framing a strong face, a soft smile on her full lips.

Also smiling, Lily eased off her blouse and it fluttered to the floor. Her breasts were full but firm, unmarked by the signs of motherhood. "We share the work load."

Lil undid her belt, her skirt tumbling into the darkness at her bare feet, undressing in the dreamlike motions of animal sensuality. Clearly, they had been expecting him as she also was wearing no undergarments.

"We share everything," the woman whispered, pinching out a candle flame and the room dimmed slightly.

Four hands began to caress the scarred youth, undoing buttons and belts, removing an endless array of weapons.

"Strong, he's so very strong," one sister whispered hoarsely.

"He better be," the other said as she went to her knees and took Jak fully into her mouth.

Lily kissed him again, and no more words were spoken through the long autumn night.

MILDRED HAD GONE TO BED early, complaining that her ankle ached, so J.B. entered their assigned room on the second floor as quietly as possible so not to wake her. The negotiations with the caravan leader had gone well, and the trip should be an easy job. Mildred was going to ride shotgun, so she wouldn't have to use her sprained foot for driving the whole way. That should please her a lot.

Opening the door, J.B. was surprised to find the room lit with more candles than anybody would have deemed necessary and some sort of sweet-smelling incense musky in the air. Covered by blankets to the neck, Mildred was lying in the big bed smiling expectantly. Her gun belt was draped over the nearby end table, the medical bag in the corner.

"Thought you were feeling poorly," the Armorer said carefully.

Mildred motioned him closer, causing the blankets to slide down to her waist and expose her full breasts.

"Come here, John," she whispered, "and see for yourself how I feel."

The candlelight glistened off her skin, and J.B. realized for the hundredth time what a truly beautiful woman she was.

The most beautiful he had ever been with. Closing the door tightly, he slid a chair under the latch to make sure there were no interruptions until the dawn.

WALKING UP THE RICKETY STAIRS to the second floor, Ryan and Krysty took the middle room and bid goodnight to Doc and Dean.

"Where's Jak?" Dean asked, scowling.

"With the barmaid," his father replied, unlocking the door to their room.

"Wonder if he noticed there's two of them," Krysty said, chuckling and fighting back a yawn.

"They were twins?" Dean asked, confused.

"Come along, young Master Cawdor," Doc said, sporting a grin for the other adults to see. "I'll explain it to you tomorrow. Good night."

"Night," Krysty replied as she closed the door.

Standing near the bed, Ryan was already stripped to the waist, checking his weapons one last time before placing them on a nearby chair. Free from the weight, he stretched, listening to his joints crack and pop.

"Been a long day," he said, sighing, kicking off his boots. "Tomorrow, as well."

"Not over yet, lover," Krysty purred, and her shirt flew across the room to land on top of his clothes.

The man turned to find the woman already naked. The lone candle did little to illuminate the darkness, but a flood of moonlight gave the room a surreal appearance as if everything were forged of purest silver laid on black velvet, including the redhead's luscious curves.

Krysty held out her arms invitingly, and he joined her in an ardent embrace, her nails lightly scratching down his muscular back and across his powerful waist. Her nipples hardened against his chest as he rose between her soft thighs.

"Pretty fast for an old man. Been a while, hasn't it, lover?" she whispered.

"Too long," he growled, and lifted her bodily off the cold floorboards.

Krysty grabbed his head and pressed it between her breasts as he blindly walked to the bed and placed her on the downy quilt. Mouths and hands roamed freely, tasting, touching, stroking in a banquet of intimacy.

A noise outside the window made them both pause to make sure the blasters were at hand, safeties off. But as the voices moved on, Ryan gently pushed her down on the bed and started to spread wide her strong thighs.

Unexpectedly, the woman wrapped her long legs around his waist and hauled him down onto the bed beside her. Then, lifting herself up on her knees, Krysty used her hands to stroke him hard and make sure Ryan was ready before deliciously lowering herself, fully engulfing him until their hips rested together and their bodies fused for a brief few seconds in perfect symmetry.

His hands gently caressed her breasts and thighs as she rocked slowly, teasingly, back and forth, the moist heat of her growing passion flowing over him as he stiffened even more to fill her by the heartbeat.

Her long hair cascaded across both their bodies, hiding and revealing as the animated locks responded to her enhanced emotional state. Private words were spoken, secrets revealed, as the couple went beyond words, every breath needed to fuel their bodies locked together in the writhing rhythm more basic and primordial than speech or thought.

Suddenly, Krysty arched her back, thrusting herself hard against the man. Ryan grabbed her hips, holding her motionless for a tick as he thrust deeper into her innermost reaches until their minds were conscious only of each other responding, touch, taste and sound combining into a wild elixir of near drunken intoxication. The creaking of the bed was muffled by their breathing as the chill vanished from the small room, and for a brief moment of time, the world was at peace for the two wanderers.

AS ASKED FOR, there were two double beds in Doc and Dean's room, along with a table, chair and a tin bucket full of tepid water with a cracked ceramic mug tied to the handle with old twine. An oil lantern lit the bare room bright enough for reading, but both of the occupants were too exhausted to think of anything but sleep.

"Ah, Morpheus claims even the giants of yore," Doc

said with a yawn, sitting on the edge of his bed. Easing off his boots, he massaged his stocking feet. "Time to surrender to his dark embrace."

"Sounds good to me," the boy agreed, rubbing his eyes sleepily. Carefully checking his blaster, Dean set it on the table between their separate beds.

"Hey, Doc?" he asked, climbing under the covers.

Already under his blankets, the oldster turned over. "Yes, my young friend?"

"Can you tell me about women? I've only had a little experience with someone I liked at school."

That brought the time traveler fully awake as if doused with ice water. So the boy was starting to notice the wonderful attractions between men and women. This should have been a question for his father, but Doc was here and there were few matters the companions didn't discuss openly. Modesty and reticence were two of the first causalities of the nukestorm that had consumed the world.

"Ahem…well, certainly," Doc said, brushing the hair off his weathered face. "Are, ah, are we discussing the mechanics of intimacy?"

Dean chuckled at the predark word. "I know what goes where," he chided. "I've seen a lot on my travels with Rona, my mother." The boy sat up in bed, hugging his knees. "I mean, how did Jak ask the barmaid and how did he know she liked him, and…?"

"I see, you wish to know the answer to the ultimate question," Doc replied. "A question that has a thousand answers, and no answers. How did our Mr. Lauren know? He did not know. He simply asked."

"But—"

"Let me explain. There is a classic tale from predark days of an ordinary man who stood in the middle of

Times Square, part of a huge ville in its day, and to every woman who passed by he asked if she would like to, ahem, copulate with him.''

"Do what?"

"Have sex."

"Really? Some fool tried that with Krysty or Mildred, and they'd get a chair busted over the head. Or worse.''

"Indeed. As did this fellow. He got slapped, punched, kicked, stabbed, shot…'' Doc paused dramatically. "And copulated.''

There was a minute of silence from the other side of the room. "So it's random, sort of a shotgun thing. You keep asking until one says yes, and with any luck, she's good folks.''

Doc nodded at his pupil. "Wise enough for this night, young Master Cawdor. Understand?''

Dean chewed that over. "Not really.''

"Me, neither.'' Doc laughed, and turning down the wick, he killed the lantern. "How my dear Emily or the sweet Lori ever succumbed to my dubious charms I shall never understand. But if you do figure out the mystery of the ages, please be so kind as to inform the rest of mankind, won't you?''

"Sure,'' the boy mumbled, rolling over onto his side. "No prob.''

ON THE COLD STREETS of the ville, two figures moved through the darkness to the creek that washed through a sluice gate and into the quarry below. One man kept careful watch as the other tossed in a plastic bottle.

"Sure they'll understand?'' the short man asked.

The bald man bared a broken-toothed grin. "Of course they will. Only dumb-ass four-eyes learn reading and such. We send them a bottle with a sheet of paper, means one thing. Bottle with a feather means another, and like that. Who needs writing?''

''But you stuffed this one full of leaves. What does that mean?''

The ville sec man watched as the bobbing bottle quickly floated along the turbulent creek and vanished out of sight into the stygian night. ''Revenge,'' he said softly.

Chapter Five

With the coming of the dawn, the companions met in the dining room of the inn and broke fast with toasted acorn bread, wild honey and bacon. Mildred inspected the bacon carefully before allowing any of them to eat the meat. Nowadays, undercooked ham in any form could give a person trichinosis, which meant a horrible death, eaten alive by the microscopic worms.

Feeling brave that morning, Doc dared to venture a cup of the cook's homemade coffee, and ruefully agreed with the rest of the ville. It looked like coffee and smelled similar, and there the resemblance abruptly ended.

They were just finishing their second helping when a blast of cold air swept the room, and Stephen walked into view from around the damaged plywood buffer. This day the fat man was dressed in tanned leather clothes, rough and durable, and rawhide boots, with none of the fancy trimmings of the previous day. A sleek longblaster was slung across his back, and a coiled bullwhip dangled from his left side. Canvas gloves were tucked into the front of his belt, a dark wool hat on his head.

As he drained his cup of sassafras tea, Ryan's opinion of the man went up a notch. At least he was dressed for travel today, and not like a baron's jester.

"Good morning," Stephen said, striding to their table. "The sun is up, so let's get moving. I want to reach the lake before nightfall, so we can avoid camping on the open road."

"Half expected Monty to be with you," J.B. said, brushing the crumbs off his shirt.

Stephen stole a slice of bread, dipped it into the bowl of cloudy honey and took a bite. "Crazy bastard woke me before dawn."

"The man sure doesn't like you," Mildred stated, rising carefully, keeping most of her weight on the crutch. "Might be wise to find another ville."

"Can't," Stephen mumbled, stuffing the rest of the acorn bread into his full mouth. He swallowed most of it unchewed. "I have to live here. Married his sister."

"Ah. My condolences."

The fat man shrugged and stole a drink from a cold cup of tea.

"Let's get moving," Ryan said, turning from the table in disgust. The caravan owner ate like a pig. The one-eyed man lifted his backpack and rifle in one hand. "The sooner we start, the earlier we arrive."

The rest of the companions gathered their belongings and started out, but a voice called for Jak.

He turned and saw Lily rushing over. She kissed him on the cheek, pressing a cloth bundle into his hand.

"Lil said to give you this in case you left before she got back," the woman said.

Jak weighed the package in his palm. "Heavy. What is?"

"A fifth of 'shine," she said. "The good stuff. So you'll think of us with every sip and not forget too quickly."

He pulled the woman close in a crushing hug and

kissed her deeply. "Won't forget," he said with unaccustomed feeling. "Ever."

Releasing her, he tucked the bottle into a pocket and buttoned the flap closed tight. Digging in another pocket of the fatigues, he unearthed a similar bundle.

"Here," he said, pushing it into her hands.

Smiling slightly, Lily untied the knot. Inside the square of cloth were a dozen .22-caliber rounds perfect for the derringer.

"Oh, Jak, we can't accept this. It's a fortune in ammo," she said and pushed it back. "Here."

He folded his hand over hers. "Keep, and think of me," he said. Then quickly added, "Gift. Not payment."

"I understand," Lily said, smiling, and kissed him again, this time long and hard on the lips.

"Goodbye." Jak lifted his satchel of supplies onto a shoulder.

"Good journey," she sniffed, and turned her back on him to start clearing the table.

As he walked from the building, Jak had the oddest feeling that he would be seeing them again soon, but under terrible circumstances. Irritably, he shook off the notion as nonsense. He was no doomie able to see the future. Probably just missing them already. Twins! What a night that had been.

Outside, the morning was damp and chilly, and Jak spied the others were already past the sandbag nest of the ville. Shifting into a run, he hurried along to catch them, the pocket of his jacket sloshing softly with every step.

"Wags are in there," Stephen said, gesturing toward a large splintery barn near the front gate. "I hired a boy to stay awake for the night and start the engines once an hour to keep them from seizing in the cold.''

"Pretty smart," J.B. admitted reluctantly. The unlit stub of a cigar jutted from the corner of his mouth. The tiny nubbin was his last, and the Armorer wasn't going to light the tobacco until he found more. Shouldn't be too hard, this was Virginia.

"I have done this many times before," Stephen boasted proudly.

"So have we," Krysty stated, not impressed.

Standing on a corner near a brick building, Monty watched them walk by, four of his armed sec men flanking him on both sides.

Wearing a bright red jacket, the squat man resembled a fireplug to Dean, but the boy wisely refrained from making that comment aloud.

"RCMP," Doc said, pausing for a second in the street. He snapped an odd palm-out salute to the security chief, and Monty reluctantly returned the gesture.

"What was that about?" Krysty asked.

"RCMP, the Royal Canadian Mounted Police," Doc explained, twirling his swordstick. "Also known as the Mounties. His family must have wandered down here during the long winter."

"The great-grandson of a predark cop," Ryan said. "No wonder Monty is such a good sec chief. It's in his blood."

Undoing a padlock, which squeaked in protest, Stephen opened the long door of the barn and threw it wide. Hurrying inside, the companions followed.

Empty horse corrals lined both sides of the structure, with a giant stack of hay at the rear of the building, and parked in the middle area were four predark vehicles standing side by side forming a tight square.

Stephen gave a small can of food to a boy who immediately bolted outdoors with the prize as the companions inspected the wags.

"A self-heat. You pay pretty good," Mildred said.

"Have to." The fat man sighed. "He's a cousin."

The front vehicles were large industrial trucks, flatbeds with wooden side rails festooned with bulging canvas sandbags, making them mobile forts. Behind the trucks were two rust-streaked vans with solid sides, no windows, with large sliding doors in the aft and huge windshields.

"Delivery vans." Ryan frowned. "Can't imagine a worse wag for fighting."

"Hopefully there won't be any," Stephen replied, hitching up his belt.

Krysty shot the man a look. "Ever done the journey without a fight?"

"Well, there's always a first time," he shot back.

"Idiot," Mildred said under her breath.

Footsteps crunching on the frozen ground announced the arrival of some people at the barn door.

"Just a tick, folks," Stephen shouted. "We'll be rolling soon."

"Okay, Mr. Stephen," a young man replied. Standing close to him was a young woman, no more than a girl, suckling a newborn baby under her blouse. There was a pile of patched duffel bags at their rag-wrapped boots.

Leaning against the barn door was a gruff pair of men dressed in clothes made entirely of animal furs, including their boots and hats. Large unsheathed knives were stuck in their belts, and each was smoking a homemade cig and held a muzzle-loading rifle as if it were part of them.

"Hunters," Jak said.

"Passengers," Stephen corrected him. "The big guys are Clem and Bob. The others are the Johnson family, Hector and Sara. Kid isn't old enough for a name yet."

"Only five, sir?" asked Doc. "I mean, four and a half?"

Jak sniggered.

"Hey, not many want to go anywhere near Front Royal these days," Stephen answered in frank honesty. Then he quickly added, "In the winter, I mean."

"Of course," Doc demurred, keeping a neutral expression.

"And this is the convoy," J.B. said, completing his circuit around the assortment of rickety vehicles. "Two trucks and two vans. All civilian wags."

"More than enough," Stephen stated huffily. "I have done this run a hundred times, and I always get through."

"Passengers, too?" Ryan asked, lifting a hood to check the engine.

"Accidents happen. What are you looking for?"

"Engine seems okay," Ryan announced, lowering the hood of the first truck.

"Told you so," Stephen chided, crossing his arms. "I take good care of my wags."

"Well, we're not going to take your word on it," J.B. said, going to the second truck and lifting the hood. The latch was stuck and required some pounding to get free. "We are passengers and will check the air in the tires if we think it necessary."

Stephen glanced out the barn at Monty, standing on the street corner. "But we're losing daylight."

"Ill-prepared is doomed from the start," Doc said, sliding open the door on one of the vans. He climbed into the seat and started the engine. It rattled and knocked for a while, then steadied to a smooth hum.

"This one is okay," he shouted out the window.

Dean slid into view from underneath a truck. "Springs okay. There's some body rust, but the thing is repaired with wood."

"Engine seem okay?" Mildred prodded, standing near.

Holding up the hood of the second truck with his hand, J.B. scowled at the greasy V6. "Yeah, I guess. No obvious problems. But I'll wrap some of the heater hoses with duct tape as a precaution."

"Tires seem in good shape," Ryan commented, inspecting the rubber for critical defects. A blowout on one of the mountain passes could tumble them into a ravine and chill them all faster than a mutie attack.

"They got me here," Stephen replied, sounding annoyed.

"Any spares?" Krysty asked.

"Two each, tied to the undercarriage."

"Blasters?" Jak asked bluntly.

"What you folks brought, and there's a brace of shotguns and a case of Molotovs."

"Homemade firebombs and two scatterguns, that's it?"

"Why would I need mercies if I had missiles and an electric minigun?"

Ryan accepted that.

Dean crawled over the trucks in a fast inspection. The first wag had the spare tires; the second truck carried all of the spare fuel. Big twenty-gallon military fuel cans were tied to the aft railing of the truck, which only made sense. They could always drop the cans as a bribe to stop folks chasing after the convoy. Or they could

release the cans with a lit fuse to block the road with a
wall of flame. Of the two tactics, he much preferred the
latter. The best defense was making the other fellow
dead, as his father always said.

"Plenty of juice," Dean announced, jumping to the
ground.

"Enough to get us there?" asked Krysty.

"Easy."

"Where did you get the gas?" J.B. asked curiously,
unscrewing a cap and taking a whiff. It wasn't the con-
densed fuel they found in the redoubts, or regular gas,
but something else. Not kerosene, either. Probably a
mixture of gas, kerosene, alcohol and anything else that
would run an engine. The Armorer hoped the man was
smart enough to add some bullet shavings and a drop
or two of used oil to the fuel to help maintain the engines internally.

"Where I find fuel," Stephen answered, glowering,
"is my biz."

He accepted the rebuff. "Fair enough."

"What's in here?" Mildred asked, rattling the door
of the second van. "It's locked."

"That's just some cargo for the baron," Stephen said
in a measured tone.

"Blasters?" Ryan asked, wiping off his hands on a
rag.

"Wheat."

"In the middle of autumn?" Mildred asked, tossing
in her medical satchel into the first van.

Stephen scowled. "Wheat," he repeated, walking toward the people waiting at the doorway.

The companions exchanged brief looks, but said
nothing aloud.

"Okay, folks!" Stephen shouted between cupped hands. "We're leaving now. Get your stuff on board."

In an orderly fashion, the passengers climbed into the back of the first van and took seats amid the packs and bags.

"We're doing a standard sandwich pattern," Ryan said to the other companions as they gathered around him. "Truck, passenger van, cargo van and truck. I'll take the lead so Stephen can show me the way. J.B., you ride in the back as gunner."

"Of course," the Armorer said, unfolding the wire stock of his Uzi submachine gun.

"Krysty take the passenger van. Doc, ride the cargo. Jak, you drive the second truck, with Mildred riding a shotgun in the cab. Dean in the back."

There was no dissension at the order, so everybody moved to their assigned posts.

Climbing into the cab of the lead truck, Ryan adjusted the mirrors to suit him, then worked the choke a few times. The big V6 engine caught the first time, black smoke tinged with blue pouring from the rusty tailpipes. The whole wag shook as the engine loudly backfired, then settled into a steady hum.

Krysty had some minor trouble starting the passenger van, but after a few tries it finally caught. Doc was surprised at how smoothly the engine ran for the cargo van. Smooth as silk. The cab was remarkably clean, and on a wild hunch he tried the air conditioner. The engine automatically revved to handle the compressor, and icy cold air blew onto the surprised man. Doc turned it off immediately.

"Impossible," he muttered. J.B. had once told him that the ammonia gas in the units easily leaked through the rubber seals and no AC would work after only the passage of a decade. A hundred-year-old air conditioner that functioned perfectly? The scholar made a mental note to tell the others about that as soon as possible. Then feeling very apprehensive, Doc looked through the tiny ventilation grille in the wall dividing the cab from the aft cargo area and stared at the array of different-shaped boxes lashed to the metal floor. Wheat be damned. What was he really carrying?

Applying the gas and shifting gears on the stick, Jak revved the big engine on the second truck a few times before trying the ignition. The predark wag jerked as the clutch was engaged, and the engine hesitantly roared into life.

"Sounds odd," Mildred said, setting her sore foot on top of an old dirty blanket to be used as a cushion. She rested the M-4000 shotgun in her lap and touched her shirt pocket, which was bulging with extra shells.

"Rotary engine," Jak said, rolling down the window. "Not piston."

"Is that better than diesel?" she asked.

"Nothing better'n diesel," the teenager replied, gunning the engine.

Loosening his blaster, Ryan laid his rifle across the dashboard and shifted into gear, slowly testing the brakes.

"Pulls to the left," he said, fighting the steering wheel.

"Still works," Stephen grumbled, slightly annoyed.

Rolling out the barn door, Ryan headed for the main gate. As the convoy rumbled forward, a crowd of white-hairs and children watched them going by without much interest. However, Ryan thought he recognized one of Phillipe's crew watching from an alleyway, then they were gone in the smoke and dust.

Monty and the sec men were at the gate, holding the double doors open wide to let the convoy pass effortlessly through. None of them waved or cheered or even smiled. As the second truck cleared the exit, the sec men closed one of the doors and two men took guard positions at the opening. Exactly the same as Ryan had first seen them do the day before.

"Head east, toward the quarry," Stephen directed, the stock of a rifle resting in his lap, the long barrel jutting out the window. "And for God's sake, stay close to the ville."

Trundling away from Rock ville, Ryan led the convoy around the town until reaching a packed dirt path that skirted the ragged edge of the deep quarry. The excavation was well over a thousand yards across, and so deep the bottom wasn't visible to Ryan inside the cab. But reflected light playing on the irregularly cut walls clearly indicated that the bottom was filled with water.

The spacing between the ville wall and the pit was uncomfortably tight, barely wider than the trucks, and Ryan scraped the bumper along the wall several times trying to stay as far from the edge as possible. Thankfully, the vans would have no trouble, being so much smaller in width, but for the trucks it was tight quarters. Loose rocks tumbled into space as the wag slipped in some loose gravel and slid dangerously toward the right.

"Careful," Stephen warned unnecessarily, swallowing hard.

"Shut up," Ryan said through gritted teeth, concentrating on the driving.

Splashing through a small creek, the one-eyed man relaxed as the wag finally went past the ville and the path angled away from the quarry toward the woods.

Lumbering through a field of dried grass, their ride evened out as the truck jounced and bounced onto a predark road of pavement and concrete.

As their speed increased to nearly 40 mph, the lead wag rolled along the four-lane highway through a thick forest. The trees still had leaves, but the green was long gone, fiery colors of the rainbow filled the forest stretching into the distance.

"Get ready," Stephen cautioned, working the bolt on his longblaster. "There's almost always an ambush somewhere along here, just outside the range of the ville blasters."

"Hey, J.B., incoming!" Ryan shouted out the open window.

Riding in the back, the Armorer thumped the roof twice in acknowledgment. Then raising his left arm high, he tightened his hand into a fist.

In the second van, Krysty hit the horn to signal she understood, but no sound came from under the trembling hood. She stuck an arm out the window and waved an okay, then relayed the same hand signal to the wag behind her.

Doc beeped the horn and passed back the warning.

Jak tried the horn with no results, so he flashed the headlights. Mildred readied the scattergun, and in the back, Dean drew his Browning semiautomatic and patted his pockets to make sure he had a butane lighter for the Molotov cocktails. The bottles were rattling in their wooden box, the thick rags tied around the long necks of the glass containers doing nothing to cushion them against the vibrations of the vehicle.

Tense minutes went by with no sign of any activity, then there was a lot of movement in the bushes on both sides of the highway. Ryan shifted to a higher gear and increased their speed.

"Here they come," Stephen said, working the action on his shotgun, chambering a shell.

Dozens of green-skinned muties stumbled into view from both sides of the forest, charging headlong at the convoy. Ryan had never seen the type before. They almost looked like norms, except for the skin tone and complete lack of hair. Then a few opened their mouths, and he saw only rows of sharklike fangs and forked tongues.

Taking careful aim, J.B. fired a burst of 9 mm rounds into the closest bunch, and several of the creatures fell to the pavement, gushing black blood. One survivor snatched for a door handle and missed, while another successfully grabbed a side mirror and the supports snapped free in its grip. The mutie hit the roadway and tumbled bonelessly directly under the van.

Choosing his targets, Ryan veered around a thick clump of the attackers, then plowed through a couple of stragglers, the steel fenders smashing them aside to the sound of shattering glass.

"That cost us a headlight, ya fool!" Stephen raged.

Zigzagging wildly, Ryan ignored the man, savagely plowing into the attacking creatures. From the wags behind them came the sounds of blasterfire, shotgun blasts and mutie screams.

Bracing himself against the random jerks of the wag, J.B. hosed the bushes on the right side of the highway with his Uzi, and more of the bleeding muties stumbled onto the road. Closely followed by dozens more of the green creatures, the naked beings waved their arms in the air and loudly hooted as if demented.

"Goddamn, I have never seen so many before!" Stephen cried, firing the rifle out the window at the darting figures. "It's an army out there!"

"Been too long between convoys." Ryan cursed, steering over some more of the saber-toothed muties. The wag lurched as crushed bodies bounced off the front bumpers, or were squashed beneath the wide tires. "They must be starving to come this close to a walled ville."

At point-blank range, Stephen fired again and again. "Too damn bad. Let's chill them all!"

The driver's-side door rattled as a mutie jumped partially into the cab, clawing at Ryan with three-fingered hands. Slamming an elbow into the creature's face, the one-eyed warrior grabbed the SIG-Sauer in a cross draw, shoved the muzzle into the mutie's mouth and triggered a round. With only half a head, the creature dropped from sight.

In the passenger's-side mirror, Ryan saw a mutie leap from the branches of a tree to land on top of the passenger van. Krysty twisted the steering wheel, trying to dislodge the thing as it scuttled for the window. Suddenly, a thunderous report filled the wag with bright light, and the mutie was blown off the roof to land sprawling on the highway. Doc neatly rolled over the thrashing creature, ending its pain with a sickening crunch.

Driving with one hand, Krysty aimed the shotgun and fired out the window at the hooting attackers.

Then, just as quickly as the attack started, it was over, the highway ahead of Ryan clear of any obstruction. Putting the pedal to the floor, he gunned the engine and watched the temperature gauge steadily climbing from the mechanical exertion.

Moments later, Krysty burst out of the hooting

crowd, then Doc and finally Jak, Mildred and Dean in the second truck. Dean shouted in victory as the wag escaped the forest muties and reached clear roadway. Then his elation dimmed as he saw the creatures running after the speeding wags, waving their arms and hooting furiously. Most of the creatures soon dropped back, but several actually started to gain on the last truck. The sleek muties pumping their arms and legs were running fast as dogs, maybe faster. Tense seconds passed for the boy as he prepared to drop a gasoline bomb in their wake before the truck finally pulled away from the tiring creatures.

"You okay?" Jak shouted out the window.

"Fine!" Dean yelled against the wind. "Keep going!"

"No prob!"

Several minutes passed with the drivers and gunners reloading their blasters and watching for treachery in the trees.

"Nice work," Stephen complimented, closing the bolt on his Remington .30-06 hunting rifle.

"That was too easy," Ryan muttered, shifting gears as the road surface changed from concrete to cracked pavement. "And I don't like the fact they hit us where the road was poor and we had to drive slow."

"Better here than at the rest stops."

"What do you mean?"

"The rest stops are where I usually rest the engines and gather wood for the campfires. The greenies often wait for travelers there. There are a dozen rest stops along this route, so I use different ones each time to confuse them."

Avoiding a large clump of weeds growing in the middle of the roadway, Ryan upped his estimation of the fat man another notch for the second time in as many days. So he wasn't a total fool. "You always change locations each trip?"

"Sure."

"Good. Then we'll use the exact same spots as the last trip," Ryan decided, holding his pistol between his thighs to slide out the used ammo clip and insert a fresh one. "That should catch them off guard completely."

"If the forest muties are smart enough. I've seen them standing for hours alongside a crashed wag waiting for more norms to come crawling out when you could see clearly through the windows it was empty."

Holstering his blaster, Ryan recalled Mildred once speaking about how the visible spectrum was different for cats, dogs and norms, so it was probably the same for the rad-blasted muties, stickies, swampies, crawlers, the whole horrid mess. However, that was much too complex to explain.

"Triple stupe," the one-eyed man agreed, gunning the engine to increase their speed as the laboring truck rolled over a hill. "We'll have to stay sharp."

"Then there are the coldhearts," Stephen grumbled, stroking his blaster as if it were a lucky charm. "They attack anywhere, anytime."

"We'll be ready for them, too," Ryan stated coldly, barely controlling his anger and wondering what else the fat man hadn't told them about this trip to Front Royal.

Chapter Six

Once past the mutie hordes, the convoy rolled on into the Virginia hills, making good time. A few hours later, they halted at a crossroads, and Stephen consulted a smudged scrap of map that he guarded as if it were pure gold, then pointed to the left fork.

Around noon, the highway abruptly stopped near a glassy bomb crater, and from then on they traveled along dirt roads and dry riverbeds. More than once, Ryan was forced to use their winch to haul one of the vans out of the red clay. A rock slide made them detour into a weedy marsh, the stagnant waters reaching dangerously over the tires before the wags could return to the dry highway.

"Prime spot for an attack," Ryan said, watching the marsh recede into the distance. "Good thing those green muties weren't waiting for us."

Stretching his legs in the cab, Stephen twisted his head from side to side to pop his neck joints. "Naw, we were completely safe. There was no smell of salt."

Both hands tight on the steering wheel, Ryan stole a sideways glance at the sleepy man. "Explain that."

"Sure. Those saber-toothed muties stink of the sea for some damn reason. We couldn't smell it before 'cause we were going too fast. But if you're ever near fresh water, and you suddenly smell saltwater—" the fat man worked the bolt on his longblaster "—then get ready to fight, because it's much too late to risk running."

Driving over the furrowed ground of an abandoned cornfield, Ryan filed that useful data away. They had to be some sort of fresh mutie from Washington Hole. The one-eyed man had never heard of greenies when he lived in this area. There always seemed to be something new trying to kill you in Deathlands.

Later that afternoon, the convoy halted as it reached a predark bridge spanning a deep ravine. The structure looked sound, but the girders were badly rusted in spots and big pieces of the concrete columns were missing.

Taking no chances, Ryan crossed the bridge himself on foot, first walking across, then returning and jumping on the road surface to check for any secondary vibrations. When satisfied, he ordered the wags to roll across individually to minimize the risk.

On the other side of the ravine, smooth fields of green grass stretched into the distance. Uneventful miles passed in easy driving, and the sun was dipping toward the horizon, when Ryan spotted the ruins of a farmhouse a short way off the beaten path. Angling the big truck to the crumbling structure, he parked near the artesian well in the front yard.

The other wags stopped in an orderly line behind the first truck, engines idling as they waited for directions.

"We'll rest here for the night," Ryan announced, turning off the engine. The hot pistons chugged by themselves for a while, then sputtered wildly and finally died.

"Why? There's still plenty of daylight," Stephen protested, not budging from his comfortable seat.

"And we'll need it to make camp," Ryan stated, taking his Steyr from the dashboard. "Have to scout the area and check the water."

"This isn't one of my regular stops."

"Exactly why I chose it." Ryan opened the side door and climbed from the high cab. "We have visibility for miles, so nobody can sneak close."

"This is a waste of time. I must reach Front Royal by the end of the week!"

Ryan slammed the door and walked around to the other side. "You want to reach Front Royal?" he asked in a no-nonsense voice. "Or only try to reach it? Taking chances gets folks chilled."

Stephen took off his wool cap, twisted it in hands, then shoved it back on and glowered at the one-eyed man. "Okay, we'll do as you suggest," he said, stressing the last word. "But if we're late…"

"Won't be," Ryan stated, turning away from the caravan owner. Placing two fingers in his mouth, he whistled sharply, then drew a thumb across his throat. The other drivers cut their engines, and an eerie silence extended over the landscape. Cicadas chirped in the tall weeds, and a sting-wing buzzed overhead searching for its evening meal. The orange sky was cloudy, the air chilly, but no breeze stirred over the land, threatening to bring a storm.

Uzi in hand, J.B. hopped from the back of the flatbed and surveyed the area. "Looks good," he said, tilting his fedora back to a more comfortable position now that there was no danger of the wind carrying it away. "I'll check the farmhouse for unwanted guests."

"Want any help?" Stephen offered, shouldering his longblaster. This was his convoy, and he didn't like these outlanders making every decision. Even if they were the right decisions.

The Armorer snorted in reply and disappeared from sight through a hole in the clapboard wall.

His boots crunching on the dry soil, Ryan walked over to the passenger van, and Krysty stuck her head out the window.

"Hey, lover," she said, smiling in greeting, "we making camp here?"

"Going to find out in a tick," he said, watching the farmhouse. "J.B. is doing a recce."

A few minutes passed with no sign of the man, and Ryan was starting to get uneasy when the quiet of the farm was violently ripped apart by the sound of an Uzi blast.

"Fireblast!" he cursed, chambering a round in his longblaster. "Krysty, stay here and give us cover. I'm going after him."

Moving fast, the redhead threw open the door to the cab and drew her blaster. Standing on the tire, she rested the wheelgun on the metal roof to steady her aim.

Sprinting for the predark building, Ryan slowed as J.B. walked casually into view carrying a huge opossum by its skinny tail.

"Dinner is served," he announced with a grin.

GRUNTING FROM THE STRAIN, the sec men pulled up the rope going out the window of the fortress at Casanova ville until the bucket full of moat water came into view. Carefully lifting it over the sill, they carried the sloshing plastic container across the bloody floor and threw its contents onto what remained of the naked woman tied to the surgical table.

Thick with slime and stinking of waste, the filthy water sluiced the blood and flies off the prisoner, momentarily awakening her.

"Everywhere!" she screamed, thrashing about, opening old wounds on her wrists and ankles, fresh red trickling down the sloped table surface and onto the sticky floor. "Assassins! Murderers! They know everything! They're here now! Behind you!" Her screams slowed to mumbled speech, then unintelligible mutters as she fainted again, her mutilated body supported only by the binding ropes.

Reaching into a vest pocket of his silk vest, Baron John Henderson extracted an antique silver snuff box, opened it carefully and took a pinch of the powder inside, sniffing it up first one nostril, then the other. The finely ground mixture of tobacco and jolt tingled deliciously, the electric sensation feeling as if it were going straight into his brain. Suddenly, his aged body felt alive again, young and strong. The sunlight streaming into the room started to take on altered colors, the hues shimmering and overlapping as if he were looking at the world through a distorted prism.

As usual, the baron of Casanova was wearing a predark business suit of raw silk and dainty velvet bedroom slippers. Tassels dangled from an ornamental saber hung at his hip, and the blaster in his shoulder holster was heavy with gold filigree. Even the holster itself was covered with elaborate embroidery. Every button and buckle on his clothes shone with polish, but his nails were cracked and deeply caked with old dirt. Unshaved, with greasy hair, there was a definite odor of urine and festering disease about the elderly man. The reek was only partially disguised by heavy doses of sweet perfume literally poured over his clothing and hair.

Walking about the breathing horror on the table, Henderson scratched at a scab on his face while surveying the monstrous work dispassionately. Her denim dress was in tatters, the encrusted strips covering nothing. The bra and panties were long gone to the interrogator's scissors. Both nipples were only glazed areas on her bruised breasts, the flesh seared smooth with white-hot branding irons. Smaller burns covered her body, and several of her teeth were laid out in a neat row on a tiny metal table next to a pair of pliers. Each eyelid was gone, and the prisoner could only wildly stare about herself, unable to even escape into the privacy of her own mind.

"Well, has she fainted again, Randolph?" the baron demanded, sniffing another pinch from the snuff box. His heart began to pound in his chest, and Henderson wisely tucked away the box for the present. When the jolt finally did kill him, it was going to be a dark day for the people of his ville. The details were all worked out. But that wasn't today, not quite yet, anyhow.

Dressed in surgical garb and tight leather gloves, a man with slicked-back hair was curiously inspecting the person on the table, taking her pulse. He hauled off and brutally slapped the woman twice. She only gurgled like a happy infant and made sucking noises.

"How very unfortunate." Randolph frowned in annoyance. Turning toward the baron, he bowed deeply, laying a crimson-stained hand on his chest. As it came away, there was a red outline of a palm on the white cloth. "Sir, I fear the prisoner has prematurely gone mad."

"How is that possible?" Baron Henderson growled, staring hatefully at the cooing woman. "You promised me she would talk first!"

Taking a magnifying glass from a pocket of his gown, Randolph looked into her darting eyes. "I must have miscalculated the level of pain she could endure," he answered, pursing his thin lips thoughtfully. "Norm females are designed for childbirth, and so can always withstand more pain than a mere man."

"But not this particular woman."

"So it would seem. And she was a virgin, too. Fascinating, actually."

"This is twice you have failed me," Henderson intoned menacingly, advancing upon the slim man. "There won't be a third time."

The sec men moved out of the way as Randolph stepped away from the baron and bowed again. "My deepest apologies, my lord."

"We should have starved her," a voice said from the doorway.

The baron turned to see his grandson walk into the chamber. Unlike the baron, and his father before, the man was wearing military fatigues, plain boots and had a functioning blaster at his side. Not a single item of clothing properly glorified the sole heir of Casanova ville.

"Starvation," the baron repeated as if he were unfamiliar with the word.

The young man walked over to the prisoner and curled a lip in disgust. She had once been so very beautiful, a fit consort for any baron, but now not even the rats would eat her corpse.

"Everybody talks when they get hungry enough. Why bother with hooks and corkscrews?" William waved a callused hand at the gibbering woman on the table. "This was completely unnecessary."

"By the blood of our fathers, you are too weak to be baron," Henderson spit, rubbing a trail of mucus off his face with a crusty sleeve. "Death is part of life. Often the best part, and you'll know that when you first kill somebody!''

Narrowing his eyes to slits, William stared at the old reprobate, limbs quivering from the jolt rotting his brain, wine and semen staining his clothes everywhere. And this mutie-fucker dared to lecture a soldier about life? What bitter irony that was.

''And you, dear grandfather, are too interested in fun,'' he retorted hotly. ''Slice her like a solstice turkey afterward if it gives you pleasure.''

A sudden rush of power flowed into the young man's voice. ''But first we get the bastard information, you ass!''

The sec men in the room recoiled at the words, and the baron stared aghast at his grandson. Then he broke into a gale of laughter. ''I see there is some iron under all that pomp and parade after all. Good. Mebbe some of my blood is in you.''

More than enough, William thought privately. The stinking junkie and his pet torturer should both be burned alive for the good of the ville as soon as possible. Then he could take over and run the place as it should be, with military discipline and instant justice. The lost glory of the fatherland would return to America someday. He would see to it personally.

''Randolph!'' he barked.

Tightening the neck straps on the prisoner, the interrogator turned to look at the young man. ''Yes, sir?''

''Were you able to get anything from her about the odd activity in the woods north of here?''

''Yes and no,'' Randolph replied, giving the leather strap a final tug. He tenderly caressed the woman's long hair. ''Pretty little Wilma-Sue said she had escaped from slavers down south and passed a construction site somewhere near the old limestone caves. The workers were talking about attacking Front Royal. They tried to capture her, rape her more likely, but she chilled one and escaped.''

"Falling right into our hands." Henderson beamed happily.

"Lucky us," William agreed, brushing away a cloud of flies from the prisoner. "So they're either BullRun coldhearts preparing to attack Baron Cawdor's castle, or outlanders planning on raiding the ville for goods or mebbe hit a passing convoy. If she spoke the truth."

"Of course she did, my lord." Randolph bowed, removing his gloves and passing them to an assistant. "My friend told me the truth, as far as she knows it."

The woman on the table started singing a wordless song, nodding her head in time to a secret tune nobody else alive would ever hear.

"However, the question remains, are we next to be attacked?" mused the soldier, searching for a chair fit to sit in. There were no clean ones, so he leaned against the doorjamb and crossed his arms. "Grandfather, have you sent spies?"

"Yes," the old man hissed in annoyance. "None have returned."

"Send more."

"I will, led by you," Henderson stated, leveling a finger. "And failure isn't a word we accept!"

Standing stiffly at attention, William clicked his heels and smartly saluted. "I will not fail, my lord!"

"Which brings up another matter," the baron said, glancing from the doctor back to his grandson. "Randolph has failed me. Twice."

William arched a puzzled eyebrow until understanding came. Drawing his 9 mm Luger, William shot the doctor between the legs. The man shrieked and fell to the floor trying to staunch the awful flow of blood from the wound with both hands.

"Again," the baron ordered, his face bright with eagerness. "Shoot him in the belly. No, a knee. Yes, cripple him!"

Raising the barrel, William fired once more, and a black hole appeared in Randolph's forehead. Exhaling softly, the man crumpled into a heap, the blood seeping from under his pink-stained clothes.

"Too soon," the baron panted, raking his own cheeks with broken fingernails, leaving bloody furrows. "He died too fast, boy!"

William holstered the weapon. "You said he failed us twice, so he was shot twice."

"You disobeyed me. Never do that again."

"Or?" the young man prompted boldly.

"Or else you will go on the table!" Henderson snarled.

A minute passed in silence with the two men staring hatefully at each other. The tension in the room was palpable, and the sec men moved between them to forestall any possible actions.

A civil war was the last thing the ville needed, especially with a possible army of enemies only thirty miles away.

"Please, my lords, a question," a corporal asked.

"Ask," the old man grunted.

"What should we do with Randolph and the woman?"

Lost in the moment, Henderson blinked a few times while shifting mental gears. "Do? Dispose of Randolph immediately. Save his shoes, burn the clothes and toss the rest to the dogs."

"At once, sir."

"As for the spy, slit her throat and boil her down for soap." He then repeated the word and laughed, displaying his awful yellow teeth. "Soap. Ha! Soap."

"Better yet, Grandfather, why don't we let the other prisoners in the dungeon have her?" William suggested, resting a hand on the old man's shoulder. He could feel the aged bones beneath the expensive cloth. Death was close by, and with it, absolute power. But the whitehair was still a dangerous foe. "Most haven't seen a woman in months, and will gladly use her for relief."

"Excellent! Let it be done." Baron Henderson smiled, weakly applauding the notion.

The corporal saluted. "Yes, sir!"

"And on the morrow, William, you will lead troops northward to recce the deep woods. We must know if there is a new baron at Front Royal, and what his plans are."

"And if I encounter Cawdor's troops?"

"Kill them."

"That could lead to war," William stated carefully, trying not to incur the terrible wrath of his patriarch. "Front Royal is strong. It would be a difficult fight."

"But not with us." Henderson cackled gleefully, taking a little pinch of snuff. "William, dress our sec men in the colors of BullRun ville. If Front Royal seeks retribution, they'll attack that blond bitch up north, not us."

"Brilliant, sir!" a teenage sec man gushed. "Hail the baron! Hip, hip—"

"Shut up, fool," Henderson snapped irritably. "If I want my ass kissed, I'll summon your wife."

"Sir," the boy replied stiffly, his face red.

"Afterward, we can seize first one ville, then the

other before they can recover," William added, warming to the idea greatly. "Supporting troops over so great a distance, even with horses and wags, will strain their exhausted supplies to the breaking point.

"In fact," he went on thoughtfully, "starting a war between Front Royal and BullRun might be the best thing to ever happen to Casanova ville."

Chapter Seven

Dusk was starting to fall by the time the campsite was secure. The four trucks were parked in a circle a safe distance from the farmhouse, and a large fire was crackling with the passengers and companions gathered around.

Doc and Jak were on patrol, and they walked through the growing darkness, looking for spoor or tracks, and finding nothing but cicadas and a rusted plow attached to the skeleton of a horse.

"Working AC?" the teenager asked.

"Absolutely."

"Not right. Tell Ryan."

"We will," Doc promised. "Once Stephen goes to sleep."

"Check boxes?" Jak asked.

"Indeed I did, my friend. They were full of wire. Insulated wiring and light switches, outlets and fuse boxes from predark homes and offices."

"Nothing more?"

"Every box I checked," the old man stated.

"Damn."

"I concur," Doc said, frowning. He kicked a clot of dirt out of his way, and it rolled off into the weeds. The cicadas instantly became quiet. "Somebody is very certain that Front Royal has electricity."

"Or will soon," Jak concurred.

Doc breathed in the night air, thinking back to his life in Vermont. Then he shook off the memories. That was another world, no longer his. "I know the fortress itself has power, perhaps wind generated, but it's used only for emergencies. Lighting the fields when there is a fight, and such. But Stephen has enough cable here to wire the whole ville and most of the surrounding hamlets, house by house."

"Wrong," Jak stated. "Where get power?"

"Indeed, my young friend," Doc said, resting his swordstick on a shoulder. "That is the big question. In a world of slave labor, where batteries are often considered magical, where do they plan to get enough electricity to power an entire ville?"

As they returned to the campsite, Dean nimbly darted between the men and dodged a parked wag to drop a load of wood on top of a stack near the campfire. The timbers were broken at the ends, severely heat discolored, and most had nails sticking out.

"Need any more?" asked the boy, dusting his dirty hands on his pant legs. "I have most of the wall down for easy pickings."

"No, thanks," Krysty replied, stirring the campfire with a green stick. "Better go wash. Dinner will be ready soon."

"Aw, they're clean enough," Dean said, displaying his slightly improved hands.

"Wash," she stated firmly, and the boy walked off as if heading for certain doom.

"How is it coming, madam?" Doc asked, sniffing eagerly.

"Soon enough," she replied, turning the roasting opossum on the iron spit. A little song from her childhood came unbidden to mind: the faster meat turns, the slower it cooks. The slower meat turns, the sooner you eat. True words.

Dried beans from the caravan supplies were simmering in a pan of water with pale lumps of salt pork mixed in. Mildred had added some dandelion greens from the weeds.

Studying the pan, Jak reached into his jacket and poured in a shot of moonshine. "Flavoring," he explained.

"Where did you get that?" Krysty asked.

"Gift." He smiled and tucked the bottle away. "From friends."

"Friends, plural?"

"Yeah."

Hiding a smile, Krysty returned to cooking. "I understand."

Skinned and gutted, the opossum suspended above the flames was so large it was bending the old iron rod she had shoved down the gullet as a cook rod. The animal was so big Krysty thought it had to be a mutie, but the others assured her that twenty pounds was normal size for an opossum. The smell was almost painfully good.

Hands dripping water, Dean returned from the well and sat near his father. "Dad, what's Front Royal like?" he asked, taking a harmonica from his shirt pocket and polishing it on his damp sleeve. He had looted it from one of the dead mercies, and after a good wash it seemed to work just fine.

Leaning against a truck tire, Ryan stretched out his legs. "Good fields, soil not that dead from the acid rains. Lots of deer and bear for food. Lots of cougar, too. Strange thing—for some reason, they like the taste of muties and help keep the area clear."

"Mighty polite of the cats." J.B. smiled, amused.

"I used to have a house cat," Doc said softly, a distant look in his eyes. "Piewacket, an old English name, a brindle tabby. I must remember to feed her tonight before sending the children to bed."

The others said nothing as the man closed his eyes and started talking softly to himself. Sometimes, Doc drifted off to another time in his life, reliving conversations with the dead.

Some folks thought the man touched in the head, but the companions knew that only a strong will could have survived everything he had gone through at the hands of the whitecoats of Operation Chronos. Besides, he came back sharp and fast if there was trouble. Doc was a valuable asset to the group, not a liability.

Tentatively, Dean blew on the harmonica and a smooth, pure flow of notes issued.

"That's pretty good," Ryan praised, a tiny flash of jealousy coming and going. His musical abilities were limited to bad singing.

"This plays the music I like," J.B. scoffed, patting the Uzi lying next to him.

"Glad you have it along. This has been an odd trip," Stephen said, chewing on a stick as he watched the pinkish meat cook. The excess fat dripped off the carcass into the fire, causing the flames to spurt, the greasy smoke disappearing toward the stars above.

"What do you mean?" Mildred asked, rewrapping her foot. Staying off her ankle for a whole day was making it feel much better, and the swelling was noticeably reduced.

"Lots of muties, but no coldhearts," the fat man explained.

"Think I know the answer to that," Ryan said, pouring a can of gas into the fuel tank of the second van. "There are no coldhearts attacking because we don't have Phillipe and his crew with us."

"Working both sides, eh?" J.B. grinned.

"I wouldn't be surprised to find these hills packed with their friends, but without the signal to attack, they might be spoiling a choice plan, so they have to wait. Might even let us leave unmolested."

"You think?" Dean asked.

"Mebbe," he repeated. "But we'll stay on triple red until we reach the ville. Only a couple more days."

"Unless," Stephen said, going pale and looking around fearfully, "the rad winds chilled them!"

"No hot spots around here to create those winds." Nevertheless, Ryan lowered the container and checked the rad counter on his collar.

"Nominal," he reported, screwing the cap back on the gas can. "We're safe."

Askance, Stephen stared at the device. "Is that really a rad counter?"

Ryan placed the can in the back of the Ford truck. "Yeah."

"I could really use one of those," the fat man said, licking his lips eagerly. "What would you take for it?"

"Not for sale." Ryan walked into the firelight.

"Everything's for sale," Stephen countered, then stopped talking as Ryan gave him a look that informed the man just how wrong he was.

"Hey, I j-just a-asking," the man stammered. "And remember, I'm your boss for this trip."

"You're the caravan leader," J.B. corrected, squirting a few drops of oil into his submachine gun and working the bolt. "Not our boss."

"Big dif," Jak said, drawing a knife and starting to whittle on a piece of wood from the pile.

A loud crack came from the dark forest, and everybody drew their weapons with blinding speed.

"Rifle shot?" Mildred asked, rising awkwardly on her crutch.

Whittling a new spoon out of the plank, Jak told her, "Tree branch."

Relaxing his stance, J.B. lowered the Uzi. "Probably another opossum."

Then a warbling scream sounded in the distance, and Krysty spun with her blaster in hand. "That sounded human."

"Cougar," Jak corrected, steadily whittling. The spoon was already taking shape under his expert skills.

Reluctantly, Krysty accepted the statement. The Cajun hunter was seldom wrong in such matters. Testing the meat with a knife point, she sliced into the carcass and found it nicely gray inside.

"Soup's on," she announced. "Grab a plate or go hungry."

Another scream cut the night air, and everybody froze where they were, plates and cups poised in midair.

"That was human," Mildred stated, placing her empty plate on the ground and drawing her ZKR target pistol.

"Where are the hunters?" Doc asked. He fumbled for their names. "Clem and, ah, Bob?"

"Gone as guards to cover the Johnson family while they wash dirty diapers at the creek. They didn't want to stink up the campsite."

A woman's scream cut the night, closely followed by the boom of a black-powder weapon.

"That was a musket," J.B. stated. He stood and

snapped the bolt on his submachine gun. "We got trouble."

"Sounded close, couple hundred yards to the west," Ryan added, working the bolt on his Steyr. "Mildred, damp down the fire. Jak, Doc, stay here with her. Everybody else, ten-yard spread. And watch your shots—we got friendlies out there. Go!"

As Ryan moved past the trucks, the darkness reclaimed the night.

The companions started to head for the distant creek when a commotion in the weeds could be heard coming their way. Without comment, they moved into a tight cluster, with every weapon out and ready, the oiled barrels sweeping the night for targets.

"There it is!" a voice cried from the blackness.

"Kill it!"

"Don't shoot!" a woman screamed.

A dark mass rose from the weeds and out charged a mutie carrying a bundle of rags. It was humanoid, two arms, two legs, one head, but there the resemblance stopped. A thick black mane of hair crested its lumpy head and trailed down the back, separating into different lines that ended at its ankles. Its muscular shoulders rose to meet the lumpy head as if the being possessed no neck. The skin was grayish with bits of dried mud, or perhaps scabs flaking off. The square eyes were yellow as if it had jaundice, and a filthy loincloth swaddled its waist, with a crude stone dagger jutting from a sheath made from human skin bearing a crude tattoo.

"Swampie!" Ryan tilted the barrel of his longblaster to fire from the hip, but then the bunch of rags it held started to cry.

"The baby!" Mildred cried, dropping her crutch. The physician went into a marksman stance, both hands wrapped around her deadly little Czech ZKR blaster. But as she trained on the mutie's head, it lurched into the bushes again, going to all fours and galloping away with remarkable speed.

"Dark night! After the bastard!" J.B. shouted.

The companions chased after the darting mutie, nearly colliding with the hunter and the parents who had been beating the bushes trying to drive it into the camp.

There was a furtive movement in the farmhouse, and Dean leaped at the mutie as it rushed through the ruins. The boy cried out in victory as he got a handful of the coarse black hair, but then the creature literally ripped itself free from his grasp and charged due east, straight for the stream.

Dropping his rifle, Ryan was already running in that direction, trying to cut it off. His lungs were laboring to draw in more air, but the warrior willed himself to go faster. Once in the water, the swampie and its tiny prisoner would be gone forever.

Man and mutie collided at the top of a low rise, Ryan driving the beast into an oak tree near the edge of the bluff. Snarling, the creature swung a webbed hand at Ryan. He ducked and the fist slammed into the tree, bark exploding off the trunk from the powerful impact. In the background, Ryan heard the splashing stream and knew he was almost out of time. A single jump and the swampie would escape with its living meal.

Risking everything, Ryan dived wildly at the creature and managed to grab a hairy leg. Panting like a dog, the swampie kicked at him with a clawed foot, and that gave the one-eyed man an idea. As hard as he could, Ryan drove a rock-hard fist directly upward between its legs. Mutie or norm, if the creature was a male, that should stop anything for a few seconds.

The mutie gasped in pain and staggered backward a step. Ruthlessly, Ryan slammed it again in the same place, then drew his blaster and fired at its knee.

The silenced weapon coughed gently, and blood erupted from the wound, as the 9 mm round plowed through flesh and bone.

Screaming in agony, the swampie dropped to the ground and started crawling toward the stream. Ryan fired again, the flash from the muzzle showing its precious bundle was still tightly held in inhuman arms.

Then others were with him, firing their own weapons at the crawling beast. The power of Doc's LeMat was so great that a single blast removed the head, the muzzle-flash illuminating the bluff for yards in every direction.

The decapitated body shuddered and convulsively released its grip on the screaming baby. As the companions watched in horror, the infant rolled straight over the edge of the bluff, and they heard a tiny splash.

"Fireblast!" Ryan cursed, charging forward. Heedless of the sharp rocks and briar patches blocking their way, nearly everybody scrambled hastily down the steep incline, grunting and gasping as flesh was torn every foot of the way. Only Krysty stayed behind.

Dropping her heavy bearskin coat, Krysty raised her hands and launched herself off the bluff, diving straight into the stream. She disappeared beneath the icy water.

Clothes and skin ripping from the thorns, Ryan and J.B. skidded down the muddy banks, dropping their blasters and wading chest deep into the freezing waters.

"Krysty!" Ryan bellowed, the icy temperatures knifing into his body. He took a breath and ducked underwater, but quickly stood again, his body shaking with the cold.

"No good," he gasped. "Can't see a thing."

"Make torches!" J.B. shouted uphill through cupped hands. "And get moving!"

Suddenly, lights washed over the bluff and a horn sounded.

"Anybody hurt?" Mildred called.

In a geyser of water, Krysty surfaced from the middle of the stream with the child in her arms.

Fighting shivers, Ryan and J.B. helped her to the shore and she laid the infant on the rocky ground, brushing away the tangles of blond hair off its face.

"Mother Gaia, no," Krysty whispered. The small form was completely still, the lips a deathly pale blue.

"Millie, we need you now!" J.B. yelled.

Gathering the child in his arms, Ryan braced himself and charged up the incline, ignoring the thorns that seemed to be everywhere. Seconds later, the man reached the top, and pushing past the weeping mother, he thrust the little body at Mildred.

"Not," he panted, "breathing. In water."

Placing the child in the beams of the truck, the physician checked for a pulse, then listened for a heartbeat. Neither was present. Opening the baby's mouth, she checked for obstructions. Then, tilting the head backward to open the throat, Mildred inhaled and exhaled into the tiny mouth.

Minutes later, J.B. and a shivering Krysty struggled to the top of the bluff, and Doc draped the bearskin coat over her. She nodded her thanks and watched along with everybody else as Mildred continued breathing into the infant's mouth without stopping.

Minutes passed in silence until, with a ragged cough,

the baby vomited some water, then started to cry as if there were no tomorrow.

"Alive! My baby is alive!" Sara cried joyously, gathering the girl into her arms. Dean gave her an old blanket from the truck, and the woman wrapped the child up like a miniature mummy.

J.B. draped his leather jacket over Mildred and helped her stand.

"Sh-she'll be fine," Mildred wheezed, trying to catch her own breath. She was close to hyperventilation from doing CPR for so long. "Just keep her warm."

"Thank you," Hector replied, sliding off his coat to drape it over the mother and child.

"Everybody in the truck," Doc rumbled loudly. "We better get you folks into dry clothes fast."

"Hey! Where's Stephen?" Dean asked, glancing around.

"Guarding the campfire."

Jak made a noise. "Yeah, right."

Gathering their weapons and clothing, the group climbed into the rear of the flatbed.

"What's your name, lady?" Sara asked, holding the baby tightly. The gears engaged with a grinding noise, and the wag started to roll over the rough ground at a good clip.

"Wyeth," answered the physician wearily. "Mildred Wyeth."

The parents exchanged looks, and the woman nodded.

"Baby's name is Mildred now," Hector said.

"Thank you. That is the highest fee I have received from a patient in a hundred years."

"Hey, I thought you guys were hunters," Dean accused. "But that swampie sure caught you by the surprise."

"Are hunters," Bob responded patiently.

"We were watching the creek," Clem explained, resting his chin on the flintlock of his musket. "But this mutie dropped out of a tree."

"Oh." The boy blinked. "So that's what was in the trees making all the noise."

Bob shrugged. "I suppose."

"Crazy thing must have been mad with hunger."

"Get hungry enough, you try anything."

"True enough."

The mixed group settled into the rhythms of the rocking vehicle, confident that dry clothes and food were only moments away.

Over in the corner, shivering under her heavy coat, Krysty violently sneezed, then did it twice more. But nobody thought anything of it at the time.

THE PATCHED SIDES of the canvas tent moved with every gust of wind, but the flaps were pegged tight and the only breeze came through the front opening. An oil lantern gave off a wealth of light, but only faint traces of heat. A few wooden boxes were used as seats by the armed men, blasters were stacked neatly near ammo boxes and the carved wooden pole supporting the roof was decorated with clusters of dried human scalps.

"Any word?" one of the men asked, a cigarette dangling from his mouth. A long jagged scar traversed his face from his forehead down into his shirt and out of sight.

"Nope," said the messenger, shifting his weight from foot to foot. "Rode here fast as I could. Spotted them at the old farm. Tangled with a mud puppy."

"Anybody die?"

"A kid, I think."

"Not an adult. Good." The big man dropped the butt onto the dirt floor and crushed it under a boot. "Still, I hate to attack without a signal. Mebbe Phillipe is working some angle we don't know about. Don't want to queer a good deal."

"Could be the others found out and aced him," suggested another man, chewing on a piece of salted meat.

"Could be," Scarface agreed, lighting a fresh cigarette off the lantern flame. Sitting back, he drew in a satisfying lungful and blew a smoke ring at the ceiling. "That would be too bad. He was good at the job. Guess we'll have to find another cheese for the trap."

"Trouble is," the messenger said, frowning, "they keep stopping at random spots and are avoiding every trap we have."

"Somebody in that group has brains. But no matter. They can't reach Front Royal without going through the pass. When will the convoy reach it?"

The messenger gave a toothy grin. "Two days, mebbe sooner."

"Then that's where we hit them." Scarface smiled, showing that his teeth had been filed to sharp points.

"Easy pickings," the messenger agreed happily. "And food for the whole damn winter."

Chapter Eight

Two days later, Ryan braked the lead truck to a rattling halt on a dirt road and stared hard around them, his hands white on the steering wheel. The land had been getting higher, more mountainous. The road they were taking now sliced along the steep side of a small mountain, a foothill compared to the rocky giants in the Shens, yet sloped enough to slow their travel to a crawl. Stephen keep insisting that the wags could take the inclines at full speed, but Ryan had no wish to blow an engine block and leave the convoy stranded in mutie territory.

But the section ahead of them was as level as a table, smooth and without potholes or rain gullies. The very fact it was in good condition made the man suspicious. A large grassy field rose sharply to the right, disappearing into a granite outcropping, and on their left was a dense wall of battered trees.

Listening to the sounds of the forest, Ryan glanced at the passenger van behind him and waved at Mildred. She flashed her lights in return. A few days off her feet and the physician was completely healed. Only now Krysty was suffering through a nasty cold and spent most of her days sleeping, most of her nights sniffling. It was odd how it had come on so fast. That dip in the creek had to have done her some damage.

"Well, what are we waiting for?" Stephen asked. "We're less than a day from Royal. Let's shake a leg."

Gunning the engine to keep it from stalling again, Ryan ignored him and checked their fuel level. Less than a quarter of a tank. Even if they could, running wasn't a viable option.

"Hey, J.B., you see this?" he called out the window.

"Not blind yet," the Armorer retorted, adjusting his glasses.

Annoyed, Stephen scanned the trees and bushes with growing confusion. "What are you talking about?" he demanded. "Keep driving—the road is clear."

"The pass is anything but clear," Ryan replied, taking the Steyr off the dashboard and working the bolt to chamber a round. He placed it on the seat between them, then checked the clip in the SIG-Sauer. "We're sitting in the middle of an ambush, and the next move I make may chill the lot of us. So shut the fuck up and let me think."

Holding on to the wooden slats, J.B. poked his head through the window. "This is really bad," he said, handing over a couple of grenades. "I don't see how we can get out of the trap."

"Buy us some time," Ryan said, turning to the caravan owner. "Take out that scrap of map and pretend you're checking something. Be casual, act natural."

Sweat dampening his brow, the fat man hurried to obey, wondering what they saw that he couldn't.

Briefly, Ryan considered they were wrong. But the facts said no. There were no birds singing in the trees, which was the first thing that caught his attention. A lack of wildlife was always a bad sign, as it usually meant someone was about. That was when he noticed the trees on the left side of the road had most of their bark removed for about a yard or more at ground level, the exposed green wood crushed and battered. With the hill to the right, it only made sense that some boulders had rolled down and crashed into the trees doing damage.

Only there were no gaps in the boulders high on the hill, and none on the road or amid the trees.

"We're in a killing box," Ryan stated, gauging the distance to the end of the pass. A hundred yards at least, so a quick sprint was completely out of the question, as was trying to back the convoy up and avoid the ambush. Only a fool would give victims a way out, and whoever designed this was no fool. He recalled the Trader once saying that when the front door was blocked, jump out the window. But where was the window here? There had to be one.

"If we're in a trap, how come nobody has attacked yet?" Stephen asked nervously, hiding behind the torn map. Then he broke into a chuckle and lowered the ratty sheet of paper. "Oh, I understand. Well, I'm not paying a bonus for battling imagined dangers. You had a chance to cut a deal for jack—now just drive the truck and stop acting tough."

Coldly, Ryan weighed the option of killing the idiot so he wouldn't do something stupid in the forthcoming fight and get everybody chilled, but decided against it. They were going to need every blaster. He might be a fool, but Stephen could pull a trigger and that was good enough for today.

"We're taking too long," J.B. said from the back. "They're going to get wise."

Pulling the choke completely out, Ryan turned the ignition a few times and let the engine rev without catching. "That should do it. Go check under the hood. Make them think we're having trouble."

"Right." J.B. jumped to the ground and casually sauntered to the front of the vehicle.

"And you," Ryan stated in a voice that brooked no argument, "go get some more fuel from the last truck, and as you come back here, give some to each wag and pass along the warning to the others."

"You really are serious," Stephen said hesitantly. "But if this is an ambush then we should—"

Ryan jabbed the barrel of his SIG-Sauer into the man's soft gut. "Git," he snarled.

"Okay, okay." Stephen jerked open the door and stumbled out, nearly falling in his haste to get away.

Shouldering his Uzi, J.B. lifted the hood in a squeal of rusty hinges. Now the two men could talk without raising their voices.

"Boulders must come rolling in from the right and slam-hit the wags," J.B. said, pretending to tinker with the distributor. "The natural reaction would be to turn and shoot the guys doing it to stop them from sending more your way."

Ryan faked a yawn and stretched his arms. "Which means the real attack will be from the left, catching us unawares from behind."

"Any chance we could drive the truck into the trees and catch them by surprise?"

"No way. The trunks are too tightly packed."

Wiping off his hands, J.B. lowered the hood and gave it a slap to lock it tight. "Which only leaves us one option."

"Yeah, I know," Ryan said, smiling and starting the engine. The two men smiled widely and shook hands as if conquering a tough problem.

"Bet these are the rest of Phillipe's crew."

"Most likely."

"Think the trucks can do it? That's a lot of punishment. One slip and we're dead meat."

"Guess we're going to find out. When you only have one choice, don't waste time dithering and worrying—get it over with."

"Done," Stephen said, climbing into the cab smelling of fuel. "What?"

"Now the killing starts," Ryan told him, passing the man a spare grenade. "Know how to use it?"

Stephen nodded and started to unwrap the tape that held the arming lever in place.

Whistling a happy tune, J.B. climbed into the rear of the wag, and thumped the roof, signaling he was in position.

"Eight-second fuse?" Stephen asked, swallowing twice before the words would come out.

Drawing in a deep breath, Ryan exhaled slowly. "Yeah, but throw on five to be safe."

Keeping a foot on the clutch, the one-eyed man started the truck forward slowly, as if he didn't have a care in the world. But his hand stayed on the gearshift.

The other vehicles tagged along behind him, keeping formation. Hands clutched blasters and eyes darted everywhere, waiting impatiently. But nothing occurred until the convoy reached the middle of the pass.

A distant rumble caught his attention, and glancing out the window, Stephen screamed when he spotted a line of boulders rolling down the hill, coming straight for them.

"Run for it!" he shrieked, pulling on the door handle.

Ryan wasted a precious tick clubbing the man quiet

with his blaster, then he shoved the truck into high gear and savagely twisted the steering wheel, turning straight for the oncoming boulders.

If this had been summer with the hill covered with green grass, Ryan knew they wouldn't have a chance, the old bald tires slipping on the slick growths. But this was autumn, and the dried dead grass gave them a slim chance of surviving the mad tactic.

The view through the windshield was pure chaos as the truck bounced onto the hill and started to climb the steep slope. Banking to the left, but staying on an angle so he wouldn't tip over the wag, Ryan fought the struggling truck to greater speeds and headed directly for the largest rock. The boulder swelled before him and they passed each other, missing by inches. Any hunter knew you aimed where a moving target would be, not where it was.

But more rocks were thundering down the slope. The deafening noise escalated louder than cannon fire, and the whole world seemed to be shaking apart as tumbling granite passed before the vehicle so close the spray of loose dirt washed over the truck, blanketing the windshield.

Temporarily blinded, Ryan hit the wipers, but only the passenger's-side wiper worked. Slowing a notch, he stuck an arm out the window and yanked his wiper into motion. His view cleared, and he savagely turned the steering wheel, but it was too late. The truck sideswiped a tree stump, and the bumper ripped off from the chassis, the impact slamming his head against the roof. As a dizzy Ryan fought to control the shuddering truck, it started to dangerously tip over, then miraculously righted itself again.

A full-throated war whoop from the back told him that J.B. had jumped position and kept them level.

The tires spun like crazy, digging their treads into the dirt as Ryan shoved the gas pedal to the floorboards. Jogging left, then right, Ryan desperately dodged a barrage of smaller rocks, ignoring the trickle of blood seeping down his face and into his shirt. For a brief second, he saw the other three wags wildly zigzagging across the hill as huge boulders rolled endlessly from the bushes at the top of the hill.

"Fifty more yards," he cajoled, crushing the wheel in his grip. "Come on, baby. Move your fucking ass!"

Another boulder came straight at him. He dodged it, and a handful of small rocks sprayed over the truck, shattering the windshield completely. Covered with tiny glass pebbles, Ryan glared at the people now visible in the bushes, struggling to shove additional stones to the edge. Somebody fired a blaster, and the Uzi chattered above him. A man screamed, followed by more gunfire.

The truck seemed to launch into the air as it crested the top of the slope and sailed through a bush to crash on top of the screaming man, his hands raised as if to knock the truck away. Shifting gears and pumping the gas, Ryan plowed into a crowd of stunned men frantically trying to load rifles. The vehicle recoiled as the dead bounced off the rusty chassis.

The wag bounced over a man caught underneath, and Ryan spun the wheel to lurch sideways and slam another. The screaming man left the ground and flew across the field to wrap boneless around a tree.

Squealing to a halt, Ryan exited the truck and shot a woman who was shoving shells into a homemade shotgun, the patched barrel held together with baling wire.

More rifles shots sounded, and the telltale chatter of the Uzi spoke of J.B. at work.

Then the passenger van appeared, followed closely by the cargo van and the second truck crushing more men under the sturdy tires. Firing steadily, the companions charged out of the wags, and a dozen more attackers dropped under the withering cross fire. Clem and Bob triggered their flintlocks, billowing clouds of smoke masking the men, but two coldhearts flew backward as the .75-caliber miniballs smashed into their chests and out the back side, leaving gaping holes the size of a grapefruit.

Moving like a panther through the battle, Hector buried an ax into the head of a coldheart, cleaving the man to the waist. As the vivisected body dropped, a sniper in the bushes caught the farmer in the arm, and Hector staggered to one knee, then rose again firing a handgun snatched off the ground. The sniper fell, bleeding from the belly, and Ryan finished him with a head shot.

Armed with ax and blaster, Hector sprang into the bushes lining the crest, searching for more hidden assailants. A scream followed by ghastly whacks announced he was successful.

As the two groups took cover behind whatever was available, the blasterfire rose to a deafening cacophony. Acrid black smoke from the homemade rounds masked the battlefield as bullets flew thick across the grassy slope. Dean headed for the truck with the Molotov cocktails, but got pinned down behind a still-bleeding corpse. Tiny dust spurts caused by ricochets constantly kicked up from the ground. A van tire went flat, and numerous holes were punched into the thin metal bodywork of every vehicle by the random hail of hot lead.

Spotting a canvas tent near a split-rail fence, Bob

charged from underneath the truck and was immediately hit by several rounds at once. The fur-clad hunter stumbled once, still grimly advancing, then sighed and fell sprawling to the ground, his flintlock thundering impotently at nothing in particular.

Crawling on his belly through the fresh blood and spent shells, Ryan advanced to the shelter of a stack of split wood stacked near the hot ashes of a dying campfire. There was a haunch of meat on the spit, and Ryan was repulsed when he realized it was the partially consumed torso of a human female. The coldhearts were cannies.

Waiting for a lull in the combat, the one-eyed man pulled the pin on his only grenade, counted to five and threw the bomb at the enemy. Somebody cried out a warning, but it came too late. The white-phosphorus charge detonated in the air, raining deadly chemical fire onto the coldhearts. Hair and clothes blazing, the enemy ran about screaming insanely and slapping themselves with burning hands until they finally collapsed, the blackened flesh split apart, exposing the charred bones inside the steaming human corpses.

Their numbers reduced to a handful in only minutes, the few remaining coldhearts hastily retreated, firing wildly. A spray of 9 mm rounds from J.B. made them dive into cover, then Dean and Doc threw their grenades. With a blinding flash, the double blasts ripped the men apart, tossing arms and legs everywhere.

As the smoke cleared, few coldhearts were still shooting. Standing amid the fiery destruction, a lone man stood bleeding from both ears and weakly pulling the trigger on a wheelgun that only clicked in response. Mildred trained the M-4000 scattergun on the man, and in spite of the range, his belly was blown apart, entrails scattering to the wind.

Popping into view for only a tick, Clem expertly shot a man directly between the eyes, then plunged a nimrod into his musket, packing in a fresh wad and ball.

With his spine pressed tight against a tree trunk, one of the coldhearts was frantically fumbling in his pockets for loose rounds, the slide kicked back on his weapon, showing the clip was out of ammo. Caught completely by surprise, the coldhearts weren't properly armed for a sustained fight, and nobody had even been able to get close to the armory in the log cabin.

His pockets proved to be empty, and the man glanced over the dead searching for a weapon. That was when he realized how many of his crew were gone—Big Charlie, Hanson, Mickey, Laura-Lee, Clint, Joker... enough.

"Head for the river!" the man yelled, throwing away his useless blaster and turning tail.

Several others followed the strategic withdrawal, but soon it was a mass rout, the coldhearts leaving behind their spent longblasters and charging headlong into the thickets.

"After them!" Clem shouted, waving his musket.

"Let them go," Ryan ordered, wrapping the leather strap of the Steyr around his forearm to steady his aim. Standing upright, the Deathlands warrior moved the crosshairs in the scope from man to man, dispatching each of the cannies without mercy until there was no more movement in the forest.

Dropping in a fresh clip, Ryan swept the field with his good eye, looking for more targets. "Anybody dead?" he demanded loudly.

"Bob," Dean answered, thumbing fresh rounds into

an empty clip. His clothes were splattered with blood, none of it his own. The boy slammed the clip into the grip of his Browning and jacked the slide.

Taking a bag of shells from a corpse with a shotgun, Mildred cracked open the scattergun and reloaded. "Looks like a clean sweep."

"Mebbe," Jak said, gesturing with his wheelgun. Several tents stood near a stout log cabin, where smoke rose from the brick chimney.

In the cab of the windowless truck, Stephen dramatically moaned as if just recovering from the blow to the head he had received from Ryan during the initial assault.

"Yellow cur," Hector growled in disgust.

Drawing the SIG-Sauer, Ryan advanced toward the cabin with a blaster in each hand. "Doc, right flank. J.B., go left. Mildred and Dean, cover fire. Jak, Hector and Clem with me."

Preparing their weapons, the companions started toward the cabin when a sharp whistle caught their attention.

"Incoming!" Doc shouted, gesturing down the hillside.

Returning to the wall of bushes edging the slopes, Ryan and the others took positions in the greenery and looked down the slope. A swarm of coldhearts, led by a huge man on a horse, was striving up the grassy incline. Their leader's face was disfigured by a hideous scar. Each cannie was armed with longblaster or crossbow, and the scar-faced man sported a huge U.S. Army M-60 machine gun, with a glittering golden belt of ammo dangling from the side port of the deadly weapon.

"Fireblast!" Ryan cursed bitterly, ducking out of sight. "That's trouble."

His lip split, J.B. spit blood on the ground and removed the partially loaded clip from the Uzi to slap in his second-to-last full one. "Must be the ground crew from the next part of the trap."

"Must be fifty of them!" Krysty cursed. Her face was unnaturally pale, and she stood with shoulders slumped, her hair limp, as if completely exhausted.

"Sixty-two," Ryan corrected, guessing the distance. Eighty yards, certainly no more than that. They were moving slow, waiting to be attacked. Ryan cradled his rifle but did nothing. His five remaining rounds weren't going to stop the charge of five dozen.

"Mebbe we can escape in the wags?" Stephen asked, sweat dripping off his pale face.

"Shut up, fool," Mildred ordered, hoisting the scattergun and working the pump. "Running would only get us killed."

"Anybody got a gren?" Ryan demanded, but their expressions told him the answer.

J.B. patted his shoulder bag. "Got some blocks of C-4, but they're useless in the open like this."

"Prep one," Ryan snapped. "A big one, just in case. Dean, any more cocktails in the truck?"

The boy grinned. "Plenty! I'll get the case." He took off with the speed of youth.

"Any more boulders?" Clem asked, glaring hatefully at the approaching crew. "What almost did us, should do them fine."

"Sure are," Hector said, pointing with his new wheelgun. "Just past the cook fire."

"Show us where," Ryan ordered, duck-walking out

of the bush. "Everybody with me. J.B., buy us two minutes."

The Armorer removed his hat. "No prob." He took careful aim down the slope, flipped the selector switch to full-auto and put a long spray of 9 mm rounds down the steep incline.

Three cannies cried out, and the rest hit the dirt, returning fire, the whole expanse of bushes shaking from the passage of bullets. But lacking a clear target, they were just shooting blind and hoping for the best.

Then the scar-faced man on the horse worked the arming bolt on his M-60, and the massive blaster began to throw gouts of flame at the ridge. "Keep going, ya dogs!" he shouted, riding the bucking military blaster like a pro. "First man on top gets a live woman!"

On the other side of the bushes, Ryan and the others were following Hector across the battlefield, jumping over bodies and blast craters until reaching a stand of trees with a scraggly collection of bushes in front. A gate of some kind was partially hidden behind the plants.

"Here," Hector panted. "I found it by accident."

The men removed the bushes, discovering they weren't attached to the ground but just sitting on top.

"Camou," Jak stated. "Nice."

Exposed was a split-rail enclosure that resembled a horse corral, large enough to hold a hundred big boulders—only a scant handful of smaller, yard-wide rocks rested behind the hinged gate.

"Shit! Have to do," Ryan growled, leveling his blaster. "Clear the path!" Neatly, he shot off the knotted rope and the gate swung aside, but the granite didn't budge.

From the ridge, he could hear Mildred discharge her

shotgun again, as J.B. inserted his last clip and started firing controlled bursts at the riders.

"Twenty yards!" J.B. yelled, switching to single-shot mode. "Nineteen!"

Growling in frustration, Ryan jumped over the fence and threw his shoulder against one of the stubborn rocks. He was surprised when it rolled easily out of the paddock, bumping the gate on the way out. Doc, Jak and Clem joined him in getting the other rocks started, and soon all six were rapidly tumbling across the sloped field. As they rapidly built speed, worn tracks in the hard ground spread the boulders out in a pattern between the bushes before they disappeared over the crest.

Scarface screamed as the line of rocks came tumbling his way. Irrationally, he fired the M-60 at the boulders as one hit a bump and sailed directly over the startled horseman to crash behind him and his mount. Unstoppable, the other boulders plowed through the startled cannies, smashing them aside in bloody ruination, and then the rocks were past them, rolling down the hill to ram into the trees on the far side of the road.

Ryan and the others reached the bushes and surveyed the carnage. Broken bodies were strewed across the hillside by the score, and no more than twenty men stood undamaged, including their leader.

Cursing bitterly, Scarface turned his mount and started to gallop down the hillside with his crew in hot retreat. The companions opened fire, but only managed to drop two more of the cannies before they reached the road and disappeared from view into the low trees.

"Think they'll return?" Dean asked, placing the case of Molotov cocktails heavily on the ground.

"Mebbe," his father said grimly. "Jak, Doc, stay here and keep watch on things. Dean, get those firebombs in the truck and help J.B. check over the wags. We might have to leave fast. Mildred, see what the hell is wrong with Krysty. Hector, make sure your wife is okay. Clem, come with me. Let's see what's in that cabin.''

Everybody hurried to their assigned tasks.

"Look at all this!" Stephen said greedily, grabbing a blaster from a corpse. Then he knelt and started to untie the laces on the combat boots. "This will triple my profit!"

Hector bumped the man in passing, and Jak retrieved the shotgun off the ground from his hands to sniff the barrel.

"Unused." The teenager cast it to the ground.

"Stephen, none of the weps or supplies are yours," J.B. stated coldly. "Those that fought get a slice. You don't."

"B-but I hired you!" the fat man raged.

"We're passengers," J.B. reminded him, working the bolt on his Uzi and pointing it straight at the man. His expression was calm. "Or do you think we still might make good mercies after all?"

Stephen slunk off muttering to himself.

"Going to be trouble there." J.B. sighed, resting the hot blaster on a shoulder. "Come on, let's check the vehicles."

"Any chance they can still roll?" Dean asked, hefting the box of bombs to his stomach and resting the bottom on his belt buckle to balance the weight.

"Sure," the Armorer said confidently. "But not for long." Then he paused and touched his head. "Where the hell is my hat?"

Checking for booby traps along the way, Ryan and Clem were almost at the log cabin when they spied a wounded man crawling along the ground toward the structure, a trail of blood stretching into the woods. Without stopping, Ryan drew his blaster and pointed it at the man, but Clem stopped him.

"Mine," he said firmly. "Bob is dead."

"Fair enough," Ryan said, holstering the weapon.

Clem kicked the man over so they were face-to-face. Weakly, the coldheart struggled as the hunter lowered his musket until the muzzle rested against the man's bare throat.

"For you, brother," he whispered, and pulled the trigger.

Ryan was already at the cabin circling the building, checking for sentries, when Clem returned, reloading as he walked. There was only one door in front, and the two small windows were covered with wooden shutters on the interior.

"Strange," Ryan whispered. "What are they keeping in there?"

Moving near the door, the two men listened for a while.

"That be crying?" Clem asked askance.

In a flash of understanding, Ryan drew the SIG-Sauer and kicked open the door. Inside the cabin was a nightmare. The small building clearly served as the cannies' armory with racks of blasters, boxes of ammo, crossbows and arrows stacked along both walls. But the rear area also served as their larder. Lacking only their heads, dressed human bodies hung gutted from rafters in orderly rows, men and women mixed together, the children and infants off to one side. The sweet air was thick with the smell of burned wood, and Ryan saw a smoker stove in the far corner, the fumes used to cure meat and make it last longer. His stomach lurched at the notion, and he tasted bitter bile in his mouth.

"By the blood of the prophet," Clem gasped, touching his heart, lips and forehead in an ancient protective gesture.

The crying sounded again, and the men spun, ready to kill anything they found, man or beast. Near a stack of seasoned wood, a man was chained to the wall. Within easy reach on a nearby shelf was a jelly jar full of water and a tin platter stacked high with roasted human hands.

"No, never," he repeated, a gasping cry marring his words. "Can't make me. Never eat. Stinking cannie freaks."

Slapping the plate away, Ryan drew his blaster and blew the chains off the wall. The prisoner recoiled from the blast and retreated into the corner.

"It's okay," Ryan said, staying where he stood. "We're not them."

The freed prisoner dared to peek out from behind his hands, and cried out in delight. "Lord Ryan! You have returned at last!"

Then the elation drained from his gaunt features, and he slumped to the floor, openly weeping. "Oh no, I've gone mad. This is only a dream. Why don't the bastards just kill me? Kill me!"

"I know you," Ryan said, dropping to a knee. "A hunter from Shersville, one of the shantytown hamlets near Front Royal. David, Daniel, something like that."

"Daffer," the prisoner breathed weakly. "Ryan, is…is it really you?"

As gently as he could, Ryan took the man's hand and helped him to his feet. "Daffer, it's been a long time."

"Indeed, it has been." The bedraggled man smiled

faintly, shuffling from foot to foot, as if ashamed of his condition.

"Clem, go get Mildred," Ryan said, and the hunter dashed out the door.

Minutes later the physician charged into the cabin and jerked to a halt staring at the hellish objects hanging from the rafters. Forcing her attention away, Mildred went straight to the man and checked his vital signs.

She fingered the back of his neck. "He certainly hasn't been fed in weeks. How long has it been?"

"Don't know. There's no day," Daffer replied, pointing at the sealed windows. "No night. A year, a month?"

"Hush, it's okay now. You're safe with us." Mildred took the jelly glass and offered it to him. "Here, drink some water. It will help with the stomach cramps."

"Never," he cried, knocking it away. The predark jar shattered on the floor, the glass shards scattering.

"What was in that?" she demanded, watching the thick fluid slowly seeping through the cracks in the rough-hewn floorboards.

"Some mutie brew," Daffer croaked, wiping his mouth. "The stuff makes you hungry as hell. Once you eat, the cannies own your soul. It's a thing they do to newcomers. Makes him one of them forever."

"An initiation," the warrior mused. "But you didn't drink a drop. Takes a real tough man to do that. The baron will be proud of you."

Breathing heavily for a while, Daffer stood straighter as he fully considered the matter. "I did refuse," he said, then broke into hysterical laughter. "Told them to go to hell, and they did! I never ate. Never!"

"Hush," Mildred said soothingly, unscrewing the cap to her canteen. "Here, drink my water. Fresh from a creek a hundred miles away.'' She took a long pull on the container to show it was safe, then pressed it in his grip, but maintained a tight grasp.

"Don't swallow the first sip,'' Mildred ordered. "Swish it around in your mouth and spit it out. Then take only small sips. Drinking too fast would be very bad for you in this condition.''

"Lord Ryan?'' the man asked, confused, clutching the container.

"Do as the healer says, Armsman,'' Ryan snapped, using the ancient predark word for a loyal warrior. He had heard his father use the term only twice, and it was always reserved for special sec men whose favor he wished to curry.

The man visibly calmed with the honor, and did as ordered, sipping and spitting until Mildred allowed him to drink freely.

"Bless you all,'' he finally said, coming up for air. "Are the cannies dead? There's one big man with a scar—he's the leader. Watch out for him.''

"The cannies are dead,'' Ryan stated. "Come on, I'll show you.''

He took the man by the elbow and helped him walk to the front door. Daffer paused at the sill as if a door were there, then with a determined face he stepped over the jamb and outside the log cabin. Mildred followed them closely, ready to catch the man in case he fell.

Blinking against the strong daylight, Daffer struggled to focus his vision, then smiled widely as he spied the bodies sprawling in the dirt, more than one face displaying its ghastly filed teeth.

"May the worms choke on your rotting flesh,'' he growled at the corpses. Turning clumsily, he stood at attention and saluted. "As my father did before me, I again swear my allegiance to you, Baron Cawdor, ruler of Front Royal!"

"I'm not a baron," Ryan stated, deliberately not returning the salute. "Never was. My nephew Nathan Freeman Cawdor rules Front Royal."

"Nathan?" the man said, slowly lowering his hand. "You don't know then, my lord?"

"We heard of trouble at the ville," Mildred replied, putting away the canteen. "But nothing more. Has there been a fight? Did it burn down?"

"The ville is fine. Never better."

The soft forest wind brushing his hair, Ryan braced himself for the worst. "Is Nathan dead?" he asked bluntly.

"Oh no, Lord Ryan," Daffer answered, confused. "Baron Nathan is alive and well. Both of them."

"Both?"

"Got a son, does he?" Clem asked, scratching under his furs. "Good. A baron needs kin like a rifle needs powder. Ain't no use without them."

"A son?" the sec man said, his unease clearly growing. "A son? Yes, but it's not *his* son. It's yours."

"Mine?" Ryan asked, startled.

"What are you talking about?" Mildred demanded.

"Front Royal is still ruled by Nathan," Daffer explained, glancing toward the east. "And by your son, Overton Cawdor, come home from the Deathlands."

Chapter Nine

A layer of mist lay over the ground, with the low hills breaking the cover like islands in a sea of smoke.

Not far from Front Royal, the companions stood amid some trees and watched the abbreviated version of the convoy roll down the cracked asphalt of the road winding toward the east. The truck in front was packed solid with tents, blasters, horse tackle, crossbows, clothes, boots and other assorted supplies looted from the cannies. Even the blaster racks on the walls had been taken. Not a single item of value remained at the ambush pass.

Chained behind the truck was the cargo van, and in the rear van Sara was at the wheel and Hector cradled the baby, as she was the one who knew how to drive.

On the horizon was a collection of predark houses and buildings. Mixed among the old homes were new log cabins and battered concrete structures resembling pillboxes.

"Is that Front Royal?" Dean asked, lowering the Navy telescope.

"No, just one of the hamlets that surround the ville," Ryan replied, compacting the scope and tucking it into a pocket. "There's a ring of small towns surrounding the fortress—River, Benton, Brown, Linden, Sherril... They act as a buffer zone against invaders."

"The fortress at Front Royal is farther down the road," Doc said, sitting on a log beside their small campfire. He was holding tongs and melting lead in a tiny crucible. "Quite a sight it is, too. The stone blocks are weathered a brownish-yellow, so it appears to be made of solid gold, like some mythological abode of King Arthur and the knights of the round table."

"Wow," the boy said, impressed.

A patched canvas tent stood behind Doc, the flap wide open so the heat from the fire could gather inside and help them stay warm at night. Before burning down the log cabin, the companions had looted the place of everything useful, including the tents, although the decorations on the tent poles were the first things to go. The armory had been a treasure trove of blasters and ammo, with enough different calibers to fit the weapons of each companion. Everybody was fully armed again. Naturally, there had been nothing for Doc's oddball .44 LeMat, but he had convinced Clem to upgrade to a bolt-action Enfield rifle, and took the hunter's supplies of black powder, cloth and lead for himself. The miniballs wouldn't fit his small .44 wheelgun, but lead was lead, and he could make ammunition from anything that melted.

In a nearby clearing, Jak was cutting branches and using them to cover the second truck, which was now their property in exchange for the loot from the cannies, now riding in the first truck. With the companions staying behind, Stephen was short on drivers, and more importantly, they would need a wag to rendezvous with Mildred at midnight.

"The fortress is very impressive," Krysty agreed from under her blankets inside the tent. "The turrets rise so very high in the sky that—" She stopped talking and broke into a ragged cough.

"Go to sleep," Doc ordered, carefully pouring the

molten lead into the aluminum bullet molds he always carried, and topping off the batch. "Mildred placed me in charge of you, and sleep is the prescription for the flu. Do you want to get pneumonia, my dear Krysty?"

The redhead buried herself under the covers again.

"Still," the boy said, unrelenting, "I sure wish we could have gone with Mildred."

Ryan walked him to the campfire. "Too dangerous, son. They know the five of us there."

"Even after so many years," J.B. added, brushing off his beloved fedora, "somebody recognized your dad immediately."

"That's not very difficult," Ryan said. "I bear a strong resemblance to my father."

"Well, they don't know me!" Dean countered, resolute.

"However, if some pretender is claiming to be my son," Ryan stated, filling a coffeepot with well water, "then my real son will be the first person he'd want chilled, or in chains."

He placed the pot near the flames to start the water boiling and opened the rusty predark can of U.S. Navy coffee. The corrosion on the exterior hadn't reached the inside of the metal container, and the grounds were clumped together into hard lumps, but it was actual coffee. The cannies had to have been saving it for a special occasion, and what could possibly be more special than their complete eradication?

No, he mentally corrected, that wasn't true. Scarface had escaped, and they would have to watch for his revenge for quite a while.

"Dad, what if he *is* my brother?" Dean asked quietly, leaning forward, hands clasped together.

Conflicting emotions filled Ryan, and he said nothing

as he looked in the direction of the departing caravan. Daffer would be dropped off close to Front Royal, so as not to stir suspicions. Armed with a new longblaster and wheelgun from the cannies' armory, he also had Clem's musket and a bag of some strange 7.62 mm bullets that J.B. thought were Chinese, but wasn't sure. Still, it was more than enough ammo to pay for whatever he might need.

However, the recce of the ville would be done by Mildred and Clem, as they hadn't been to the ville before. And there were so many questions to answer. Who was this Overton? Why was Nathan going along with the liar? Or did the baron believe the stranger was truly Ryan's son?

The water started to boil. Ryan poured a handful of lumpy black grounds into the big pot, and instantly the mix started to smell like coffee brewing.

"What if Overton is my brother?" the boy repeated.

Thoughtfully, Ryan stirred the bubbling brew with a green stick, his face a mask of consternation.

"Dad?"

"I'm still considering that possibility," he stated, for some reason feeling very much alone even though surrounded by family and close friends.

DOWNSHIFTING, Mildred steered the battered truck past a washed-out section of the roadway. The asphalt had completely crumbled over the ages, and the winter rains undercut the soft dirt beneath until the entire side of the road had slid into the mists to their left.

Colorful birds skimmed along the tops of the swirling clouds, and there seemed to be treetops just out of sight below, so Mildred put a touch more pressure on the gas pedal to hurry them along. She didn't want to think about how high they were.

The front seat of the truck was an awkward fit with the three of them jammed in tight. But Clem was riding shotgun, and Mildred had no intention of letting Stephen alone until absolutely necessary.

"Remember our deal," Clem said, resting an elbow out the window, thankful for the few extra inches of space it afforded. A cool breeze rich with the smell of pine trees ruffled his fur coat and long hair. "You don't talk to nobody about Ryan and the others. Right?"

"Hey, I always keep my word!" Stephen stated, managing to sound offended. "I'm an honest man!"

Clem scowled in response. Anybody who called himself honest almost invariably wasn't.

"We keep our word, too," Mildred said. "You best remember that."

Stephen forced a smile.

The miles passed quietly, the silence broken only by the rattle of the engine and the throb of the off-balance wheels. There were many things Mildred wanted to discuss with Clem about their recce mission, but with Stephen sitting between them it wasn't deemed a safe topic of conversation.

"Daffer going to be okay?" Clem asked across the plump obstruction in the cab. With so much starvation these days, he really didn't trust anybody with fat on their bones.

"He'll live," Mildred replied, paying close attention to the serpentine road. "But that's about all I can promise. What I wouldn't give for a full field-surgery kit. Even a first-aid pack would do fine."

Roused from his nap, Stephen burst into laughter. "A predark med bag? A man could buy a whole ville with one of those! And you would use it on a half-crazed cripple?''

"Why, hell," Mildred said in an even tone, "I'd even use it on you."

The laughter stopped hard, and the man glanced at her then at Clem on his other side for several minutes before finally accepting the rebuff. "Healers," Stephen muttered softly under his breath. "Crazy as a shithouse rat."

"Hunters, too." Clem grinned, working the stiff bolt on his new longblaster and adding a few drops of oil. The Enfield .30-06 was just a marvel to the man. It was much shorter than his old smooth-bore musket, hardly over three and a half feet in length, and it weighed only about ten pounds. Oddly, the ammo clip didn't come off, but instead he was supposed to load in six rounds from the top through the firing chamber by pulling back the bolt. Six shots! Think of the time that would save in a fight. And he could shove in single rounds if necessary instead of taking the time to reload a full clip into the magazine.

Clem patted his new ammo pouch, packed with over fifty cartridges. Lovely little thing, too. There was a wide red stripe around the wooden stock, and a small crown etched into the blue barrel. The sights were a bit of a bitch to adjust for windage, but this was surely the best blaster he had ever owned. Hell, there was even a knife you could attach to the end of the barrel to gut folks. J.B. had called it a bayonet.

"Must you constantly do that?" Stephen complained as the man worked the bolt action again and again.

Clem smiled as he finally realized that the bolt wasn't sticking. It just required some muscle to operate. "Man who don't know his weps," the hunter said, "is just a walking corpse looking for a place to lay down."

"Amen, brother." Mildred chuckled.

THE BURNISHED COPPER SUN was high in the purple sky when the convoy rolled across a trestle over a raging river, the spray forming rainbows in the air above the turbulent water.

"Is this the Sorrow?" Mildred asked, glancing below. The water was wild, a raging torrent of white foam that crashed over the exposed boulders with unbridled fury.

"Worst water in the Shens," Stephen replied. "That river kills more often than a baron. Didn't get that name for nothing."

"Seen worse in Kentuck," Clem drawled, taking a plug of some dark fibrous material from his pocket and biting off a piece. He chewed contentedly for a few minutes.

"Is that tobacco?" Mildred asked, interested.

He swallowed. "Sure. Want a chaw?"

"Good Lord, no! I mean, no thank you," she hastily amended. "But, ah, any chance there are cigars available?"

"This is tobacco country," Stephen noted with a tone of pride. "Bet your ass they got cigars. I hear they're rolled on the thighs of virgin girls during the full moon."

"Always thought seasoning was mighty important myself," Clem snorted, taking a fresh bite of the plug.

The joke was crude, but Mildred was forced to smile in spite of herself while downshifting gears again. Damnation, if the road was in any worse condition they'd never be able to reach Front Royal without resorting to walking.

"Cigars a gift for your man?" Clem asked, stroking his blaster and watching the countryside pass by outside.

"His only bad habit," the physician answered wryly. "But he does loves them so, and we haven't found an intact cigar since—" Mildred bit a lip, stopping herself. "Since the Deathlands," she finished coolly.

The redoubts the companions used to travel across the continent were the biggest secret of the predark world, and even more so now. The very existence of the subterranean forts wasn't to be mentioned in front of strangers under any circumstance.

Eventually, the road climbed higher and the truck rolled onto a barren field. Gutted tracks marked the soft soil, showing where numerous horses and wags had plodded along the identical path.

"We must be close," she said, using a free moment to check the shotgun. The blaster was within reach and fully loaded.

In agreement, Clem worked the bolt on his Enfield, chambering a cartridge. J.B. had offered his Uzi for the journey on the opinion that firepower was the best replacement for numbers. But the hunter felt confident that if he couldn't chill something with this deadly beauty, then it just plain couldn't be chilled.

Soon, the ground on either side of the crude roadway took on a more cultivated appearance, with fields covered with a thick growth of a blue-green plant with fat leaves.

"Soybeans," Mildred marveled. "Ground cover to protect the soil from the acid rain?"

Stephen stared at the woman as if she had just solved

the mystery of the universe. "That's correct," he said slowly. "It was the new baron's idea. Seems to work pretty good."

"Beans," Clem scoffed, and he spit brown juice out the window. "Ain't fit food for man or dog."

"The farmers don't eat the soybeans, just plow them under in the spring to feed the real crops, taters and corn and such." Stephen made a face. "Boy, you ever eat a soybean? Tastes like a used sock."

"They need to be treated first," Mildred stated. "After that, they can taste like anything."

"Really now," Stephen said, warming to the topic. "Could be a lot of profit in that. Treat them how?"

"Slow," Clem warned, easing the blue barrel of the Enfield closer to the window.

The afternoon sun was burning off the mists, and clearly ahead of them was a fork in the road, one branch going to the north, the other continuing east. However, a military outpost was at the fork, tripods of logs lashed together with barbed wire to form an imposing array along the sides to retard escape attempts. Exiting the road wouldn't be possible until they were past this section.

A log cabin surrounded by a low sandbag wall stood prominently at the junction, and an armed sec man rose from a rocking chair at their approach. He called to somebody inside the cabin, the words lost over the rumble of the old engine.

"Stop when he tells you to," Stephen said. "This is just a checkpoint for Front Royal."

Mildred scowled, noticing the barrels of several long-blasters sticking out of narrow notches cut into the walls of the fortified log cabin. They seemed to be mostly muskets, except for the telltale muzzle of an AK-47 assault rifle amid the others. That was the sec boss, without a doubt. "Checkpoint? You mean tollhouse. Pay or die."

Clem glanced around. There was an empty gallows alongside the road, and a set of darkly stained crosses, with old rope dangling loose from the killing bars. "No customers."

"They don't kill here unless you disobey or try to smuggle in contraband. It's merely pay or go back," the fat man corrected. "Baron Cawdor rules a tight ville, but he's no bastard. Well, no more than any of the others."

"How much do they want?" Mildred asked, slowing gently. Then panic hit the woman, and she drew her blaster. "If it's me they're after..."

"Nothing of the sort," Stephen denied. "Because I don't pay tolls. This is a private shipment for the baron himself."

Clem motioned with his head. "What's up that side road, a shantytown?"

"A hamlet, yes. Shersville. Farmers and hunters. Nothing there to buy, and they don't have enough to buy. I was there once, and that was enough."

Cleanly dressed in a bright blue shirt as if he were a police officer from bygone days, the ville sec man walked boldly into the middle of the roadway and waved at the wag to halt. Working the clutch, Mildred applied the brakes and squealed to a halt only a few yards away from the man.

"Welcome to the border of Front Royal," the sec man said, sounding slightly bored. "No jolt or muties allowed. If you got any, leave it or dump it in the ravine. We find any, you get chilled on the spot. No trial, no blindfold."

"Clean and fast," Clem said. "Sounds good."

The sec man studied the man. "Mountain man?"

"Tennessee valley lowlands," the hunter corrected, as if that were an important distinction.

Stephen leaned across Mildred, coming uncomfortably close to the woman in her opinion. "Hey, Brian. It's me. We're finally here with the baron's goods."

"Oh, it's you. Made good time this trip," the guard said, easing his stance. A hand still rested on the grip of his holstered weapon, but a finger was no longer on the trigger. "Any trouble with the muties?"

"Mostly coldhearts. But we saw their work on the road," he said, keeping to the story they'd agreed upon.

"You don't say." Brian studied the vehicle in tow, and the van behind. "This your whole crew, just four folks? Where are the rest of the mercies?"

"We lost a lot in the hills," Mildred said.

The sec man produced a cigarette and lit it with a match he struck on his pants. "Sorry to hear that. I'll pass that info along to the shift commander."

Mildred filed that phrase away. Sounded very military.

"Say, any chance you know a sec man called Daffer?" she asked. "Short guy, brown hair, big nose."

For the first time, the guard looked at her directly. "Yeah. He was chilled a month ago by a cougar, or so we think. At least, Daffer's not in the ville anymore."

She jerked a thumb. "We got him in the rear van. Not in great shape, but he'll live."

The sec man's stern visage softened. "Nice to hear he's still alive. Was it a cougar?"

"Cannies. He was almost dinner himself when Ry— When we saved him."

Stephen added, "They tortured him for defense info

on Front Royal so they could raid the hamlets, but he never talked. Tough little bastard, should be a sergeant!''

The genial expression on the sec man's face melted away with those words, and Brian stuffed two fingers into his mouth giving out a shrill whistle. Squads of sec men charged out of the cabin and from the woods. Mildred realized that they had been surrounded from the moment they saw the toll. Then she noticed they were wearing crisp blue shirts and carrying AK-47 assault rifles. All of them. There was enough firepower here to start a war, much less protect a ville.

"We have a possible sec breach!" the corporal shouted, drawing his blaster, a 9 mm Beretta in perfect condition. "Double all patrols! Shoot anybody suspicious. I'm going to report to the baron in person."

The armed men rushed about, and a crew expertly began to set up what looked like a .50-caliber machine gun behind the sandbags. Where the hell had they found that?

"Corporal, this isn't necessary," Mildred chided, leaning out the window. "Daffer didn't talk."

"Mebbe, mebbe not." The sec man climbed onto the back of the truck, holding on to the slats. "But until we know for sure, this post is going triple red and staying as hard as a prayer in hell. Baron Cawdor takes military threats very seriously."

"No shit," Clem drawled, watching the activity.

The corporal thumped the cab. "Let's move, the baron is waiting for you."

Having no choice in the matter, Mildred started the engine with a sputtering roar, and the truck rolled past the checkpoint. In the taped-together pieces of the rearview mirror, she saw sec men swarm over the cargo van, forcing Hector and his family out at blasterpoint, then carrying out Daffer on his litter.

"Good luck," she muttered.

Beyond the toll, the road evened out, raked smooth for miles. Aside from the occasional piece of predark highway still intact, it was the best road she had ever seen. Then the truck passed by a crew of sec men whipping a gang of prisoners bound in heavy chains, the men and women smoothing out the roadway surface with their bare hands.

"Mighty harsh justice," Clem said, scowling.

Coming out of the forest, Mildred rode across manicured grasslands before Front Royal rose into view. Granite blocks formed the high walls of the fortification, stones aged to a soft golden color from the acid rains that came every spring. A homemade American flag fluttered from the top of the central keep, while armed sec men walked the parapets.

There were no shanties, huts or tents surrounding the fortress, just acres upon acres of trimmed lawn. The halcyon fields were hideous in their beauty, because Mildred could guess how the grass was maintained in that pristine state. Slave labor, or rather criminals working as slaves.

"Bet there are a lot of laws in the ville," she said aloud. "Tricky ones, real easy to break by mistake."

"Yeah," Stephen said suspiciously. "How did you know?"

"Common sense."

"Besides, the baron has to get his slaves from somewhere," Clem drawled, hunkering low in his seat. He took out his plug of tobacco, almost took a bite, then tucked it away again. The man desperately wanted a chaw, but spitting might be illegal here. Damn city folks were plum crazy. For a tick, he fiercely wished Bob were here to advise him, then Clem forced away those thoughts and put on his best poker face. Stay loose, stay low, just as if he were hunting a bear.

A cobblestone drawbridge crossed a wide moat. Armed sec men in blue, and some in brown, watched as Brian directed the rattling wag through a barbican, the portcullis of the brick tunnel raised flush into the ceiling to allow easy passage. But Mildred knew the single slice of a sharp knife would send that ton of spiked iron crashing down to seal off any possible invasion. Or escape attempt.

A courtyard spread out before her, hundreds of yards wide and long. Horses were corralled at stables, and a mill was grinding wheat. Loud clanks came from a blacksmith shop, the blazing hearth masked by dense clouds of smoke. Sec men marched by in orderly columns as if on parade, women carried baskets on their heads, children ran by chasing dogs, a man was being whipped at a wooden post, songs came from a tavern, with a gaudy house on the second floor. The sluts leaning over the balconies displaying their wares to potential customers.

From long talks with Ryan, Mildred knew the huge, sprawling fortress was truly a city unto itself. The numerous buildings and structures interconnected via a series of closed arbor and tunnels. An invading force would have hell's own trouble searching out the defenders, and narrow slits notched every wall to offer perfect firing views for the defenders.

"Park over there," Brian directed, hopping off the wag while it was still moving.

Nosing in close to a wall, Mildred killed the engine and put on the brake.

"My thanks for the ride. I must report to the duty sergeant immediately, but you can go about your biz," he said, patting his uniform here and there.

Mildred had seen Ryan and J.B. do the same thing a thousand times. The gestures were the unconscious actions of a battlefield warrior making sure his weapons were in place. This man was not just a mercie in a uniform.

"Good journey," she said.

"Freedom and duty!" he cried, snapping a stiff-hand salute to his chest.

Awkwardly, with the steering wheel in the way, Mildred returned the gesture. He nodded as if she had done the correct thing, then spun on a boot heel and marched away quickly.

"How did you know about the new salute?" Stephen demanded, sounding annoyed.

Without answering, Mildred opened her door and climbed out, dragging her med kit from behind the seat. "We part company here," the physician said. "But this is Ryan's old home, and he has lots of kin here. So mind our bargain."

"Or else," Clem added, joining her on the street.

"Deal is a deal," Stephen said stolidly, trying to smile in a friendly manner and failing miserably.

Just then a horn beeped and a crowd of people quickly separated, allowing the cargo van to pull alongside the truck, sandwiching the people between the wags. Sara set the brake and exited the wag, running around to open the door for Hector, who handed her a wiggling bundle before climbing down from the wag.

"Glad you folks arrived safely," Mildred said happily, walking closer. "I got worried when the sec men hauled you out of the van. Everybody okay?"

"Certainly," Sara said, tucking the blanket tighter around the baby. "They checked some papers Stephen had given us, then gave us an escort into the ville as if we were royalty."

"Whatever is in those boxes," Hector said, "must be mighty important."

"Wheat," Stephen said. "Grains to plant this spring. Just a lot of raw wheat."

"Sure," Clem drawled.

"Papers?" Mildred asked.

"If you knew all of my biz," the man huffily said, "then you wouldn't need me."

"Don't need ya now," the hunter replied, loosening the lacings on his fur coat. Underneath, he wore tanned leather pants, shirt and vest. A bandolier of ammo was slung across his chest. Two sets of belts rested on his hips, supporting a blaster and a hand ax, and the top of a complex tattoo was visible above his low-cut shirt.

Stephen turned from the other man. "Well, here we are safe at Front Royal, and I have more biz to do. Goodbye to you all. Perhaps we'll journey again sometime."

"Not likely," Mildred stated bluntly. "Just remember our deal. You stay alive for as long as you stay quiet."

"I remember everything, outlander. Farewell!" Stephen cried, executing a stiff-arm salute. Then the fat man walked into the bustling crowds and was gone.

"He a sec man?" Sara asked puzzled, gently rocking the baby in her arms.

Hector shook his head in disbelief. "Can't be. No way."

"Mice got teeth," Clem observed, hooking his

thumbs behind the bandolier. "And sometime they do bite."

"I agree. We best be leaving," Mildred said, gathering her backpack and kit. "He'll be coming back with an escort, and it might not be wise if we were here to bother the sec men in their many duties."

"We'll keep a watch on the fat man," Hector said, slinging his new longblaster over a shoulder. "Chain his ass to a rock and toss him in the moat if necessary, but he won't be talking to any sec men today."

"Lady healer, we can never thank you enough," Sara gushed, tears making tiny diamonds in her black eyes.

"Taking care of little Millie is more than enough," she replied, hugging the woman.

"If you need to find us," Hector added, "my cousin is named Miguel. He's a carpenter at a barrel maker's. I'll also be working there, hopefully."

"You will be," Clem stated. "Can feel it in my bones."

Mildred nodded. "I'll remember that name. Godspeed."

"Good journey."

The group shook hands, and the family pushed its way into the crowd. Mildred caught glimpses of Hector amid the strangers, and then he was gone.

"Time to go," Mildred stated, heading in a different direction than the others.

"Where first?" Clem asked, shortening his stride to match her pace. Then he quickened his walk to try to keep up with Mildred. She was short and stocky, but full of energy.

"Nowhere," she replied, studying the parapets rising on every side. A single stone tower rose high above the other buildings, and she wondered what function it served.

Just then a clock began to chime the hour. Startled by the noise, Mildred double-checked the tower, but that wasn't the source. She recalled that Ryan had mentioned there was a clock tower in the exact middle of the ville, so everybody could see it easily. The machine was the pride of the ville, even if nowadays nobody had any conceivable use for precise schedules.

"Let's just wander for a while, go with the flow and see where the crowds take us," she suggested, "then decide where to go next, a bar maybe, or a tavern. We can learn a lot with ours mouths closed and ears open."

"A quiet hunter eats regular," he said solemnly.

Mildred patted the tall man on the shoulder. "True words, my friend. Maybe we can even find someplace to buy food. Don't know about you, but I'm starving."

"Not going to eat meat for a while," Clem said with a frown, touching his rumbling stomach. "But bread and beer will do. Hell, mebbe even some damn beans."

Strolling through the milling throng of the busy courtyard, the man and woman found the public market by following the noise. Shouting farmers were selling scrawny vegetables from wheelbarrows; brewers offered drinks by the cup from an open keg of homemade beer; nearby, an old man with a bedraggled guitar was pandering songs for a drink.

"Any cigars?" Mildred asked a dealer whose table was covered with sun-dried leaves of tobacco. She had no idea the things were so enormous, well over a yard long and half as wide.

"Just pipes," he apologized, carefully whittling a calabash from a piece of driftwood.

"Damn. Oh, well."

Clem eyed the plugs of chaw dubiously. It was all third-grade lug, not worth an empty brass.

Fishermen yelled about the freshness of their catch of the day; a hunter dressed very similar to Clem was dickering over the sale of an entire bear; some wandering gaudy sluts were plying their trade in alleyways for the impatient; small dogs and kids were constantly underfoot tripping people; hot taters were being sold straight from a little brick stove by a blind man; gamblers rolled dice made from carved bone for tarnished bullets; horse tackle and other leather goods were hawked by a hundred people; a thief was caught stealing an arrow from a fletcher and beaten to death on the spot by the blue shirts, as the people called the new sec men. The guards were carrying AK-47 assault rifles, the barrels gleaming with oil. Mildred and Clem moved quickly away.

Everybody seemed to be trying to outshout the other hucksters, the noise level growing steadily. Clem was a bit apprehensive, but Mildred reveled in the chaos. Even crude civilization was better than none, and she had seen more than her share of that in Deathlands.

Front Royal was obviously very prosperous. There was actually food for sale and open commerce, just incredible. It was the new Manhattan of America. No wonder it was the center of so much attention.

Then a line of chained slaves shuffled by, the overseer cracking her bullwhip across the backs of the sluggish. Mildred's hand went for her blaster, and she had to force herself to relax. She was here to gather info, not start a fight.

Not wanting to draw attention by paying for food with ammo, they instead bartered the cured opossum skin and a spare knife for a pair of decent shoes. Then they exchanged the shoes with a baker whose son was barefoot for all the stale bread they could carry. Half the bread bought them a dozen winter apples from a suspicious farmer.

Pockets jammed full, Mildred and Clem ate slowly as they meandered through the market, sidling close to any group of folks arguing and avoiding the sec men whenever possible. Mildred's ZKR was tucked out of sight, but the Enfield drew looks wherever they went.

"Can you wrap that in your jacket?" Mildred asked. Aside from the sec men, they were the only folks displaying firepower of any kind.

"Wouldn't be able to reach it should the need arise," he said, finishing off an apple. "What kind of blaster do those blue boys have? Pretty fancy. Ain't never seen anything like that before."

"I have," she stated, but would say no more on the subject.

Over the next couple of hours, they roamed from one end of the huge courtyard to the other, and then back again in a continuous circle, listening to the snatches of conversation with growing unease.

"Awful lot of people hate the new baron," Mildred said, gnawing on a heel of bread. "And most can't understand why Nathan is letting him take over, even if he is the son of Ryan."

"Lord Ryan, they say. Folks here worship the guy," Clem agreed, tossing away the apple core. A rat darted out of a drain, snatched it and ran away chased by a mangy dog.

"Maybe Overton is just some guy who wants to be baron. So he claims to be the son of a local hero to get his foot through the door."

"Why?" Clem asked, licking his fingers clean. "He

got enough sec men and blasters to take this place if he wants to.''

"Does he?''

"Sure seems so.''

"Maybe that's why he's playacting, trying a scam. He needs the whole ville prosperous to feed that many.''

"Rabble will turn on you if they're unhappy,'' Clem drawled. "Then you got a real fight.''

"Could be,'' she admitted. Then she added hotly, "Only, where did he get those brand-new AK-47s? And where the hell does electricity come in on the deal?''

"Tell me what that is, mebbe I know,'' he offered.

Just then a busty gaudy slut walked by suggestively wiggling her hips and smiling at the men.

"Whew, ain't she something? Mebbe I'd like living here.'' Clem grinned, then he squinted. "Hey, what's happening over there? Some sort of speech?''

Glancing around, Mildred spotted a growing crowd of people forming a half circle before a blank wall of the fortress.

"Let's go see,'' she said, heading in that direction.

Pushing their way to the front of the waiting mob, Mildred and Clem saw a line of sec men with rifles facing a man chained to the wall. The surface around the captive was heavily pockmarked with bullet holes. Another man in clean clothes and sporting a fancy blaster was reading off a list of crimes.

"Speech, hell,'' Clem drawled, crossing his arms. "This be an execution.''

"Hush,'' Mildred said, trying to hear every word.

"...and so, as baron of this ville,'' the handsome man finished, folding the sheet of paper, "I condemn you, Quinn Marley, to death by firing squad.''

"But I was only drunk, Lord Nathan," he whispered, head bowed. "Just drunk, is all."

"Drunk while on guard duty, you mean!" Nathan snapped, his face a mask of fury. "An unforgivable act of treason! This ville survives by the diligence of its sec men, and when they fail us, lives are risked. Plus, this isn't the first instance. You've been publicly whipped already, and I told you plain what would happen the next time this occurred."

"But I was only drunk!" the man screamed shrilly and began to rattle his chains, kicking at the wall. "Please, my lord, have mercy!"

"No. You have received enough mercy. Now it's time for justice." Nathan raised his hand high. "Firing squad, ready..."

The sec men lifted their blasters and worked the bolts, chambering rounds.

"You got to listen to me!" Quinn pleaded.

"Aim..."

The sec men took a firing stance, the barrels pointed at the prisoner.

His lower lip quivering, the man burst into tears and shamefully soiled his pants. "No! Please, don't chill me, Lord. It was a mistake, and it'll never happen again. Please, don't shoot me!"

Arm poised ready to drop, Nathan waited for a few ticks to let the terror seep into the struggling prisoner. Quinn was a superb gunsmith, the best he had ever known, a valuable asset to the safety of the ville. But his flagrant dereliction of duty had to stop today. A natural tech, Quinn was a special man with unique gifts, and Nathan was willing to overlook a lot of shit from the top-notch gunsmith. But nobody could be allowed to directly challenge the authority of the baron.

Technically, being drunk on duty could be considered an act of treason, and a harsher baron would simply make an example of the sec man. But master gunsmiths were few and far between, so Nathan had decided to give the damn fool one last chance and a taste of what could have occurred. Hopefully, that would set him straight. A ruler had to be merciful, as well as strong. However, if it ever happened again, Nathan would personally heave him in the dungeon for a hundred years.

"Hold!" somebody roared within the anxious crowd.

Reluctantly, the people parted to make way for a large man striding toward the execution. As he came into view, Mildred dropped her jaw in astonishment. What the hell was this?

The man was tall, well over six feet in height, and his skin was deeply tanned, as if he'd just come from the desert. His black hair was long and curly, swept off a stern face with a square jaw and piercing blue eyes. He was dressed in a dark blue shirt like all of the other sec men, but this one also had matching pants and knee-high jackboots. A blaster rode in a holster at his right hip, another under his left arm. The curved sheath for a panga slanted up from his belt for a quick cross draw.

"Son of a bitch," Clem muttered. "Looks just like him."

Mildred was forced to agree. Whoever this man was, he strongly resembled a young Ryan Cawdor. He even carried a panga! The physician had never even heard of the strange weapon before meeting Ryan, and never seen another since.

"Baron Cawdor," Nathan said through gritted teeth. "We're in the middle of something that isn't your concern."

"That is incorrect," Overton replied, marching to the

bound man. The firing squad watched him hard, their hands dangerously close to triggers.

Reaching Quinn, the baron drew a .45-caliber Desert Eagle from his belt and shot the prisoner in the face. The muzzle-flash washed over his features, and the man's head literally exploded, bones, brains and blood splattering the rear wall.

"You dare!" Nathan roared, drawing his own weapon and starting forward, only to grind to a halt as if reaching the end of an invisible rope.

The people murmured angrily among themselves. Only a few scattered voices cheered for the new baron and swift justice.

"Why did you do this?" he asked in a hoarse whisper.

"Typical waste," Overton shouted to the masses. "Eight bullets used where one would do."

"Quinn was a sec man and deserved a military execution," Nathan argued, returning the blaster to its holster with a trembling arm. He released the Glock as if casting it into the sea. "Not being shot like a rabid dog."

"He was a traitor!" Overton retorted. "His drunkenness put this whole ville in danger of attack by muties. And traitors die."

The people voiced a hundred opinions, many in agreement.

"As a formerly loyal sec man, he deserved no more than a painless death for his years of service. That he received." Baron Overton turned to address the confused crowd, and spread his arms. "Can any here say I made him suffer?"

Approving sounds were heard, and somebody started to applaud. More did the same, but it soon died away.

His hands opening and closing at his sides, Nathan drew in a deep breath and exhaled slowly. "No, of course. You're correct once more. Waste nothing! Including our time. This matter is over. Good day, Baron," growled Nathan, and stalked from the execution area hunched over against a wind only he could see or feel.

As the firing squad unchained the body, the crowd began to disperse. Mildred and Clem joined the exodus and moved deeper into the throng, staying out of sight of the barons and their troops.

"To hell with waiting, let's leave now," Mildred said. "I've seen enough."

"Yeah," the hunter drawled in agreement. "Stinks worse than skunk shit, don't it?"

STANDING AS IF ON DISPLAY, Overton stayed where he was, watching the people and studying their reactions. A lot more than usual were listening to him. Soon, he would have no need of Nathan. Suddenly, he noticed a movement coming his way. Overton tensed for battle, but relaxed when he saw it was only his chief sec man, Jian Hwa Ki.

"My lord," the man said quietly, turning his back to the crowd, "look to the east, near the stove of the blind man."

Puzzled, Overton scowled in that direction, froze motionless, then slowly grinned. She was with a hunter wearing leather and furs, but it was definitely Dr. Mildred Wyeth—short black woman, stocky build, long beaded hair, Olympic target pistol in her belt. It couldn't be anybody else.

Overton took the sec chief by the shoulder and together they walked toward the fortress at an easy gait.

"Excellent work, Jian Hwa. If the physician is here, then Ryan and the others are close."

"We could detain her," Jian Hwa suggested.

"Let them leave. She probably came here to recce the ville before the rest dare to come. A very smart move. But soon they will return with Ryan."

"And then, my lord?"

Overton laughed. "Then, old friend, we slaughter half the ville and finally begin our real work here."

Chapter Ten

Springing silently from the bushes, the cougar landed on the young buck deer and mauled it to the ground. Sharp white teeth sinking into the animal's hide, the big cat ripped away a mouthful of flesh from its living prey and swallowed. The cougar started to purr with satisfaction. The cat began to play with its food, raking claws across the hide, letting it crawl away a few yards before pouncing on it again and chewing at its legs. The mutie deer whimpered and cried, which only made the cougar continue its game.

In a wild thrashing of tentacles, something dropped from the branches above and wrapped its flexing limbs around the cougar, pinning it helpless. The terrified animal struggled insanely, blind panic filling its eyes with madness, as the amorphous mutie sank the horned tips of its tentacles deep into the soft fur of both animals. The ropy lengths of the translucent limbs visibly began to pump warm red blood along their lengths.

Bleating in horror, the mutie deer pawed at the ground, again trying to crawl away as the cat fully extended its claws, desperately seeking a purchase to strike from. But both actions were to no avail; the terrible feasting went on and on.

A vibration grew in the soil and the air, startling, then frightening the three creatures, the noise rising to deafening levels, the whole forest shaking. Then the bushes

fell over and a huge metal machine rolled over the hunters and hunted, crushing the creatures beneath its eight
churning tires and mashing them into the soil. Only a
little of the blood splashed upon the angular sides of
the armored personnel carrier.

Rumbling onward, the APC moved toward a clearing,
as another of the wheeled machines came in from a
different angle, smashing aside small trees as the juggernauts headed for a low hill protruding from the Virginia landscape.

The black mouth of a cave yawned in the rocky face
of the swelling, and an armed sec man in a clean blue
shirt waved them closer. Even if they hadn't been right
on schedule, he would have recognized the transports—
a brace of mint-condition Bradley Fighting Vehicles,
designation LAV 25, Piranha type, assault class, fully
armed with a 7.62 mm machine gun and 25 mm rapid-
fire cannon on the top turret.

The two machines parked some distance from each
other, their turret cannons sweeping the area for possible hostiles. After a few minutes, the rear doors of the
wags swung aside and disgorged sec men carrying AK-
47 blasters. The last man out was a tall slim man in a
starched blue uniform, a silver blaster in his hand.

"Spread out," the sergeant ordered, gesturing to the
troops. "Gerrold, take five men and secure the perimeter. O'Connor, start digging a fire pit and gathering
wood for dinner. Hemeniez, get some water."

The sec men moved quietly and quickly.

"Boil it first?" asked a private with a bucket.

"No need. The Shens are clean."

"Which is why we're here," the lieutenant added,
doffing his cloth cap. "Not going to build a forward
base in the middle of a rad pit."

The officer's uniform was crisp and clean despite the long hours in the confines of the APC. His dark hair was combed flat, wings of silver at the temples. His dark eyes were quick and seemed to notice everything. "What do you think, Sarge?"

Resting the stock of his blaster on a hip, the big man studied the wooded glade. "It'll do," he conceded finally. "Good trees for the cover, we're centrally located to all three of the villes and not a sting-wing in the area."

Puzzled, the lieutenant looked around. "How the fuck do you know that?"

"Too many nests in the branches. Birds would build the homes inside hollow trees for protection if sting-wings were in the area."

"Excellent. Tomorrow we start felling trees, one mile due south and east. I want a log wall eight feet high and encompassing the entire area. Once up, we'll top it with the concertina wire."

"Nasty stuff."

"Deadly stuff."

"Does it have to be that large?"

"Going to be a lot larger before we're done. Carry on, Sergeant." Holstering his piece, the lieutenant walked to the men waiting patiently at the mouth of the cave.

"Freedom through duty!" they chorused, snapping a stiff-arm salute to the chest.

The officer returned the gesture with force. "We came as fast as possible. What is the emergency? Trouble with the locals?"

The interior of the limestone cave stretched back for a good hundred yards. The floor was smooth with ripples that resembled the surface of a pond. The broken butts of removed stalactites covered the irregular ceiling, and insulated power lines crawled along the moist rock with covered lightbulbs dangling at regular intervals. Far in the rear was a humming gasoline generator, perched safely on a pallet to keep it from ground seepage, and a shortwave radio on a nearby table crackled with static. Stacks of large boxes were arranged in rows, according to their contents. More than one hundred empty folding cots lined a rough wall.

"No, sir. Some hunters found us," the corporal said. "We have them buried in the back under some rocks."

"It's these wired muties," the private continued. "Ropy things drop from trees and drain your blood unless you get them off fast. And if their stingers get under the skin, you die from blood poisoning. Triple bad. You go crazy screaming and shitting yourself. Tom bit off his own fingers!"

"I'd rather take a bullet in the belly," the corporal added.

"How many have we lost?" the lieutenant asked grimly.

"Fourteen. Bill and I here are the only men left."

"It was getting bad, sir, the flapjacks—we call them that sir, 'cause that's what they look like—well, they were getting bold. Hell, we found one of the suckers inside the cave."

"So we disobeyed orders, sir, cracked open some crates of grens and went hunting," the corporal said nervously. "Pretty damn sure we got them all, sir."

The lieutenant waited a few minutes, watching their faces, then relaxed and cracked a smile. "Must have been tough. Well done, troopers. My compliments."

"Thank you, sir!"

A piercing scream sounded outside. Slapping the

bolts of their blasters, the sec men rushed out of the cave to find the sergeant running around the clearing with a translucent pulsating mass on his back. The writhing tentacles were wrapped around his chest and face, the clear, ropy limbs visibly pulsating as the mutie drained off his blood.

The corporal rushed forward brandishing a knife, but a dozen other sec men burped their blasters, the rounds tearing the mutie apart. The riddled mess hit the ground and was torn to pieces by another fusillade.

Staggering away from the dead mutie, the sergeant fell to his knees, bleeding from a dozen open wounds.

"Help me...." the man croaked, his face and neck bristling with the torn-off stingers.

"Poor bastard," the private said, raising his blaster.

"Don't" the lieutenant snapped, slapping it aside.

Rushing to the side of the fallen sec man, the officer brushed the matted hair off his sweaty face. "Easy, old friend," he whispered, drawing his handcannon. "You're going to be fine. Just fine."

Foaming at the mouth, the dying man convulsed, blood welling freely from the slashes and punctures. The blue cloth of the uniform was now black over most of his body.

Clicking the hammer on his piece, the lieutenant chuckled. "Hey, remember when we found that farm with the three beautiful daughters, so we shot their folks and did them until we just couldn't do it anymore?"

Wheezing for breath, the man fell over on his side, fingers clawing the empty air.

"Remember those three blondes!" the lieutenant demanded, going to a knee and shaking the man's shoulder. "The blondes!"

"What?" the sergeant asked weakly, clearly disoriented. "The girls...yeah, they were so pretty—"

The blaster discharge slammed the body flat, the muzzle-blast setting fire to the mutilated shirt. The sergeant made no attempt to move, and in seconds the tainted blood ceased flowing from the wounds.

"Sweet Jesus," a sec man gasped from the turret of the LAV 25. "You chilled one of your own men!"

Snarling in rage, the lieutenant swung the weapon on the driver of the APC. "Say that again, and I'll open you like a self-heat. Charlie was a buddy, and I made his last thoughts happy. There was nothing else anybody could do. He was already dead."

"It's the truth," the corporal said from the cave. "He did the best thing, the only thing."

Confused murmurs arose from the rest of the troops, and they reluctantly accepted the information. Now they fearfully watched the trees, hands twisting on the stocks of their blasters.

The lieutenant holstered his weapon. "Corporal, you're a sergeant now. Take ten men and sweep this whole forest. Kill anything you find. Deer, birds, mice, men. I want a fucking clear zone eighty yards in every direction!"

"Sir!" The new sergeant turned to address the others. "Okay, you apes, let's move with a purpose! Unless you want one of those stinking muties sucking out your guts some day!"

Snapping the bolts on the Kalashnikovs, the grim sec men swept through the forest, the stuttering fire of their predark weapons rattling the dense greenery in the clarion call of death.

"And we sure as hell aren't going build the new capital of America in the middle of a mutie pit, either," the lieutenant said softly, the mountain winds carrying away his words long before anybody else could hear.

IN THE CENTER OF Front Royal, a stout tower rose from amid the lesser structures of the imposing ville. Thick growths of ivy climbed the walls as if trying to consume a foe, and sec men stood guard on the rooftop alongside ancient gargoyles, imported from Ireland generations earlier to do exactly their job—protect the keep from evil.

Orange clouds heavily laden with toxic chems flowed across the horizon, thunder rumbling softly in a purple sky streaked with fiery slashes of yellow. A low wind from the south moaned over the ville, bringing the first hints of true winter. Splintery and gray from the acid rains, the thick oak shutters covering the windows were closed tight on every level, except to the fifth floor. There the wood was thrown open wide, admitting what sunlight there was, and offering a commanding view of the green fields and even hints of the distant shanty-towns.

The window glass was long gone, consumed by the world-shattering flash and concussion when Washington, D.C., reaped the reward of its foolishness, but stout iron bars still protected the openings from climbing intruders. The breezes wafting into the top floor of the keep smelled faintly of boiling laundry, wood smoke, baking bread and horse manure. Somewhere in the ville below came the sound of troops marching, a horse neighing, slaves singing a work song, a woman crying, a fistfight, chopping wood, a gas engine sputtering into life and then dying.

In the top room of the keep, several men stood around an old table studying the maps and charts spread out over its smooth surface. Their clothes were clean and without patches, their boots shiny with polish. Well-oiled blasters jutted from every belt and shoulder holster.

Behind them, the walls were lined with wooden racks holding rifles with scopes, wax-covered boxes of ammo stacked neatly underneath for easy access. Next to the only door, a small plastic box rested in a wall niche, the joining edges of the case sealed with candle wax, making it absolutely airtight. Battered wooden chests near the windows were packed with Molotov cocktails, and plastic buckets of sand stood guard in wall niches ready to quench any accidental fires from spills. A chandelier of six oil lanterns hung from the rafters of the room, and more stood unlit in wall niches. A tapestry bearing the crest of the Cawdor family covered one section of the walls; another bore a tattered flag of the United States retrieved from a burning library.

This was the war room of the fortress, although few called it that anymore, aside from the newcomers who stood belligerently among the local chiefs and sec men. The room was full, but nobody stood side by side. A respectful distance was maintained between every occupant. The distance also gave the men room to draw weapons should the need arise.

Nathan Freeman Cawdor sat at the head of the table. His elbows rested on the chair arms as he bent forward to study the detailed maps and charts strewed across the tabletop.

On the opposite side, Overton impatiently watched the baron shift the papers as if dealing cards. The others in the room stood quietly while their leaders decided an outcome to the matter.

"This treaty will assure us peace for a hundred

years," Overton stated forcibly, brandishing a fist. "We'll be strong, invincible!"

"Yes, I can see the many advantages," Nathan said slowly, sitting back in his chair. His face was heavily lined from lack of sleep, but his voice was still strong. "A mutual-defense pact is a clever idea—I don't know if it has ever been done before. If somebody attacks Casanova, BullRun and Front Royal come to their aid, and then each does the same. Combining our strengths would make this triad of baronies absolute rulers of the entire Shen area from the ocean to the Blue Ridge Mountains."

"Exactly!"

Nathan pulled a chart closer, then tossed it into the middle of the table. "However, it will never work. Mutie attacks never last for longer than a few hours, and there hasn't been a coldheart mob large enough to threaten the ville for years."

"True, but—"

"Besides," he continued, "it takes a day for horses to ride from one ville to the next, and nobody has enough to mount troops. On foot, the villes are several days apart. Thirty miles is no small distance to cover. Fuel is more scarce every year, and we constantly cannibalize the broken wags to keep the remaining few operating.

"Plus, how can we communicate with one another? Even our most powerful radios won't reach more than a mile because of the nuke trash in the air, and batteries grow weaker each year. Riders would take too long and are easily stopped." Nathan ticked off the items on his fingers. "We can't communicate with one another, and rescue troops would take too long to ever arrive in time to help. Unifying the baronies is a masterful idea, brilliant, but it will never work.''

The attending sec men coughed and shuffled their boots, waiting for an outcome to the discussion. This was baron talk, and not really their concern until one of the men drew a weapon and the expected bloodbath began. None of them could understand why their leaders had waited this long to chill the other man.

''Oh, I have a way,'' Overton said softly, a smile playing on his lips.

''Good. How?''

Suddenly, the sound of blasterfire erupted outside and people began to shout.

''Are we being attacked?'' Overton demanded, striding to the window. Privately, he raged over the incompetence of the fools. They weren't supposed to attack the ville until they got his signal! The baron glanced down but could only see the courtyard below and a thin slice of the moat around the fortress.

''I don't hear the alarm bell,'' Nathan said, rising wearily from the chair to head to another window. The sec men there made way for him, and the baron leaned out as far as the iron bars would allow.

On the main road to the walled ville, a lone wag was drawing near. The predark vehicle was surrounded by people waving their arms and faintly shouting, but at that distance it was only noise. More and more people joined the mob around the wag, some of them firing their blasters into the air in celebration.

''What the hell is going on?'' Overton demanded, unsnapping the flap of his covered holster, the butt of his Desert Eagle jutting backward from the holster.

It was a seemingly ridiculous thing to do with a blaster, but Nathan had seen the man cross draw with either hand equally fast and knew the truth of the matter. Overton was a gunner, and a bastard good one. Perhaps even as good as he thought he was.

"We have important guests," Nathan said, trying to suppress a smile. The cries of the crowd were finally becoming discernible, and mixed in with the general hurrahs was a single word—a name, actually.

Overton stiffened as he finally caught the name the crowd was shouting, and he slammed men aside as he rushed from the war room with blaster in hand.

THE FLATBED TRUCK STOPPED at the foot of the drawbridge, the cheering throng so thick that Ryan couldn't drive any closer. Endlessly, the dancing people waved their hands in the air and chanted his name.

Killing the engine, Ryan stayed behind the wheel as the rest of the companions climbed from the rear of the truck. Everybody that was, except Mildred and Krysty, as they were still at the campsite. Krysty's fever had finally broken, but the woman was much too weak to take into a potentially dangerous situation, so Mildred volunteered to stay and nurse her back to health. Besides, J.B. had added sagely, it never hurt to have a few folks in reserve when boldly walking into a viper's nest like Front Royal. The plan made sense, and Ryan agreed reluctantly.

"They sure like you," Clem drawled, standing at ease with the Enfield cradled in his arms.

"Appears so," Ryan admitted, beeping the horn to try to clear a path to the drawbridge. The noise only made the crowd shout louder and fire more blasters skyward. It was a triple-stupe waste of ammo, and the chanting was starting to get on his nerves. This was why the one-eyed warrior hadn't even attempted to sneak into the ville like their last visit. His scarred face was just too well-known here.

"I had hoped all that crap about me arriving on a white horse," he growled, "and firing golden bullets would be forgotten by now."

"Indeed, no, sir," Doc stated, basking in the attention and waving to the crowd with his swordstick. "Even in the best of times, people always need their mythic heroes. You are that to them. A new symbol of hope."

"Horseshit," the man snarled, pounding on the horn again.

Graciously, Doc smiled. "Agreed, my dear Ryan, but still true, nonetheless."

"Not everybody is delighted we're here," J.B. stated, tilting back his hat for a clearer field of vision. The Uzi was slung over a shoulder and dangled at his side, ready for instant use. "Spot them yet?"

"The blue shirts? Yeah, I got them zeroed." Even before stopping the truck, Ryan noticed the gathering of the sec men armed with AK-47 blasters. There were a lot of them. But he was also noticing other sec men dressed in brown shirts staying near the blue shirts. Wherever the blues went, the browns followed and in greater numbers.

"Nathan's troops?" Jak asked through the passenger's window.

High in the cab, Ryan craned his neck for a better view. "Makes sense."

"Sure going to be easy to know who to chill if it comes to a fight," Clem observed, taking out a plug and biting off a healthy chaw.

"Can't see how it could end any other way," Ryan stated. "Doesn't take a doomie to know that."

"Winner take all," Doc said. "Loser gets buried."

"Exactly."

Still in the rear of the truck, Dean couldn't stop staring at the cheering people and the golden fortress. This was his heritage, his true home. Some day, if he wanted, he would be the baron here. No, wait a second—that was wrong, the boy corrected himself. His father had given up the title, and Nathan's children would rule the ville. Dean wasn't quite sure if he was happy about missing that bullet of responsibility or angry as hell about not getting the title and authority. It would require some serious thinking. Did he even want to be a baron?

"Ahem," Doc said, indicating a commotion near the drawbridge. People were going quiet as something pushed through them at a good clip.

"Nathan?" J.B. asked, resting a hand on his Uzi.

"Gotta be wag," Jak said.

"Can't tell yet," Ryan stated, moving the carefully cut wooden stick closer to the gas pedal. If trouble came, he was going to jam the stick on the gas pedal, flooring the engine, and send the flatbed truck crashing into the fortress while Dean lit the fuse on the case of Molotovs. The rest of the companions would scatter into the crowd. They were ready to talk, fight or escape.

In growing silence, the crowd hastily parted, several folks almost going into the moat as they cleared away from a big man wearing a blue uniform.

"That's him," Clem said, resting a finger on the trigger of his blaster.

Overton ran swiftly across the drawbridge, unbuckling his gun belt and dropping weapons every few yards. When he reached the shore, the would-be baron was only wearing clothes.

Cig lighter poised near a cloth fuse, Dean wondered

what the man was doing. Suspecting the truth, Ryan unlocked the cab door as a precaution.

"Salutations and greetings," Doc said, but the man went straight past him.

Reaching the truck, Overton slammed a fist through the open window and directly into Ryan's face. The one-eyed man was caught by surprise—not by the attack, but by the speed of it. He managed to roll with the blow, but it still rattled him hard. Then combat reflexes flared, and he kicked open the door, slamming Overton to the ground. The big man landed sprawling, and Ryan climbed down with a hand on his blaster.

"Get up," he ordered, drawing the weapon.

Slowly, Overton stood and threw dirt in Ryan's face. He instinctively fired twice, and the other man grabbed him in a bear hug. Powerful arms wrapped low around his back began to squeeze, trying to break his spine. Ryan head-butted his adversary twice before he finally let go. Then, before Overton could get clear, Ryan slammed his boot into the man's groin. Overton loudly grunted in pain but didn't drop.

He was either a eunuch or he was wearing padding, Ryan realized, leveling the SIG-Sauer. But Overton kicked it away before he could fire. A red mist of rage took hold of Ryan, and he jabbed the flat of his hand into the other man's throat. Hacking for air, Overton turned sideways and kicked Ryan in the gut, slamming him against the side of the truck.

Bouncing off the metal, Ryan drew his panga and started forward in a crouch.

"Don't do it!" J.B. cried out, raising his empty hands in surrender.

Forcing himself to heed the warning, Ryan slowly stood and sheathed the blade. Overton stood ready for combat, balanced on his boots, his knuckles cracked and oversize from a lot of brawling. Subtly, Ryan shifted his weight, and the other man altered his stance slightly to counter the move.

"Who the hell are you?" Ryan asked gruffly, his muscles tensed and ready for more combat.

"Don't you recognize me?" Overton countered through gritted teeth, his hands partially extended.

"No," Ryan answered truthfully. "Should I?"

The big man snarled. "My name is Overton Cawdor!"

"And he claims to be your son, Uncle Ryan," Nathan said, walking across the drawbridge through a corridor of people, his boots clicking loudly on the hard cobblestones.

Unobserved, Dean retrieved his father's blaster from where it had fallen, and tucking it inside his shirt for safekeeping, started working his way toward the truck.

Stopping a short distance from the two combatants, the baron of Front Royal paused. "Oh, sorry. I forgot you hate being called by your name from kin. My apologies, Uncle."

Keeping a neutral expression, Ryan said nothing at the bald-faced lie. One of the first things he ever said to Nathan was not to call him Uncle; he had a name, so use it. This backward version of that was a message of some sort. But what exactly did it mean?

The three men stood in a circle of anxious people, brown shirts and blue scattered throughout the assembly. The tension was thick in the air. Nobody in the crowd was talking, some barely breathing. Then a fish jumped in the moat, catching an insect.

"Want to come over here and talk with me for a tick, Nathan?" Ryan asked, crossing his arms, the fingers of his right hand dangling dangerously near his knife again.

"I'm not a prisoner," Nathan said smoothly. "Overton and I currently...share the duties of being baron."

"Why?" Ryan asked.

"Out of necessity," Overton replied, the wind ruffling his hair. "I arrived a few months ago with my sec men to see my ancestral home."

"And stayed," Ryan added.

"We...I asked them to," Nathan finished, quickly correcting the mistake. His stomach tightened at the thought he might already have condemned them both to death with that tiny slip. "The ville has been under constant attack by gangs of coldhearts and needed more troops badly. They arrived when sorely needed."

Slow and careful, Doc walked to Ryan and passed him the SIG-Sauer.

"So you saved the day," Ryan said, checking the blaster for damage and tucking it into his holster, but with the safety in the off position, "and claim to be my son."

"I am your son, Father," the man stated, not relaxing his stance. "Your bastard son, abandoned twenty years ago in the Deathlands."

Both arms full, a blue sec man went to Overton and returned his arsenal of dropped weapons. The new baron armed himself, but never took his eyes off Ryan.

"Well, you certainly have the manners of a bastard," Ryan agreed, trying to provoke a response. "And just who the hell was your mother? Anybody I know?"

Overton shoved his own panga into a sheath. "Remember a gaudy slut down in Texas named Havila?" he said, hate plain in his voice.

"Havila? Yeah, I remember. I spent a night with her."

"You might have been with her for a single night, but you were the only customer that night, so when mother found out she was carrying me a month later, there was no question as to who the father was."

Instantly, Ryan knew the story was a lie. He and Havila hadn't done that kind of loving. She used her hands and mouth on him several times, but it had been her time of the month, so he declined anything further. Havila knew her trade, all right, but she would have to be some kind of a supernatural mutie to get pregnant down the throat. So either Overton was lying, or he believed it was the truth and somebody else had lied to him. There were wheels within wheels here.

As Ryan glanced about casually, as if deep in thought, he saw a brief flash of reflected light from the roof of the keep. A double flash would have been binocs; a single meant a telescope, or a scope on a high-powered sniper rifle ready to remove his head. Then a second flash from the trees caught his attention, and Ryan realized he was caught in their cross fire. By stopping the truck outside the ville, he had hoped to force Overton into an awkward position, but instead had played right into the man's trap. The original plan was probably for Ryan to be killed by a silenced shot from the keep while he and Overton fought. Who would notice a small-caliber wound in the body of a man already bleeding? It was a good plan. However, ambushes always fell apart if the victim didn't do exactly what was expected.

Taking a hesitant step, Ryan extended his arms toward the younger man. Overton recoiled as if expecting a strike but stood resolutely his ground.

"Yeah, I can see Havila in you," Ryan said, forcing some emotion into his voice as he walked closer. He felt like a triple-stupe fool, but an excited hush fell over the watching crowd. "And we look so much alike...it must be true. You're my son. My long lost son!"

Lunging forward, Ryan hugged the total stranger. Overton stood there as stiff as a board, completely baffled by this unexpected turn of events. Then, ever so slowly, he returned the hug, and the crowd erupted into wild cheers. Surging forward, the people lifted both men onto their shoulders and carried them triumphantly across the drawbridge and into the ville.

Chapter Eleven

Clouds of acrid smoke drifted over the battlefield at BullRun ville. The dead and the dying lay everywhere, destroyed wags and crushed horses burning under the fiery sky. Even the fortress itself, barely visible above the line of trees separating the ville from the war zone, had several large holes punched through its thick granite walls.

Standing amid the destruction, a large blond woman in ripped Army fatigues dug loose 5.56 mm rounds from her shoulder bag and hastily thumbed the bullets into the exhausted clip of her repaired military blaster. When it was full, she grabbed the M-16 leaning against her leg, slammed in the clip and worked the bolt with practiced ease.

The predark M-16 was a mismatch. The barrel came off an MR-4, the recoil spring was cut down from a Stoner, the carrying strap made of horsehide and the replacement stock hand carved by a local carpenter. But the deadly blaster functioned smoothly, and that was the most important thing.

Blinking the sweat from her eyes, Baron Susan Markham started to walk through the destroyed cornfield. Dead sec men and residents lay everywhere, many of them missing arms or legs. She wanted to avert her eyes, but forced herself to look at each and every one of them. These were her people, and their deaths were a personal matter.

Scattered among the locals were the dozens upon dozens of Oriental men dressed in black. Even their faces had been masked, leaving only a tiny slit for them to see through.

"Baron!" someone called.

Susan spun on a heel, and exhaustion almost made her fire purely on reflex. "Chatty, is that you?" the baron demanded.

Out of the billowing clouds came a small man wearing a garage mechanic's jumpsuit, the loose pant legs tucked into hiking boots. A bloody tourniquet was wrapped around his right arm, the hand tucked into his belt to keep it still. Fresh blood trickled down his cheek from a shallow gash in his scalp. The leather bandolier crossing his chest was empty of rounds, the knife sheath at his hip empty and the staggering man carried a shotgun with a bent barrel. But he was still standing and seemed fiercely proud of the fact.

"Did we get him?" the baron asked anxiously.

Sec chief Charles Chattington nodded wearily. "The bear traps we laid killed his horse, and the archers put enough shafts into him for us to use the bastard as kindling."

"What about the bomb he was carrying, that satchel thing? I heard a blast, but it sounded distant, muffled."

"It was. We sank a butcher's hook into the samurai, tied it to the saddle of a horse and whipped the beast until it galloped off a ravine. Hell of an explosion."

"Hell of a fight. How did that happen?" the baron asked, gesturing at his broken blaster.

"I found one of our sec men wearing their black, figured he must be the traitor and decided to convince him what a bad idea it had been to rat us out," Charles said. With an effort of will, he forced his fingers apart and the weapon dropped to the ground with a clatter. "Take my word on it. The matter is settled."

"Good," the baron said, handing him the reloaded M-16 hybrid. "Here. Can't walk around naked, and I've still got my Webley."

The sec chief nodded his thanks and took the blaster, resting the hot barrel on his shoulder. "Thirty?" he asked, shaking the machine gun as if he could gauge the amount of ammo left by the noise it made.

Wiping the sweat off her face, Susan almost smiled. The sec man never missed a trick. Even a weapon from his own baron was suspect.

"Yes, the clip is fully loaded—thirty live rounds."

"Good." He surveyed the cornfield around them. "Did we get them all?"

"Yes and no," the baron replied, a terrible sadness welling within her chest. "We stopped their charge, but a handful escaped to the south."

"Bad news for somebody else."

"Not our problem."

"Too true."

In the distance, wounded men staggered through the battlefield, helping others to their feet and taking blasters from the hands of those who couldn't use them anymore.

"What about the leader?"

Susan gestured and walked through the litter of corpses until she reached a blackened crater in the ground. The pit was twenty feet deep and over thirty wide. Nothing was at the bottom but some tiny scraps of debris.

"That him?" Charles asked.

She nodded. "Davis in the high tower got him with the sniper rifle just as he was going to launch another rocket from the RPG. He lost his grip, and the weapon discharged straight down at the ground."

The baron glanced at the smashed barricade that blocked the main road to BullRun ville. The timbers and concrete were scattered like broken toys from the devastating rounds of the predark bazooka. Plus, gouts were missing in the granite block walls of the fortress where the rockets had struck but failed to penetrate. Sophisticated blasters designed to chill predark tanks were pretty useless against the tons of heavy stonework.

"Blew the hell out of our troops, though," Charles commented as if reading her mind.

"Fucking samurai bastard was clever," she muttered. "Too damn clever."

"Not anymore." The sec chief glanced at the high tower jutting from the ville, partially hidden by the trees. "That's a hell of a shot."

"You were smart to risk half of our .50-caliber ammo so he could practice and learn how to use that huge-ass rifle properly."

"Called a Barrett. She's a bitch to control, but the best sniper rifle there is. Steyr is good, Weatherby even better, but neither of them have the range and power of a Barrett Light Fifty."

"How do you know so much about blasters, anyway? Always wanted to ask."

"Don't," he replied wearily. "It's really not important."

Just then a soft moan came from somewhere near, and both of them quickly spread out until they located the source. Sprawled on the ground was a legless man, his black robes torn asunder, exposing a bulky leather vest wrapped around his chest. Dark blood was pooled around his waist and trickled from the corner of his mouth.

Charles leveled his rifle and fired a single round into the twitching man, who jerked at the impact and went still.

Susan then hawked and spit on the enemy. "He wrapped their bodies in wet leather and let it dry good and tight, so even if we belly shoot them, their guts don't fall out and they can still fight. They're dead, but could still fight."

"Heard he gave them some drink before battles to make them brave."

"Drugs to kill the pain of a wound?"

"Don't know. But makes sense."

"Never heard of such tactics before."

"Brilliant, he was fucking brilliant."

"Thankfully, now he's fucking dead."

"Agreed, my lady. Any ideas of the damages?"

She gestured vaguely. "We lost over half our sec men, and almost all of our ammo. We couldn't stop an attack by rabbits today. Take us at least a week to make more black powder for the cannons."

Susan looked at the line of trees edging the field. Even though she knew exactly where the muzzle loaders were hidden, the baron still couldn't easily detect the cannons. Each primitive weapon had been painstakingly salvaged from city parks, VFW halls and museums across the whole Shen valley. The iron barrels of the ancient weapons had been blocked with soft lead, which proved very easy to remove once the barrels were heated over a forge. Then the lead that poured out made cannon balls, and a high-school textbook had revealed the secret of how to make black powder from kitchen matches and their own night soil.

"We lost two cannons," Susan said, squinting at the hole in the forest. Bloody splinters were scattered for yards around a flattened area of charred soil. "The crew overpacked the blasters, or the barrels were too old. Whatever. But the explosion killed more of us than the samurai ever did."

"Just bad luck," Charles stated grimly. "It was the cannons that stopped their charge. Their leader never even got close to the fortress. Thank God."

"Yes, thank God."

Another shot rang out in the field as the ville sec men found another Oriental warrior not quite dead enough to suit them.

The two started walking slowly toward the fortress. "Have the whitehairs and children sweep the field for any of our men still alive, and then establish a collection point where all of the recovered weapons and ammo can be gathered and inspected. We want to make sure each sec man has a working blaster and the correct rounds."

"What about the swords?" he asked, stepping over the tangled corpses of a samurai and a sec man who had died chilling each other. "There's going to be a lot of those."

"I don't know, Chatty. Pile them somewhere and we'll decide later if we want to learn sword fighting or grind them down into knives."

Blaster in hand, he gave a salute. "By your command, Baron."

She returned the gesture. "You know," she spoke in unaccustomed honesty, sheer exhaustion forcing the words out, "I really didn't think we would survive today, much less win."

"We had to be victorious," Charles said, resting on the upturned M-16 as if it were a crutch. "I was in charge of ville defense, and I never lose. Didn't I ever mention that?"

"Oh, shut up, asshole," Susan said, and was astonished to find there was a chuckle in the words.

He grinned. "By your command, Baron."

Suddenly, a man sprinted toward them from the fortress. The baron and her sec chief stood patiently, waiting for him to reach them. If he had the energy to run, there was no need for them to move.

"Your lordship." The man snapped a crisp salute.

The baron returned it wearily. "What is the matter, Corporal?"

"Another attack?"

Susan barked a laugh. "And who would attack this time? There's nobody left."

"Front Royal, Baron," the corporal replied. "We just got a report from some of the hill folk we trade with that Front Royal has over a hundred new sec men and crates of blasters. Autofiring blasters. Something called an AK-47."

"AK-47," Charles confirmed. "Black dust, crates of blasters, you say?"

"That's the report, yes, sir."

"What the hell is Cawdor doing?" the muscular blond woman mused. "Could Front Royal be preparing to attack?"

The sec chief frowned deeply. "A hundred new troops, plus those packs of wild dogs they use—who needs that kind of defense? No, he's planning something, but what?"

"Chatty, we can't hold off another attack," the baron stated in bitter truth. "Front Royal could take us in a day. Mebbe we should cut a deal with them, buy us some time."

"Or," the sec chief suggested, "we could use that special person again."

The woman blanched. "Sullivan? I thought he died after chilling the last baron of this place."

"And waste a valuable resource like that? Never, my lady! I gave him a small cabin in the woods and let him practice on coldhearts and condemned prisoners. We gave him freedom and food. Sullivan is very loyal to us."

"To you," Markham corrected pointedly.

"That's the same thing, Baron. The man will happily perform any dirty chore we ask of him."

"Hardly a man," she snorted.

The former baron of BullRun had enjoyed torturing prisoners and relatives by forcing them to have intercourse with muties captured from the radioactive hellzone of Washington Hole. Many died in the attempts, a few offspring were born, but those were always deformed and died within minutes. The one exception was Sullivan. He not only survived, but also grew tall and incredibly strong, killing the baron at age ten when the fool tried to drown the mutie child in a river.

Now over six feet tall, Sullivan could physically pass for a norm, his loose clothing hiding any major physical irregularities. His finely chiseled features were almost too perfect to be called handsome, his head smooth and hairless, but whether from shaving or a natural condition was unknown. Sullivan rarely spoke and never seemed to eat. He never laughed, but constantly bore a gentle smile as if greeting an old friend. Small-caliber rounds such as .22s and home-loads would bruise his odd skin, but didn't penetrate. He had once chilled a man who laughed at him by crushing his skull in one hand, the man's head busting apart like ripe fruit in the iron grip of the monstrous half-breed.

The former baron tried many times to duplicate the creation of the horrible mutie, but with no success. Even though the humanoid muties were once true norms, something had been altered within them by the radiation, and no matter how often the baron forced prisoners and condemned men to try, Sullivan remained unique.

"Give the thing whatever it wants, then send it off to Front Royal to chill the baron."

"Nathan Cawdor?"

"Or anybody who is in charge, I don't care. That should buy us enough days to get prepared for a fight."

"And afterward?" Charles asked pointedly.

"Kill the mutie freak," she ordered, and started for the fortress once more.

SMILING AND WAVING to the people in the corridor, Overton closed the door to his rooms in the fortress and spit out a virulent oath. "The one-eyed gimp didn't fall for it!" he raged. "Ryan is supposed to have this terrible temper. Faced with a bastard usurper, he was supposed to fly into a rage, attack me, and then snipers would kill him and Nathan, wounding me. Our blues kill the snipers, and I become the undisputed ruler of Front Royal."

"Yes," said the other man in the room.

Overton kicked a footstool out of his way. "How could such a simple plan go wrong?"

Sitting in a chair near the window, Ki looked down on the courtyard filled with cheering people. The area was dark, lit only by the occasional flash of lightning and the pale moon struggling to show through the boiling orange clouds of toxins.

"Mebbe he's smarter than we were told," the sec man ventured. "That would be most inconvenient. Or perhaps he believes you *are* his son. The story is just crazy enough to be true."

Overton grunted in reply. His mother had been a gaudy slut, all right, but not down in the south somewhere. He knew who his real father was. The man had taken a week to die, Havila tossing the match herself to set fire to the gasoline-soaked man who had abandoned them.

"What should we do?"

"What *can* we do is a better question," he retorted angrily. Crossing the room, he yanked open a cherry-wood cabinet and chose a bottle of wine at random. "At present, I'm throwing a party to welcome home the man I want dead."

"Poison?"

"Don't have any."

"Get him drunk and push him off a balcony?"

"Love to. But when will we ever be alone?"

The sec man stood. "Mebbe we should just shoot and risk open rebellion from the locals. We can beat this bunch of uneducated hicks in a straight fight."

"Mebbe," Overton said thoughtfully. "But not for certain. Those packs of dogs they have are a formidable weapon.

"Besides," he added, annoyed, "our boss wants everything low-key and quiet. Don't let the neighbors know what's going on here until it's too late for them to do anything."

"Bah," Ki said, making a face. "I detest stealth."

"Tough." Placing the dusty wine bottle on a rolltop desk, Overton took a key from a pouch inside his belt and unlocked a drawer. Reaching inside, he withdrew headphones, clicked the switch and worked the dial on a old-style portable shortwave radio. Frowning, he flipped a gang bar, boosting the flow of power from the nuke battery to the maximum. After several minutes, he turned off the electronic machine.

"Still too much static," he said, removing the headphones and tucking them beside the shortwave radio. "Damn thing will never reach the cave, much less headquarters. Better send a pigeon. Do we have one?"

"Six came in the caravan with Stephen."

"Tell the boss what happened and ask for instructions."

"At once. However, there are many sting-wings about nowadays, and sometimes the birds don't arrive."

Locking the drawer, Overton nodded in understanding. "An interesting idea, but we dare not try. The sec men are loyal to him and the great project, not to me."

Ki gave a bow of respect. "What now?"

"I'm going to a party," Overton growled, brandishing the bottle as if it were a club. "You stay with Nathan. Monitor his every move. Don't ever let the man talk privately with Ryan."

"And what about the others?" the sec man asked softly.

"Send some of the boys to see what they know."

"But be sure to leave them alive," Ki suggested. "So we don't incur Ryan's famous temper. A hostage, perhaps?"

"We have enough of those," Overton snorted. "Kill his friends, rape them, castrate them, nail them to a wall and feed their guts to the hogs. I don't care. Just get me some information!''

As the door slammed shut behind the baron, Ki chuckled softly and withdrew a long thin knife from a sheath attached to his forearm. The blade was abnormally thin, as if a regular knife had been honed to beyond razor sharpness.

"By your command, my lord," he said with a chuckle, stabbing his palm with the blade and watching the blood drip like rubies onto the cold stone floor.

OVERTON HEARD THE CELEBRATION long before he entered the main dining hall; badly played music and off-key singing were rampant in the fortress. People cheered his approach for the first time ever, servants bowed with respect and sec men in brown shirts actually saluted.

He returned the gesture smartly, all the while marveling over the incredible change. That vagabond from Deathlands gave him a hug, and now the people who were ready to die protecting their baron bowed before him in homage.

Stupid cows, he sneered privately. They all deserved to die.

Throwing open the doors to the great hall, Overton was buffeted by the waves of heat and light, the smells and cheers of the people and the musicians in the corner struggling to force tunes from their instruments.

"Here it is!" he cried, slamming the bottle down on the table. "The last of the predark wine."

A steward produced a corkscrew and opened the bottle, intending to let it breathe for a few minutes. But someone grabbed the container and started to fill glasses.

"To the new allegiance!" cried a drunken sec man, slopping some of the wine onto the table.

"To peace," Nathan said, lifting his mug listlessly.

"To victory," Overton added, forcing a smile on his face.

"Death to our enemies," Ryan finished, slamming his mug into theirs so hard the pewter was almost knocked from their hands.

Everybody else at the table lifted mugs along with the Cawdors, J.B., Doc and the others sipping their well water and acting as if it were strong home brew.

As the three Cawdor men tossed off their drinks, servants poured new ones from clay jugs.

"It's been quite a while since you were last in this room in happy times, hasn't it, Uncle?" Nathan said.

"Having just as much fun," Ryan admitted.

"I'll bet you are, Ryan." Nathan chuckled. Then he paused. "I'm sorry. You hate that. I apologize, Uncle."

Ryan kept his face neutral and toasted the man with the cup. He preferred to be called by his name, and Nathan knew it. This was another hint that things weren't as they seemed. The tension crackled like electricity in the air, and every time Ryan's chair was bumped by a passing servant, he started to draw his weapon. The hall was filled with celebration, but underneath it was a current of violence and hatred that rivaled anything he had encountered in his long travels.

Desperately, he searched for some pretext to be alone with Nathan, if only for a few minutes. But wherever the man went, the baron was closely followed by his own sec men and a squad of the blue shirts. Overton traveled in the same fashion, each shadowed by the other's troops. Checks and balances, a Mexican standoff. Baronial allegiance, his ass.

For a fleeting instant, the red rage filled his mind, and he forced down the urge to flip over the table and chill Overton on the spot and damn the consequences! But Nathan could have done that any time; if he hadn't, there was a reason.

"By the way, dear Father," Overton said, lowering his glass to the table. "I have planned a hunt tomorrow in your honor."

Placing aside his untouched mug, Ryan smiled at the stranger across from the table. Fireblast, so soon? He certainly knew a trap when he heard one.

"A bear hunt, by any chance?" he asked.

Overton beamed a happy smile. "Exactly!"

"You mean Cyclops? That old one-eyed mutie griz that's been bothering this ville for years?" Ryan glowered and rubbed his leg, wincing slightly. "I'm not going near that thing again. I pass, son. But thanks for the offer. You kill him and show that mutie bastard what a Cawdor is made of, eh?"

The table roared its approval, and Overton toasted the plan with his mug. He then rose, excused himself and hurried from the hall.

Once out of sight, Overton strode down a branching corridor that went directly into the kitchen. Past the double doors, the air was foggy with steam and richly scented with the smells of roasting meats. Darting servants froze motionless as the baron strode past them and headed toward the plump woman frying forest mushrooms in a skillet above the huge wood-burning stove.

"You there!" barked the baron, pointing.

Both arms carrying a tray stacked high with dirty dishes, an elderly man near the soapy sinks gawked. "My lord?" he squeaked.

"Yeah, you!"

The dishwasher offered a wan smile. "Of course, Baron Cawdor. How can I be of—?"

"Is there a one-eyed griz in the local woods," he interrupted, towering over the trembling whitehair. "A giant that mauled Ryan in the leg?"

The cook stopped stirring the mushrooms, and the scullery maid ceased her chopping as silence filled the kitchen. There was only one possible answer to that.

"Of course, my lord," the old man replied. "It's called Cyclops. A nasty brute, ate my cousin—"

Turning on a heel, Overton stomped from the kitchen and turned left in the corridor, heading for the lav.

"That was close," the cook whispered, hurrying over to make sure there was nobody in the hallway.

Collapsing on a stool, the steward wiped his brow on a sleeve. "Yes and no, my dear. Every baron's family knows the staff listens to their conversations to see if the meal is to their liking."

"So Ryan was hoping we would cover the lie?"

"Yes." The man scowled. "Go hunting with Overton, and it's certain you come back draped over the horse."

The plump woman pursed her lips, then spun and began stirring the mushrooms again. "I don't like this," she muttered. "I don't like this one bit. I have a feeling that Overton would make us long for the bloody rules of Harvey Cawdor and his bitch wife."

"Shh! We shouldn't say such things aloud," the dishwasher said nervously. "Stay low, and live. That's my motto."

"Words to live by," the steward agreed with a frown. "But sometimes that isn't enough, old friend."

As the scullery maid continued chopping vegetables,

the cook expertly tipped the iron skillet to fill a wooden bowl with the mushrooms and not miss a drop of the garlic sauce. A serving girl took the bowl and placed it on her tray atop a decorative doily. Hurrying from the kitchen, she paused by the steward for the man to spit on the food, then she burst through the double doors, heading for the dining hall.

"Special treat for Baron Overton!" she called, entering the dining hall. Placing the steaming bowl at the head of the table, she gave a curtsy and departed for the next course.

Ryan eyed the slimy mess in repulsion, wondering what the staff had done to the food. Spit or piss? Probably spit. It carried less flavor. Rumor was that Harvey had mostly dined on the saliva of the kitchen staff for his whole life. A wise baron never bullied the cooks.

"To Ryan!" a sec man in brown shouted.

"To Overton!" a man in blue replied.

"To Baron Cawdor!" Doc shouted, curtailing yet another fight at the table.

The people roared their approval with true gusto.

Appearing from the crowd, Overton sat heavily at his chair. "So tell me more about your journeys, Father," he said, spearing a mushroom on a fork and eating the delicacy with gusto.

The conversation turned to tales of battle and lies about women. Nathan excused himself at midnight, and it was near dawn before Ryan finally managed to leave without suspicion.

As he climbed the stairs to the western wing of bedrooms, several blue shirts followed in his wake, with several brown shirts close on their heels. Acting much drunker than they were, Doc, Clem and J.B. collided in the doorway, blocking the stairs in a drunken tangle of limbs, until Ryan was long gone from sight, his destination unknown.

Chapter Twelve

The music faded into the distance as Ryan climbed the stairs, turning and ducking down hallways and through curtained alcoves. As children, he and his brothers had played this game many times, but the Deathlands warrior never dreamed an intimate knowledge of the fortress would ever come in handy this way, evading armed pursuers.

Pausing at an intersection, he waited with the SIG-Sauer in hand to see if he was being followed. After a few minutes, he holstered the weapon and continued onward. Squeezing through a short sloping tunnel made of brick, the purpose of which was lost in predark history, Ryan emerged into a long hallway lined with closed doors—guest rooms. Overton and his personal troops had taken over the east wing, with the rest of his sec men billeted in the barracks, leaving the entire west wing empty and barren. At the end of the passage, Ryan eased open a heavy door and climbed another flight of winding steps higher and higher until exiting on a parapet, the stonework balcony curving gently from the side of the ville and overlooking the southern acres of farmland, pastures and forest.

Stepping onto the chilly parapet, Ryan spotted a dark figure in the shadows. The person stood as if hunched against a fierce wind, both hands tight on the stone railing cresting a low wall.

"Crops were good this summer," Nathan said, seemingly out of nowhere. "We'll last the winter without short rations. First time in years."

"Good news," Ryan answered casually, walking closer. The tension from the man was palpable, like heat radiating from a furnace. "We'll be glad to help with the eating and the drinking."

Closing his eyes, Nathan didn't smile at the joke, and he tightened his grip on the railing. "Look at that view," he said, extending an arm. In the distance, the rocky Goliaths of the Shen Mountains of Virginia rose to challenge the sky, the slopes faintly bluish from the dense growth of Scotch pines and spruce trees. "A thousand years ago, somebody saw the exact same thing, and a thousand from now somebody will again. Mountains last forever."

"Unless they get nuked," Ryan snapped irritably.

"True. Too bad your woman Krysty couldn't be here." he said.

"She is," Ryan answered, standing next to the baron. "Krysty and Mildred, a friend, were only a couple of hours behind us. Krysty had a fever, which broke shortly after we departed, and they arrived a little while ago. She's been in the dining room since midnight, eating everything not nailed down."

Nathan spoke slowly. "A fever, you say?"

"She throws off these things quickly. Tough lady."

"Good," Baron Cawdor said. "Good for her."

"Now let me tell you a little secret about my woman," Ryan chuckled, laying an arm across his nephew's shoulders and drawing him closer.

"Okay, what the fuck is going on here?" Ryan demanded softly in his ear.

"I'm being replaced as baron," Nathan answered,

almost too low to hear, his lips barely moving, "and I can't stop the process."

"How?"

"We were attacked in the summer by muties, hordes of them." Nathan shook his head. "It was like a nightmare where you shoot a man only to find another behind him, and so on and so on endlessly."

"Swampies?" Ryan asked. "We tangled with one of those coming here. Pretty tough. Had to head-shoot the bastard twice."

"Swampies, yes," the baron answered. "And stickies, and scalies, and a dozen more we have no names for. Waves of them."

For one terrible moment, Ryan had a flashback to Kaa's army, then he shook off the memory. The mutie king was dead, and his army scattered. There would never be another Kaa.

"You're still here," he stated bluntly. "So it couldn't have been too bad."

"A southern hamlet was attacked at night. The muties killed every man, woman and child. A runner brought the word, and we galloped there on horseback with blasters firing, and every dog I have came along with us."

He paused. "The triple-damn things had hatchets."

"Armed muties?" Ryan scowled. "Bullshit."

Wordlessly, Nathan pushed up his sleeve and showed a badly healed scar that ran from his shoulder to his elbow. He let the sleeve drop back into place. "The blades were roped to their arms. The muties couldn't drop the weapons if they wanted."

Ryan remained silent. There was nothing he could say. A cool breeze was blowing in from the Shens, carrying with it the faint smell of the forest and the ville below. Wood smoke, horse dung, soap, tar—the smells of life. But there was also the stink of gasoline, the sounds of marching boots, the crack of a whip and a prisoner's scream of pain. The music from the dining room didn't seem to reach into the courtyards of the ville.

"They were eating the dead, the living. You know muties."

"Thought I did," Ryan said skeptically.

"Me, too. We went through the hamlet once and didn't find a soul alive."

"So you set fire to the place."

"As your grandfather taught us to, yes. The muties went mad and attacked in a suicide rush. We slaughtered the things, but the horses got wounded, dogs died by the dozens...." His voice trailed off, then came back strong. "We won, but what a loss of lives! Over half of my sec men got chilled that night."

Ryan knew where the story was going. "The mutie attack was a diversion," he said. It was stated as a fact, not a question. "And the next day, Overton arrived, posing as a mercie and offered his services. Once inside the walls, his troops started to take over."

"Not quite, Uncle," Nathan said, which meant that was exactly how it occurred. "Now we share the ville, as I train him to be my replacement. He controls the walls and the food warehouses. My men control the dogs and the armory."

Controlling the walls meant Overton's troops had seized the front gate also, the only way in or out of the ville. Nathan was a prisoner in his own fortress. It was a classic stalemate. But Nathan should have fought to the death to stop the invaders once he discovered their plan. When Overton finally took over, the first thing he'd do would be to chill Nathan and every loyal sec man. His own life was on the line, yet the man was merely stalling for time instead of fighting back. There had to be a reason.

"Why?" Ryan asked. There was no response, so he grabbed the man and roughly spun him. Nathan jerked away from the contact, his face contorted in anger.

"Watch yourself, Uncle," he growled. "I'm still the baron here, not you!"

"Just wanted to see if you lost your balls in that battle," Ryan countered, losing control and speaking loudly. "There's Cawdor blood in your veins, man! What's going on here? Why are you letting Overton take over?"

Surreptitiously, Nathan glanced out of the corner of his eyes at the stained-glass window nearby. The scene was of an armed hunter with a stag at bay.

"Guess I'm just getting old," the man replied, measuring each word carefully. "Happens to each of us. Even Red Roger. Remember him? Time takes us all down, Uncle."

Releasing his grip, Ryan did indeed recall Red Roger, and his gut tightened in suppressed fury. Fireblast, so that was the problem.

"Perhaps you're right, nephew," Ryan added, deliberately using the word to let the man know what he said next was a blatant lie. "Besides, Overton is my son. You can see it in the very way he walks. That man is Cawdor to the bone."

"To the bone," Nathan agreed listlessly.

Laughing, Ryan slapped the baron on the back. "Well, enough politics. I'm off for some sack time with my woman. Let me know if you want to go fishing later on. Still lots of trout in the moat?"

Nathan blinked in shock. Fish in the moat? Only minnows and sunfish not worth catching if you were starving. Then his face took on a neutral expression. "Certainly, lots of them in our special hole. Think you could find it after so many years? What has it been, twelve?"

"Twelve," Ryan repeated, brushing the wild tangles of black hair off his scarred face. "Later, nephew. Talk to you tomorrow."

"In the morning, Uncle."

"Tomorrow," Ryan corrected.

As his uncle departed, Nathan took a cigar from his shirt and used a disposable lighter on the tip, puffing until it glowed cherry-red. Taking a single draw, he then tossed the smoke away, watching the glowing cheroot tumble the five stories into the moat. It drifted slightly to the left from the wind.

Baron Cawdor stood silent on the battlements, contemplating the dark waters below for several minutes before Jian Hwa Ki stepped from the shadows.

"You did well, Nathan," he said with a smirk. "The fool believed every word. I'm pleased."

With a snarl, Nathan spun and grabbed a fistful of the slim man's collar, bodily lifting him off the stone floor. The sec man began gagging and choking for air.

"Please..." he wheezed.

"I'm Baron Cawdor to you," Nathan snarled, spraying spittle on the man's red face. "And if not for the life of my unborn child, I would wash this ville with your blood, and the blood of your stinking master!"

Strangled gasps were the only reply.

Nathan raised his right hand. "Do you understand me?" A slap punctuated each word.

Blood flowing from his nose and mouth, Ki nodded frantically.

"Bah, you're not worth the effort to chill." Disgusted, the baron threw the man away, and he hit the floor a yard distant. Nathan turned from the sec man and looked into the black night again. In the east, the sky softened in color with the approach of dawn. A new day was being born, quite possibly the last of his life.

"Leave," Nathan said in a normal voice. "Or die. Your choice. I'm beyond caring."

The taste of blood filling his mouth, Ki slunk from the balcony and hurried inside the fortress, closing the hallway door quietly. Inside the building, the sound of music was louder, and the merriment only fueled his rage and shame. Going to his room, Ki inspected the damage in a mirror. There would be no scars, but the memory of being handled like a child—worse, like a slave—by an overseer, filled him with mortification.

"That was the worst mistake of your life, Baron," Ki muttered, his mind already working on the details of a fitting revenge.

THE DYING LIGHT from the crackling fire threw strange shadows on the trees surrounding the small forest clearing. Green sticks supported a metal rod upon which hung the roasting carcass of a coney. The skin of the rabbit was draped over a tree branch, already scraped clean of tissues and dripping with urine as a preparation for proper tanning.

Sipping a plastic cup of coffee sub, Daniel Lissman wrinkled his nose at the smell. Urine had a lot of tannic acid, and was an excellent beginning for curing hides to keep them from going bad. In addition, it would help mask the smell of the kill and reduce the number of predators who might be interested enough to investigate.

Resting his back against the rough bark of the pine

tree, Daniel smiled in remembrance. This had been a very good day. Stopping at a ville to rest his feet, the healer offered his services to help deliver a breech baby. The father hadn't been able to offer anything in barter, but his shapely daughter had, and after the child was wrapped in an old Army blanket and suckling on its mother's breast, Daniel joined the daughter behind the woodpile and did something similar for a while. Then it was her turn.

Daniel finally left the farm feeling tired, but in high spirits. Then, wonders of wonders, he had came across a man alongside the road trying to bandage a busted leg. The white splinter of bone from the compound fracture jutted from the torn skin of his leg. After confirming the wounded man was alone, he slit the fellow's throat and acquired a fine pair of walking shoes and some ammo for his blaster. Everything else was junk, so he threw it and the corpse into a swampy bog to hide the deed. Mountain folks often had kin, and some of these uncivilized hill men took the idea of revenge very seriously. Even on a healer.

A stick cracked in the darkness outside the clearing, and Lissman drew the blaster in a smooth motion. The .38 Ruger Police Special was small but powerful, and in his capable hands more deadly than an autoblaster. Rising slowly, he tried to hear over the noise of the fire. As a standard precaution, Daniel had dragged wild rosebushes into a circle around the clearing. The sharp thorns held off most animals and muties that might attack in the night. Only norms would pass through the briars.

Blaster balanced in his grip, the healer dragged his backpack closer and eased out a sawed-off, double-barrel shotgun. Loaded with homemade black-powder charges and packed with gravel and rock salt, the crude blaster would kill only at very short range. But the salt would blind an opponent, giving Daniel the chance to operate again. Few lived who felt the angry touch of his cold little knives.

Another stick cracked, closer this time.

"I know you're out there," he said, a blaster in each hand. The heavy weight of the weapons made him feel confident. "Show yourself, or I start blasting randomly. On the count of five. Four...three..."

"No, please," a voice gasped, and a large man stumbled into view, holding a bloody rag to his neck.

"Come into the light," Daniel ordered, relaxing neither his stance nor pressure on the triggers.

"I saw...the fire," the handsome male wheezed. "Fell...bear trap..."

"Does look bad," agreed Lissman, lowering the blaster. "Is the blood spurting out, or flowing?"

The newcomer coughed raggedly.

"Now, now, fellow. Don't try to answer," he said in a soothing voice. "I'm a healer, and can fix you as good as new. Got some clean rags and a sewing kit here in my bag." He kicked the canvas satchel on the ground.

"Thank you," the man squeaked, weaving a bit as if ready to collapse.

Holstering his handblaster, Lissman walked over and pulled on a piece of rope attached to the thorny brambles, dragging a large rosebush out of the way. The wounded man stumbled into the clearing, and Daniel used the shotgun to shove the bush back into position.

"That is, fix you for a price," the healer continued, holstering the blaster. "Got any jack?"

"No." He barely spoke in a whisper.

"Spare ammo?"

The stranger shook his head.

Slightly annoyed, Daniel sat down and placed the primed shotgun across his lap. The stranger was too big for Daniel to use his clothes, and he owned good walking boots now.

"So how will you pay?" Daniel asked bluntly, tossing another log onto the fire for more light. "Got any food? Booze? I can use jolt or Dreem, but no wolf weed. I have no use for that shit."

The man staggered and leaned against a tree. "Nothing," he panted. "But strong...travel with you...bad country ahead..."

The healer burst into laughter. "Are you proposing that I fix your throat, then haul your sorry ass along with me to the next ville for free? Am I supposed to feed you, too? Go away and die. I have no time for idiots."

"Please..." the man whispered, slumping to the ground.

With a sigh, Daniel stood and drew his belt knife. The bowie was sixteen inches long, the needle tip of the steel blade reflecting the firelight like a mirror.

"Guess I'll be operating tonight," he said, walking closer. "But don't worry, friend. I always do this as painlessly as possible."

"No! Please...who...who are you?"

"Who am I?" Lissman laughed, amused. "My name is Daniel Lissman. Happy now?"

"Yes, thank you." Sullivan smiled, exposing a big-bore Army Colt .45 automatic pistol from within the folds of his loose clothing, the hammer already cocked and in the firing position.

Lissman dropped the knife and clawed for the Ruger on his belt.

Calmly, without any emotion, Sullivan triggered the military blaster and a massive dumdum round blew the healer's chest apart, red blood and organs spraying across the campsite.

Before the dead man hit the ground, Sullivan rose to his full height, tucked the blaster into its holster and threw the bloody rag from his undamaged neck.

When he'd found the fresh corpse in the bog, it seemed only natural to use some of the blood to pretend he was wounded himself, and follow the trail of the killer. It had been too long since Sullivan last killed in combat, and he desperately needed to know if his skills were as good as ever before taking on the baron of Front Royal.

Stepping over the corpse, Sullivan tossed some more wood onto the fire, building it to a roaring blaze, and inspected the dead man's belongings. There were four more blasters in his pack, along with predark cans, a wad of jack tied with string, vials of jolt, two sticks of dynamite coated with wax to keep them fresh, a switchblade knife, a can opener and several pieces of silver cutlery. It was a fortune, but Sullivan recognized the items as a litany of human suffering packed into a dirty canvas satchel.

In the background, grisly bits of the dead healer were still dripping off the trees as Sullivan slid the switchblade into a boot. A good fit. Then the half-breed kicked the head of the corpse for a while. Making a decision, Sullivan tucked the bowie knife into his own belt and exchanged his polished Colt for the other man's rusty wheelgun.

Dawn was starting to brighten the sky above the thick foliage. Not a cloud was in sight, which was always a good sign. The sky was only a light orange in color, streaked with some soft purple and a few minor burning hues. It was about as clear a day as it got in Deathlands.

Squatting on the ground, Sullivan reached out with his bare hands and ripped some strips of meat off the roasting rabbit suspended above the flames.

"Dan Lissman," he said between bites, trying different tones and inflections. "Hello, I am Daniel Lissman, a healer. How can I assist you, Baron Cawdor?"

Chapter Thirteen

As Mildred closed and locked the door to their suite, Ryan checked the ledge outside the windows, while Dean looked under the bed and J.B. did a quick recce for secret doors and such in the walls. Doc probed the closet, Krysty searched the washroom and Jak stood guard in a corner watching their backs. Clem did the same across the room.

"Clear," the Armorer reported, dusting off his hands and pushing back his fedora. "Okay, what's this about?"

"Overton has Nathan's pregnant wife held hostage," Ryan said, pulling a chair from under a rolltop desk. He turned the chair around and sat down with his arms resting on the back. "And unless he turns over the ville, she and the baby die."

"Wife? I heard some of the staff mentioned his wife—Tabitha, I think they called her. Supposed to have died in the mutie attack."

"If she is believed dead," said Krysty succinctly, "then nobody would try and rescue her."

Ryan scowled. "Exactly. He's got every base covered."

"Clever bastard," Clem muttered, leaning against the corner and crossing his arms. He looked for a place to spit, but saw no sign of a spittoon or bucket. Damn, what a backward fortress.

"Overton dies," Jak stated, tilting his head forward so that the snowy hair tumbled forward and masked his features. A knife slid into his palm, and he tested the edge on a thumb. His own wife and child had been killed a long time ago, but the pain of their loss was reborn with this news. The teenager had coldly witnessed the deaths of hundreds over the years, but the murder of women and children stirred a fire in him that no amount of revenge could satisfy.

"Dies slow," the Cajun added grimly.

"Sounds good to me," Clem agreed amiably.

"How can we do that?" Mildred asked pointedly. "You saw Overton at dinner. He went to the damn lav with bodyguards trailing along. They probably wipe his butt. The man's always surrounded."

"Exactly like Caligula and the praetorian guards of yore," Doc rumbled, working his swordstick. "As I recall, after numerous failed attempts, the mad emperor was finally murdered, but the assassins were killed within moments by his bodyguards. Rome was set free, but at a terrible price."

"Only terrible for some," J.B. amended, fanning himself with his hat.

"Get me close." Jak flipped a knife into the air and expertly caught it by the blade between thumb and forefinger. With a twist, he tucked the knife away into his clothes. "That's all need."

The conversation stopped as bootsteps went by the door, then faded into the distance.

"How do you know this?" Krysty asked, her hair waving gently about her shoulders. She still felt a bit weak from the flu, but it was nothing she couldn't handle.

Ryan jerked his head toward the parapets. "When I

was talking with Nathan, he mentioned a man, Red Roger. The same thing happened to him. A prisoner escaped from the gallows and hid in his house, holding the farmer's pregnant wife hostage so Roger would swear the man wasn't there to the baron.

"It worked," he continued without emotion. "And when the sec men went away, the prisoner chilled them both. Nathan knows what will happen the minute Overton seizes control. He took a big chance telling me this."

"That's what Overton has to control Nathan," J.B. said, resting his backside on a corner of the desk, one boot dangling freely. "What does the baron have to hold back Overton?"

"His troops control the hunting dogs, plus the armory."

Dean whistled and J.B. cursed.

"Indeed," Doc said, playing nervously with his swordstick. "So if Overton pushes too hard, or terminates Tabitha…"

"Front Royal gets loudly removed from the landscape," Krysty finished. A bout of coughing made her stop talking for a minute. Ryan looked at Mildred in concern, but the physician waved the incident aside.

"Just phlegm," the doctor explained. "Perfectly normal."

"Are there enough explosives in the armory to really destroy the whole fortress?" Dean asked, sitting crosslegged on the bedspread. "It's an awful big place."

"More than enough," his father stated. "We know how to make black powder here, and the ville gunsmith stores the excess in barrels for selling to other barons. He's a drunk, but a friend. We can count on help from him and his staff."

Sadly, Mildred and Clem informed Ryan of the earlier execution. The man's expression didn't change, but they knew his confidence in the plan was reduced.

"A blasterfight in a powder mill," J.B. said, removing his hat completely and rubbing his hair. "Dark night, what a shit-hole we've walked into."

"Kin helps kin," Mildred stated. "Nathan would do the same."

"Yeah, he would, I suppose," the Armorer relented.

"We need to stage a diversion," Krysty said. "Get the sec men busy doing something else, then we can chill Overton."

"Have to be big," Mildred said.

"Really big," Ryan agreed. "Any ideas?"

Withdrawing his knife, Clem started dry shaving his neck to the sound of sandpaper on stone. "Sure, we rescue the wife," he said. "Fortress ain't that large. How tough can it be?"

"Nathan must have already searched everywhere for her," Mildred chided.

"We look someplace he ain't yet."

"Which is where?"

"The barracks," Ryan said, sitting upright. "Fireblast, Overton's troops have taken over the old barracks! That would be the only place Nathan couldn't search. Hell, there's even a punishment room in the basement. My father used it when a sec man needed discipline but he didn't want to whip the man in front of the people."

Slowly, J.B. nodded. "Sounds good to me."

"I'm for it," Dean said.

"No," Krysty stated forcibly. "We don't free Tabitha."

The companions stared at the woman, then began to smile among themselves.

"She's right." J.B. grinned. "We don't free Tabitha. We free everybody in the barracks. Gotta be more than just her in there. Man has got a lot of enemies."

"The sec men will go crazy hunting down the escapees. Without the hostages, Overton is powerless."

"Allowing us to get Overton," Clem added, cracking a smile. "Told you it was easy."

"I'll ask the staff to bring me lots of hot water for tea," Mildred said, dragging her medical kit closer and opening the flap. "This is a pregnant woman we'll be hauling around, and we better be ready for anything. The excitement of a rescue could cause an early birth, depending upon what trimester she's in."

Then she closed the flap. "No, damn it, I can't ask for hot water. They know I'm a healer. It's too suspicious."

"White sheets," Jak said, pointing at the bed.

Dean and Krysty moved off the bed, as Mildred yanked off the blankets and closely inspected the sheets. "Lightly bleached, no starch. These will do fine," she decided. "But I'll also need some clean twine and a sterile knife. Jak?"

The teenager produced a slim blade. "Sharpest I got."

J.B. donated a spare bootlace, as the companions sliced the bedsheets into usable pieces. Mildred carefully stored them in her bag as swaddling for the newborn, while Jak cleansed the knife blade over a candle flame. That, too, was wrapped in the clean cloth and tucked into the bag.

"After we get Tabitha," Krysty said, "we better hide

her someplace good. The sec men will go mad trying to get her back into their custody.''

"What about Daffer?'' Clem asked, polishing his longblaster. "He sure owes us. Hide her there. After the sec men let him go, he went to Benton. That hamlet is only ten minutes away by wag.''

Digging in a pocket, Ryan jingled the keys. "Want to ride guard with Mildred?''

"Done so before,'' the hunter drawled. Then he winked at the physician. "I think I can stand her for a little bit more.''

Ryan tossed the keys, and the hunter caught them, tucking them into his vest.

"Time is against us,'' Ryan said, pushing away the chair. "The longer we stay, the worse the situation gets for Nathan.''

"And after the baron,'' J.B. added, "we're next on the hit list.''

"Only if we fail.'' Kneeling on the floor, Ryan used the point of his knife to scratch an outline on the flagstone. "Here is the barracks, the buildings alongside, an alleyway leading to the moat for trash, main street, side street, horse corral and tack room.''

"Open courtyard with almost no cover,'' J.B. ruminated sourly. "Going to be tough trying to sneak through the door. Any chance of a roof hatch or a coal chute, something like that?''

"Nothing. The building is as tight as a drum. That's why it was chosen as the site for the barracks,'' Ryan said, resting on his haunches. "But mebbe we don't have to sneak in. Mebbe we can make them invite us inside.''

"How we going to do that?'' Clem asked skeptically. "Ask pretty please?''

"Yes," Ryan said unexpectedly. "Exactly correct. Hell, they'll beg us to get inside fast as possible."

The hill man raised an eyebrow but didn't comment.

"What bothers me," Krysty said hesitantly, "is how much information Overton has about this place, and about you. Where you used to get laid, the layout of the ville, where to hide Nathan's wife."

"There's a traitor, somebody working with Overton who knows you extremely well and hates Nathan."

"Yeah," Ryan growled, low and dangerous. "I know."

"No idea who?"

The Deathlands warrior stood, the panga tight in his grip, the razor-sharp edge of the blade reflecting candlelight across the people in the bedroom.

"If I knew who," he muttered, "they'd be dead already."

"Sure you want in on this, Clem?" J.B. asked the man in the corner. "This is our fight. You can just walk away."

"Be bloodbath," Jak agreed.

"Yeah, it sure could. And Bob wouldn't have helped. Would have said it weren't none of our biz," Clem drawled, working the bolt on the Enfield rifle. "But me? I'm just itching to try out this fancy blaster. Six shots! Damn."

Ryan clapped the man on the shoulder. "Glad to have you with us, amigo."

"Well, course you are." Clem grinned. "Shit, who wouldn't be?"

The companions chuckled at the bravado, and the bedroom soon filled with metallic clicks and clacks as weapons were prepared for battle.

"When do we move?" Dean asked impatiently, jacking the slide on his Browning Hi-Power.

Walking over, Ryan squinted at the boy. "You tell me. When would Overton least be expecting any action on our part?"

Knowing this was another test, Dean thought hard for a few minutes before answering. "It's almost dawn," he said, weighing each word. "We should wait until nightfall, then hit the barracks at midnight.

"No, wait a tick," the boy said, hurriedly changing his mind. "The clock in the bell tower will wake everybody up, make them alert. So we go tomorrow night, say, thirty minutes after midnight. Just enough time for the guards to relax again."

"Nice to have known you," J.B. said grimly, checking the contents of his munitions bag.

"Bad call," Ryan stated, slinging the Steyr over a shoulder. "The longer we wait, the worse our position."

"And we need every ounce of surprise to pull this off," Krysty added, rubbing out the scratches on the floor.

"What, now?" the boy asked, surprised. "At dawn?" Outside, some birds were chirping and a horse whinnied as it was forced awake to start the work of the day.

"Yes, right now," Ryan confirmed, working the slide on his handblaster and chambering a fresh round as he headed for the door.

A FEW MINUTES LATER, there was a loud knock on the front door to the barracks, and a sleepy sec man rose from his wooden stool to swing open the tiny conversation hatch in the thick door.

"Yeah?" the corporal asked, sleep making his voice rough.

"We have a new prisoner," a smiling guard in a blue shirt said through the grilled portal. The sec man stepped aside, and the dirty face of Ryan Cawdor filled the view for a second.

"Hot damn!" the corporal cried, and he rushed to push aside the iron bolts locking the door. "How the hell did we get him so soon?"

"Didn't," Ryan said, firing through the crack of the opening door. The silenced pistol was no louder than a cough, but Overton's sec man staggered backward, his chest spraying blood from the multiple wounds. He groaned, then slumped onto a table, rattling the dirty dishes and wine bottles.

"What the hell was that noise?" somebody called out.

Rushing inside, the remaining companions dragged in two more dead guards from the street. Hauling the live blue shirt aside, Jak brutally rammed the head of the captive against the wall. The sec man sighed and folded to the floor, leaving a crimson trail along the rough bricks.

Holding an AK-47, Clem stayed outside trying to act casual in his tight blue shirt and baggy trousers. The Enfield was strapped across his back, his long hair tied in a ponytail and tucked into the collar of the shirt. Only the most cursory glance would fool anybody that he was one of Overton's neatly dressed troops.

"Get the wag," Krysty ordered through the door grille, as she slid home the bolt.

Clem nodded and dashed down the street out of sight.

"Sarge?" a worried voice called from down the hall-way.

Wiping the mud off his face, Ryan took a position near a locked blaster rack as J.B. went to work on the padlock holding the chained weapons in place. The device clicked in less than a minute, and the companions all took an AK-47 blaster, then stuffed their pockets with extra clips. J.B. closed the padlock and broke off the tip of his lock pick inside the mechanism.

"I wish them luck opening that again," he said, his tone triumphant.

"Get ready," Ryan warned, gently pulling the bolt on the submachine gun until it loudly clicked. "Once we start, there's no going back."

Just then a group of armed sec men walked into view, the man in front pulling up his pants by the suspenders. At point-blank range, Ryan shot him in the face, brains and bone fragments spraying onto the guards behind him. On the left side, Doc lunged forward with his sword, stabbing one in the heart, and Jak threw a knife into the throat of the other. Sighing into death, the falling bodies were caught and dragged out of the way.

Weapons at the ready, the companions moved deeper into the quiet of the enemy barracks as the clock in the ville bell tower loudly began to chime the arrival of dawn.

Chapter Fourteen

Ten more sec men died quietly as the companions moved like ghosts through the sleepy barracks. Another locked door blocked the main corridor, and J.B. easily got them through in record time.

Now a hallway dimly lit by oil lanterns stretched ahead of them, multiple doors on each side. The first two opened into large rooms lined with empty bunk beds, and the faint stink of stale sweat and cigarette smoke permeated the air.

"That's forty," J.B. counted. "Should be twenty more here asleep and twenty on patrol duty."

"Should be," Krysty agreed. "But then how many more in the east wing?"

"Probably the same," Ryan answered, watching for movement in the shadows. "If not more."

Another door proved to be the linen closet; the next was to the lav. Oddly, faint light seemed to be coming from the bottom of the pit visible through the hole in the wooden seat.

"So you don't miss in the dark?" Dean guessed.

Ryan scowled, but said nothing.

The last door opened to another bunk room, but this one was full of snoring men, boots on the floor, blasters hanging off the end of bedpost newels. Assuming a marksman's stance, Ryan leveled his silenced blaster to give them cover fire, while Dean and Doc moved quietly among the sleepers gathering their longblasters. One man started to awaken, and Dean clubbed him unconscious with the butt of his pistol, the sharp blow delivered expertly to the temple. The sec man snorted and went limp on the mattress.

Exiting the room, J.B. placed an armed Claymore mine on the floor and closed the door, locking it with a twist of the key.

"That's my only mine," he whispered, backing away from the room. "It better chill most of them, or we're in for a hell of a fight."

Reaching the end of the hallway, Ryan knocked softly on the door. A voice mumbled a question, and he muttered something unintelligible. After a few moments, the door swung open, exposing a sec man with a greasy napkin tied around his neck and a plate of food in his hands. The sergeant froze motionless as the business end of the SIG-Sauer was pressed against his throat. Silently, he walked backward into the office, and Krysty closed the door.

"Master keys," Ryan demanded.

With some difficulty, the sergeant swallowed the food in his mouth before speaking. "Top drawer of the desk, left side, behind a blaster."

J.B. walked across the room and searched for traps before checking the drawer. Mildred kept watch, while Doc and Jak moved to a blaster rack filled with longblasters and started to dig into the breeches with knives, snapping off the firing pins.

"Well?" Krysty prompted.

"Got them," J.B. replied, examining the ring of keys. "Seems legit."

When Doc and Jak were finished, Ryan jabbed the

blue shirt with his blaster, the sharp muzzle cutting his pudgy skin. "Where's Tabitha Cawdor?"

"Cellar," the sweaty man replied. "She's in the cellar. But honestly, I had nothing to do with—"

In a rush of anger, Ryan buried his left fist into the fat man's stomach. The guard doubled over, vomiting, and the one-eyed man clubbed him to the floor. Blood welled from the gash on his head, but the sec man was still wheezing for air as they departed.

"Cellar?" Krysty asked.

Ryan gestured. "Should be this way."

Turning a corner, they found a sec man sleeping in a chair, his longblaster laid across his lap.

"Hey," Ryan called.

The man awoke with a start and stared in astonishment at the invaders. With a curse, he pawed for his weapon and died in the chair, a soft chug from the SIG-Sauer knocking him from the chair.

As J.B. undid the cumbersome lock, the companions noticed a faint, unpleasant stench reminiscent of a sewer. As the door opened, the pungent reek of night soil filled the air, the smell thick enough to cling to the tongue and bring tears to their eyes.

Oil lanterns hanging from nails illuminated a short flight of stairs leading to the water-stained floor one flight below. Holding their noses and breathing shallowly, the companions proceeded down the rickety stairs into the dank basement. Immediately, they could see dozens of prisoners manacled to the walls. The men were skeleton thin, little more than skin covering bones, their clothes rotting rags. Not one lifted his head to look at the approach of the companions.

Keeping a grip on the banister, Ryan still almost slipped when he stepped onto the floor, realizing almost too late that the water wasn't a thin puddle, but more than a foot deep. Worse, the floating solids in the liquid clearly showed it had been used as a makeshift toilet by the poor souls chained to the dirty walls. Then he recalled the light from underneath the guard's lav, and realized they had done the same.

"Jesus, Mary and Joseph," Mildred whispered, crossing herself.

Ignoring the filth in the water, Ryan stepped into the raw sewage, the material almost cresting the top of his Army boots. "Free them," he snapped, feeling a red madness fill his mind, and this time he did nothing to stay his temper. This was beyond even the initiation of the cannies. They starved prisoners to make them recruits. This was done purely for sadism. Another item to settle in blood with Overton.

"J.B., open the chains. Doc, Jak, get them upstairs. Krysty, look for Tabitha."

Slinging his weapon, J.B. sloshed across the horrid water and, fumbling with the keys, unlocked the first person on the wall. He stopped for a moment, thinking the sec man was dead, but then the eyelids fluttered and the head weakly lifted.

"F-fuck you," the man hoarsely whispered. "Long live Nathan Cawdor."

The manacles came free with a snap, and J.B. gently pushed the stick figure toward the stairs. "Get going!" he commanded. The Armorer knew there was no time to explain. Just give orders, and make them move. Food and sanity would come later. Quickly, J.B. moved to the next living man and unlocked the manacles, then the next, and the next. There were almost as many dead as there were alive.

Trembling with the effort, the first freed prisoner

splashed toward the stairs. Doc assisted the man up the steps, while Dean kept watch in the hallway above.

"Fireblast, I know these men," Ryan stated, his hands knuckle-white on his blaster as he watched them go by. "He was the leader of the ville sec man. This man was the best hunter we had, that dead one the gate-keeper."

"Loyalists," Mildred said, guiding another to the stairs. "Captured men who stayed true to Nathan and wouldn't bend to the new baron."

"And this was their reward," J.B. muttered, freeing another.

The prisoner stumbled and started to fall, but Jak caught the man in his arms and carried him upstairs as if he weighed nothing.

"We can't set these men loose as a diversion," Mildred stated, helping a sixth man get free from the shackles.

"They go with Tabitha in the wag," Ryan replied. "Screw the plan. We'll find another way to distract the blues."

One of the sec men going for the stairs fell to his knees into the slimy water, then he suddenly plunged his head into the disgusting liquid and began to slurp greedily.

"Water!" he whispered, raising his dripping face into the air to catch a breath. "Sweet water!"

The rest weakly took up the cry.

In that instant, Ryan fervently wished that the sleeping blue shirts upstairs would awaken and give him something tangible to beat to death with his bare hands. He had seen many horrors in his life surviving Death-lands, but rarely was his heart touched with pity. His red fury changed in that moment into an icy determination, and Ryan silently vowed that Overton would die at any cost. Even his own life.

Sliding an arm under the drinker, J.B. hauled the man to the stairs and pushed him toward the light. "The baron commands you to go and obey the boy upstairs," he said softly.

"Y-yes, my lord," the former officer replied, weeping, and he began to crawl up the stairs as if the effort of walking were completely beyond the limits of his physical strength.

A sharp whistle from Krysty cut the terrible moment, and Ryan thankfully sloshed forward through the quagmire. In the rear, an open doorway led to another room a step up from the sewage, the concrete floor dry and only stained from boots coming out of the muck. Mildred was close behind.

The cinder-block walls were green with mildew, the air worse than a freshly opened grave. The sharp tang of the mold almost masked the reek coming from the other area. Several empty tables leaned upright against a wall, the leather straps and dark stains showing their purpose and frequent usage.

A surgical cabinet stood nearby, and Mildred marveled at the glistening array of scalpels, forceps and hemostats. She tried the handle, but it was locked tight. Smashing the glass with the barrel of her weapon, Mildred began to stuff the instruments into her medical kit uncaring of the sharp glass that ringed the opening.

Heavy curtains closed off one end of the room. Pushing them aside, Ryan found Krysty holding the hand of a pregnant woman strapped to another slanted table. She was naked, her huge distended belly covered with bruises, one eye swollen shut, her nose clearly broken.

"No," she cried weeping, "not again, no more…

please, my baby. You'll hurt the baby...." And the woman desperately clenched her legs together.

"Hush, everything is fine now," Krysty said softly.

Whipping out his panga, Ryan slashed the curtains loose and draped them over the nude woman.

"Thank you," she whispered, trying to focus her good eye.

"Are you Tabitha Cawdor?" Ryan asked, sawing at the straps. The predark woven material was tough but soon gave under the razor-sharp steel.

"Yes, who are you?"

The first strap parted, then the second. "Ryan Cawdor, a relative. We're here to take you to Nathan."

"Nathan?"

"Fireblast," Ryan growled. The third strap was different from the others. Some sort of resilient steel strands had been woven into the material. The panga wasn't getting through.

"Look away," he ordered and, placing a hand over her face, triggered the SIG-Sauer at the locking buckle.

The metal exploded and the woman jumped from the stinging report at such close quarters. Yanking the strap through the smashed buckle, Ryan did the same on the other side and helped to woman to sit upright.

"I'll take her," Krysty said, lifting the pregnant woman off the table. Even without her mutie strength, the redhead was nearly as strong as Ryan and this tiny slip of a girl was no real burden. Besides, at that precise moment, Krysty believed that she could easily have pulled down the whole fortress.

"Move fast," Ryan directed, leading the way. "Overton's men will wake soon."

Sloshing their way to the stairs, the companions herded the freed prisoners out of the barracks and into the rear of the waiting truck. Clem stayed at the wheel, watching for trouble as Mildred helped the scrawny sec men climb into the wag. Loose hay filled the rear of the truck, and the men collapsed into it and went to sleep, totally exhausted by the terrible ordeal of a twenty-foot walk. Ryan got the door to the cab, and Krysty placed Tabitha on the front seat, tucking her in with the old curtains. Clem wrinkled his nose at the stink but made no comment. If this was what came out of the barracks, he could only guess at what they'd found inside.

A few people passing by took in the strange sight and kept walking. Armed people were to be avoided in Front Royal.

"We'll send word when it's safe to return," Ryan said, passing up a spare AK-47 blaster. "Stay low, move fast and don't hesitate to shoot."

"No prob," Clem drawled, working the gears and releasing the clutch. Mildred waved goodbye as the truck started to pull away, then she buried herself out of sight under the hay with the rest of the human cargo.

The wag was halfway across the courtyard, heading for the distant drawbridge, when a thunderous explosion shook the barracks, blowing the glass out of the windows while tongues of flame licked out the doorway. As the companions got off the ground, they heard piteous screams from inside the burning building.

The fire bell began to clang.

"Now it begins," J.B. said grimly, looking around. There was no sign of the blue shirts, but that would change at any moment.

"Be careful," Ryan warned, jacking the slide on his handblaster and holstering the piece. "I've seen Overton draw and he's fast as me. Mebbe even better. Don't know if he's accurate, so the second you see him, no conversation, just keeping banging away until you are sure he's dead.''

"Sounds like a plan to me," J.B. said, snapping the bolt on the Uzi, then the AK-47.

"Okay. Let's go."

The companions scattered to their chosen positions— Ryan behind the water trough, Doc in a side street, hidden in the shadows of the rising sun, Krysty down the alleyway behind a pile of refuse near the garbage chute, Jak in the tack room amid the ropes and horse harnesses, J.B. in the horse corral. They laid out the extra clips, checking the grens in their pockets, and prepared for the onslaught of blue shirts.

They didn't have long to wait before a platoon of sec men raced around the corner, blasters held at quarter-arms as if they were in a damn parade.

"Platoon, halt!" a sergeant called, raising a hand.

On that cue, the six friends cut loose on full-auto, a deafening hellstorm cutting down the troops, their bodies jerking wildly under the hammering of brutal cross fire. The sec men died without firing a shot.

Ryan called a halt, and the companions moved across the cobblestones and spent brass, quickly relieving the bodies of spare clips and a surprising numbers of grens. Grabbing extra blasters, the friends moved quickly inside the fortress, giving the stolen military weapons to random members of the house staff, and shooting on sight anybody wearing the telltale blue shirt.

Rushing to a window, a young serving girl threw open the shutters. "Everybody listen! It's here!" she yelled in delight to the people outside. "The revolution is finally here! Death to Overton!"

A blue shirt in the street fired his weapon at her, the string of rounds stitching a path across the stonework of the window, and the girl fell back with half of her head removed.

Screaming in rage, an elderly steward holding an AK-47 rushed outdoors and emptied the clip into the murderer, tearing the man apart into bloody gobbets until the weapon cycled dry. Panting from the adrenaline, the steward rushed to search the corpse for another clip. A chimney sweeper took the dead man's longblaster. The two men exchanged looks, nodded and went their separate ways.

Cries were starting to spread throughout the streets, random sputtering of automatic blaster fire dotting the crisp morning air, and the fire bell stopped ringing. Soon it was replaced with the much louder danger bell, its brassy rings summoning every able-bodied person to come to the defense of the ville.

HIS BARE FEET PERCHED comfortably on a cushioned footstool, Overton carefully sliced a summer apple.

"Stop worrying, Ki," he said, munching on the juicy piece. "I have the ville completely under my control. By the end of the week, I'll be baron."

Jian Hwa Ki took an offered slice and ate it without enthusiasm.

A soft pattering noise came from the courtyard below, followed by several screams, then silence.

"What the hell was that?" Ki demanded, rushing to the window.

With a shrug, Overton ate another slice of fruit off his knife. "My sec men executing a thief, or just target practice. Relax, old friend. Ryan is no more a danger to us than those serving wenches we bedded last night. Mine was pretty good, fought like a wildcat. How about yours?"

"There's a lot of commotion," Ki warned nervously, straining to see into the distance. "And smoke's coming from the direction of the barracks. Mebbe we better sound the alarm."

Overton rose languidly, brushing the sticky apple bits off his robe. "What kind of commotion?" he demanded, amused. "Anybody running around firing a blaster and throwing grens?"

Just then, the low boom of a gren shook the room, closely followed by the long rip of a blaster on full-auto. More blasterfire was followed by another explosion. The sounds of battle didn't stop, but escalated in volume steadily.

Standing brazenly in the window, Overton spread his arms as if to embrace the world. "At last!" the big man shouted in delight. "The rabbits have finally been roused. The rebellion is here!"

Overton turned with a smile. "Colonel Ki?"

Bent over the desk, Ki was already at the radio, trying to contact the barracks. But the speakers only crackled with unmodulated static. "Yes, sir?" he asked.

"Kill the hostages!" Overton snapped, pulling on pants, then boots. "Send off a pigeon to the cave and get us reinforcements, plus the LAV 25. Hell, both of them. All of the reserve troops, the heavy machine guns and the flamethrower. And tell the snipers it's open season. They can shoot anybody they wish. Anybody not wearing blue, that is."

"At once, Commander!" The man saluted.

Bare chested, Overton belted the Desert Eagle about his waist. "I'm going after Ryan personally."

Chapter Fifteen

Daffer hobbled over to the small fire in his hut and tossed another handful of twigs on the flames. A whole chicken was roasting on the spit in his fireplace, crackling above the wood fire, but he hadn't been able to force down more than a few mouthfuls. Mildred had claimed his stomach would have to stretch again, having shrunk from starvation. That sounded reasonable, but the sec man knew better. Wings resembled hands far too closely for him, what with all those little bones, and legs were legs. But Daffer had been able to spoon some of the rich drippings over a loaf of stale bread, and that was a fine meal. No complaints.

His wife had left him while he was gone, and moved northward to new territory. Daffer couldn't blame the woman. She had little future except as a gaudy slut with her husband dead and so few unmarried men in the area. So his home had been deserted on his return, aside from a few rats and a miniature bear. How they had gotten inside, he had no idea. The walls were solid concrete, predark material as strong as granite, the windows had been bricked shut for some unknown reason by a prior tenant, and the door, although streaked with rust, was metal in a metal frame. These were the reasons why he had chosen it for their home in the first place, strong and safe. Sure was a hell of a lot better than a log cabin with winds cutting through the door as if it weren't there.

The chimney! Cracking a smile, he studied the field-stone chimney he'd built so many years ago. The little animals had to have simply climbed down the open flue! Well, of course. Once you figured it out, the mystery was plain as a blaster in your face.

Situated by itself away from the other ruins of the predark ville, Daffer believed it was a jail or bunker of some kind. There were some letters set above the door lintel, but he never could figure out what DPW Substation stood for. Had to have been something special to be this well made.

Shuffling over to the table, Daffer poured himself a drink of red 'shine—mountain wine, as it was called—and took a sip. The cool brew went down easy and took the pain from his joints. Mildred advised him to drink a lot to replenish his tissues, and that sounded fine by him. With the bag of bullets the outlanders gave him, Daffer could damn near drink himself to death. Sometimes at night, it was almost enough to stop the nightmares and make him sleep.

Pulling close a chair, Daffer sat down and continued to disassemble the blaster Lord Ryan had given him for protection. The internal parts were small and his fingers clumsy, but Daffer tried again to take the weapon apart to clean every nook and cranny. A Webley, he called it. Odd weapon. Instead of the cylinder swinging out from the side as normal, the blaster broke apart at the top, the cylinder staying with the barrel. At first it seemed as if the revolver had broken in two, but he was slowly coming to appreciate how easy it was to load the blaster with so much space for his hands. Damn thing was a real handcannon, too. The fat .44 cartridges were as thick as cigar butts. As an experiment, Daffer tried to load the blaster with just one hand, and a precious cartridge fell to the concrete floor and rolled away.

Mumbling in annoyance, he crawled under the table to reclaim the live round. Holding the blaster backward by the barrel, as Ryan had showed him, Daffer now easily dropped in the six rounds and closed the heavy blaster with a satisfying clunk. Aiming it across the room, he saw how the firelight glistened off the blued steel, the forward aiming fin streaked crimson with a dab of paint to make it easier to target. The monster should stop a bear in its tracks, much less a man. The bullet would probably go through the first guy and chill the one behind him before slowing enough to stop.

Which meant a brutal recoil, and he made a mental note to fire the cannon with both hands or else he wouldn't hit anything but sky.

But even with that minor flaw, it sure as shit was better than his old .22 zip gun. As a child, Daffer once saw a big miner from the Kentuck coalfields take six .22 bullets straight in the chest from a coldheart, and the miner still managed to kill the man—much to the surprise of both of them. The miner lived for years afterward and finally died due to injuries sustained in a big mutie attack in another hamlet. But Daffer would never forget how the big man took half a dozen of the little bullets in the chest and still survived. It wasn't a lesson easily forgotten.

There came a soft knock on the door.

Standing, Daffer lifted the oil lantern in one hand and the massive .44 Webley in the other. Standing behind the light would make it difficult for others to clearly see him.

"Who is it?" he asked gruffly. Strangers in the night

were always trouble. His first impulse was to put a
round through the door, but he wasn't sure if even the
big-bore .44 could punch through the predark steel.

"Mildred," said a woman's muffled voice.

He started forward happily, then stopped. "Prove it."

There was a short pause. "Ryan called you Armsman
in the cabin."

"Damn right he did!" Daffer replied, walking over
to throw the two big bolts and pull open the door. Mildred entered quickly, carrying a heavily wrapped bundle
in her arms.

Daffer spied a flatbed truck outside that seemed familiar. That Kentuck hunter was behind the wheel. The
man nodded at Daffer, and he did the same in reply
before closing the door again.

"Sorry about asking, but a man's got to be careful
these days," he said, sliding the bolt into place. "I
heard that lots of folks answered the door and were
never heard of again."

Mildred was already across the room, placing her
bundle in his lumpy bed. She fussed with the covers
before facing him.

"I know," Mildred said. "We found most of them."

"Don't sound good," he stated.

The physician went to the table and poured herself a
shot of red 'shine. She drank it with pause and slammed
the plastic tumbler onto the table. "It wasn't," she answered.

"Another?" he offered.

"No, thank you," Mildred said, wiping her mouth on
her sleeve. "But by God, I surely needed that one. And
we need your help."

Tucking the blaster into his loose belt, Daffer kicked

a chair toward her and sat at the table, pouring himself a small dose of 'shine. "What's the problem?"

"Overton," the physician spit, as if the name were a curse word.

He nodded. "I understand. Who's in the blankets?"

"Tabitha."

His eyes went wide. "The baron's wife? Sweet Jesus, she's still alive?"

"Yes, and carrying."

Glancing at the woman in his bed, Daffer grinned with happiness. "A kid? Nathan has an heir to follow him? Hot damn, that's great...." The grin faded into a dark scowl. "That's why he didn't fight Overton. The scum-sucker had his wife and babe hostage."

"Worse, a lot worse than that," Mildred said.

Daffer raised a hand. "Don't want to hear. Only cloud me with anger when straight thinking is needed."

Mildred regarded the man with new respect. Nathan chose his security chiefs well.

"What do you need?" he asked, pushing the drink away. The lantern shone through the 'shine, casting red lights across the man as if he were painted with blood.

"Hide her until the fighting is over."

"Because you're going to be much too busy to care for a pregnant woman, eh? Consider it done."

"And this is for you," she added, laying a long wad of cloth on the table.

He frowned. "You saved my life back there. Don't want no payment, won't take no payment. I owe you. Besides, Nathan be the best baron we ever had."

"Fair enough." She touched the wrapped item. "But this isn't payment. It's a loan to help you do the job."

Curiously, Daffer unwrapped the layers of cloth and recoiled when the AK-47 assault rifle came into view.

"Black dust!" he whispered, reaching out a finger to touch the autoblaster as if he couldn't believe it was really there. Then he jerked his hand away. "You can't be serious. This…this is for barons, not sergeants. And you folks going to need every wep if you're going against Overton and his blue boys."

"We have enough, and better than this." Then Mildred added a lie, knowing the honest man simply wouldn't accept the priceless weapon as a gift. "And we damn well want it returned afterward or it's your ass. Friend or not!"

"Fair enough," he said softly, and lifted the weapon as if it were made of fragile glass already filled with cracks. The balance was excellent, and the stock fit snug in his palms as if the machine were made just for the sheer pleasure of chilling.

"These adjustable sights?"

"Yes, the little screw over there."

"I see it. Any spare clips?" he asked.

Mildred placed three full magazines on the table, the curved metallic boxes smeared with blood. Daffer made no comment at the sight.

"You got to show me how to work this thing," he admitted sheepishly. "Wheelguns and bolt actions are all I know."

Over the next hour, Mildred ran through the basics with the man. Already a seasoned fighter, he learned quickly.

"Short burst, you say, don't ride the trigger like a runaway horse."

"Beginner's mistake," she agreed, checking on Tabitha. Her pulse was good, breathing easy and regular. The mother-to-be was simply asleep. "Burp the rounds, unless there's a whole gang of people, then pull the trigger hard and move the barrel fast in a sideways figure eight.''

"A what?"

Dipping her forefinger in the 'shine, Mildred drew the figure on the tabletop. "See? Like this."

"Leg to head, then again. Oh, I got it. Smart."

Standing, Daffer rested the heavy assault rifle on his shoulder and experimented, dropping a spent clip and slapping in a reload. The fireplace crackled loudly, filling the hut with waves of warmth. Tabitha moaned softly in her sleep.

A pebble hit the door, and Mildred dropped into a crouch, blaster drawn. Going to the door, she slid the bolts and peeked outside. The truck was gone, and a squad of sec men in blue shirts was going from hut to hut, kicking open doors and checking the occupants at blasterpoint.

"Overton?" Daffer asked, awkwardly holding the AK-47 in his trembling hands. "Let's send them to hell!"

"There are way too many," Mildred stated, glancing around the small fortress. "Is there another way out of here?"

"Nope. Except the chimney."

"Got a cellar, a back room?"

"Don't even have windows."

Frantic, Mildred walked to the wall and kicked it resoundingly with her steel-toed boot. The material neither shook nor dented.

"Damn, damn, damn!" she cursed. The guards were a minute away, maybe less. The truck was gone as expected. There was no sense in everybody getting captured again. She might escape alone, but then the blue shirts would have Tabitha as a hostage again, and Daffer would be killed on the spot. They could lock the door and make a stand, but one gren down the chimney and they were toast.

Mildred glanced at Tabitha, lying on the bed softly sleeping.

"No," the physician stated, undoing her blouse. "The bastards aren't going to get her away from us. Strip."

Daffer blinked and almost dropped the blaster. "Eh? What was that?"

Mildred dropped her shirt and undid her bra with one hand, while struggling with her belt buckle. "I said strip, man, if you want to save Lady Cawdor and her babe!" Next to go were her beaded plaits.

STANDING ON THE DARK street of the ville, Krysty motioned for Ryan and the others to advance into the fortress. They raced past her, and she stayed behind to cover their rear. Satisfied nobody had spotted them, Krysty started to casually walk toward the drawbridge to make sure their escape route was kept open.

"Hey, you there, Red!"

Icy adrenaline flooded her body at the cry, and Krysty turned, her AK-47 leveled. A platoon of blue shirts was running toward her, armed with longblasters, wheelguns and grens. One large man even carried what resembled a flamethrower, a hideously deadly weapon at close quarters.

"Yeah, that's her!" a sec man cried. "Ryan's bitch!"

"Get her!" the leader roared, charging forward. The sec man raised his blaster, but another slapped it down.

"Alive, you fool!" he barked. "You want to go to the baron's private room?"

The officer paled and lowered his blaster while vigorously shaking his head.

Alive, eh? Good. Krysty went into a crouch and snapped off four fast shots. Three of the men dropped, clutching their bellies, but instead of scattering, the rest kept coming. Their terror of Overton overwhelmed any fear of death.

Baring her teeth in rage, the redhead turned and sprinted down the street, firing wildly over her shoulder and reloading as she ran, searching for a fast escape. She couldn't head toward Ryan and the others, as that might give away the attack on Overton. Krysty had to play for time and hope for the best.

Taking a corner, the woman emptied the AK-47 at the mob of sec men coming up the road. A dozen of the men collapsed to the ground, and one threw a brick. She ducked and ran, her heart pounding in her chest. If that had hit her head, she would have gone down for the count. And after seeing Overton's torture room, Krysty would rather chill herself than be taken alive by the madman.

Ducking into an alleyway, the red-haired beauty was blinded by the rising sun but ran for her life, dropping the spent magazine of her weapon as she reloaded for the last time. Thirty rounds, and she would be down to her wheelgun, useless against that many men.

Krysty slammed into a wall, losing her AK-47. The sec men shouted in victory behind her, their voices coming closer. Desperately, she clawed the surface of the barrier, searching for a door or some way over the wall. But the new wooden planks were solid and without purchase.

Voices filled the darkness of the alley, and Krysty moved to the corner where the wall met the barrier, expecting to find a rain barrel, but the area was bare. Impossible! There were always barrels to catch rainwater or snow, and buckets for garbage. That was what an alley was for!

Suddenly, the barrier shook and Krysty moved away just in time to avoid being crushed as the door swung downward, laying flat on the cobblestones. Brilliant electric lights washed over the alleyway, and she could dimly see a dozen more sec men clustered around a predark LAV 25 war wag.

"Mother Gaia, save me," she whispered, leveling her blaster and firing steadily. It was Overton's private garage for his war wags.

A powerful tingle started to flow into her body as the woman summoned her mutie strength. Masculine hands grabbed her from every direction, and Krysty fired her weapon directly into faces, the features of the men flashing into view for one split second before exploding from the deadly impact of the .38 hollowpoint rounds. When the blaster clicked empty, she dropped it and grabbed a sec man by the throat, crushing his neck. Somebody punched her in the stomach with no effect. Feeling as if she were in a dream, Krysty slapped him to the wall, broken teeth flying.

Another sec man grabbed her legs, and she kicked him away to fly across the alley and hit the brick wall with a sickening crunch. But then something hard rammed her head, and her vision blurred from a concussion. Drawing her belt knife, she slashed wildly, blood spraying across her body from severed arms and throats. A rifle barrel jabbed into her side, and Krysty wrestled the blaster away from its owner and reversed the deadly autofire on her attackers.

But as she pulled the trigger, it only clicked on an

empty magazine. Tricked! Smashing the rifle over a sec man's head, Krysty dashed for the LAV, planning to lock herself inside. Scrambling up the sloped side, she lifted the heavy hatch and a rifle stock slammed directly into her face. There was a moment of pain, then the world went completely black.

LONGBLASTER AT HIS SIDE, a sec man wearing a blue shirt stood at the top of a flight of stairs inside the fortress. A tremendous stained-glass window dominated the end of the hall, the morning sun filling the passage with a rainbow of hues. Listening for any sign of the baron or his officers, the guard decided to risk lighting a cigar. Gratefully, he drew in a deep lungful of the smoke and exhaled with great satisfaction. Then he felt something like a bee sting him in the chest, and a purple spot appeared on his shirt. The stain spread fast and wide as a numbing cold filled his body and he finally slumped to the floor, crushing the cigar underneath his cheek, the glowing tip hissing as it was extinguished on his bare skin.

Barging from an alcove, Ryan and the others crossed the top of the stairs and entered the east wing. Almost instantly, they dived for cover as a score of volleys flew toward them.

"Fireblast," Ryan cursed behind a credenza, the heavy oak sideboard shuddering from the impact of bullets, the ancient china plates stacked neatly inside shattering at every strike. "The son of a bitch has got half his troops here!"

"Good!" J.B. shouted as he stood and threw a gren down the long hallway. The firing stopped, and one man dived from cover to grab the explosive and lob it straight through the stained-glass window at the end of the hall. One moment later, the predark window shattered from the outside blast, spraying rainbow glass everywhere.

"Do it again," Ryan ordered, firing blindly around the credenza. "Shorter fuse."

"Can't," J.B. grunted, dropping the AK-47 and pulling the Uzi around to his front. "That was my last gren."

"Doc?"

"The same, my dear Ryan."

"Me, too," Dean reported, firing controlled bursts from underneath an ornately carved mahogany chair. Then his longblaster stopped, and he tossed it aside, drawing his Browning Hi-Power. He worked the slide and clicked off the safety in the same move, and commenced firing again. But much more carefully, placing his shots instead of just banging away at anything that moved.

Safely ensconced behind heavy steamer trunks and from inside doorways, the company of blue shirts down the hallway sprayed streams of bullets at the companions. The fusillade chewed a path of destruction along the walls, destroying priceless family portraits, mirrors and vases. Swords and riddled shields tumbled to the floors, flattened rounds ricocheting randomly, pounding on the doors and clearing tables of candelabra and oil lanterns. Several lanterns burst into flames, the spreading pools of burning oil generating volumes of thick black smoke.

The head of a sec man appeared above the top step of the stairs, his eyes darting about, only the tip of his weapon in sight. Dean waited until he rose a little higher and shot him in the ear as he turned. Limply, the dead man tumbled from sight.

Staying low, Doc crawled along the hallway, grabbed two more lanterns and threw them toward the sec men and down the stairs. Both of the lanterns crashed into fireballs, blocking any possible attacks from that direction for a few minutes. The blue shirts shot at the overhead rafters in reply with no appreciable effect, the bullets burying themselves in the massive oak timbers.

Dropping the exhausted AK-47, Ryan checked the Steyr and worked the bolt. This sally was a total failure. He had hoped to catch Overton unprepared and end the fight in the ville quickly. But Overton had expected such a risky plan, and while he didn't have them trapped yet, two directions were already cut off, and there was no doubt the other hallways would soon be sealed also.

"Enough of this crap," Ryan declared, firing and smoothly working the bolt action on the Steyr as fast as he could. A sec man in a doorway jerked and fell, but another filled the post, his AK-47 firing steadily. "First chance, we head for the southern parapet!"

"Regroup?" Jak demanded, sliding his last clip into the hot belly of the Kalashnikov.

"Retreat," Ryan corrected, jerking the bolt to clear a misfire.

"We're going to the parapet?" J.B. asked, peering owlishly through his glasses. "You're out of your mind, Ryan. That's a dead end!"

"Not for us," Ryan said, raising the longblaster and shooting at the ceiling. The support chain of an unlit chandelier snapped, and the massive fixture dropped, crushing four sec men.

"Charge!" he barked, starting in the other direction.

As the sec men prepared for a rush, the companions hastily ran through the alcove.

Nearby, a door opened a tiny crack, and a man wear-

ing a blue shirt peeked out. Ryan almost fired, but
stopped himself just in time when he realized it was the
steward from the dining hall in a denim nightshirt.

"They're on the roof," the man mouthed, then closed
the door.

Maintaining cover fire with the Steyr, Ryan appreci-
ated the warning. Once outside, they would have to
keep moving or else get caught in another deadly bot-
tleneck. Just how many men did Overton have, anyway?
Ryan had to have chilled twenty already just by himself.

At a branching corridor, J.B. laid a handful of
7.62 mm rounds on the carpet.

Low on ammo, Doc asked a silent question.

"Don't touch those," the Armorer warned. "It's a
special gift for the blue shirts. Trust me."

Just then, a sec man appeared through the smoke and
died from a volley of fire from the companions. But
others followed close behind the brave fool. Darting
from doorways to tables, the friends made it alive to a
set of winding stairs. Abandoning defensive actions,
they bolted up the steps until reaching an ornate stained-
glass doorway. It was locked, but smashing through,
they piled onto the parapet overlooking the southern
acres of Front Royal. A team of prisoners was in the
distance, cutting grass and stacking it as winter food for
the cattle. Clouds moved low in the sky, and the morning shadow of the fortress stretched across the fields and
forest.

"Give me a hand here," Ryan grunted, struggling
with a decorative gargoyle set in a niche. Jak and Doc
joined the man in rocking the granite statue to and fro
until it dropped in front of the open doorway. The
curved horns snapped off, but the figure was otherwise
undamaged by the short fall.

Crouching behind the outstretched wings of stone, J.B. sprayed a wreath of copper-jacketed 9 mm rounds down the stairs, the slugs bouncing off the curved walls and whining out of sight, but there came no answering cries of pain.

"What these?" Jak asked, dropping his spent shells and thumbing fresh rounds in his Colt Python. Several canvas backpacks lay on the parapet, and he regarded them warily.

"Gifts from Nathan," Ryan said, grabbing a pack and slinging it across a shoulder. "I told him we would be here if the rad hit the Geiger."

A group of blue shirts appeared on another parapet opposite from them and started to shoot. The companions ducked, flying granite chips from the misses hitting them with stinging force. The rough stone of the parapets pressed hard into their spines, a cold breeze tugging at their clothes as the men frantically reloaded.

"It has," J.B. said, firing controlled bursts from the Uzi at the dodging sec men. A man cried out, blood spraying from his shoulder.

Hopefully, Doc ripped open a pack and found food, candles, matches and lots of mixed ammo, but no grens.

"I am less than pleased with the choice of accoutrements," Doc rumbled in annoyance. "A dozen grens would have done us a world of good."

Suddenly, a powerful explosion rocketed the stairs, and a billowing cloud of acrid smoke blew out the shattered door and expanded over the parapets. Wails of agony came from below, along with bitter curses and virulent oaths.

"They found my gift," J.B. stated with a grin, adjusting his glasses.

"What was that?" Dean asked, picking up a backpack.

"I emptied the gunpowder from the bullets and packed them solid with C-4. Not a blaster made can contain that detonation. The fools took off their own arms and hands using my ammo."

"'Thou shalt not steal,'" Doc recited, casting away the AK-47 and drawing the LeMat. "Most appropriate."

J.B. judiciously fired the Uzi at the other parapet, while the others cut loose at the men trying to sneak up the curved stairs.

"They have us trapped," Dean announced grimly, his left hand holding his right wrist to steady the blaster and get maximum accuracy. "As soon as we run out of ammo, we go into the cellar."

Doc shuddered, clearly recalling his prior days as a captive to another mad baron fond of torture. "I would rather die fighting," the time traveler said resolutely.

"We're not going to surrender," Ryan said, releasing a shard of colored glass from the broken door and watching it tumble into the moat. The wind took it a bit to the left. "And we're not going to die. We're going to jump."

"Jump?" J.B. repeated, dropping a spent clip and replacing it with a fresh magazine. His munitions bag was alarmingly light in weight. Stretching his neck, the Armorer stole a peek at the choppy waters below. "Dark night, it's five freaking stories, and that's a shallow-ass moat, not a river. We'll hit bottom and break every bone we got!"

"Not if we jump exactly here," Ryan retorted, patting the railing.

"Nine o'clock!" Jak warned loudly, shooting upward.

Twisting at the waist, Ryan tracked sec men climbing along the roof of the castle through the crosshair scope of the Steyr. The longblaster spoke, and a screaming man flew off a gable. Ryan fired again, and a second rolled off the slanted roof to bounce off another gargoyle and plummet downward. The fellow missed the moat by a yard and hit the ground with a grisly thud.

The rest of the blue shirts on the roof scurried over the peak for cover.

"Why here?" Dean asked, pressing loose rounds into an exhausted clip. The boy was down to his last few bullets.

"There's a deep hole down there. My brothers and I used to jump off this balcony, and we always made it okay."

"You sure?"

"Been a while," Ryan admitted, dropping a fresh clip into the breech of the Steyr, "but I'm sure."

A hail of bullets peppered the parapet, clipping a fang off the sideways gargoyle, and J.B. felt a tug at his fedora. "Lead the way!"

Slinging the longblaster across his shoulders, Ryan climbed onto the railing, took a breath and jumped. The blue shirts paused in their attack, confused by the bizarre suicide, and the other companions took advantage of the lull to follow Ryan over the railing, staying as close to him as they possibly could.

Their fall through the sky was brief, the fortress flashing by as the moat expanded below. The chilly air buffeted their clothes and a tingling feeling filled their stomachs, then they hit the icy water. The companions plummeted straight down into the stygian depths. Each man braced himself for the killing impact against the rocks on the bottom, muscles tightening in preparation for the pain. But their descent gradually slowed, and soon the companions began to float upward.

Following the bubbles, they broke the surface, gasping for breath. The shore was only a few yards away, and they swam to it easily. The stone blocks edging the moat were slippery with algae, but Ryan directed the others to a set of worn steps cut into the foundation. The men dragged themselves out of the freezing water to fall on the dewy grass.

"Dark night," J.B. said, gulping in air. "We did it!"

Voices cried out from the balcony, and shots flashed in the shadows overhead. Ryan felt a hot buzz go by his face, and he rolled away fast.

"The trees!" he cried, and started off at a run.

A large splash came from the moat.

"They're still following us!" Dean yelled, turning to fire.

"Not for long!" J.B. shouted, and lobbed a block of something silvery at the fortress. It hit and sank, then the surface of the moat bulged and a roar of steam erupted from the bubbling moat. The swimming sec man shrieked as the water actually began to boil, the cooking flesh sagging away from his bare bones. The horrible cries thankfully ceased as he sank beneath the roiling chop.

"Thermite," Doc said, his long hair plastered to his scalp, clothes dripping. "I did not think you had any left."

"Sure," J.B. grunted, retrieving his glasses from an inner pocket. "Just couldn't use it in the fortress because of the close confines. But it's safe out here."

"How long?" Jak demanded, wiping off his face.

"Ten minutes, mebbe more."

Another man dived off the parapet, landing far away from the boiling waters. He went under and stayed there.

"Underwater spikes," Ryan explained. "I don't think any more will be following us along this route. And it will take them forever to circle around the ville, even in a wag."

The ground spurted at their feet from the impact of numerous bullets, and the companions raced across the smooth field into the safety of the trees, the thick canopy of branches closing off any view of the brightening sky.

"What now, my dear Ryan?" Doc asked, wiping off the blade of his sword on a soaked sleeve. The LeMat at his hip was dribbling black powder and wadding through the bottom of the holster, the blaster useless until it could be thoroughly cleaned and dried.

"Now?" Ryan repeated, straightening his eye patch. "We attack again immediately, of course."

Chapter Sixteen

The unlocked door to the substation was violently kicked open, and the armed sec men marched inside.

Completely naked, Daffer cried out in shock and Mildred, beneath him, raised a knee to hide their joining. The nude couple was lying on a tangle of old blankets loosely thrown over a small bed in the corner of the room.

"Noble, ah, sirs?" Daffer sputtered, trying to hide his nakedness. "What can I do for you this, ah, night?"

Amused at their predicament, the sergeant snorted a chuckle as the other sec men did a brief recce of the tiny building, checking behind the woodpile and inside the wall cabinets. "Is there a back room?" he demanded.

Daffer blinked, sweat dripping off his face. "Here? No, sir, not even a cellar. I had planned on digging one, but when I was captured by the cannies last month..."

The leader of the sec men waved that away. "Yeah, yeah, we heard. Bad for them, good for you."

"This hole is clear," a private announced, smiling at the trapped couple. "Unlike others."

Scrawny shanks exposed to the cruel light of the lantern on the table, Daffer bent his head in shame. Contrarily, the naked woman under him raised herself on an elbow and ran a hand through her wild mane of hair.

"Look any harder, boys, and it will cost you," she

stated, cupping a plump breast as if offering it for inspection. "Hey, Sarge, you want to wait a few minutes, and I'll take you next. Daffy here is almost done and hardly wets me at all."

The troops roared with laughter.

"A gimp and a slut," the sergeant muttered, heading for the door, shaking his head.

Still chuckling, the sec men walked out of the bunker, leaving the metal door wide open.

Easing out from between Mildred's legs, Daffer lowered himself to the floor and, padding barefoot across the floor, closed and bolted the door.

"It worked," he whispered, dragging his pants off the chair and pulling them on quickly.

Mildred swung her muscular legs off the bed and stood, reaching under the pillow and retrieving her ZKR blaster. "Idiots are easily fooled," she said, checking the clip.

Facing away from her, Daffer whispered, "And my deepest apologies."

Mildred laid aside the weapon and walked to the shaking man, resting a hand on his shoulder. He flinched at the contact.

"There's nothing to speak of," she said softly. "I know you haven't been with a woman for a long time, and tucked so close to each other, certain physical masculine—" the physician fumbled for a polite word "—reactions were to be expected."

Buttoning his shirt, the man didn't speak.

"Besides," Mildred added sternly, "weren't you willing to die to protect the wife of your baron?"

"Certainly!" Daffer snapped. "I took an oath to my liege lord!"

She crossed her arms and smiled. "Then what's a little embarrassment?"

Daffer mumbled a reply and headed for the door. Undoing the bolt, he peeked outside, then closed and locked it again.

"They're gone," he reported.

"Good," Mildred said, pulling on her pants. Buckling the belt, she tucked her target pistol into the holster, then slid on her other garments. Touching her wild Afro, Mildred sighed. It would take her and Krysty a great deal of time to get her hair under control once again. She wondered if she should simply cut it off.

Turning the lantern higher for more light, Mildred pulled the blankets away from the bed, exposing Tabitha beneath on the bare concrete.

"You can come out now," Mildred said, offering a helping hand.

The tendons sticking out on her neck, the pregnant woman was drenched with sweat, her fist jammed into her mouth to keep from crying out. An AK-47 was held tightly in her other hand, the bolt primed and ready. Her legs clenched together and trembling, the floor beneath her damp with a clear fluid.

"Oh, no," Mildred said, kneeling on the floor.

"What's wrong?" Daffer asked, bringing the lantern closer. "Did we hurt her pretending to bounce on the bed?"

"Her water broke. She's in labor." The physician took the weapon from the woman and placed it aside. "Help me with the bed."

Daffer rushed over. Together, they lifted the furniture and moved it out of the way.

"You sure?" he asked nervously. "It's much too early."

"Tell that to the child. They come when they decide, and that's life."

"Or death," he said, glancing at the door.

Brushing the damp hair from Tabitha's ashen face, Mildred placed a palm on her bulging belly and counted. The contractions were only seconds apart. Tabitha gave a muffled cry of pain, as Mildred knelt before the woman and eased her legs apart. Then as gently as possible, the physician tested the birth canal with fingertips.

"Why, you're already at ten centimeters," Mildred complimented her soothingly. "This will be such an easy birth."

The panting woman writhed in agony as another contraction shook her whole body, and this time she cried out, "It hurts!"

"Always does," Daffer said, trying to be helpful.

"Not this bad. Get my med kit," Mildred snapped, pointing. "Over there by the chopping block. Start boiling water in that clean pot, and bring that bottle of moonshine!"

'Shine? Daffer stared in confusion at the physician but did as requested.

Tabitha shuddered in terrible pain, as Mildred probed inside her in a different manner. Her fingers touched something that felt like a foot.

Placing the bag nearby, Daffer asked a question with his expression.

Rolling up her sleeves, Mildred nodded. "It's a breech. The baby's coming out backward and strangling on its cord."

"Don't," Tabitha gasped, through clenched teeth, "...let die."

Yanking open her bag, Mildred didn't reply as she

laid out the shoelaces, the clean cloth and her jar of sulfur, then placed the sterilized knife from Jak on a separate square of bed linen. That was for emergencies should everything else go wrong.

"Easy, now," she said, placing a folded piece of leather into the woman's mouth for her to bite down on, although losing teeth was the least of her worries at that moment. "There, better, isn't it? Daffer, bring the moonshine. Now, Tabitha, try not to push on the next contraction, okay? I know how much you want to, but don't push. Understand? Do not push."

The woman nodded, clawing blindly at the floor, cracking fingernails and leaving bloody trails.

"Pour the moonshine on my hand," Mildred ordered, holding out her arms. As Daffer complied, she washed thoroughly, paying special attention to under her own nails.

"Now what?" Daffer asked, hugging the empty bottle.

Mildred picked up the knife and inspected the edge in the flickering light. "Pray," she whispered.

THE BLACKNESS FADED into a red haze, and sluggishly Krysty awoke into a world of pain. Her head was throbbing and her mouth tasted of blood. In a rush of fear, the woman suddenly knew that she was standing against something cold and metallic with her hands tied. Forcing her vision to clear, Krysty realized she was tied spread-eagle to the side of the LAV 25, her shirt was unbuttoned to the waist, her bra was missing and several grinning sec men were roughly squeezing her breasts.

"Ryan's bitch is nice and juicy." A man guffawed, pinching her nipples hard.

Another man started to unzip her jumpsuit the rest of the way. "Let's get to it!"

Revulsion and fury welled within the woman, but she was as weak as a kitten and totally helpless. Frantically, Krysty glanced around as the laughing sec men dragged her jumpsuit down to her ankles. The garage was large enough for several wags, but only one Bradley was parked inside. Another door off to the side led somewhere, and the garage door she had mistaken for a wall was closed tight. The troops were gathered close around their prisoner, grinning and rubbing their crotches—ten, maybe fifteen blue shirts and one officer. He was the only man shaved and wearing a side arm.

Dimly, Krysty could hear the sounds of warfare outside—the rattle of a machine gun, the boom of a shotgun, a scream of pain and the insistent clanging of the alarm bell.

Dirty hands fondled her intimately, and the woman braced herself for the gang rape. These animals wouldn't dare kill her, because the baron would be furious. Her death would come later in Overton's private chambers.

"Line up, boys," said a big sec man who sported a bushy mustache that he stroked lovingly. Oddly, he stood a bit away from the others. "We can each have a turn with the slut!"

The sec men eagerly formed a line to the right, slapping one another on the back and making vulgar comments.

"Officers first," a lieutenant stated, unzipping his pants.

"Sure," said the sec man and, leveling the blaster, he hosed the lieutenant with a stuttering burst of rounds. Shifting the barrel, he then moved quickly down the row, spraying them in a classic figure-eight pattern. The last few tried to grab their weapons, but to no avail. At that range, the rapid-firing Kalashnikov assault rifle tore them into pieces.

Disoriented, Krysty could only stare in wonder at the man, as he slammed in a fresh clip and shot the blue shirts some more just to make sure everybody was dead. When he was done, the sec man shouldered the AK-47, drew a knife and started sawing at her bonds.

"Have you free in a tick," he grunted, putting pressure on the blade. The knotted hemp rope was thick and didn't cut easily.

"Why?" Krysty whispered, staring at the man. It was the only question she could think to ask. He was so close she could smell his sour sweat and the stale smoke on his breath.

"The name is Orin Wyndham, ma'am," he said as the first rope parted. "I hold the rank of sergeant in the sec force of this ville's lawful ruler, Baron Nathan Cawdor."

"A brown?" she gasped, rubbing her aching wrist. The skin was rough and sore, but not bleeding.

"Never heard of spies before?"

The second rope parted, the knife blade hitting the armored hull of the LAV with a clank, then the sergeant knelt to work on the lower ropes. "There are six of us in Overton's troops, miss. We're not quite as dumb as he thinks." The lower ropes didn't offer anywhere near the resistance of the early bonds, and in seconds the man stood and turned his back on Krysty so she could get dressed.

There was a rustling of cloth for a few minutes, then a hand grabbed his shoulder and spun the loyalist.

"Thank you," Krysty said softly. She knew the

words were completely inadequate, but what else was there to say? "I...thanks."

Twitching his mustache, Orin bowed slightly, then stood with the gun belt of the dead officer in his hand. "Let's get the fuck out of here," he suggested.

As her own weapon was nowhere in sight, Krysty belted on the bloody leather and checked the handcannon in the holster. It was a .357 Magnum Smith & Wesson with a four-inch barrel. Cracking the cylinder, she found it fully loaded with homemade dumdums, and the ammo pouch on the belt held several reloads, both .38- and .357-caliber. That confused her for a moment, until she remembered J.B. once mentioning that certain Smith & Wesson revolvers could take both cartridges with perfect safety. That made it a near perfect survivalist blaster, as that feature doubled the type of ammo a person could use.

Krysty took a longblaster off the floor, then slowly went along the row of corpses stuffing her pockets with extra clips. One private also had a nice thirteen-inch knife that she took and shoved into her boot as a spare.

"Sounds quiet out there," Wyndham announced, ear pressed to the garage door. "Don't know if that's good or bad."

"It's too soon for either side to have won, so it probably means everybody is digging in," Krysty said, pointing at the interior door. "Where does that go?"

"It's a storage closet, filled with wires and cables, and odd predark things. Don't know where he got them."

Krysty stared at the blank door. So that was where they hid the electrical supplies brought in by Stephen. The cables had to be very important to Overton for him to guard the equipment so well.

The sergeant studied her for a moment. "Are you okay, miss? You're very pale."

"It'll pass, and the name is Krysty," she snapped irritably, a flush immediately rising to her cheeks. Mother Gaia, she was still too weak from summoning the Earth Mother's power to charge into the streets and do anything but get chilled. However, an alternative plan offered itself.

"We're taking the LAV 25."

"Excuse me, the what?" Orin asked, confused.

"The APC." She pointed. "That thing."

"But Krysty, I don't know how to drive."

"I do," she replied, working the bolt on the longblaster. Walking to the rear of the military wag, she took a stance and yanked open the double doors. Nobody was hiding inside.

"Get in," Krysty ordered, moving to the front of the wag.

Placing the AK-47 on the line of wall seats, Wyndham stepped inside and closed the doors, throwing a stout locking bolt.

"Not half bad," the sergeant said, crouching a little to avoid hitting his head on the armored ceiling. "Usually only officers get to ride inside these."

"It'll do. Any chance you know how to fire a machine gun?" Krysty asked, looking at the chain gun in the turret. The machinery seemed in good shape, and the ammo bin was filled with a linked belt of brass shells.

"Of course I can," he replied smugly. "It's a blaster, isn't it?"

"Good. I'll start the engines and get you some power for the turret motors," she said, moving to the front of the wag. The wall bins for grens were empty, which was hardly surprising, but the control board in front of the driver's seat looked good, the indicators alive with electricity. There was lots of juice in the nuke batteries, hydraulics were normal, and almost a full tank of gas.

"With this, Lord Cawdor can grind Overton in the dirt," Wyndham stated, awkwardly climbing into the turret. The passage wasn't designed for a man with his wide shoulders. "Send the outlander and his bastard blue shirts straight to hell!"

"That's the plan," Krysty agreed as she dropped into the driver's seat, and almost didn't hear the telltale *tick-click* of a trigger mechanism setting.

"Let's move this can!" the sergeant shouted from the turret, only his boots visible.

"Can't," replied the redhead, sitting absolutely motionless, her temples pounding.

"Is the engine broke?" the sec man called down, worried.

"No." Krysty swallowed with difficulty. "I'm sitting on an armed booby trap."

ELSEWHERE IN THE FORTRESS, armed sec men strained to keep still and not rush outside as the sounds of warfare in the corridors and streets grew louder, then dimmed, returning once more to ebb and fade. The sounds were coming through the grilled ventilation slots high in the granite block walls. The formidable door to the armory was built of sturdy oak beams, not just flimsy planks, and held together with wide bands of wrought iron riveted firmly into place. Four large hinges supported the door, and at least two men were needed to push it aside even when unlocked.

"Sir, the ville is being attacked!" admonished a frantic sec man. "Let's grab some blasters and help defend our home! Folks are dying!"

Rows of empty blaster racks lined the walls, and almost every box of cartridges was gone. Only a few of the older muzzle-loading longblasters, and some rusty wheelguns waiting to be repaired, were still on the shelves and worktables. The men guarding the armory were armed only with axes and crossbows. Nothing that might destroy the precious hoard of powder.

"And what if it's a trick?" the captain asked in forced calm. The man was sitting on a small keg of black powder next to a full-size hogshead of more explosive gunpowder. Embedded in the top on the big wooden container was a wheelgun, the handle jutting out and the hammer cocked for instant use. One pull on that trigger and the huge barrel of explosives would detonate, spreading a fiery chain reaction to every other barrel, keg, drum, box and crate in the armory building, an explosion that would level the fortress.

"Huh? A trick?" asked another brown shirt. The five others shared his confusion.

"Overton wants to chill us and seize the armory. What better way than to stage a fake attack using his own men to pretend to be locals, and then wait for us to rally to their aid."

"So what do we do?" asked one man.

"What can we do?" another added.

"We sit tight," said the captain of the guards, taking a plug of tobacco from his pocket and biting off a chaw. Smoking—and striking a flame—in the armory was beyond forbidden. Even the light came from some predark contraption called a safety lantern hanging from the rafters. Supposedly, the tiny flame inside the glowing mesh wick behind the glass flue wouldn't ignite gas fumes in the air, and was allegedly safe to use near raw gunpowder. The baron had paid a fortune to buy it from the widow of a coal miner killed in a brawl.

The sec men glanced nervously at the large hogshead barrel cushioned on a bed of dry straw to keep it away from the moisture on the floor.

"We just wait," a sec man repeated, licking dry lips.

"The way soldiers always have," the captain agreed. "We stand our post until Baron Cawdor gives us the signal to join the attack."

In deliberate slowness, the officer placed an arm on top of the hogshead, his fingers only inches away from the primed pistol. "Or we send Overton straight to hell."

A STEADY RAIN of bullets chattered from the palisades of Front Royal, the tattered leaves falling from the trees as Ryan and the other men retreated deeper into the forest until reaching a woody glen.

"We'll be safe for a few minutes," Ryan said, dropping the Steyr and a canvas satchel. On the parapet, he had noticed spare clothes inside the bags and wanted to double-check that the items were dirty. He lifted a shirt to find it sweat stained and horribly smelly, something worn by a man who had toiled in the hot sun all day. There was only one possible explanation for Nathan giving them dirty clothes to wear.

The one-eyed man glanced toward Front Royal and almost smiled. "You crafty bastard," he said in praise. "Triple clever, nephew. Well done."

"Safe enough for what?" J.B. demanded, retrieving his hat from inside his shirt. Slapping the fedora against his leg, he beat the water from the fabric.

"Until it's safe enough to return," Ryan said, "and finally chill Overton."

"How are we getting back inside the ville?" Dean asked, vigorously shaking the water out of his blaster. The sealed brass cartridges wouldn't be damaged by the brief soaking in the moat, but any floating debris in the water could impair the ejector mechanism, causing it to jam while firing.

"Drawbridge closed," Jak stated, laying the other satchel on the ground. "Gotta be."

"Indeed," Doc stated, shivering slightly. "Unless the man is a complete fool, the ville is now sealed tighter than the proverbial drum!"

"Good. That'll work in our favor." Yanking apart the drawstrings holding the canvas bags tightly closed, Ryan started to haul out the dirty clothes.

"Strip and put these on," he ordered, tossing the filthy garments to the others. "Socks, underwear, change everything."

"Mine aren't that bad," Dean said, water pooling around his boots. The shirt and pants were reeking, stiff with dried sweat and even a few bloodstains.

"Do it, Dean," his father ordered gruffly, ripping off his own shirt. "And do it quickly."

"Better than nothing, I suppose," J.B. said, exchanging his soaking clothes for the relatively dry items from the satchel. "Would have been nice if Nathan could have given us clean stuff to wear."

"It's the only thing that might save our lives," Ryan countered, buckling an old worn belt. The pants were too big, the shirt too small and his skin itched from the contact with somebody else's pungent laundry. Hopefully, it would be powerful enough. It was a dangerous plan, but a lot better than his idea of running on foot to the Ox Bow stables and stealing horses to ride back to Front Royal.

"Worried about pneumonia?" Dean asked, puzzled.

"No," Ryan answered brusquely.

After getting dressed, the companions moved into the cover of some bushes and used the ammo in the bags to quickly reload their blasters. There were plenty of rounds for everybody, including a small plastic jar of black powder and cotton wadding for Doc's huge LeMat.

"The copper nipples of the primers should be fine," Doc said, purging the compartments of his revolver and stuffing in fresh powder and shot. He gingerly added the clean wadding on top, then pressed each compartment in the cylinder down tight with the built-in arming lever. A touch of grease from his soaked ammo pouch sealed each hole, and the monster handcannon was ready for use again.

"Nathan thought of everything," J.B. stated, thumbing fresh rounds into a spare clip for the Uzi.

"That he did," Ryan agreed, working the bolt on the Steyr to check the action. It was a little stiff, taking a fraction of a second off his firing time. Damn, some of the lubricant had to have washed off in the moat. He would have to watch for that in the coming fight.

Just then, a steady pounding sounded over the distant blasterfire from the fortress, and the ground began to vibrate as if an earthquake were coming.

"Cavalry!" Jak spit, drawing a knife and his Colt Python. "Hide trees!"

"Don't move!" Ryan commanded, slinging the longblaster. "Lower your weapon, make no threatening gestures and don't talk!"

Before the others could ask questions, a dozen horses

thundered into view from the trees, the riders wearing blue shirts and bent low, urging the straining animals to gallop faster. Racing past the companions, the mounted sec men rode across the glen at a full gallop. Seconds later, a pack of dogs appeared, sprinting low across the ground, chasing the terrified riders. Oddly, none of the hounds were barking.

"Dark night," J.B. whispered, aghast. "Nathan unleashed the bastard dogs!"

Bred and crossbred for generations after skydark, the dogs of Front Royal were its first line of defense against invaders. The huge bull mastiffs, their coats black as midnight, were heavily muscled, possessed oversize jaws and never barked or growled to give away their presence. As quiet as death itself, the colossal hounds flashed toward their victims in unnerving silence.

The riders were halfway across the glen when the dogs reached the horses, circling their prey to the front to stop their escape. A sec man fired his AK-47, the stuttering rounds churning the ground but coming nowhere near the darting dogs. Then a large bitch bit the horse in the leg and the animal reared in pain, dropping its rider. The sec man hit the ground, and another dog ripped out his throat, blood gushing into the air.

The other sec men wildly sprayed the weapons everywhere, struggling to control their mounts. A dog charged and ducked, causing two horses to collide. Nearly losing his seat, one blue shirt shot another sec man and wounded a horse. The rider dropped away and the bleeding horse bolted for the trees. Converging on the fallen man, the hounds savagely tore out gobbets of flesh, then broke apart, offering no mass target for the chattering blasters.

Ryan knew this was Nathan's new training. The former baron simply starved the beasts and let them eat the victims. But a full belly made the hounds slow. Now the mastiffs removed a throat or opened a belly, then moved to kill again. The sec men were cursing, firing their automatic weapons randomly, the bucking horses screaming, the dogs silent and constantly underneath the mounted animals where they couldn't be fired upon. The bizarre scene was unnatural, unlike anything Ryan had ever seen before, and the man felt as if he were watching somebody else's private nightmare.

Trying to insert a fresh clip into a hot Kalashnikov, a sec man dropped the magazine and a dog leaped onto his horse, clawing open his chest until the man dropped to the ground. Another blue shirt fired, killing man and dog. Then a bull mastiff leaped upward and grabbed the blaster by the barrel, yanking it free from the man's grip. He cursed and tried to draw a handblaster, when another dog slammed into him from behind, toppling him off the horse. Tumbling, the man stood and back-handed a charging hound with the blaster, shattering its jaw, then two more hit him in the face and groin. Wildly shrieking in pain, the gory blue shirt disappeared beneath a pile of dogs and abruptly stopped making any noise.

Following the tactics of their leader, the other hounds stole blasters from the last few men. Unarmed, the sec men drew pistols and fought on, but without the volume of fire of the assault rifles, they were soon dragged into reach and brutally slain.

Clutching a wheelgun, the last man blindly staggered for the imagined safety of the forest with the dogs racing around and around him, nipping out chunks of flesh from his arms and legs. Weakly falling to his knees, the crying sec man put the barrel of the revolver to his head and pulled the trigger, but the empty blaster only clicked in response. Now the dogs converged upon their victim and he died in seconds, warm blood steaming slightly as it pumped out onto the cold autumn leaves.

Unharmed, the horses galloped away, reins flapping freely as the hounds circled the glen a few times, checking the dead. Coming near the companions, a bull mastiff jerked its boxy head in that direction and sniffed loudly, the first sound Ryan had heard any of the beasts make, aside from breathing.

Padding closer, the black animal walked through the bushes and faced the companions directly. Baring its teeth, the hound raised its haunches preparing for a jump. J.B. made a move toward the Uzi, and Ryan grabbed his hand in an iron grip.

"Don't move," he whispered hoarsely. "Make no threatening gesture. Just follow my lead."

Doc nodded. The swordstick was in his hands, but the blade still nestled in its ebony sheath. Jak swallowed hard, hands tucked into his pockets, knives tight in his grasp.

Twitching its ears, the animal walked around the companions, coming close to Ryan and bumping hard into Dean. The men did nothing, and the animal sniffed their clothing, backing away a few feet, snarling and bobbing its head, clearly confused. More of the animals arrived, stepping from the bushes with only the noise of their claws on the dirt to announce their arrival. The pack of killers circled the companions, sniffing away, and a bitch licked at Doc's pants. The man's eyebrows arched upward, but he forced himself to do nothing.

"Confused," Jak said, frowning. "We smell wrong."

"Smell right, you mean. These are Nathan's clothes,"

J.B. said quietly, watching the hounds study them closely. The head of the bull mastiff reached his gun belt. On its hind legs, the dog could look him directly in the face. A chilling concept.

"I knew what he had in mind when I saw the dirty clothes in the bags," Ryan said out of the side of his mouth. "Now start toward Front Royal. Nice and slow. No sudden moves."

"We could have been halfway there by now," Dean said.

"No, we had to let them smell us first," Ryan replied, taking a step toward the fortress. "If they saw us moving while they were excited from a kill, they would have attacked immediately."

The boy accepted the statement, fighting to stay calm. As the smallest member of the group, he was that much closer to the dogs and could smell the fresh blood on their breath. Sweat broke out on his brow, and the boy realized in horror that soon his own scent would overpower the stink of the old clothes.

"What about the snipers?" Doc asked, forcing a smile on his face but keeping his mouth closed. A toothy grin was a deadly challenge to most animals.

"Head north," Ryan answered, pausing with a boot off the ground to avoid touching a hound standing in the way. He didn't make eye contact with the beast, and after a few seconds, it moved aside. They were being tested for hostile intent, and failure meant swift death. "There's a tunnel used to release the dogs without lowering the drawbridge. Only the family knows the location."

"A tunnel?" J.B. asked, sweat trickling along his jaw. "Hate those. Had a bad experience in those once."

At a slow walk, the friends proceeded through the

bushes into the trees. The dogs stayed with them every step of the way, circling constantly, exposing their fangs and sniffing at the bare flesh of hands.

"Keep hands pockets," Jak ordered in a pleasant tone. "Don't let smell!"

Ryan led the way past a tangle of thorn bushes, finally locating an outcropping covered with ivy. Climbing over the rocks, he clambered down a sloped incline covered with wooden boards. The way would be an easy climb for a dog, but a difficult descent for men, which was the design. At the bottom, Ryan gratefully stood in a pool of sunlight on a brick-lined passageway. Ahead was him was a low tunnel no more than a yard high, the sunlight only reaching a short distance into the darkness.

"Cover yourselves," he directed, pulling his sleeves over his hands as the others joined him.

Going to his hands and knees, Ryan started to crawl into the tunnel, his head rubbing against the ceiling to help him steer past the many traps ahead.

In single file, the companions entered the absolute blackness of the subterranean passage, the bloody hounds mixed between them and sniffing constantly.

Chapter Seventeen

The sound of sporadic firing came from the streets, the brown shirts in the windows of the keep spraying the people below with their AK-47s. The floor was slick with spent shell casings, the atmosphere of the second floor misty with fumes from the volumes of expended cordite rounds.

"What the hell do you mean he's still alive?" Overton roared, grabbing a sec man by the throat.

"Dogs attacked the riders in the forest," the man wheezed, struggling to breathe in the iron grip. "We saw most of it through our longblaster scopes."

"And the dogs didn't attack Ryan?"

"No! Just sniffed around them."

After a moment, Overton released the messenger. "Nathan," he growled furiously. "I don't know how, but Nathan is behind this."

Leaning against the stone block wall, the messenger merely nodded, massaging his bruised neck.

"Ryan freed the hostages, the people have risen in revolt, then he escaped our trap, slaughtered over a dozen mounted sec men and by now is most likely long gone." Jian Hwa Ki rose from the table covered with maps of the ville and magazines for the longblasters. "Perhaps we should take the LAV and leave while we can."

Fists clenched, Overton directed a furious stare at the man. "Now? When we are so close to victory?"

"When we are close to getting chilled," corrected the sec chief of the blue shirts.

"Leave? Never!" Overton snapped, drawing his Desert Eagle blaster and brandishing it. "I would rather attack the armory and make them blow their own ville to bits first!"

The sec men in the windows slowed their attack on the defenders in the street at those words, then continued with renewed vigor. Clearly, the situation had shifted to victory or the grave. So be it. Death was part of a sec man's job. Some of them were veterans, some green fish, but all knew the way of the world. If you wanted to win everything, then you risked everything.

"Yes, sir!" Ki said, snapping a stiff-armed salute to his commander. "Then what do you suggest, sir?"

Holstering his piece, Overton chewed on a lip for a minute. "How many men do we have?" he demanded.

"Eighty here in the keep," Ki replied, tilting his head in thought. "Mebbe another fifteen guarding the APC and motorcycles in the garage."

Digging in a pocket, Overton tossed the little man a ring of keys. "Take a platoon of men, get the APC and start sweeping the ville with its chain gun and cannon. These hillbillies can't have anything that can stop that armored war wag."

"As you command," Ki said, tucking the keys into a pocket in his blue pants. "However, what about the men in the armory?"

The black-haired impostor sneered. "Use the poison-gas containers in the APC and chill them like rats in a cage. Nathan may be free to act against me at last, but

Ryan is long gone, and we still have more blasters, better blasters and the APC.''

Turning to a window, Overton drew his blaster and started to fire at the furtive brown shirts, the booming large caliber rounds blowing holes through whatever cover the men hid behind and chilling them.

"This fight is only just beginning!" He laughed, standing brazenly in the window and shooting anything that moved.

A FAINT LIGHT APPEARED in the distance, diluting the solid darkness of the long tunnel. Ryan crawled a little faster at the sight and soon emerged into a well-lit area inside a tall cage made of iron bars. A dozen armed men stood behind the bars.

Standing, Ryan moved out of the way so the others could leave the tunnel and join him near the door to the cage. Their claws clicking on the concrete floor, the black dogs milled about the companions in a threatening manner until Nathan stepped away from the sec men and gave a sharp whistle. Instantly, the animals froze, then sat and stared at their master, tongues lolling from their open mouths.

A brown shirt unlocked the door to the pen, and the companions slowly walked out of the dog pen as Nathan tossed a handful of meat scraps to the mastiffs, speaking softly, using each dog's name in turn. The leader of the pack offered its head to the baron and was rewarded by a brief scratching behind the alert ears.

"I was hoping you would understand the dirty clothes," Nathan said, turning from his deadly servants.

Yawning and scratching, the hounds spread out, some drinking at a water bowl, others chasing their own tails until falling asleep on the floor.

"Almost didn't," Ryan stated, shaking the man's hand. "Thanks for helping."

"No prob."

"Sir, three dogs are missing," a sec men said.

"Damn, you're right. Are they wounded?" the baron asked hopefully. "Still in the tunnel?"

"Chilled," J.B. stated bluntly.

"But they got all ten of the riders chasing us," Dean added.

"Three for ten," Nathan said, frowning deeply. "Shitfire, Overton's men are good. Too damn good. I shouldn't have lost a single dog today."

"Excuse me," Doc said, gesturing with his swordstick at a table laden with clothing and backpacks. "Are those ours, perchance?"

Nathan waved at the supplies. "I brought them along so you could change. There's also food and cold coffee sub. Thought you might be hungry."

"You thought right." J.B. grinned.

The companions fell upon the supplies, changing clothes and stuffing food into their mouths. The coffee sub was only warm, not cold, and took the fog of exhaustion from their minds. It had been a long night, and the day was only just starting. It couldn't be much past noon.

With a soft belch, Ryan finished his second cup and shoved it aside. Any more and he would get the shakes. "How's the fight going?" he asked, draping a bandolier of rotary ammo clips for the Steyr across his chest.

"Stalled at the present, I'm afraid," Nathan replied, taking a stool while a sec man poured more coffee. "I had no idea if you freed Tabitha yet, so most of my troops are protecting the armory in case Overton tries to seize control."

"She's alive," Jak said, after swallowing a mouthful of bread.

"Indeed, sir," Doc added, nibbling some hard cheese. "Lady Cawdor should safely be in one of the hamlets by now. Mildred and Clem took her and several of your captured sec men on a flatbed into the hills."

Nathan stood straighter, a new expression of determination on his haggard face. "Then I can finally chill that outlander." He spoke so quietly and firmly that the dogs whimpered, thinking their master was displeased with them.

Slapping a venison steak between two slices of homemade bread and wrapping the sandwich in a cloth napkin for later, J.B. then dragged his munitions pack closer and did a quick inventory, finding most of the explosives gone. "Where's my stuff?" he asked, annoyed.

"Taken and used already," Nathan answered, checking his handblaster. "Weapons are getting scarce. We've been stealing blasters from the dead, and are dangerously low on ammo. There are no grens or dynamite."

"Incorrect, sir, there are plenty in the barracks," Doc stated, ruffling the frills on his dry shirt. With his hair neatly combed, food in his belly and wearing clean clothes, the old man felt revitalized. "Along with quite an impressive array of ammo for the longblasters."

"Excellent! I'll send troops to gather them."

"Not deserted," Jak warned, hiding his leaf-bladed throwing knives in the secret places of his clothing. His white hair was already drying and starting to fan about his shoulders.

"Good," the baron replied firmly. "Now that we don't have to worry about the hostages, my men will rip the fucking door off with their bare hands to get us more weps.''

''By the way, how's Krysty?'' Ryan asked, drying off the SIG-Sauer 9 mm with an embroidered napkin.

Baron Cawdor frowned, then glanced at his sec men. They shrugged and shook heads. ''Thought she was with you,'' he replied.

''Fireblast,'' Ryan growled, rubbing his unshaved chin. ''Hope she's okay.''

Reshaping his crumpled fedora, J.B. gave a snort. ''Krysty is probably at the drawbridge with a blaster to the guard's head, making sure the riders can't get in, and we leave.''

''Hopefully,'' Ryan said, deeply worried. ''But if she's a prisoner, we're back to square one.''

''CAREFUL, NOW,'' Orin said, tightening the second belt around the seat of the APC. ''That should do it, I think.''

Krysty tried not to wiggle as the leather straps underneath her moved. The plan was her own idea, and it had taken more than an hour for the sergeant to get enough strong, long belts, without cracks or worn spots, from the dead sec men in the garage and slide the leather under her, cinching the straps until compressing the seat cushion—hopefully hard enough to simulate her weight.

The booby-trap charge under the seat was a full block of C-4, not just a small antipersonnel to chill the driver. Both Krysty and Orin knew that the five-pound block of high explosive would vaporize anybody inside the APC. Even the APC itself would be permanently damaged from the staggering blast. Apparently, Overton was a believer in destroying what he couldn't possess, and would rather see the predark war wag reduced to shrapnel than allow the browns to get control of its advanced weapons systems. Smart man.

"Wait," she said suddenly.

The sergeant looked up from the floor. "Trouble?"

"Open the turrets and back doors, both of them."

Orin breathed quietly for a few moments, then nodded in understanding. That could spread the force of the detonation outside the vehicle, lessening it tremendously. They would still die in any blast, and the wag would probably never roll again, but the turret blasters might be salvageable.

He got to work quickly. The top hatch the driver used to steer by opened easily. The gunner's hatch was more stubborn, but finally yielded. However, the commander's didn't move an inch no matter how much strength the big man exerted.

Sighing in frustration, Orin went to the rear and swung aside the double doors, using a seat cushion to keep them from swinging closed again. Then he dutifully returned to the woman in the chair.

"Ready?" he asked, taking both her hands.

"Ready," Krysty replied, heart pounding in her chest.

Without further notice, Wyndham yanked her bodily off the chair and they hit the metal wall together. Both waited a few seconds for fiery annihilation, only slowly allowing themselves to relax with the assurance of continued existence.

"Nuke me, it worked." The sergeant laughed in relief.

"Let's go," Krysty ordered, already moving, her cascade of red hair waving wildly about her shoulders from her tense state of mind.

Exiting the wag, the pair closed the doors and put some distance between them and the LAV.

"Think we can get the chain gun?" Orin asked, studying the turret.

Krysty cracked her knuckles. "Better not chance it. The slightest vibration—"

The world went silent as blinding light emanated from every ventilation hole, turret and hatch of the armored transport as it lifted off the ground. Krysty and Orin found themselves flying through the air from the strident concussion, hitting the floor and skidding along the smooth concrete for yards until slamming into the far wall near some motorcycles.

Gamely, the stunned man and woman tried to stand in the ringing silence, blood flowing from their ears. But they were unable to focus enough to regain their balance. Vaguely, they were aware the armored chassis of the vehicle had to have stopped the brunt of the detonation, the open doors channeling the blast safely away from them exactly the same way a barrel on a blaster did the muzzle-flame. The wall behind the wag was cracked and peppered with smoking bits of chairs and internal machinery. The door to the closet was completely gone, and the motorcycles were riddled with shrapnel holes, gas and oil leaking from the big engines. The detonation would have killed at close range, the few yards they retreated out of common sense changing the crushing effect to merely stupefying.

Weakly, Krysty clawed at the reeling Orin as she noticed a yellowish gas streaming from the punctured saddle bags of a motorcycle, the thick cloud quickly expanding across the enclosed garage and coming their way.

SMOKING A CIG, a blue shirt in the doorway of the fortress jerked unexpectedly and died as Ryan and the companions approached with Nathan and a dozen of his loyalist sec men. The group stepped between the ornate columns and looked across the ville.

Holstering his silenced blaster, Ryan studied the battlefield of the courtyard. Dead blues and browns were strewed about everywhere, along with dozens of villagers. A wag burned near the execution dock, filling the noon air with the faint smell of roasting taters to mingle with the sharp stink of black powder and the reek of the newly deceased. Near the horse stables, a human head was perched on top of a hitching post, the anguished features staring across the decimation.

Somewhere, an assault rifle softly chattered, emptying a full clip in mere seconds, then fired again in short bursts as if doing cleanup work.

Dean took the blaster from the blue sprawled on the steps and shared the man's extra ammo clips with Jak and Nathan, who were both low.

"I'll check the drawbridge," Doc said, staring into the distance as if he could see the gatehouse of the drawbridge. "Maybe Krysty is there."

"Secure the area," Ryan ordered, pulling the bolt of an AK-47. "Cover our exit."

Doc saluted with his swordstick and dashed off at a brisk run.

"Pretty spry for a whitehair," Nathan remarked.

Ryan made no comment.

"This is a good location," he said instead. "We can see the streets leading to the drawbridge, and the stables. Jak, Dean, take position here and cover our rear. Nathan and everybody else with me." Ryan raised the

Steyr and his borrowed Kalashnikov. "Let's go shopping."

HIDING THE AK-47 under a dead horse, Doc started hobbling toward the gatehouse, leaning heavily on his cane and mumbling to himself. Turning the corner, he found the short tunnel through the ville wall was full of blue shirts. A door on the right he knew led to a small room used for different things by different barons. To the left was the guard kiosk with bars covering a window so the people inside could monitor who entered and exited the ville. From his last visit, Doc knew that inside the small room were the pulleys and wheels controlling the portcullis and drawbridge, which was down at the present, probably to let the mounted sec men back inside after chilling Ryan. But if Overton had hidden troops in the woods, it also allowed them access into the Front Royal. The old man knew in cold certainty that was big trouble. The bridge had to be raised immediately.

"Excuse me, young man," Doc called, hobbling closer and smacking his gums. His frock coat hid the presence of the deadly LeMat, and hopefully he resembled just some old whitehair confused by all the loud noises. "Young man?"

"Piss off, Grandpa," a blue shirt snapped, Kalashnikov cradled in his arms. "Gate is closed by order of Baron Overton. Go home."

"Okay," Doc agreed amiably, still walking closer. Krysty might be tied up in a corner somewhere. He had to get a better look inside the kiosk. "Say, are you Jimmy?"

"Who?" demanded another sec man in annoyance. "Ain't nobody here by that name."

"Go home, Gramps," a third snarled. "This is men's work."

"Jimmy?" Doc asked, peering inside the kiosk. There was only a single person behind the grilled window, and the Oriental nearly fell over his chair in his haste to draw a weapon.

"Kill that man!" Ki cried. "He's one of Ryan's men!"

Doc dived to the ground, drawing and firing the big LeMat twice, the thundering booms filling the confines of the passage with volumes of black smoke. There was a rush of boots and Doc shifted position, firing twice more. This time he heard screams of pain. A movement in the smoke made him jerk to the side, and a shiny bayonet at the end of a Kalashnikov stabbed past his head, missing by an inch. Grabbing the rifle barrel, Doc used it to guide his aim and shot twice at point-blank range, high and then low. Still clutching his weapon, the sec man reeled backward, bleeding from the neck and belly.

"That's six, Grandpa," cried a grinning corporal, stepping into view from the smoke. "That wheelgun is empty. Get him!" The sec man charged with two privates bracketing the rush to forestall any attempts at escape by the unarmed whitehair.

Doc chose his targets and fired three additional rounds from the oversize blaster, shooting the blues in cold blood. The corporal died with an expression of total shock, completely unable to comprehend how any wheelgun could fire more than six rounds.

"Now that trick gun is out," Ki snarled, rising behind the grilled barrier.

Switching the selector pin to the second barrel of the

Civil War handcannon, Doc leveled the blaster at the chief of the sec men. "Freeze!" he commanded.

Ki sneered in contempt at the feeble bluff, then saw the raw determination in the whitehair's face and clawed for his own blaster.

The stubby .63-caliber smooth-bore shotgun vomited lead and smoke, a barrage of pellets hitting the stonework and bars of the window. Screaming, Ki clawed at the ruin of his face, teeth shattered, blood squirting with every heartbeat, one eyeball dangling on his cheek at the end of its cord. Half-blind, the man slammed shut the door and twisted the key in the lock, his hands slipping in the volumes of blood.

"Never get in," he cried madly.

Arm extended, Doc lunged at the bars, the Spanish sword darting between the bars and stabbing the sec man directly in the heart. The twitching man exhaled once, a rattle sounding in his torn throat, and he collapsed out of sight.

Fishing about with the gory blade, Doc managed to catch the ring of keys and delicately haul it through the bars. Unlocking the door across the passageway, he dragged the bodies into the storage room, then opened the kiosk and took a position behind the barred window with a stack of AK-47 blasters by his side. The only door to the ville was again under Nathan's control, and Overton would get no fresh troops from outside. That was a major point in their favor of regaining control of the ville, but his main objective hadn't been achieved.

"Where could Krysty be?" Doc demanded rhetorically, watching both directions of the tunnel while reloading the LeMat with expert speed.

RYAN, J.B., NATHAN and the others converged on the barracks, weapons at the ready. The thick door was ajar, the interior black and smoky from the earlier fire.

Suddenly cheering sounded from above, and the armed troops looked up to see the villagers waving at them from the second- and third-story windows.

"Shut up!" Nathan ordered. "Want to tell the bastards where we are?"

The people recoiled in fear and closed the window shutters in a series of wooden bangs.

"Goddamn idiots," a sec man growled.

"We'll cover the street," Nathan said, hoisting his weapon. "Take five of my men and see what you can find. Even one more blaster would be a big help."

"Agreed. But I'll take four men in a standard two-on-two defense formation," Ryan replied, slinging the Steyr and drawing his SIG-Sauer. "Ready?"

The brown shirts looked blankly at Ryan, unsure of where to go or what to do.

"Fireblast," he growled. "You four watch each other's asses. I'm on point, and J.B. covers the rear."

"Go," J.B. said, leveling the Uzi.

Swift and silent, the six men entered the damaged building. The barracks was completely different from when they were last there only hours earlier. Corpses lay underfoot everywhere, and the fire from the Claymore had consumed huge sections of the structure until the sky was visible in most areas.

In the front, the blaster rack was burned to ashes, the remaining weapons destroyed by the heat. However, several boxes of ammo had fallen free and survived the ravages of the flames. The sec man gathered the crumbling boxes eagerly, filling their pockets with the shiny brass shells. Outside the bunk room, the stack of blasters in the hallway was untouched, merely covered with hot ash. The excited sec men gathered armloads of the precious weapons, and two carried the first batch outside to the waiting troops.

Standing dangerously near the sagging doorway, Ryan could see that beds and the floor of the room had tumbled into the watery basement, swamping the cesspool and masking its purpose. Several roasted corpses lay amid the destruction, their clothing reduced to ashes. It could have been anybody until Ryan noticed the good boots. They were blue shirts, but Ryan hoped the suffocating smoke and awful heat of the fire had aced them, and not the fast clean blast of the powerful Claymore.

Reaching the rear office, Ryan darted into the empty room first. The browns stayed in the hallway as J.B. followed his friend with the stubby Uzi leading the way.

The office was bare, not even a corpse on the floor from the blues they had rendered unconscious.

"Deserted," Ryan stated, shoving aside the chair to glance under the desk. Nobody was hiding there. "And they took damn near everything not nailed down. Overton must be going for a last stand at the keep."

"Too bad for him," J.B. commented, moving to a corner of the charred office. Some timbers had fallen from the ceiling there, and he kicked away the covering to expose a partially melted plastic box.

"Bingo," he said softly, taking the case and putting it on the desk. Carefully inspecting for traps, the man then opened the lid and beamed at the weapon laying inside on a cushion of crunchy gray foam. The pistol was short and fat, a breech loader with a maw large enough to shove in a gren. On either side were neat rows of color-coded, waxy cylinders.

"That's a Navy flare gun," Ryan said, holstering his

blaster. "My father used to have one. He used it to signal troops during large battles so he wouldn't have to relay orders by shouting."

J.B. caressed the signal gun as if it were gold. "Yeah, a Veri pistol. I spotted it when we were here before. Had no use for the thing then, but now..." The wiry man smiled. "Now it's our key to killing Overton."

"How the fuck are we going to bust open the keep with that?"

"Come on," J.B. said, closing the case and starting for the door. "I'll show you."

Chapter Eighteen

High above Front Royal, the blue shirts in the war room of the keep looked down at the ville below, sweeping the streets with the scopes of their longblasters, hunting for targets. There was a huge reward for the man who chilled Ryan or Nathan, and so they were concentrating their attention on anybody with black hair, man, woman or child.

Suddenly, there was a flash of light from a nearby rooftop, and something streaked their way to hit the outside of the keep and bounce off the hard stone.

"What the heck was that?" a sec man demanded with a nervous laugh.

"Must have been a homemade rocket," someone answered. "Piece of shit didn't even explode."

"We better close the shutters anyway," another man suggested, bending out of the window and reaching for the drawstring.

Just then another burning object streaked in to impact on the wall, spraying sparks everywhere. The sizzling blue light was blinding, and it gave off volumes of thick sulfurous smoke. Raggedly coughing, the men knocked the object to the floor and stomped on it until the blazing illumination died while another grabbed a bucket of sand from a wall niche. Then a second blue flare entered the war room and glanced off the closed door to land on the table, setting fire to the maps and charts.

The nearest sec man grabbed the flare with his bare hand and tossed it away but missed the window. It hit the floor as a crimson-red flare smashed against the wall, spraying sparks and embers in a pyrotechnic geyser. Another red flare flew in to ricochet wildly, followed by a green, then a blue. The room was stifling with the awful heat, the air barely breathable from the reeking fumes. A chair caught on fire, then a blaster rack. Yanking the blasters off the burning wood, the blue shirts beat at the flames with blankets and threw buckets of sand onto the flares. One sec man tried for the door to escape, but couldn't find the exit in the hellish light that seemed to pierce his closed eyelids. Another man shouted directions, the words lost in the loud sizzling of the incandescent rockets.

More flares shot in, crashing into an oil lantern, smashing a glass case full of crossbow arrows and landing in the middle of a crate of Molotov cocktails. A screaming guard dumped the last bucket of sand on the flare in the gasoline bombs, but it was already too late. A blue shirt, covering his face with his hands to block out the terrible light, heard a new sound, a deep hissing, and squinted in horror at the crossbow arrows tipped with sticks of dynamite. Plunging his bare hands through the jagged glass, the man slashed his arms into ribbons grabbing for the lit fuse.

RUTHLESSLY SHOOTING civilians and brown shirts alike, Overton and his personal contingent of guards proceeded along the main street of the ville. In the distance, they could see the keep rising above the smaller sections of the fortress, an indomitable column of stone rising skyward.

Turning into the mouth of a small alley, the blue

shirts stopped in their tracks, staring at the door to the garage.

"Hell!" Overton cursed. Traces of yellow gas were seeping from the top of the doorway, and there was a definite stink of chemicals in the air. The bloody fools had to have tripped the gas canisters. Now the war wag was unreachable until the poison naturally dispersed.

"Shoot that door!" Overton commanded.

"Sir?" a sergeant asked askance. "But our men are on the other side!"

"Anybody inside the garage is dead," the baron retorted. "Now shoot the fucking door to help vent the gas. I need that wag operational to defend the keep before Nathan and Ryan mount a serious attack. It's our last refuge here."

Obediently, the troops aimed their weapons and started to shoot the door to pieces, blowing away chunks of the ancient wood paneling. Soon they could see the ruin of the APC inside the garage. Suddenly, the whole ville seemed to shake from a massive explosion.

"What the hell was that?" a corporal demanded, pointing his weapon about frantically.

Feeling ill, Overton had a terrible suspicion that he knew. Rushing into the street, the man could see a huge fireball engulfing the top of the keep. Debris from the blast was spreading across the ville, body parts and furniture raining onto the fortress, burning timbers tumbling from the sky. Blocks of cracked granite plummeted downward to punch into the tiled roofs and crash resoundingly into the cobblestone streets.

"Ryan," he said bitterly, watching the smoke ring of the blast rise into the sky, forming the classic mushroom shape of any high-temperature explosion. It was time to leave. The barracks was burned, half his troops dead, his best men trapped outside with those damn dogs, the Bradley unreachable and now the keep was obliterated.

"Back to my suites in the east wing," Overton ordered, turning and striding away. "We must smash the radio and kill the pigeons."

"We've lost?"

A fluttering piece of flaming table crashed into the street in front of them, and the blue shirts were forced to detour around the crackling obstruction.

"Lost? Corporal, you're a jackass," Overton stormed. "We're simply retreating to regroup. And when we return, no more of this diplomacy shit. Everybody dies! End of discussion."

STANDING BEHIND the columns at the front of the fortress, Dean grabbed Jak and pulled him into the building and behind a giant tapestry. Holding their weapons tight, the youths listened to a parade of boots going into the main hall and out of range.

"Who?" Jak demanded softly, peeking out from behind the heavy velvet tapestry. There was nobody in sight.

"Overton and some troops," Dean answered excitedly. "Should we go after them? We have the element of surprise."

"How many?" Jak demanded.

"Twelve, mebbe fifteen. But it could be more. I didn't get a good count."

"Too many." The albino teenager gave the boy a shove. "Get Ryan. Move!"

Pausing only a moment, Dean took off at a spirited run. When his friend was safely outside, Jak went up the stairs to the second floor and proceeded along the servants' hallway, switching the selector switch on his Kalashnikov from single shot to full-auto.

Reaching the balcony, he peeked over the ornate railing and saw Overton crossing the dining room surrounded by a gang of his blue shirts. Jak leveled the blaster, but the chandeliers blocked a clear shot. Dashing down the hallway to another balcony, he stepped boldly into view only to find the enemy gone.

Cursing, Jak debated going after them or staying there for an ambush. It took only a moment to decide, then he lurched into action.

A WHIFF OF FRESH AIR bringing a moment of relief to her aching lungs, Krysty lifted her throbbing head from the rough floor. A yellow cloud floated in the garage, hovering a few feet off the floor like mist above a lake. Vaguely, she realized the breeze from the broken door was keeping the gas at bay. There were a hundred holes in the wood paneling, almost as if a firing squad had been using it for target practice. Had to be shrapnel damage from the C-4 explosion.

Looking for Orin, she spied the man sprawled on the floor, his clothes darkly stained. Crawling closer, Krysty checked for a pulse, but there was no question he was dead. The wounds appeared to be from bullets, not shrapnel. Whispering a quick prayer to Gaia for the brave sec man, Krysty searched wildly for the pulley rope used to open the garage door. She found it on the wall directly above the sergeant. In pure bad luck, Orin had stood to get the door open so they could escape and been shot for his struggles.

Unfortunately, the breeze from the riddled wood was forcing the yellow cloud to hover in place above the man, with the rope dangling tantalizingly just out of reach. Knowing there was no other way out, the bruised woman took a deep breath, closed her eyes tightly and leaped for the pulley. She made the catch, fingers wrapping tightly around the old rope, but the garage door only moved an inch, then stopped, the wheels in the guiding tracks caught on the loose splinters from the damaged paneling.

Tugging feebly, Krysty hung suspended from the rope, the gas painfully searing into her exposed skin and hair.

WEAPONS AT THE READY, Nathan and Ryan walked through the streets of Front Royal with the sec men fanned out in a patently offensive formation. Finally, the troops were on the hunt.

After the destruction of the keep, the ville sec men rallied and invaded the lower levels, executing the stunned blues without mercy. Now the victorious troops were doing a fast recce of the main streets, shooting every blue shirt they found. Some fought back bravely, some hid or ran away, but it made no difference. If the blues outdistanced the blasters of the brown shirts, then Ryan chilled them with a 7.62 mm round from the Steyr SSG-70. Inside the walls of the ville, if Ryan could see it, then the target was in range, and not one blue escaped. However, a few suspicious men were encountered not wearing any shirts, one stark naked, and the cowards were taken into custody for later judgment.

"Hey, J.B.," Nathan said, studying the rooftops for snipers as they walked on patrol, "any chance you'd stay and work for me? I need a new sec chief."

"Don't like staying any one place too long," the Armorer replied, his Uzi balanced in both hands. His munitions bag was stuffed with the Veri pistol and the last three rounds.

"Besides," he added, "Ryan can't stay here, and where one of us goes, so does the other."

"We're a team," Ryan stated in unaccustomed frankness.

Adjusting his glasses, J.B. grinned. "Sure are, Chief."

A blue shirt popped into view from behind a water trough and was cut down by a volley from the browns.

"Well, at least design me a new keep," Nathan said, shaking the bolt of the Kalashnikov to work loose a jammed round. The ammo was good, but it seemed the blues had never cleaned their weapons, and constant maintenance was the daily price you paid to have a working blaster.

"Use smaller windows," Ryan said gruffly.

"And store the dynamite in metal boxes," J.B. added. "Glass cases let you know how much of the stuff is left to use, and that's good, but much too vulnerable."

"So I noticed," the baron replied. "And that's it for the next keep, smaller windows and metal boxes."

"Yep."

"Fair enough. Thanks."

There was a sudden motion in an alleyway, and the men fired their weapons into the shadows. A bleeding blue shirt stumbled into view, and some of the browns finished the man off with their bolt-action longblasters. The ammo for the assault rifles was almost gone, so the sec men were using their older weapons first and saving the fancy autoblasters for any potential trouble spots.

As the brown shirts moved into some alleys, Ryan noticed a distant figure running their way, just one per-

son and apparently unarmed. As a precaution, Ryan zeroed his scope on the incoming target, but released the
trigger instantly when a familiar face appeared in the
crosshairs.

"Trouble?" Nathan asked, squinting.

"It's Dean," Ryan said, then added, "My real son."

The baron studied his uncle closely. "Truthfully?"

"Only son I know about," he replied bluntly.

Placing fingers between his lips, Nathan whistled
sharply twice, then once long, and the browns parted to
let the running boy get past them without hindrance.
They closed ranks behind him and continued walking.

"Hey!" Dean cried breathlessly, stopping in front of
the three men.

"Hello, cousin," Nathan said, giving a casual salute.

Caught by surprise, Dean strained to keep his expression neutral. "I beg your pardon, sir?"

"Nathan knows," Ryan said. "I told him."

"Oh." The boy beamed a smile. "Hi, Nathan."

"Why the rush?" his father demanded. "You
wouldn't leave a post without a reason."

"Is Jak okay?" J.B. asked, tilting his rumpled hat
backward.

"He's fine. But Overton is in the east wing with
twenty sec men," Dean reported. He still wasn't sure
of the numbers, but decided it would be better to err on
the plus side. "Jak is keeping a watch on them."

"Any sign of Krysty?" Ryan asked. There was a
touch more emotion in the question than he would have
preferred. "Does he have her prisoner?"

"I didn't see her with the blues, Dad. Sorry."

Trying to control his rage, Ryan scowled, his mind
racing back through the years to remember the side

streets and alleys. But it was too long since he'd had any sleep, and nothing definite was coming to mind.

"Fireblast!" Ryan cursed in annoyance. "Nathan, what's the fastest way to the main hall from here?"

The baron pointed. "Shortcut this way."

"Watch for an ambush," Ryan warned, removing the partially used clip from the Steyr and inserting a fully loaded one. "This could be a trap."

"More for the slaughter," J.B. said, checking his Uzi.

"Attention! Overton is in the fortress!" Nathan shouted through cupped hands. "Who wants a piece of his hide with me?"

Waving blasters, the sec men roared their approval.

Although not pleased with publicly announcing their intentions, Ryan understood the need for keeping the morale of the sec men high. They were winning at the moment, but how many of them had died already? He had to keep their minds off dead friends and focused on chilling the man responsible.

"Double time, march!" the baron shouted, and the browns charged forward.

Taking a side street, the armed group traveled for a block, then angled into another side street. Going past wreckage from the keep, and some dead civilians shot in the back, Ryan noticed what seemed to be a blank wall starting to move at the end of a small alleyway. He slowed to watch as the damaged expanse of wood paneling sluggishly lifted into the ceiling of a small room, exposing a battered LAV 25. On the ground were a dozen seemingly dead blue shirts and a redheaded woman slumped against the left wall, her long fiery hair waving as if stirred by secret winds.

"Krysty!" Ryan shouted, charging headlong into the garage.

TURNING A CORNER inside the fortress, a blue-shirted sec man fired his AK-47, and a maid holding a broom was cut to pieces from the deadly hail of slugs. Stepping closer, a corporal lowered his blaster to dispatch the wounded servant.

"Please, no," she whimpered, blood flowing down her clothing and dripping off her trembling hands.

"Don't shoot her!" Overton ordered sternly. "Are you mad?"

"Sir?" the corporal asked, worried.

The baron sneered. "Idiot. We'll need every round we have to get out of here should the brown shirts find us. Don't waste a single bullet."

"Yes, sir. Sorry." Kneeling, he slit the crying woman's throat, and the troops moved onward.

Armed pointmen swept the grand staircase, checking for enemy sec men before allowing the main body of troops surrounding Overton to advance. Then they did the same for the east hallway. Finally reaching his former suite, Overton ordered a corporal to kick open the door, and a brace of troopers sprayed the room with their assault rifles, cutting down three brown shirts waiting in ambush. The fusillade of rounds tore them apart, driving one man out the window in a crash of stained glass. He screamed all the way down to the street and abruptly stopped.

"You there, kill the pigeons," Overton directed, furious over the lapse of secrecy. "You, rip the wires out of the radio and take them along."

A private reached into the cage and took the trusting birds by the throat and snapped their necks one at a time. The other private removed the guts of the communications unit and stuffed the wires into a pants pocket.

Moving to the armoire, Overton inserted a key and unlocked the heavy ironwood doors. Inside was an arsenal of blasters, grens and a fat canvas bag.

"Everybody fill their pockets with spare clips," Overton ordered, stuffing some grens into his pockets.

The sec men looted the armoire as Overton grabbed a squat Thompson with a huge cheese-wheel ammo clip. He pulled the bolt, and the predark blaster was ready for war. Despite its size, the Thompson fired .22 rounds, but the oversize clip held 600 rounds, which was enough to blow them a path to freedom.

Yanking open the canvas bag, Overton lifted into view a monstrous blaster, the likes of which none of the others had ever seen before. The weapon sported a pistol grip attached to a breech-loading mechanism and a fat barrel only a foot long. Feeding sideways into the blaster was a flat wheel from which jutted a circular series of fat soup-can-size compartments.

"Corporal, take this," Overton said, handing him the bizarre weapon.

"What the hell is that?" asked an awed trooper.

"Something special from the boss, an MM-1," Overton replied, snapping off the safety for him. "And it's our key out of here. It launches twelve 38 mm grens. Right now, it's loaded with a mix of high-explosive, shotgun rounds and white phosphorus. If the wind is with us, we can set fire to half the ville and be long gone before they figure out what happened."

The sec man practiced with the balance of the strange blaster. "What then, my lord?"

"We regroup at the cave and come back here. No tricks this time, no clever plans. We're just going to take over and chill anybody who dares to try and stop us.''

''About fucking time,'' a private grunted.

As he agreed wholeheartedly with the sentiment, Overton allowed the lapse in discipline. But he made a mental note to punish the man later for insubordination.

Returning the same way they came, the sec men were halfway across the dining room when they heard a steady chatter of gunshots. Oddly, nobody was killed or even wounded on the floor, nor was any furniture damaged from missed rounds or ricochets. The machine gun chattered once more, and the old chains supporting the enormous crystal chandeliers snapped, dropping the entire row onto the sec men, crushing most of them to death instantly.

''Ambush!'' Overton cried, spraying the balcony with a long stuttering burst from the bulky Thompson. Wood chips flew off the banister along the entire front of the room, as he turned and hosed the walls randomly, hoping for a lucky strike. When satisfied, Overton raced out of the dining room and down the front corridor.

At the front door, he stuck out the Thompson and sprayed bullets around in a circle. Cries of pain announced multiple hits, and he charged out of the fortress still shooting indiscriminately. As he reached the street, a glance at the tiny indicator on top of the weapon showed it was only down a hundred rounds.

Firing sporadically at anything that moved, Overton reached the barn and chilled a trio of civilians hiding there among the bales of hay. The horses were whinnying in fear in their stalls, but saddles hung in front of each gate. Fumbling with a saddle, blaster tight in his grip, Overton chose a big stallion that looked as if it had lots of stamina. Throwing on the saddle blanket and leather saddle, then cinching the girth tight, he dropped the stirrups and climbed on the horse.

Guiding it toward the doorway, Overton cut loose at a group of men entering the barn. The chattering Thompson decimated the civilians, who jerked and flinched as if stung by a million hornets. Blood splattered everywhere. Then his horse reared at the noisy weapon, and Overton was forced to stop firing to use both hands to control the beast.

The terrified horse didn't want to walk through the morass of fresh bodies, so the big man drew his knife and pricked the animal in the rump, swearing over the fact he had no spurs.

Nickering, the stallion walked forward, occasionally stepping on a hand or a leg when it couldn't be avoided. A few of the people screamed in pain, but that only hurried the animal along and soon Overton reached the street.

Turning in the saddle for a moment, the would-be baron sprayed the other horses in the barn with the Thompson, waving the flaming barrel as if conducting an orchestra. Dust and splinters erupted off the stalls from misses, but one by one the trapped animals dropped, his own mount trembling fearfully now at the awful smell of horse blood.

When every mount was bleeding profusely, Overton kicked his stallion into a canter and headed for the drawbridge, shooting at any open window and door just to be safe.

THE IRREGULAR BLASTERFIRE sounded distant to Doc in the gatehouse, but the plodding steps of a horse coming toward him were loud and clear. Snatching an AK-47, Doc waited behind the barred window trying to breathe calmly. There had been a loud blast a short while ago, and the top of the keep was no longer visible above the parapets. But did that mean Nathan and Ryan were winning the fight, or had already lost the battle for control of the ville? Was this relief coming or an execution squad?

The hoofbeats had a sharp sound to them, which meant shod hooves. No plow horse, then, but a baron's mount, or an officer's. And just a lone animal, so it wasn't a hunting party or troops. Perhaps one of the baron's horses escaped and was running away from all the noise. That made sense.

The clatter of iron hooves on cobblestones grew louder until a magnificent dappled stallion rode into view. In the saddle was a well-dressed figure, carrying a canvas bag and a huge blaster.

"Overton!" Doc whispered in a mix of delight and shock. The baron seemed just as startled to see him in the kiosk instead of his blue-shirted sec men. Aiming the AK-47 to avoid hitting the horse, Doc fired the weapon at the hated enemy.

The rounds hit Overton several times in the chest, and he hosed Doc with the stuttering Tommy gun, the tiny rounds striking the kiosk, floor, walls and bars with ringing force. A pain stabbed Doc in the shoulder, and he was thrown to the side, dropping the AK-47. Doc fought the pain and tried to draw his pistol.

Twisted sideways in the saddle, Overton was too high up to target Doc. He sprayed a wild burst from the odd blaster before leaning in to the kiosk and tripping the lever to lower the drawbridge. He then kicked the stallion into a full gallop and rode over the drawbridge and across the grassy fields.

"Egad, a vest!" Doc fumed in outrage. "The dastardly blackguard is wearing a bulletproof vest!"

A tiny piece of his mind wondered where the man was getting this predark military equipment, but he shoved that question aside for later as he scrambled to his feet and rushed into the tunnel. Fisting the LeMat, he ignored the pain in his arm and tightly held the blaster in both hands, aiming it at the hastily departing baron. Carefully, Doc tracked the rhythmic gait of man and horse as they raced over the ground. Seconds passed, and Overton was perilously near the trees when Doc finally fired.

The handcannon boomed, and Overton bucked in the saddle, nearly falling out, blood spraying from his left thigh. Dropping the Thompson, he struggled with the reins and managed to stay on the horse as it galloped into the woods and out of sight.

A FEW MINUTES LATER, Ryan and the others arrived at the gatehouse, panting from the long run.

"Dark night!" J.B. raged, throwing his hat on the ground. "We saw the bastard on the bridge but couldn't chance a shot because we were afraid of hitting you."

"Well, I did hit him," Doc said, holding a hand to his upper arm. Blood was seeping between his bony fingers, but only a small trickle. "Shot him several times, in fact, but the egg-sucker is wearing a vest!"

"Bulletproof?" Jak asked, scowling.

"Most assuredly."

"Son of a bitch."

"Now, where did he find one of those?" Nathan asked, resting his longblaster across his shoulders. "Hell, where did he get any of his supplies?"

"Who cares?" Dean wheezed, holding his side to

help ease a stitch from the long-distance running. The others had done this only once, but it was the second time for him. "L-let him go. We won the fight!"

"But did we win the war?" J.B. asked succinctly.

"Unknown," Ryan snarled, brushing the hair from his scarred face. "The son of a bitch will only return with more troops. I've meet his type before. They never stop until they're dead."

"Any more horses?" Doc asked, leaning against the brick wall.

"Too weak," Jak said, touching the man on the shoulder. "Shot."

Doc winced at the contact, but stayed firm. "Nonsense. That trifle will not even slow me!"

"Doesn't matter," J.B. stated glumly. "He killed all of the horses in the stable. Or at least badly wounded them."

"Did Clem return with the truck?" Ryan demanded, clenching a fist.

"Not through this locale," Doc answered. "At least, not since I have been here."

Nathan grimaced. "We have several wags. But unfortunately, they are at Ox Bow, near the fuel dump. My sec chief wanted them away from Overton in case of emergencies. And I wasn't planning on leaving the ville alive."

A good notion that just backfired on them.

Ryan stepped farther into the tunnel as if going to chase after the man on foot. There had to be something they could do. He couldn't let the coldheart escape alive to strike at them again. This matter would never be over until one of them was buried in the dirt with his throat cut.

"Hey, Dad, weren't there some motorcycles in that garage?" Dean asked, scratching his head in thought.

Chapter Nineteen

The sun was creeping toward the horizon when a roaring sound filled the ville courtyard. Ryan charged through the gatehouse tunnel, hunched low over the handlebars of a badly battered motorcycle. The windshield was gone, only jagged pieces of glass remaining to line the support bar like a wall of transparent daggers. The engine was discolored from the C-4 blast, the frame shook at every bump and blue smoke poured from the exhaust. But it did run, and this was the best of the three bikes from the garage.

How Krysty had survived the explosion he chalked up to sheer luck. By all accounts, she should have been blown to bits. Yet according to J.B., she had never been in any real danger from the poison gas, since it was lighter than air. Maybe Overton had brought the stuff along to toss into the front door of the keep and have it waft up the stairs, clearing out Nathan's sec men if they had made a last stand there.

"South!" Doc shouted at the top of his lungs as the motorcycle sped by at forty miles per hour.

Slowing to try to control the shakes caused by the irregular cobblestones, Ryan shot the man a puzzled glance, then nodded in understanding. Overton had been spotted by somebody. Good. Twisting the throttle on the handlebars, he gunned the 200 cc engine to the max and roared off again, spewing oil and gas in his wake.

Along with the assorted damage, the bike possessed a holster that was a perfect fit for an AK-47, so Ryan had one of the blasters tucked in there, but he had his Steyr and another Kalashnikov strapped across his back. It would be hours if not more before Nathan could get another motorcycle fixed, or have people run to Ox Bow near the Sorrow River and drive back a wag. Ryan was alone on this chase, so he brought along every blaster he could carry. There was even a spare knife from Krysty tucked into his boot, a thirteen-inch parkerized blade, sharper than a lie from a friend.

Even with the extra armament, Ryan knew he was at a serious disadvantage. The bike made a lot of noise, and the horse was quiet. But the bike had ten times the speed, and hopefully that would make the difference.

Roaring through the forest road, Ryan waited for a clear section of road and killed the engine. The soil crunched beneath his tires, the wind sighed past his ears and the hot metal of the internal combustion engine ticked as it contracted. Ryan tried to hear beyond those noises, and distinctly heard a horse whinny in the distance. To his left?

It sounded again. Yes, to his left. Twisting the handlebar throttle, Ryan restarted the engine and eased in the clutch, jumping forward with renewed speed. An unseen rain gully almost toppled him from his ungainly mount, but he fought the wobble in the bent frame, staying erect and moving.

The road took a curve, and suddenly a fork was ahead of him. Ryan stopped the bike and killed the engine, trying not to breathe so he could hear. But nothing was discernible except the chirp of the cicadas in the tall weeds, an owl hooting, a cougar's scream claiming the whole valley as its personal territory.

"Come on, you bastard, curse the horse," Ryan muttered to himself. Silence ruled the darkening Virginia forest, and the autumn sun was already touching the tall treetops.

Squinting, Ryan studied the ground, but the light was waning. He dared not turn on the bike's headlight, if it still worked, as that would announce his presence more than the roar of the blasted engine. Unfortunately, a galloping horse and running men churned the dirt equally, so he glanced around for horse droppings, or blood from Overton's wound. But there was nothing, not a clue.

The right branch headed for Shersville, the left roughly south toward the limestone hills of a predark battlefield. There were caves, but those were the abode of a deadly group of blood-drinking muties. Much farther south, the road led straight to a glowing blast crater, one of the many misses from skydark. The rad count was so high there that even driving by the glass-lined hole in a speeding wag gave a person a fatal dose of rad poisoning. Right was the logical choice, but would Overton go south exactly because it had no clear destination? The choice was fifty-fifty. Time for a gamble.

It took a few tries to restart the bike, and Ryan was dismayed to see how much fuel he had used in so short a trip. The ramshackle machine would be drained in another half hour.

Charging up the right fork, Ryan pushed the motorcycle hard, watching the tachometer climb dangerously as he dodged rocks and potholes. The noise of the bike would give Overton a chance to get off the road and hide. Only speed would let him catch the man, but the faster he went, the more fuel he used. It was all a wild gamble at that point, so Ryan settled it, concentrating on keeping the rattling piece of junk from falling over as he sped through the growing twilight.

Then it occurred to him that he wasn't being covert anymore. He could use the headlight to gain himself dozens of yards of visibility. He tapped the switch, and the big light flared on in supernatural brilliance, the beam a stark blue, illuminating the roadway ahead for a good hundred yards.

Halogen lamps, he realized, his first lucky break.

The speedometer climbed to the fifty mark and stayed in the vicinity, as the miles flew beneath the clattering two-wheeler. Ryan's suspicions grew as did the distance, and finally he was forced to accept the fact that either Overton had outmaneuvered him or taken the other fork.

Braking to a stop as quickly as possible, Ryan dragged the rear wheel about in a fast turn and started back down the road at breakneck speed. Zooming past the fork, he reached a flat section of ground and opened the throttle completely. The hungry engine thundered between his thighs, making his bones throb. The needle on the gas gauge was dropping visibly, the engine temperature at redline, ready to blow. Ryan was going seventy when he spotted the galloping horse.

Coaxing a few extra miles per hour from the struggling machine, he roared past the racing animal, leaving a contrail of blue smoke in his wake. The horse screamed in terror and reared on its hind legs, toppling and crashing to the ground.

Braking to a shuddering halt, Ryan wheeled about and returned much slower, the silenced SIG-Sauer tight in his grip. The animal galloped into the bushes at his approach, tripping on fallen trees in its haste to get away. Instantly, Ryan knew Overton was nowhere nearby. The man had killed other horses in front of this one, so the animal wouldn't be running toward the murderer. Horses were extremely smart and very proud. They remembered riders by their smells and faces, and they recalled every indignity they suffered. If Overton was in the area, the animal would have a definite direction it would run from. This was merely chaotic charging. The would-be baron had to have abandoned the animal earlier down the road and gone into the woods.

Breathing heavily, his legs almost burning from the awful heat of the bike, Ryan tried to guess when the coldheart first set the animal loose. He guessed the timing at a mile. But Overton had to have jumped off as soon as he heard the bike, so…say another quarter to a half mile before that.

"Fireblast, that's a lot of ground to cover," Ryan muttered angrily, wiping the sweat off his face with a sleeve. This job was fast becoming impossible. Now he was guessing on top of guesses.

Returning the way he had come, Ryan counted off a mile, then chose a point one-third of a mile beyond. When in doubt, go for the middle, as the Trader used to say. That always gave you some leeway in case of a miss.

Kicking down the stand, Ryan throttled the engine to an irregular idle with the brilliant headlight washing the roadway and into the trees. Crossing to the other side in the shadow of the beam, Ryan walked slowly, looking for any indication of where Overton might have jumped off. The Deathlands warrior knew that time was against him, but it was his only chance. At dawn, Ryan could come back with a hundred sec men from Front Royal and sweep this area of the forest. However, Overton would be long gone by then. There had been hardtack and blankets in the stable for ville sec men to take with them on long rides, but Overton hadn't grabbed any, even though the grub was in plain sight.

Blaster in hand, Ryan proceeded along the dim shoulder of the roadway, total darkness descending as the sun dipped behind the trees. Without food, running away couldn't be his plan. The bastard had some local goal in mind, close enough so that food wouldn't be a problem.

A stuttering sound erupted up in the trees, and the headlight of the bike shattered, plunging the road into darkness. Dropping to his belly, Ryan grabbed a stone and, throwing it into the bushes, screamed in pain. It landed with a clatter near the bike.

The tree branches rustled, and a figure in black lowered himself to the ground, cradling a longblaster of some kind. The weapon fired a long burst at the motorcycle, a flower of fire ringing the vented muzzle of the sleek assault rifle. The bullets noisily punched through the machine, and the engine whoofed into flames. Since the wind was coming from the north, Ryan cupped his hands and gave a low moan, hoping the sound would travel.

The sniper seemed to buy the trick and as he started to walk closer, he dropped the spent clip and reached for a fresh magazine. With his enemy unarmed, Ryan aimed the silenced barrel of the SIG-Sauer at the man and fired six times. Sparks flew from the rounds as they struck the Kalashnikov, but the other bullets garnished meaty thumps, and the would-be killer crumpled to the dirt road. His heart pounding, Ryan quietly stood and walked forward to see whom he had just chilled.

The dancing light of the burning bike cast bizarre shadows across the surrounding forest, and Ryan had to drop to his knees to get a close look at the dead man. The face was clean shaved, the hair long. Mentally crossing his fingers, Ryan flicked his butane lighter and saw it was just another blue shirt and not Overton. The sec man was heavily armed, but so was Ryan, so he left the corpse with its blasters and ammo. Only a fool took more than he could carry. Being slow was as deadly as being unarmed in the Deathlands.

Scrambling down the gravel incline of the roadway into the forest, Ryan moved stealthily through the bush, circling into the greenery until the gasoline fire was a flickering spot of light. Now anybody else waiting in ambush would be silhouetted by the flames, and a perfect target.

Stepping from mossy rock to bare stones, Ryan avoided the dry autumn leaves and headed deeper into the trees, searching for the reserve man in the ambush. Overton wouldn't be stupid enough to send only one man to try to chill him. Caution was called for here. The swift always died first.

The thick canopy of branches overhead blocked any possible view of the stars. Then a cough made Ryan go motionless. There was a brief flare of spitting light, and a man's face was illuminated as he lit a cig. He shook the flame out, briefly showing the Remington shotgun cradled in the crook of his arm.

Drawing his panga with his free hand, Ryan circled around the guard. Contentedly, the man puffed away before finally dropping the butt and grinding it under his heel. As he stood straight, a cold sliver of metal rested on his throat and gouged his flesh.

"Not a word," Ryan said, easing the shotgun out of the man's grip and tossing it aside. "Any more guards around?"

"No."

"Good, then you get to live for a while." Ryan walked in front of the man and pressed the barrel of the SIG-Sauer against his temple. "Where's Overton?"

The sec man stood in the darkness breathing heavily, estimating his chances for a break, so reluctantly Ryan rapped him across the face with the blaster. Gasping in pain, the man dropped to his knees, blood flowing between his fingers.

"You bastard," he choked.

"Overton," Ryan demanded once more.

"Fuck you, traitor," growled the blue shirt, glaring hatefully upward.

The word caught Ryan by surprise. "Traitor?"

"We were going to repair America, make her great again by chilling the muties and cleansing the rad pits," the man said, painfully standing. "But you stopped him. A man whose boots you aren't worthy to lick."

"Clean the nuke blaster craters? You're crazy," Ryan said, leveling his blaster. "Overton is just a man, like you and me, nobody special. Nobody can repair the world, make it like it was again."

"Screw the world," the man snarled. "I said America. Let the rest of the half-breeds and Commies die in the rad pits and acid storms. What do we care?"

Ryan nudged the sec man with the blaster. "Right. Overton knows some way to stop the acid rains. And exactly how was this miracle going to happen?"

The blue shirt seemed startled by the question, his face taking on a cunning demeanor. "You don't know," he said as if just coming to the realization. "No, I can see that you have no real idea of what was happening at Front Royal."

"So tell me."

"Of course," he said coolly, and breathed deeply.

In sudden realization, Ryan knew the man was going to shout a warning, and no mere blow would stop him. With no other choice, Ryan squeezed the trigger, and the SIG-Sauer coughed softly in the night. The corpse folded to the ground, hardly disturbing the dry leaves.

Ryan started forward, the silenced muzzle of the deadly 9 mm blaster leading the way in the stygian greenery. If the man was going to shout for help, that meant others were close enough to hear him. Moving in a spiral search pattern, Ryan tried to concentrate on the task, but he kept hearing the man's last words. The blue shirt had truly believed that Overton knew some way to repair all of the damage caused by skydark. Complete crap. Yet the absolute conviction of the man bothered the Deathlands warrior.

You have no real idea of what was happening at Front Royal.

He shook it off. It was just bullshit from a man trying to talk his way out of death. Ryan had seen it before, and done it himself on occasion. Condemned men being walked to the gallows claimed to be the President of the United States, or able to cure the red shakes, and all sorts of crazy things. Kept making wild claims until they dropped the floor out from underneath him. That was all. Just crazy talk. Nothing more.

Starting to part a bush, Ryan felt something odd on his hand and drew it back to see. There was a line of blood across his palm.

Using the blade of the panga to separate the leaves, Ryan found coils of concertina wire strung through the greenery, attached to each tree in a long curving line. It was an imposing barrier to animals and muties. Listening with his whole body, Ryan seemed to hear steps coming this way. Perhaps it was a perimeter guard walking patrol. Good.

Crouching low, he readied the panga. The arc of the knife was perfect for slitting throats. Then Ryan reconsidered and drew the silenced SIG-Sauer instead. The man knew he was tired when such simple decisions had to be debated. Perhaps he should leave and come back in the morning with fresh troops.

But Overton might be doing the same, and instead of them hunting down the escaped baron, it could be full warfare between their sec men. More important, if the bastard had an LAV 25 hidden in the ville and carried AK-47 assault rifles, what other military hardware might he have access to come dawn? No, better to strike now, while Overton was wounded and on the run.

As the darkness coalesced into a man-shaped figure, Ryan waited until he saw the Kalashnikov and blue shirt, then chilled the sentry on the spot. Moving along the wire, Ryan found six more perimeter guards, and each followed the first into death.

Past a stand of trees, Ryan found a crude roadway with tripods made of sharpened tree trunks. Oil lanterns hanging from poles washed the path with deadly illumination. Clearly, that wasn't the way inside if Ryan wanted to keep breathing.

Knowing that the sentries would be missed soon, Ryan retreated a hundred feet, then cut through the lowest section of the concertina wire with the serrated spine of Krysty's knife. Already the weapon had proved its worth. Sliding through the small opening, he eased past the trees. Soft light was shining ahead, and Ryan went to ground, crawling closer until he reached the edge of the bushes encircling a huge clearing.

A low hill protruded from the ground, the curved

crest of the natural limestone hill lush with plants. He spotted a satellite dish, and the sight chilled his blood. There were no more working satellites that he know about, and the few the companions had ever encountered had always been trouble in spades, though one had once saved their lives. Sighting through the scope of the Steyr, Ryan relaxed a notch when he saw loose cable dangling from the dish. It wasn't working yet.

The mouth of a small cave fronted the hill, the opening squared off with timbers and some fresh brick work. Inside were stacks of crates in neat rows, as if organized into categories.

A mint-condition LAV 25 was parked outside, its angular prow pointing outward so the men in the hill could climb safely into the rear doors of the wag. That was when Ryan spotted another of the deadly war wags off to the side of the clearing. Both were fully armed assault platforms, Piranha class, with electric chain gun, cannon and minirockets. They were two horribly lethal juggernauts from another time, their armored bodies clean and rust free, the tires shiny black. In their present positions, the machines would give optimum cross fire on any enemy coming through the break in the trees.

Directly across the clearing, squaring off the cave, the LAV and the dirt road, was a granite outcropping, or perhaps a boulder, set in a small indentation in the forest. It was a perfect spot to spy on the campsite.

Avoiding the area completely, Ryan crawled through the tangles of thorny bushes until reaching the second APC. He shimmied underneath the chassis, watching for antipersonnel mines or sensors. But there was only the smell of dirty grease and lubricants from any transport used to cross wild country.

Peering out between the heavy studded tires, Ryan

observed a crackling fire hidden in a low pit. Squatting around the flames was a platoon of sec men, sipping coffee sub brewed in a huge steel pot suspended over the fire by a metal grid. Their conversation was low and unhurried, as if they had nothing to worry about.

Ryan quickly abandoned his plan to try to capture or kill Overton. This wasn't a campsite; it was a military outpost. Whatever Overton was doing here would have to wait until morning when Ryan could return with more troops from Front Royal.

Backing away under the predark vehicle, Ryan froze as Overton limped out of the cave. The man was wearing clean clothes, and using the stock of an M-60 machine rifle as a cane.

Hobbling closer, Overton asked the men around the fire a question. They responded, and the black-haired man lifted a whistle to his lips and blew hard, the shrill noise shattering the peaceful night.

"I know you're here, Father," he shouted, the words echoing slightly in the woods. "There's an electric current flowing through the concertina wire. When you cut the strands, it instantly informed us of a break. One might be an animal or an accident, but four mean it's you. The hole is now covered with ten armed sec men, the wire already replaced."

Could be true, could be bullshit, Ryan thought. But there had been a slight tingle when he cut the wires and he thought nothing of it at the time. Now he was in their camp, with the noose closing. Glancing at the dirt path, Ryan saw blue shirts walking the wooden tripods across the road, trailing glittering coils of the concertina wire to seal off the exit.

Quickly, Ryan reviewed his weapons. He'd lost a longblaster with the bike, but he still had the Steyr with five reloads, an AK-47 with one extra clip, the SIG-Sauer with three magazines and a couple of knives. It was nowhere near sufficient for a stand-up fight, especially when he was outgunned and outmanned. Okay, when losing at a crooked card game, a wise man kicked over the table.

"Come out, Ryan, and we can talk this over like gentlemen," Overton shouted, staring into the darkness.

Ignoring that nonsense, Ryan placed a hand on the belly of the wag above him, but felt no movement. Taking a risk, he eased open the belly hatch with his knife-point the way the Trader had taught him so long ago. As Ryan swung aside the steel plate, a sec man in the driver's seat turned and gasped. Then the blue shirt rocked backward, the handle of Krysty's knife protruding from his neck. As quietly as he could, Ryan pulled himself inside and closed the belly hatch, then slid home the heavy sec bolt that nobody ever used. It simply took too long to open if you were trying to get out in a hurry.

The driver was struggling with the seat belt, trying to get free. Ryan neatly finished off the dying man with his panga, retrieved Krysty's knife and checked the indicators. Plenty of fuel, nuke batteries at full power. He flipped a couple of switches and moved to the turret.

"Ryan?" Overton called, bringing the huge M-60 to rest on a shoulder as if it weighed no more than a common rifle.

Climbing up the step, Ryan fumbled with the ammo belt for the 25 mm cannon, finally getting it to feed properly into the breech by sheer determination. Without the big Detroit engines to supply electricity, the batteries would soon drain from operating the electricity-driven weapon. But in those few minutes, Ryan would blow himself a hole to freedom straight through Overton.

"All right, then—die, traitor!" Overton shouted, working the bolt of the M-60 and chambering the first round of the long ammo belt dangling from the side of the weapon. "Alpha, full perimeter sweep! Beta, secure the cave. Gamma, stand by me."

"Traitor, my ass," Ryan said, tripping the controls. The cannon jerked at his delicate touch and started hosing the campsite with 25 mm shells.

Dropping his weapon, Overton dived for cover as powerful detonations raked the clearing. Men simply disintegrated under the hellish barrage and the ground seemed to boil. The mouth of the cave collapsed explosively, partially sealing off the opening. In a screech of tortured metal, the antenna dish folded over and tumbled off the hill, crumpling as it impacted on the grass.

One sec man stayed sitting near the campfire, a cup of coffee sub in his hands. Ryan thought the man was paralyzed with fear until he noticed the sliver of metal sticking through the man's chest, nailing him in place to a wooden crate behind.

The headlights of the other LAV clicked on as the big engine roared to life. On battery power, Ryan wasted precious seconds completely destroying the other APC, the predark depleted-uranium rounds punching through the thick military armor as if it were cardboard. When the first wag burst into flames, the Deathlands warrior finally dared to move onward, raking the forest and road with thundering death.

Bright flowers of muzzle-flashes dotted the darkness from return fire, and a hundred rounds bounced off the APC, sounding like rain on a tin roof. The hot spent shells rained upon the metal floor at his boots, the ringing noise deafening without protective covering on his ears. With the trigger locked into position, Ryan turned the turret in a full circle, shooting into the trees and bushes. Screams peppered the nonstop explosions, and fires were burning all over the clearing.

A gren boomed near the LAV, throwing dirt onto the hull. Then another hit the prow, igniting with a swell and casting a thick sheet of fire across the wag. A wave of searing heat flooded in through the vents, carrying the metallic stink of thermite. They were trying to melt the APC from underneath him!

Just then, a warning light started to flash as Ryan swept the clearing again and the cannon stopped abruptly, the ammo bin completely empty. Dropping out of the turret, Ryan hit the munitions locker and grabbed a fresh belt of 25 mm rounds. The linked shells were incredibly heavy, and it was an effort for him to drag the belt into the turret. Reloading was supposed to be a two-man job.

Blinking away the sweat running off his face due to the rising temperature inside the wag, Ryan fought apart the hot breech of the cannon, then spied Overton walking out of the cave carrying a short plastic tube. He extended the tube to nearly double its length, a sight popping up from the top and a pistollike handle dropping down from the bottom.

With a bitter curse, Ryan dropped the ammo belt and scrambled from the turret. Clawing at the handle of the rear door, he charged into the cool darkness.

A lance of flame reached out from the tube to slam into the fire-coated APC and violently explode, the blast lifting the wag off the ground and throwing it sideways. The noise of the massive blast rumbled over the forest.

Still running, Ryan was slapped against the ground by the sheer force of the concussion.

"Now!" Overton commanded, and the night vanished in a crash of illumination, clusters of halogen bulbs on the top of poles lighting the area as bright as day.

Caught totally by surprise, Ryan found himself trapped in plain sight. Yards away from the forest, he dived behind the crumpled ruins of the satellite dish. Drawing his blaster, Ryan emptied an entire clip at the closest pole, and the lights died as the glass shattered. But that was only one out of many.

"You're trapped!" Overton roared, working the bolt on the M-60, being extra careful not to break a finger on the powerful spring. "Chill the son of a bitch!"

A score of blasters from every direction spoke at once, sending waves of rounds into the resilient plastic dish. Designed to withstand the worst possible of storms, the antenna still cracked under the fusillade of bullets. Then the M-60 spoke, the large 7.62 mm rounds stitching a line of holes clear through the material.

Crouching low behind a crushed corpse, Ryan seized the man's AK-47 and fired a return volley. A mound of loose dirt was at his rear, offering some protection, but the dish was being torn to pieces, and he was still horribly outnumbered. Ryan knew he better get clever real fast or else he was meat in a box.

The barrage slowed for a moment, and Ryan stood, emptying the AK-47 at the fuel drums inside the cave. But the angle was wrong, and he couldn't reach the barrels without dangerously exposing himself to lethal return fire.

"You had a chance to surrender," Overton snarled, laying a fresh belt of linked ammo into the hot breech of his big blaster. Spent shells lay at his boots like golden offerings to a primitive war god. "Too late now, dear Father!"

As a reply, Ryan stood and threw his only spare ammo clip for the AK-47 into the smoldering campfire.

"Incoming!" Overton cried, as the rounds started to cook off, bullets flying every which way in a totally random pattern.

Inside the cave, a sec man cried out, a red stain spreading over his stomach. A crate burst apart, spilling MRE packs, and a fuel barrel dented deeply enough to start oozing fuel like tears from a dead eye. But there was no detonation.

"You three, maintain cover fire!" Overton shouted from behind a timber from the fallen entrance of the limestone hill. The man was brandishing a huge hand-cannon, with the deadly M-60 lying near the campfire. "Shoot in shifts, one reloading while the others keep firing. You four, circle to the right, you and you to the left. Block his escape and chill the bastard on sight!"

Bullets drilled into the curved expanse of the antenna steadily, ricocheting off the metal support struts.

Staying low, Ryan didn't dare stand, knowing it was certain death. Pawing through the bloody clothes of the dead men under the dish, the one-eyed man found the wrong half of an AK-47, a bent knife and a single gren.

Bullets zipped through the trees on either side, the cross fire closing in like the mandibles of an army of killer ants. Mentally, Ryan tried to gauge the distance to the fuel dump. The resulting blast would obliterate this whole outpost, chilling him just as surely as the blue shirts. But if Ryan Cawdor was going to die, then he would take Overton and his troops along for the ride.

Pulling the pin, Ryan stood and prepared to charge.

Chapter Twenty

A loud crashing in the trees behind Ryan made him turn, gren and blaster at the ready.

Incredibly, a flatbed truck festooned with sandbags smashed through the burning bushes. Trailing coils of concertina wire, the truck braked to a halt between the smoking wreck of the LAV and the battered satellite dish. Clem was at the steering wheel, with Mildred in the passenger's seat. Throwing open the doors, both started to fire their blasters as the rest of the companions and twenty Front Royal browns cut loose from the rear of the bedraggled vehicle. A dozen blue shirts dropped before the rest could shift positions and return fire.

Suddenly, Nathan Cawdor jumped from the truck and pointed at the limestone hill. "Kill!" he shouted, and a pack of Front Royal hunting dogs surged out of the wag to silently charge across the clearing.

Screaming in fear, two of the sec men dropped their weapons and ran for the cave. The dogs tore them apart in passing and kept going. But the rest of the blue shirts stood their ground and cut the beasts to pieces. One bleeding hound managed to reach the sec men and leaped, burying its fangs into a man's throat before the others could blow off its head.

The wounded man lay on the ground screaming, blood squirting into the air, until Overton himself shot the man. Amid the confusion, Ryan darted for the truck, pausing to throw the gren. It bounced off a wooden crate of MRE packs and sailed into the interior. A second later, the cave shook from an explosion, but again the fuel dump didn't ignite. Then the halogen lights on the tall poles clicked off, plunging the campsite into darkness. Only the tiny fires of burning wreckage and the red embers of the dying campfire marred the black night.

"Nice to see you alive," J.B. snapped, firing the Uzi at some darting figures in the shadows.

"Same here. How the hell did you find me?" he asked, dropping the spent Kalashnikov and working the bolt on his Steyr. "Use the dogs?"

"Indeed, my dear Ryan," Doc answered, discharging two rounds from the LeMat.

Krysty stood and snapped off some rounds from her wheelgun, and a cry told of a hit. "The engine was leaking so much oil we could have followed your trail ourselves."

Smoothly reloading the Uzi with a spare magazine from his munitions bag, J.B. gave a sideways glance at Mildred's partially untangled hair for the hundredth time. "Can't believe that fooled the blue shirts," he stated incredulously.

"It was dark," the physician answered, snapping off rounds from her blaster. "And Daffer helped divert their attention."

"How?"

Squeezing the trigger carefully, Mildred chilled a sec man with a round directly into the jugular vein of his exposed neck. The man fell back, spraying blood over the others in the cave. "Details later!"

"Spread out," Jak said, tossing aside his longblaster as the weapon emptied. "Truck big target."

"Hey, look there!" Dean cried, pointing. There was an indentation in the line of trees, and in the center of the hollow was a large granite boulder. "That's a great place to shoot at the cave!"

"Not bad," Clem agreed, coolly firing the Enfield again.

Dropping his Kalashnikov, a blue shirt spun as the heavy-caliber slug took him in the ribs and he fell out of sight behind a crate.

"Let's go!" Eagerly, Dean started off, intending to circle the clearing.

J.B. grabbed a fistful of shirt, stopping the boy. "Stay away from there," the Armorer warned.

Nathan dropped a clip from his AK-47 and slid in his last. "Why?" he asked. "Looks perfect."

"It is," Ryan said, searching for Overton through the scope of his longblaster. "That's the problem."

Shoving shells into a shotgun, the sec man next to Nathan cried out and fell sprawling, a crimson stain spreading across his brown shirt.

"What the—? He was back-shot!" Ryan stated, and he whirled, firing from the hip. "The bastards got behind us somehow!"

Barely visible in the dying firelight, men were climbing over the ruined barricade on the dirt road. Rummaging in his munitions bag, J.B. quickly armed and fired the flare gun into the sky. As the rocket ignited, brilliant green light washed over the clearing, showing dozens upon dozens of armed sec men dressed in the fancy embroidered livery of Casanova ville.

"Look, that's Baron Cawdor!" a sergeant shouted, pointing triumphantly.

"We found the secret base of Front Royal!" another cried out.

"So they *were* going to invade us!"

"Kill everybody!" roared a lieutenant, and the fresh troops opened fire with crossbows and a wide assortment of blasters, muzzle loaders, zip guns and patched bolt actions, apparently anything that could discharge a live round.

"Volley fire!" Overton ordered, and the blue shirts in the cave commenced a massive attack, emptying clips in seconds, only to slap in fresh magazines from a seemingly inexhaustible supply.

The tires blew out on the flatbed truck, headlights smashed, and the body rocked from the sheer amount of incoming lead. Caught between the two enemies, the companions hit the dirt and crawled away from the tilted vehicle, seeking refuge at the satellite dish. It offered less defense from bullets than the wag, but at least it had the loose dirt behind to cover their asses and didn't have a gas tank to ignite.

"Road blocked, sec men coming in, truck gone, no way to reach the trees alive," Doc muttered. "We are trapped."

"Squeezed," Jak said, brushing the snowy hair from his face. A furtive movement caught his attention, and the teenager spun and fired. A blue shirt cried out and died.

Clem calmly reloaded his longblaster. "Seen worse."

Their lieutenant shouting orders indecipherable to the companions over the gunplay, the Casanova troops moved into the clearing, intent on taking the cave, but Overton's weapon forced them back. The enemy troops took position behind the boulder, sniping steadily at the cave opening. Ricochets zinged off the rock walls, rock chips and splinters peppering the companions.

"Look where they are!" Dean spit, slapping a fresh

clip into his Browning. "I told you it was a perfect spot to attack the cave. They got a clear view of us and Overton, but we can't hit them back!"

Unexpectedly, a blue shirt dashed from behind a pile of crates, heading for the campfire pit. He was viciously cut to pieces by the withering Casanova cross fire.

"Yes, it is perfect," Ryan stated, thumbing a fresh rotary clip into his rifle.

Minutes passed with the three groups exchanging fire, but nothing more.

With a growing feeling of unease, Nathan realized that he was holding back in the fight, not daring to risk overexposing himself to the enemy fire. The news from Mildred had shaken him greatly, even though it was all good. His wife lived, and they had a son, an heir to the ville. But the baron couldn't die until knowing for certain that Overton was dead and they were safe. The survival of his family was paramount, infinitely more important than the ville and its people. A good baron would die to protect his ville, but a father owed more than that to his family. And Nathan had a son, damn it. A son!

"What's Overton waiting for?" Ryan demanded irritably.

The Deathlands warrior knew the boulder was a trap of some kind, probably buried explosives with hidden fuses. Fairly standard deployment, and it explained why the rock was so far away from the cave. Only a fool would leave a perfect location for enemies to snipe at his campsite completely unguarded, and for all the things he was, Overton was no fool. Hell, the Trader had used the same trick himself many times in the past. Ryan, too.

"Mebbe they were damaged by the gren you threw

in,'' J.B. suggested. "No, if they were hit by the blast, they should have ignited.''

"Under collapse?'' Jak asked, firing randomly at both groups. No cries of pain answered his shots.

"Or they're not in the cave,'' Ryan said slowly, levering in another round. "Could be hidden elsewhere.''

"Where?'' Mildred asked, choosing her targets carefully with her ZKR revolver. J.B. passed her the shotgun, and she removed the shells from the shoulder strap and quickly loaded the scattergun.

Following their lead, Nathan switched his AK-47 to single shot to conserve ammo. "Might be anywhere.''

"However, if the fuses aren't in the cave,'' Krysty said, "then fuses for the cave should be there, too.''

The woman had recognized the trap as soon as they entered the clearing. However, all swords had two edges. If there were secret fuses leading to bombs to blow up invaders, there also had to be more explosives hidden inside the cave in case the enemy seized the limestone hill and Overton had to destroy his own weapons so they couldn't be used against him. Those fuses could end this whole battle for either side in only seconds. Only, where the hell were they?

"Fuses?'' asked Dean, confused.

Frowning, Clem studied the battlefield. "Only one way to find them, you know,'' he drawled.

"Yeah, I know,'' Ryan growled. "Makes me sick just to think about it, but we got no other way. It's this or die.''

"Well, heck,'' the hunter replied. "Ain't no choice there.''

"Hey, Overton!'' Ryan shouted through cupped hands.

Silence from the cave.

"I know you can hear me," the one-eyed man called. "We need to talk."

"You need to die, traitor," came a shout, and a grenade bounded out of the cave.

Mildred fired the shotgun, showering the area with shrapnel but harming nobody in particular.

"Cut the shit and tell us where the fuses are hidden," Ryan shouted. "They're obviously not in the cave, or else you would have used them already."

More silence.

"Tell us, and we'll use them on the others!"

Nothing.

The words tasted as bitter as ash in Ryan's mouth, but the Trader had always said only a fool fought to the death when he had another way out. "Tell us, and I give my word that you and your men live."

A bellowing laugh. "Live as starving slaves in the baron's dung pit? Fuck you."

Some Casanova men tried a sortie to reach the truck, and never made it halfway there.

"We let you live and go free," Ryan stated. "Keep your weapons, food, I'm talking a full truce. Never bother us again, and we won't go after you afterward. That's a promise."

"Horseshit," came a reply. "We don't need your help!"

"Yes, you do, and you know it, jackass!"

A softer voice said, "Sir, what if he means it? We're dead men if we stay in here."

"Listen to your man," Nathan shouted, slapping in his last clip for the longblaster. "I also give my word of honor, as the baron of Front Royal."

"We help each other, or die," Mildred added, over the booming shotgun.

Firing at the Casanova troops, Ryan added, "Your call!"

Minutes passed.

"Agreed," Overton shouted, blowing thunder at the enemy with his huge M-60. Every man hit flipped over as if struck by a cannonball. But more of the Casanova sec men darted amid the wreckage and the rock. "They're over here, under the avalanche."

"By the Three Kennedys!" Doc intoned, staring at the small mountain of dirt and grass covering the left face of the hill. "How are we supposed to move a ton of dirt while under attack?"

"Any C-4?" Jak asked.

J.B. shook his head. "Not a thing. I'm out."

"I was saving this for our retreat," Nathan said unexpectedly, dropping his backpack, "but now I see it'll serve us better as a shovel."

"Rock out of range?" Ryan asked gruffly.

"Unfortunately, yes."

"Excuse me, my lord," said a sec man, fumbling to load his rifle with a bloody hand. "But now that we know where the fuses are..." He left the sentence unfinished.

"I gave my word, Sergeant," Nathan said coldly, kneeling to open the pack.

"Yes, sir. Of course. My mistake."

Tugging open the canvas sack, Nathan withdrew the ungainly object from within. It was the MM-1 multiround gren launcher from the fortress. Angling the wide barrel of the weapon upward slightly, Nathan took a stance and fired. The blaster gave a soft thump, and the 38 mm gren smacked directly into the loose dirt, blowing away a huge gout of soil, but more immediately tumbled down the slope to fill the hole.

"Sure hope that doesn't set them off," Krysty said.

Doc snorted. "If it does, what difference does it make?"

"Good point."

Again and again, the baron triggered the gren launcher, slowly digging a hole in the crumbling dirt until the wooden top of a buried crate was exposed.

"That's it," Ryan said, dropping his heavy coat and readying his weapons. "Get those bastards busy while I take care of business."

"Got you covered," J.B. announced, and he fired another flare into the woods to the right of the boulder. The Casanova troops cried out, running away from the bright light, and retreated into safety behind the large rock. The Armorer fired again to the right of the boulder as Ryan took off at a run.

Then Nathan triggered the grenade launcher, but this time aiming for the boulder. The 38 mm rounds fell short, but when they struck the ground the blasts threw clouds of dirt into the air. Each time he fired, the weapon bucked in his two-handed grip, then the exposed wheel under the barrel rotated one notch, feeding a fresh gren into the huge maw of the ungainly weapon.

Krysty dropped her own backpack and withdrew the Thompson .22 Overton had dropped outside the ville. It had poor killing power, but should keep the Casanova troops ducked out of sight until she ran out of ammo, which would be quite a while.

"Hit them!" Krysty shouted, the Tommy gun chattering.

The rest of the companions joined her. Dean grabbed an AK-47 from a dead brown shirt and fired the weapon on full-auto. He only had a vague idea what his father was doing but had learned long ago to always trust the man. If his father thought this was their best bet, Dean agreed. End of discussion.

"Horseshit," Jak muttered, reloading his blaster quickly.

Holding the LeMat between his legs, Doc was purging the chambers of the antique wheelgun of spent powder before packing it with fresh powder and ball.

"Most assuredly, my young friend," the old man whispered, his hands moving in the ballet of military ritual. "We cannot trust Overton any more than we can the Casanova troops."

"Less," Clem said, rummaging in his pockets for loose cartridges.

Dodging the corpses and blast craters, Ryan zigzagged his way across the battlefield heading for the hole in the ground. Explosions filled the clearing, and he felt something sting him between the shoulder blades, but he kept going. Diving into the pit, he hit the dirt rolling and came up in a combat crouch. A Casanova sec man peeking out of a bush gasped at his unexpected appearance and swung a crossbow in Ryan's direction. But the one-eyed warrior already had his SIG-Sauer out and blew the man away with a shot to the temple. Half his head gone, the man flopped backward as if exceedingly tired and had decided to lie down for a nap.

Holstering his piece, Ryan started shoveling handfuls of dirt out of the hole, trying to clear away the wooden planks buried underneath. Suddenly, Overton landed sprawling alongside him. The self-proclaimed baron flipped over with his Desert Eagle handcannon out and ready, only to find Ryan pointing his 9 mm pistol at him.

For a short eternity, they stayed frozen in that position, their blasters motionless while the world outside the hole raged in combat.

"Didn't want me to use the second set of fuses leading into the cave, eh?" Ryan asked.

Overton could only stare at the man in wonder.

"Use it or lose it," Ryan stated in a voice of solid ice. "We got no time for this. Seconds count."

Relaxing his stance, Overton tucked away the blaster. "Fuses are over here."

Together, the enemies cleared away the loose dirt, then used their combat knives to pry up the boards. Below was a small wooden room, a packing crate buried in the dirt. Several plastic pipes stuck out of the slats, four heading toward the boulder, four more going toward the nearby cave. What appeared to be dirty strings dangled from the open ends of the pipes.

The men climbed inside, and the noise of the battle diminished.

Taking hold of the northern fuses, Overton patted his pockets and cursed. "Nukestorm, I dropped the matches!"

Tucking his blaster into his belt, Ryan pulled out a small butane lighter. "Any order?" he snapped impatiently.

"What?"

"Is there a sequence, damn it!"

"No," Overton replied, glowering at the older man. "No sequence. Just light any one."

"Damn amateur," Ryan grumbled, and lit every fuse there was in the northern pipes. Almost instantly, the burning strings vanished out of sight with a sizzling hiss.

Turning quickly with his blaster drawn, Ryan found

Overton in the exact same position. This time neither relaxed his stance.

"How did you know about this trap?" Overton demanded, beside himself in rage. "How did you know! Do we…do I have a traitor in my troops? Tell me, or die!"

"So much for your word of honor," Ryan said, disgusted. "But I really didn't expect any better from radblasted trash like you."

"Tell me!"

"About the fuses and the trap? Fireblast, boy, it couldn't have been more obvious. It's exactly what I would have done."

"WHAT ARE THEY DOING?" the lieutenant demanded, peering out from the side of the boulder.

The private packed his muzzle loader with a ramrod. "I think they're digging in for cover."

Struggling to clear a jam in a patchwork machine gun, a corporal growled unhappily. "Crap, it'll take us forever to squeeze them out."

"Orders, sir?" the sergeant asked, thumbing fresh rounds into a homemade shotgun.

Scowling thoughtfully, the lieutenant started to speak when the ground thunderously erupted beneath their boots, sending their broken, twisted bodies hurtling into the starry sky.

"Artillery!" shouted a sec man, backing away from the steaming blast crater.

Two more tremendous explosions occurred on either side of the gaping hole, spreading the destruction wide, claiming a dozen more men and spraying a wave of shrapnel across the rest, killing and maiming a dozen more. Breaking loose from their restraints, the terrified horses plowed through the stunned sec men, galloping madly away into the night.

"Retreat!" the sergeant ordered, and the Casanova troops broke ranks and charged for the dirt road.

Already burning, the underground fuses outraced the attackers, and a fast series of strident explosions ripped apart the dirt road, annihilating the wounded men, bloody gobbets of flesh raining across the forest for hundreds of yards.

"HOLY SHIT," Nathan whispered, lowering the gren launcher. A single live round remained in the breech of the predark cannon.

"It worked!" a brown shirt shouted.

"That's called a sequence strike," J.B. said, lighting a cheroot. "First confusing the enemy, then making them run straight into the main charge."

"Nasty," Mildred commented.

"Efficient," the Armorer corrected.

Clem and Jak made no comment, taking the opportunity to reload their weapons.

"Where's my dad?" Dean asked, looking across the dark clearing toward the well-lit cave.

"DONE," RYAN SAID, glancing at the fuses leading in the other direction, and that was when Overton made his move.

Pretending to be in pain, Overton tossed away his blaster, the movement catching Ryan's attention for a vital split second. The other man grabbed the one-eyed man's gun arm and batted the weapon to the floor.

Ryan pulled out his panga just in time to block a strike from a massive bowie knife.

"Now you're done," Overton grunted as the combatants circled each other warily. His blade was covered with ornate silver filigree, but the edge was shiny sharp. It was pretty, but highly functional.

Shuffling his feet, Overton jabbed for a quick kill, and Ryan easily blocked the thrust to his armpit. Damn, the man knew how to knife fight. That was bad news. Amateurs went for the face or belly. Pros tried for the armpits or inside the thighs. Those were the locations of major arteries, and a cut there killed quickly.

Contemptuously, Overton tossed his knife from hand to hand in a steady pattern designed to frighten and disorient a novice knife fighter. But Ryan knew that no trained knife fighter ever let go of his weapon, and that hand-to-hand thing was for idiots. It was much too easy for a quick man to kick the blade away, and you were defenseless. So only a fool would do such a thing. Or, he added, a highly trained fighter who wanted you to think he was stupid and lure you into a sucker attack.

Ryan stepped away from the giant, and he stopped.

"You're smarter than you look, old man."

"Just smarter than you is all."

The men charged. Blades clanged as they met and were deflected. Overton tried for a reverse slash, the flat side of the blade cushioned along his forearm. Ryan bent effortlessly out of the way and slashed for his forehead, drawing blood.

Shaking his head to clear his eyes, Overton flipped his blade into the air, caught it by the tip and threw. Ryan ducked again, the blade slamming into the wood slats behind him. Then he lunged and slashed at the big man's groin, but only sliced into the leather gun belt.

Smiling, Overton now drew a matched pair of knives from sheaths behind his back and advanced slowly, constantly shifting his stance and faking thrusts.

Needing a distraction, Ryan brushed a hand across his own face pushing away his eye patch. In spite of himself, Overton's gaze flicked to the puckered wound, and Ryan charged. Once more their blades clanged, throwing off sparks. Only this time, Ryan got a slice on the back of his hand, the cut nearly deep enough to sever the tendons.

Sucking on the rivulet of blood, Ryan reached into his boot and withdrew his own second knife, the parkerized Junglee Krysty had given him. The blade was strong, but no light reflected off the perfectly dulled surface of the military alloy. It wasn't pretty, just a tool for killing. Nothing more.

Overton glared at the blade, which was difficult to see in the dim light of the partially buried room. Outside, he would have a better chance of winning, but there was no way to climb to the surface without getting chilled in the process. So be it. This was their final arena.

Risking all, Overton spun fast to disorient Ryan, then lunged again, low and fast. But the Deathlands warrior met his attack with double steel, and they parted, both alive, but both bleeding from minor wounds.

Overton ran a finger across his forehead and brought it down to see the blood. The big man laughed as he licked it off. "Old trick, blinding the enemy with his own blood."

"Usually works against children," Ryan said, hoping to get a rise from the man. In circumstances like these, an angry opponent was a dead opponent.

They clashed once more, and parted, each wounded in new locations. Ryan felt blood trickle down his arm and saw Overton wince as he shifted weight to his right leg. Each was hurting, but Ryan was starting to feel his lack of sleep, and knew he was going to tire long before the giant. Time to kick over the tables again.

Throwing both knives at once, Ryan turned and yanked the blade from the wooden slat behind him, and ducked. Overton stabbed the wall full force, and Ryan stood to bury the stolen knife into the big man's chest.

Stepping clear, Ryan watched as his enemy stumbled against the wall, hacking for breath. Then, impossibly, Overton stood and gave him a wide red smile.

"B-bulletproof vest," the black-haired giant stammered. "Didn't stop the blade, never do, but slowed it enough."

Backing away, Ryan glanced around for the thrown knives, the weapons lost in the darkness.

"Goodbye, Father!" Overton roared, raising his knife high. A steady chattering sounded from beyond the pit.

Dropping the blade, Overton tumbled backward as the stream of .22 bullets stitched him from knee to shoulder, then zigzagged across his belly. Bleeding profusely, the would-be baron stood on wobbly legs for a moment, staring incredulously at the multitude of tiny wounds. Slowly, he sat on the floor and toppled over with a deep sigh.

"You gave your word, sir," said a blue shirt, lowering a smoking Thompson.

Epilogue

Within the hour, the lights of the limestone cave were working once more and brilliant illumination washed over the grisly clearing in somber clarity. Wreckage and bodies were everywhere, fire burned in the trees and the ground itself was torn asunder, the spent brass casing of a hundred blasters sprinkled across the ruined expanse.

Alertly, J.B. and Krysty stood watch as the last fifteen blue shirts piled some belongings in a Hummer and drove off into the night, destination unknown.

"Hate to let them go," Nathan said, a loaded AK-47 slung over a shoulder, his pockets bulging with clips. "But as the man said, I gave my word."

"However, sir," Doc admonished, cheerfully gesturing at the cave with his swordstick, "observe the cornucopia of supplies they have left behind for us. Crates of MRE packs, enough to feed hundreds of people. Blasters galore, a literal ton of ammunition, a second electric generator!"

"It will all be useful in rebuilding the ville," the baron agreed. "That's for damn sure."

Inside the cave, several brown shirts were going through the collection of supplies, making a quick inventory.

"And don't forget the three busted armored personnel carriers," Clem added, polishing a stain off the stock of his bolt-action Enfield. So far, there was no ammo in his caliber stored in the cave, but the hunter had no plans on giving up the new blaster until kin pried it from his dead hands.

Then Clem gave a wry smile. "What the hell, mebbe we could make one good APC out of the mess."

"Possible," Jak agreed, stropping a knife before tucking it up his sleeve. "Odd, the radio."

"You mean the way they pretended to accidentally smash it?" Nathan frowned thoughtfully. "Guess I might have done the same in their place."

"No," Jak corrected, sliding the whetstone into a pocket. "Radios don't work. Why break?"

"Why indeed," the baron mused.

Diplomatically, J.B. shifted his cigar stub from one side of his mouth to the other, but made no comment on the incident with the radio. He had a crazy idea, but wanted to discuss it with Ryan first.

Chewing on a dehydrated sandwich from an MRE pack, Dean approached the group from the cave, the light casting a long shadow ahead of the boy. "We finished removing the rest of the TNT sticks, so nobody can blow up the site underneath us," he reported with a full mouth. "Now what?"

"Inventory," Nathan said wearily. "Then we start hauling the stuff to Front Royal. The runners have already left. With luck, the wags should be here by dawn."

"Sounds good. Any word on the horses?"

The baron laughed, the sound seeming alien amid the massive destruction. "The Casanova horses are gone and forgotten. Those animals won't stop running until they reach the ocean."

Accepting that, Dean paused for a long overdue swallow. "So, what about Dad?" he asked, jerking a thumb. Over by the hole in the soil, Mildred was bandaging Ryan's wounds. There were lots of them covering his muscular form, but nothing major. Mostly scratches, cuts and bruises.

"Your dad is fine," Krysty said, sitting gratefully on a wheel blown off one of the LAVs. She ached everywhere.

"I meant the other guy."

Doc made a rude noise. His opinion of the matter was easily readable from his expression.

"Oh, him," Clem drawled, a hand tightening on the loaded longblaster. "Mildred said she would keep a close watch and let us know when it's official."

"Good," the boy said grimly. "I'm looking forward to it."

"OKAY, YOU'RE DONE," Mildred stated, pressing the last adhesive strip onto the bandage. "It was only a flesh wound, a lateral dermal slash with no depth worth mentioning."

"Thanks," Ryan said, standing and tucking in his shirt. The new garment was a rich blue, taken from the stores in the cave. He hated the color, but at least it did fit. He'd replace it as soon as possible.

"Go get some food," she said, packing away her meager medical supplies, now depleted nearly to nonexistence after treating so many wounded. "I think the browns have started raiding the MRE packs."

"That's close enough to food for me," Ryan agreed, and the man shuffled off, too tired to lift his boots any higher than necessary.

Fighting off a yawn, Mildred rubbed her weary eyes. God, they all needed sleep badly, but the work wasn't finished. Not quite yet, anyway. Strange that there were enough blasters in the cave to start a war, but not a single medical bag or first-aid kit.

Walking over to the square hole in the ground, the shape too reminiscent of a grave for her comfort, Mildred climbed inside the crate. An oil lantern bathed the dying man in bright light. His face pale and waxy, Overton lay sprawled on the dirty floor, a bloody blanket covering the worst of his injuries. The bulletproof jacket had taken the brunt of the Thompson attack, but a score of small-caliber wounds peppered his shoulders, limbs, throat and, worst, his stomach. There was simply nothing more painful than getting belly-shot. Survivors said it was like having your guts on fire, while being eaten alive by ants from the inside. Mildred had personally witnessed several people take their own lives to escape the incredible pain.

In agonizing pain, the man panted steadily as if running away from death. But Mildred knew that race was already over. Overton was dying, and there was nothing she could do, even if she wanted to. It was simply amazing he had lasted this long.

With a strangled cry, Overton writhed under the blanket, clawing madly at the air. ''Kill me,'' he gasped, the dark stains spreading on the blanket.

''I can't,'' Mildred said, brushing the hair off his sweaty face.

''Please...''

Debating with herself, the physician rummaged in her medical bag and unearthed a plastic film canister. A strip of duct tape kept it closed airtight. Removing the tape, she popped the top and yanked out the cotton wadding to expose three tiny capsules that resembled vitamins. With extreme care, she broke one in two and placed it up the nose of the dying man.

"Sniff," she commanded, closing his other nostril. "Sniff hard."

Overton did and cried out, "It burns!"

With his mouth open, she poured the other half of the gelatin capsule down his throat. He hawked and coughed, gagging on the double dose, then calmed strangely, muscles relaxing, and a great peaceful calm washed over the man.

"Thank you," he said, sighing. "Oh, thank you. The pain is gone."

"Gone forever," she whispered. "I gave you a shot of pure quill jolt, enough to kill six men. There will be no more pain. Ever."

Already in a dreamy state, his eyes glazed as the wild drug mixture took him on a private lethal journey.

"Why?" he finally asked.

"I don't torture people," she replied simply. The man's face was ashen, his pulse racing over ninety. Mildred knew he wouldn't last much longer. Nobody could with that much of the hellish drug coursing through his shattered body, but that was the only amount large enough to do any good. Even in the redoubts, she hadn't encountered morphine or ether. Pain was a part of life these days, as inescapable as Deathlands itself.

"Torture…?"

"You're already dead. No sense in making you suffer."

"I would have," he said, slurring the words.

"Yes, I know," she whispered, dampening a cloth and washing the sweat from his face.

A shudder shook the man, his eyes rolling backward until only the whites showed. Mildred started to reach out, but there was nothing more she could do. Even with the facilities of a full predark hospital, the physician didn't believe he could have been saved. The tiny .22 rounds reflected off bones, piercing vital organs in a wild orgy of destruction before exiting. Youth and rage had carried Overton this far, but even those were failing now. She removed her blaster and laid it out of his reach. If things got any worse, then she would end the matter as fast and as painless as possible.

"Pay debts…" he whispered, drooling out the side of his slack mouth. "Always pay debts…nothing free…"

Overton clawed weakly at the chron on his wrist. Mildred helped him to remove it, thinking he meant to give the watch to her as payment for the drug. But as it came free, he tossed the device away and slumped. Confused, she glanced at the strip of bare white flesh on the tanned arm. There was a small tattoo there.

"Dear God in heaven," Mildred gasped, then turned and yelled, "Ryan, get down here!"

A minute later, Ryan sauntered in sucking stew right out of the MRE envelope. "Need some help?" he asked casually.

"Clem would be happy to shoot him some more," Krysty added, appearing beside the man.

"Look at his wrist," Mildred said, pointing.

In no apparent hurry, the Deathlands warrior and the titian-haired beauty came closer, then paused, their faces altering into total shock. The number 352 was tattooed on his pale skin in black ink.

"The code to open the doors of a redoubt," Ryan said hoarsely, dropping the military ration pack.

Her hair fanning out, Krysty turned and drew her blaster, making sure that nobody else was close enough to hear the conversation. A brown shirt was coming their way, and she leveled the weapon.

"Sorry, private conversation," Krysty said, clicking back the hammer. "Baron stuff, you understand."

The sec man nodded and limped away.

Ryan leaped into the crate and knelt next to the dying man. "Where did you get that number?" he demanded in barely controlled fury.

Overton raggedly coughed, blood trickling from his mouth.

"Who told you? Do you know about the—?" Ryan started to say *mat-trans unit* and cut himself off. "The special room with six walls and only one door?"

"The jump room." Overton smiled dreamily. "Oh, sure…how we got here…lots of blasters, you know. Going to save America, kill all the muties from above."

From above. What did that mean? Ryan ground his teeth in frustration. This news turned their victory into a complete disaster. The secret of the redoubts was out, as was the access code to enter the predark installations. But it seemed that Overton kept the code a secret from his own men. They might know the redoubts existed, but not how to get inside. That was something. But how had he learned the code? Where and from whom?

"Mildred, save him," Ryan ordered, clenching his fists. "We have to know where he got this information!"

She shook her head. "Nothing can save him at this point."

Ryan started to grab the man by the throat, and Mildred blocked his hands, shaking her head.

"That wouldn't do any good," she snapped. "He doesn't even know where he is."

"Where?" Overton repeated in a whisper. He worked

his mouth as if speaking, but no sound came out. The physician leaned closer, holding her ear only inches away from his blue lips.

"Shiloh…" Overton exhaled and went terribly still.

"He's dead," Mildred said, sitting erect and closing his eyelids with her fingertips.

Knuckles white, Ryan could only shake with repressed fury. "He knew. Redoubts, the codes, everything!"

"So what do we do?" Krysty asked, frowning.

"First, burn that number off his skin," Ryan ordered, starting to leave, then he paused to glance at the dead man. "After that, we're going to Shiloh."

A CRISP, CLEAN DAWN was breaking over Front Royal as a tall man in loose clothing wandered over the drawbridge. Busy sec men armed with fancy blasters gave him a cursory inspection before returning to their work.

Inside the walls of the ville, the dead and the dying lay everywhere, and a dank haze hung over the streets, a mixture of morning mist and smoke from a burning building. A whitehair was sweeping colored bits of glass off the cobblestones. More were dragging the corpses of horses into the rear of a wag. A child cried somewhere, and a woman wailed in heartbroken grief.

Shuffling along, a very tired-looking sec man with his arms full of bandages hurried by the newcomer, and the man stayed the trooper with a grip of iron.

"Hey!" the brown shirt cried out. "Watch it, asshole! I almost dropped these, and we need them for the wounded!"

"I'm truly sorry, sir," the tall man apologized, removing a hat showing his strangely bald head. "But my name is Lissman, Daniel Lissman, a trained healer. Can I be of service here?"

Don't miss

GAIA'S DEMISE,

the second
exciting volume of

THE BARONIES TRILOGY,

coming in October.
Here is an excerpt for your
enjoyment.

Chapter One

Whimpering in fear, the child stumbled through the unfamiliar fields of dried grass. It had been early morning when her mother left to gather wood for the fire, and now it was late afternoon. Susie was painfully hungry, but dared not eat the dead squirrel before the meat was cooked. That was how her daddy died so many months ago. She missed him so much, and often woke up screaming from bad dreams, once more seeing him thrash about in agony, foaming at the mouth until her mommy cut his throat with the big knife to end the terrible pain.

"Mommy?" she called, tears rolling down her sunken cheeks. "Mommy, I'm hungry! Where are you?"

Only the whispery winds in the trees answered the call.

Following a game trail through the woods, the little girl watched the bushes for signs of muties that might attack, clutching her tiny knife for protection. She was supposed to run away from strangers and animals, but if something was hurting her mommy, Susie would kill it dead with her knife.

Suddenly, the girl cried out in delight as she spied some bushes heavy with summer berries. Odd that the forest creatures hadn't eaten them all. As Susie greedily stuffed her face with the mushy blueberries, rivulets of purple juice flowing down her chin, a strange noise sounded in the trees. It was a weird crackle, as if a giant were stepping on fields of dried leaves.

Popping one last handful into her mouth, the child curiously walked through the trees. The noise came again, louder this time, and she heard faint voices.

Susie started to shout for her mother, then stopped. People were dangerous. Even the right ones without extra arms and such. Her mother had warned her to avoid contact, and the little girl carefully obeyed the warning.

Wiping her hands on the bark of a tree, Susie followed the faint noises through the foliage until she reached the top of a steep hill. Spread throughout the valley below was a spectacular ville, unlike anything she had ever seen. There were houses made of brick, and many people, some in chains and others beating them with whips. A squat building near a river had six big chimneys, with black smoke pouring into the purple sky, masking the angry orange streaks of the coming rains. Thick rope, or wire, or something, stretched from the building to a machine, then spread out across the ville like a spiderweb.

More people dug into the side of a rocky hill, chained slaves dragging stone blocks to a wall they were building around the whole area. A wall of stone. Susie had never seen such a thing before. It was wonderful! Certainly no mutie or nasty coldheart could get through that.

The billowing clouds parted for a moment, exposing a tremendous machine that dominated the middle of the ville, a huge shiny white thing that towered over the chimneys casting the land underneath into dark shadows.

"Hold it right there, kid!" an adult voice growled.

Still holding her little knife, Susie turned and looked up at the two big men standing in the weeds. They were wearing clean blue shirts and carrying longblasters.

"Hello, sec men," she said, dropping a curtsy. Her mother said to always be polite to sec men or they would tell the baron on you. "I'm looking for my mommy, have you seen her?"

"This must be that bitch's kid," the tall man said irritably. "Crap, I was hoping she would run away and get lost, or something."

"Well, she didn't," the other sec man snapped, doing something to his weapon. "And you know what that means."

The tall man ran a hand over his face. "Hey, she's too small to work in the fucking mines."

"And we can't let her go. No exceptions, or it's our necks. That's what the boss said." The other man lowered his blaster.

"But she's just a kid!" He sounded very angry for some reason.

The blaster fired once. "Not anymore."

"Black dust! She's still breathing, you asshole. Can't you even chill a little girl who's standing still?"

"Must have flinched."

"Horseshit. Finish her off!"

"And waste a bullet? Screw that." He drew a knife.

"Fuck you. I'll do it. Goodbye, kid."

A handblaster boomed, followed by the sound of soft soil being turned. In the background, the whips cracked steadily, black smoke filled the stormy sky and the giant machine continued to slowly revolve in perfect synchronization to the unseen stars, beyond the polluted Kentucky clouds.

THE RUMBLING APC rolled off the broken asphalt and crested a low sand dune, coming to a gentle stop. There was the sound of movement inside the armored transport, then the rear doors swung open wide and out climbed several heavily-armed people.

Weapon in hand, Ryan Cawdor walked forward and looked over the utter desolation spread before the vehicle. He had never seen anything like it before in his life.

Stretching for perhaps a full mile were the ruins of a predark city along the shore of the Lantic Ocean, and these ruins were crumbling apart even as he watched. Bricks fell from the side of a building and hit the ground, bursting into their component ash, the powdery cement blowing away as dry dust. A depression in the ground contained the remains of fish, as if it were once a pond. Even the soil itself was slackened as if charred by a terrible fire. Yet countless trees still stood, the bark peeling off the gray trunks, brittle leaves carpeting the ville even though it was only early autumn. A field of brown crops stretched to the north and south, every breeze snapping the stalks and clearing whole areas. The corpses lay everywhere, their clothing flaky ash, their crispy skins split apart exposing gray flesh and black bones. Sprinkled across the horrible landscape were the bodies of tiny birds, wings outstretched as if still in flight. Only the windows of the collapsing buildings seemed to be undamaged, the glass remarkably clear and sparkling clean. Straight ahead were the choppy waters of the ocean. The broken pylons of a pier reached into the water, only the twisted metal beams and support rods remaining to rust in the salty spray. The beach was smooth and shiny, the sand fused into a single rippling sheet of crude glass that reached in either direction going out of sight.

"Son of a bitch. You sure this is the right place?" Ryan demanded gruffly, tugging the patch covering the ruin of his left eye into a more comfortable position. The man's face was a network of scars, courtesy of his old brother Harvey, the lines creasing his forehead and cheeks his legacy of years of travel in the wasteland known as Deathlands. A blaster was tight in his grip, his bolt-action longblaster slung across his powerful shoulders.

"Yeah," J. B. Dix replied, tilting his fedora. A Smith & Wesson shotgun was slung across his back, and a compact Uzi submachine gun hung at his side, a scarred hand nervously resting on the deadly weapon. "I double checked the sextant. This is, or rather was, the town of Shiloh, North Carolina."

Movement in the ruins caught their attention, and the companions saw skinny rats scampering among the destruction, clearly searching for food, but none touched the many corpses.

"Not much of a town," Krysty Wroth stated, the overwhelming feeling of death seeping into her bones. The checkered grip of a revolver jutted from her belt, and the redhead shivered.

"Not much of anything, dear lady," Doc Tanner rumbled in his stentorian bass, holding a swallow's-eye handkerchief to his mouth to keep out the bitter ashes. Wearing a frilly white shirt and an outlandish frock coat, the tall man would have been a strange sight even in his own time period. A seamed face and a resplendent crop of silvery hair made Doc appear much older than he really was. He held an ebony swordstick casually in his right hand, and a massive blaster jutted from the Civil War gunbelt around his waist.

At those loud words, the artesian well in the middle of the ville broke apart, the wooden beams bursting into ash and the stones plummeting out of sight into the ground. Minutes passed, but there was no sound of a splash from the blocks striking water.

Frowning, Krysty hugged herself, the long lengths of her fiery hair moving and flexing, animated by her intense emotional state. She had witnessed death many times in their travels, but nothing resembling this.

Behind the companions, the hot engine of the predark wag ticked softly as the metal slowly cooled. Then the top hatch of their armored vehicle squealed open on stubborn hinges, and a pale teenager with long snowy hair rose into view. The youth was dressed in camou-colored fatigues, decorated with bits of metal and glass sewn into the lining. Though knives were Jak Lauren's weapons of choice, a big .357 Magnum Colt Python rested in his easy grip. Even with the armor and weapons of the Bradley surrounding him, Jak was clearly uneasy amid this desolation. He said nothing, but his expression was one of intense scorn.

"A simple village returned to its primordial state," Doc announced. "Not even a humble cottage remains to be balanced by a river's brim."

"Walt Whitman?" Mildred Wyeth asked, squinting, thumbs hooked into her gun belt. Instead of the physician's usual orderly array of beaded plaits, her hair was held in place by a bandanna, a single stray plait dangling down the side of her face.

"Me," the man replied, smiling broadly. "Just me, this time."

"Did the rads do this, Dad?" Dean Cawdor asked quietly.

Scowling, Ryan checked the tiny rad counter pinned to his collar. "Reading clean," he announced. "And acid rain sure as shit didn't do this."

A soft breeze from the ocean moved over the blackened fields, the plants were crumbling to dust and blowing away. Then a section of a building broke apart, the bricks and mortar separating as the masonry tumbled to the ground.

"Well, lightning didn't do it, either," J.B. stated, wiping clean his glasses. "Or any poison gas that I ever heard about."

Opening the med bag hanging at her side, Mildred stooped to the ground and lifted a small sample of the crispy soil with forceps. She carefully inspected it in the light before sniffing it.

"No chemical burn that I can recognize," the physician stated, tossing the piece of dead earth away. "Not napalm, thermite or even willy peter."

Shifting his combat boots, Dean mentally translated the term. It was a slang word for white phosphorous. The chem burned ten times hotter than napalm, but was controllable, unlike thermite. Once you ignited that stuff, all a person could do was run away fast, or die.

Thunder rumbled, and Krysty looked up to see fiery streaks of orange slashing across the purplish sky, a billowing array of dark chem clouds ravaged by the endless hurricanes of the upper atmosphere.

Glancing down, Mildred saw the line in the soil where the strange effect stopped and the green grass started once more. The boundary was sharp, as if a line had been drawn with engineering tools. What weapon could do that?

"See the disembarkation?" Mildred asked, her fingers tracing the edge of the destruction. "Whatever this was had precise control. Lasers come to mind, but the effect is wrong, and who the hell has that kind of weaponry anymore?"

"Whatever it is happened fast, too," Krysty added, jerking her chin. Off to the side lay the still body of a bear with a sea trout in its jaws, half the furry form in the circle of destruction, the rest on cool green grass.

Puckering his lips, Doc turned the silver lion's-head handle of his walking stick and extracted a full yard of shining Spanish steel from the ebony sheath. Placing the sharp tip against the soil, he put his weight on the sword and it easily sank all the way down until the handle touched the surface. Withdrawing the blade, he examined its unstained expanse.

"No resistance," he rumbled. "Whatever this was, penetrated deep into the earth."

"Mebbe there's a new volcano in the ocean," Dean said, "and the ville got cooked with steam?"

Mildred waved a hand at the waves breaking on the glass shore. "Lava doesn't do that," she stated.

"I don't like this," Ryan muttered, crackling his knuckles and walking deeper into the ville. "Hell, they didn't even have a wall to keep out the muties!" A rat scurried by, and Ryan resisted the temptation to shoot it out of sheer annoyance.

"Mebbe the blue shirts destroyed the ville to throw us off the track?" Krysty asked, turning slowly. The woman's eyes were a deep emerald green, like the sea in a predark oil painting lovingly created by a grand master.

"No way this was their HQ," Ryan stated, glancing around at the hellish vista. "If it was, why didn't Overton attack Casanova first, then? It's closer and has got just as good a wall and fortress as Front Royal.''

"Maybe they have," Doc postulated. "Maybe Casanova no longer exists."

Nobody spoke for a few minutes, thinking seriously about that possibility.

Removing his hat, J.B. grimaced as he smoothed the brim. "Crap," he announced. "There's not a blaster, or a war wag in sight, and the blues were lousy with predark military supplies. Overton had more weapons than Wizard Island and the Anthill combined!"

"Mebbe this was an object lesson to the locals," Krysty said slowly. "To show others what somebody could do."

"Or removing potential enemies?" Dean suggested. "Chill before getting chilled."

J.B. put his hat back on and tilted it to a comfortable position. "Testing the weapon is more likely. If it is a weapon and not some bizarre natural effect of the Deathlands."

"Like St. Elmo's fire, ball-lightning?" Doc guessed with a scowl. "Now that hardly seems likely, John Barrymore."

"Name," Jak said loudly, rubbing the barrel of the 25 mm cannon in the turret alongside him.

Thoughtfully, Mildred tucked a loose strand of hair back into place. First opportunity, she had to have Krysty finish plaiting her hair. This loose stuff was incredibly annoying. "You think somebody did this because it was called Shiloh?" she said aloud.

"Mebbe only wanted one," the teenager guessed.

"Possible," Ryan mused, rubbing his unshaven chin. "J.B., are there any other villes with the same name?"

"Give me a minute," J.B. said, rummaging in his

shoulder bag and retrieving a plastic gas station map. With loving hands, he unfolded the antique and studied the index.

"We were so positive it must be this place, I didn't look for other villes by the same name!" he snarled. "There's a goddamn Shiloh in Georgia, another in Pennsylvania, Ohio, Illinois, Alabama...no that's a crater. One in Tennessee. No that's also a bomb crater, one in Jersey and one in Kentuck!"

The Armorer angrily stuffed the map into a pocket of his leather jacket. "There was a Shiloh in Virginia, but it was situated right on the Ches Bay. Just part of Washington Hole nowadays."

"Fireblast! Seven villes named Shiloh," Ryan swore, shaking his head slowly. "That's a lot of miles to cover. What's the closest?"

Stretching out an arm, J.B. pointed directly south. "Alabama. Straight across this bay and down a ways. I know that the LAV is supposed to be amphibious, but with all the repairs we've done, I'd just as soon not trust the wag to deep ocean."

"Agreed," Ryan said with a half smile. "We stay on dry land until absolutely necessary."

"A thought just occurred to me. Are any of these villes near a known redoubt?" Doc asked, his silvery hair blowing in the breeze.

J.B. checked the map again. "Hell yes. Good call there, Doc. There's a redoubt we've been to only a few miles from the Shiloh in Kentuck."

"The one near Hazard."

"That's it."

"Hot pipe! Mebbe that's where they're getting the military supplies," Dean suggested eagerly.

Turning away, Ryan hawked and spit to get the taste

of the ashes from his mouth. "Sorry, son. But that redoubt is completely empty... Fireblast! I forgot about the tunnels under the base. They run for miles, and we never did more than a quick recce. Anything could be down there."

"Sounds like Kentuck should be our next stop. But do we have enough fuel for that long a journey?" Krysty asked. "We started from Front Royal with six spare cans, and we've already used two."

"Just have to get more on the way," Ryan answered grimly. "Buy it, steal it. If none is available, we go on foot. But these bastards have got to be stopped!"

"Absolutely," Mildred agreed, tying closed the flap on her med bag. "If only to protect the redoubts. If the blues have found a way to get inside them—"

A sharp whistle from behind caught their attention, and the companions spun with weapons at the ready.

Crawling bodily out of the crispy soil in front of the LAV 25 was something from a nightmare. The misshapen creature sported fangs and claws, its boxy head filled with different size eyes. The serpentine body was covered with alligator hide dripping with heavy manes of brindle fur. Massive muscles rolled beneath its skin as the creature shambled closer on four legs, two more shriveled limbs dangling impotently from its hideous body.

In the turret, Jak had both hands poised on the 25 mm cannon, tracking its advance, but the beast was directly between him and the others.

Taking a gren from his munitions bag, J.B. pulled the pin, but held off throwing the charge. The mutie was already too close. The blast might get them, too.

"Shit!" the Armorer cursed, but didn't return the pin

to the gren. Instead, he transferred it to his left hand and awkwardly pulled the bolt on the Uzi with his right.

"What is it?" Dean asked softly, drawing his own blaster.

Retreating a few steps, Ryan worked the bolt on his longblaster. "Hard to tell," he growled. "Some mutie animal mated with another and this was the result. Aim for the head, that usually chills them. Ready…fire!"

The companions opened fired in a ragged volley, the beast screamed in agony as it was slammed backward against the wag, the barrage of lead and steel tearing apart its mutated form. But as they stopped shooting, the growling mutie rose again. The bullet holes, leaking a greenish ichor, closed by themselves and the bleeding stopped.

"By the Three Kennedys!" Doc intoned, switching the selector pin on his LeMat from the smooth bore .63 shotgun, to the .44 cylinders. The LeMat was old, slightly cranky and difficult to use. But in the expert hands of the gentleman from Vermont, the Civil War blaster was a deadly killing machine.

Furiously working the bolt, Ryan pumped two rounds from the Steyr into the beast, stalling for Doc until he was ready. The long 7.62 mm cartridges did only minimal damage. J.B. added a spray from the Uzi, concentrating on the chest. The weird clear blood spurted with every hit, the wounds closing almost instantly, as if the mutie were accelerating the healing process.

Suddenly, Doc leveled his handcannon and the massive black powder weapon discharged, vomiting flame and smoke from the wide muzzle. The beast jerked from the impact of the miniball, but the ground behind it puffed from the impact of the round going clear through it.

"Dark night!" J.B. snarled, releasing the Uzi and swinging the S&W shotgun to the front. He worked the pump and fired two rounds at the creature, the spray of fléchettes tearing its head apart. But the bleeding pieces of flesh slid together, then a pair of scorpion tails arched from its back, the barbed tips glistening with moisture.

"Poison!" Mildred warned, targeting its face with her ZKR pistol. Several of its eyes exploded from her soft lead rounds, and the beast started forward directly toward her, the other orbs distended in their pain and fury.

Hastily, Krysty thumbed fresh rounds into her revolver as the creature rose once more, a rill of porcupine quills extending protectively along its neck. "Gaia protect us, the creature is regenerating!" She dropped few rounds, but reloaded in record time. The redhead closed the cylinder with a snap of her wrist and fired again immediately. "How the hell are we going to chill something that can do that?"

"We're going to blow it to pieces!" J.B. shouted and threw the gren. The mutie ducked its head and the scorpion tails snapped forward, knocking the sphere aside. The gren bounced into the nearby ruins and exploded, the searing blast raining chem fire over the crumbling structures. Flames started to spread across the layer of dry leaves covering the entire ville. Dozens of squealing rats darted from the shadows, racing madly away from the growing conflagration.

"It knows weps," Dean whispered, almost dropping a fresh clip before managing to insert it into the grip of his hot Browning.

Dodging to the left, then darting to the right, the mutie came ever closer, a forked tongue running hungrily along its mottled jaws.

Stealing sideways glances as he fired, Ryan looked quickly around them and saw only flat land stretching into the desiccated fields and to the ocean. There was no place to hide, or even get some protection for a few seconds. They were trapped in the open.

"Shoot it again!" Krysty ordered, but their weapons achieved only the same meager results. The wounds closed without scars after weeping a few drops of the weird transparent liquid.

"Run for the pier!" Ryan shouted, firing steadily as he headed in that direction. "Mebbe it can't swim! We've got to get some distance so Jak can use the cannon!"

Just then the big diesel engines of the LAV 25 roared into life. But the armored wag started forward with a lurch, heading directly for the mutie only a few yards in front of the hastily retreating companions.

James Axler

OUTLANDERS™

OUTER DARKNESS

Kane and his companions are transported to an alternate reality where the global conflagration didn't happen—and humanity had expelled the Archons from the planet. Things are not as rosy as they may seem, as the Archons return for a final confrontation....

Book #3 in the new Lost Earth Saga, a trilogy that chronicles our heroes' paths through three very different alternative realities...where the struggle against the evil Archons goes on....

Killers' ransom...

DON PENDLETON's

MACK BOLAN®

HELLFIRE STRIKE

In an effort to stem the flow of heroin into the U.S., the President issues an ultimatum to the Southeast Asian drug lords. To add some muscle to this diplomatic move, Bolan is sent to deliver a clear message—comply or be eliminated.

The drug lords still have one ace up their sleeve—a tie to the highest levels of the U.S. government....

Available in August 1999 at your favorite retail outlet.